1 2023

Praise for *Getting His Game Back*

"A thoroughly satisfying love story with a big, beating heart."
—*Publishers Weekly* (starred review)

"This book is emotional, steamy, and sweet—a triple threat! De Cadenet tackles mental health, gender stereotypes, and interracial romance with care and creativity. I loved it!"
—CHANTEL GUERTIN, author of *Instamom*

By Gia de Cadenet

Getting His Game Back
Not the Plan

NOT THE PLAN

NOT THE PLAN

A Novel

GIA DE CADENET

DELL

New York

Not the Plan is a work of fiction.
Names, characters, places, and incidents are the products of
the author's imagination or are used fictitiously. Any resemblance
to actual events, locales, or persons, living or dead,
is entirely coincidental.

A Dell Trade Paperback Original

Copyright © 2022 by Gia de Cadenet
Book club guide copyright © 2022 by Penguin Random House LLC

All rights reserved.

Published in the United States by Dell,
an imprint of Random House, a division of
Penguin Random House LLC, New York.

DELL is a registered trademark and the D colophon is a trademark
of Penguin Random House LLC.
RANDOM HOUSE BOOK CLUB and colophon are trademarks
of Penguin Random House LLC.

LIBRARY OF CONGRESS CATALOGING-IN-PUBLICATION DATA
Names: De Cadenet, Gia, author.
Title: Not the plan / Gia de Cadenet.
Description: New York: Dell, [2022] |
"A Dell Trade Paperback Original"—Title page verso.
Identifiers: LCCN 2022014870 (print) |
LCCN 2022014871 (ebook) | ISBN 9780593356647 (trade paperback) |
ISBN 9780593356654 (ebook)
Subjects: LCGFT: Novels.
Classification: LCC PS3604.E12253 N68 2022 (print) |
LCC PS3604.E12253 (ebook) | DDC 813/.6—dc23
LC record available at https://lccn.loc.gov/2022014870
LC ebook record available at https://lccn.loc.gov/2022014871

Printed in the United States of America on acid-free paper

randomhousebooks.com
randomhousebookclub.com

2 4 6 8 9 7 5 3 1

They may have called you a victim,
but after everything you're still here.
That's not a victim. That's a survivor, baby.

NOT THE PLAN

CHAPTER ONE
Isadora

I can do this.

Isadora Maris took a deep breath, squared her shoulders, and maneuvered her luggage into the San Diego airport. Bags checked and through security, she stopped at a coffee shop before heading to her gate. *Flying is no big deal. How many times a year do I fly? Nothing bad has ever happened.*

She had a few moments, so she took a seat at one of the small tables in front of the shop. Maybe she should buy a magazine. Something light and fun to read? She popped the lid off her cup and tried to ground herself with the aroma and taste of the latte. She was safe, she was fine. *Everything's cool. I've got this. If I can handle stonewalling senators and aggressive lobbyists, I can handle a flight.*

"Babe, I would totally die for you." Isadora caught a man's voice murmuring a table over. She glanced at the couple just as his blond companion let out a kittenish giggle.

"Kenny, sweetie, you are *so* dramatic," she said.

Isadora suppressed an eye roll as the couple leaned into each other open-mouthed. It wasn't that she was averse to public displays of affection. But how long had it been since someone looked at her like that? Touched her like that? It didn't matter; right now she had too much on the line. This time next year, her boss, Daniel Etcheverri, would be president pro tempore of the state senate, and as chief of staff, her hard work and drive had helped get him there. From there, she'd manage his (hopefully) successful race for U.S. representative and she'd reach her childhood dream: congressional aide in Washington, D.C.

"You know," the guy said after smacking his lips, "after last night, the plane could fall out of the sky, crash and burn, and I'd die a happy man."

Isadora choked on her coffee, a wave of terror charging over her skin from her scalp to the soles of her feet. She wrenched her phone out of her bag, unlocked it, and tapped on an icon on her home screen. She scrolled down to the most important line in the article.

The odds of dying in a plane crash are one in eleven million. The odds of dying in a plane crash are one in eleven million.

"If we crashed into the water, we—"

Isadora *had* to get away from these people. She grabbed her phone and the cup, pushed her chair back, took one step, and promptly collided with something tall and warm. She watched in slow motion as her latte shot out of the cup, arced into the air, and exploded against a white dress shirt.

"Dammit!" came a low, deep voice above her.

"Oh! I'm so sorry." She grabbed some napkins out of the dispenser on the table, fingertips clumsy and buzzing. When she glanced up at the man's face, she stopped dead. Green eyes framed by dark hair stared back through nerdy-cute glasses. He was well over six feet tall, had sun-kissed olive skin, and was hot. Cover model hot.

She'd just scalded the sexiest man she'd ever seen.

"Here." She offered him the napkins.

"You must be in a hurry," he said, taking them and dabbing at the coffee.

"No. Well . . . I mean, yes."

"Maybe watch where you're going next time." Just her luck, the demigod was pissed at her.

"Maybe *you* should watch where *you're* going," she snapped. "The tables are *right there*."

He narrowed his eyes at her, looking her up and down. She

wasn't going to give him a pass to talk to her any kind of way, just because he was gorgeous.

"If you'll *excuse me,* miss, I need to go get cleaned up."

She narrowed her eyes back at him. She'd taken a step away and was stuck between him and the wall of the coffee shop.

"You're in *my* way," she said.

Waving the hand holding the napkins out and bowing in a sarcastic display of gallantry, he let her by. "Have a nice day," he called after her.

She shot him a dirty look over her shoulder and headed to her gate.

Isadora adjusted her earbuds and started her pre-takeoff ritual. *The odds of dying in a plane—*

"Well, isn't this a surprise?"

She opened her eyes as the demigod's messenger bag slid onto the seat next to hers. Heat blasted into her cheeks as a bright flash of embarrassment crackled over her already frayed nerves when she realized he'd changed into a moss green shirt.

"Uh . . . yeah," she mumbled, tugging at the cuff of her cardigan. "Nice shirt." She snapped her mouth shut. *Great. My nerves are making me snarky.*

He chuckled, taking his seat. "Thanks. I started the day with a white one, but some crazy lady spilled coffee all over it and I had to change."

Swallowing over the lump in her throat kept her from clapping back. Why did he have to be so hot? She smoothed her cardigan sleeve, trying to ground herself again. She was going to be next to him for nearly two hours. And you catch more flies with honey than vinegar.

"Maybe it's for the best," she said.

He raised an eyebrow.

"That color works better for you than plain white."

"Does it?"

She nodded, proud of the ability to flirt while strapped in a giant steel tube about to be blasted into the air. The corner of his mouth dipped down, and a hint of red crept up his neck as he leafed through his bag, found a magazine, and tucked it in the seat pouch in front of him.

Is the demigod a little shy? She suppressed a chuckle.

"It's also a good cut for you," she said. He slid his bag under the seat. "It fits your shoulders just right."

Demigod raised both eyebrows and gave her a genuine smile. He had a chiseled jaw. And full, inviting lips. And dimples. Literally, the sexiest man she had ever seen. Her heart dipped as his gaze caressed her cheek and the hollow of her throat.

"I'm Karim," he said, offering his hand.

"Isadora. I am sorry about your shirt."

"No, it's nothing."

"At least let me have it cleaned."

"Really, it's no big deal. I already rinsed it in the restroom. I doubt the stain will set."

"That's good." Unsure of what to say next, she returned her earbuds to their place. She didn't want to be impolite, but it was a habit, part of her method to get into an acceptable mental space before takeoff. The flight attendants were about to start their safety instructions and her ritual included following along. She'd mastered the art of watching disinterestedly with her earbuds in place. Nobody else knew that her music was off, and she was actually hanging on to every word, willing her heart to stop pounding. But now it was going a little fast for a different reason. Her preflight ritual did not include basking in Karim's cologne. Or . . . what was that smell underneath? Him? Deep, calming breaths let her conceal her investigation.

Oh God . . . he smells amazing! Deep and woodsy and—something brushed her cheek. She opened the eyes she didn't know she'd closed. The curved headrest saved her from utter mortification after she'd leaned toward him. She stole a glance with her peripheral vision, hoping he hadn't noticed. His attention was on the magazine in his lap, but he might have been watching her out of the corner of his eye. Shifting as far over as possible in her seat, she feigned interest in the view out the window while listening to the flight attendants explain what to do if they were facing imminent demise.

She needed to focus on something else. She undid the low bun she always wore for flights. Running her fingers through her blown-out hair, she twisted it back into place, then ended up knocking an earbud loose. Karim was unwrapping a piece of gum and offered her one.

"I hate having to pop my ears later," he said.

"Thanks. I hate that too." She focused on the explosion of gooey mint across her tongue as the engines roared. His eyes were shut, so she didn't have to hide the fight to slow her breathing as the plane left the ground. She chewed and chewed and chewed, trying to get back to a calm place. The grating whine of the wheels coming up into the body of the aircraft sent a flash of thick moisture over her skin and she had to send her mind in a different direction.

"I don't understand your priorities," her mother had sighed on the phone the previous night. "Things haven't been easy for me."

The same call, the same words, the same guilt, every time.

"It's a thankless job, being a parent. Especially when you're on your own."

What do I have to do for it to be enough? Do I have to thank her for raising me every time we talk?

"It's not like he died on purpose," Isadora had said, as always.

Her mother continued, unhearing or uncaring, as always.

"You don't understand my pain. I don't think you'll ever understand."

How could I understand? He was just my dad. It's not like his death hurt me too.

Her gaze fell to the window, but she saw nothing. Pulling in a chestful of recycled air, she willed the tears back down. She pulled her phone out of her cardigan pocket, put the meditation playlist on, and closed her eyes. About twenty minutes into zen, Karim startled her, brushing his fingertips along her arm. She took out her earbuds.

He nodded at the flight attendant, a row ahead of theirs, distributing beverages. "Would you like a drink, Isadora? I'm going to get a coffee, but I'll do my best not to pay you back," he said, smiling.

The depth of his voice sent pleasant tingles through her, the pain she'd dredged up washed away. Smiling, she let herself fall into a present that excluded the rest of the world.

"Guess I deserve that. A sparkling water would be good. It's nice of you to offer."

"My pleasure." He asked the flight attendant for their drinks and handed Isadora's to her with care. His casual way of ordering for her was a pleasant surprise. A touch of chivalry. She thanked him and started to put her earbuds back in, but he spoke again.

"These early flights are tough, huh?"

"Yeah." She sipped.

"Do you usually fly business class?" He put his coffee down and caressed the edge of the tray with the pad of his thumb. *Lucky tray.*

"I try. I like to get off as quickly as possible." He raised his eyebrows and she caught how that had sounded. Face burning, she took a quick breath. "You know, um, I mean, the plane. Get off the plane."

"Yeah," he said, smiling a little. "I understand. Always seems to take forever when you're at the rear."

"Yeah," she echoed. *What to say?* He was nice. She didn't want to just pop her earbuds back in and seem rude.

"Um . . . do you like the rear of the plane?" she asked. "I've always had trouble sitting back there. It bounces around too much for me."

He lowered his gaze a millisecond, lips curling in a tiny hesitation. Then he darted a quick glance at her, like he was trying to make a decision. "Really?" he finally asked, meeting her eyes. "I quite like the rear. The bouncier the better."

Um . . . She swallowed. "Is that so?"

"It is."

Is the demigod telling me he checked me out?

"I dunno." She warmed her voice and leaned toward him. "I gotta disagree with you. I prefer it over the wings where you can feel the *thrust* of the airplane. You know? When it's fast and strong and you can't help but let yourself go."

"Is *that* so?"

"It is. You don't like the thrust of takeoff?" she asked, eyes wide.

"Oh, I do," he said. "It's . . . exhilarating." He smiled, drawing her attention to his lips. She ran the tip of her tongue along the inside of hers, imagining what his tasted like.

"Exhilarating. Good word choice," she said.

"So, what do you do, Isadora?" he asked, raising his cup to his lips.

She frowned inside. Talking about work with strangers was almost always a mistake. She loved what she did, but politics rarely made for good small talk. After wrinkling her nose, she shook her head.

"Let's not talk about work," she said.

He smiled again and put his coffee on his tray.

"What if I guess?" he asked.

"Guess?"

"What you do. Will you tell me if I guess right?"

She folded her arms, turning toward him. Most people didn't realize that her job even existed, so he'd never guess.

"All right," she said, nodding.

He shifted toward her, then tapped a finger to his lips as though he was thinking. She noticed he wasn't wearing a wedding band.

There's no reason to notice that. No time for men right now.

He glanced back at her.

"Got it," he said. "You're a therapist."

"A therapist?" she asked. "What makes you say that?"

He tilted his head to the side, glancing down to her chin and back up to her eyes.

"You seem like a warm, caring person. Easy to talk to."

She raised an eyebrow. That was a lot to assume from their brief conversation.

"And," he said, "I bet you don't like talking about it because people either ask you to break confidentiality for *interesting stories,* or they take one look into your inviting eyes and want to talk about all their troubles."

She flushed a little. Karim-the-demigod thought she had inviting eyes.

"You're very kind," she said. "I'm not a therapist. But—"

The plane slammed downward, and Isadora clutched the armrests until her knuckles burned. A hard shift to the right and the pilot turned on the fasten seat belt lights.

"Passengers, this is your captain speaking. You'll have to excuse us. We've hit a patch of turbulence and there's likely more ahead. We still have a while to go before we reach our destination, and the ride is going to be bumpy. The crew will come by and pick up any garbage you may have. Please stow your belongings and put your trays in the upright position."

The flight attendant was next to them in a flash, with a forced customer service smile that didn't reach his eyes. A woman behind Isadora gasped as the plane shuddered and bounced. The flight attendant stopped a moment, his hand clamped, bracing himself, on the seat in front of Karim. *"Brace." That's the word they use when we crash.* Roiling nausea splashed through Isadora as she passed the flight attendant her empty cup with quaking hands. Karim tried to make eye contact as she followed the pilot's instructions.

"This part sucks, huh?" he asked.

"Yeah," she said. "It does." She stuffed her earbuds back in, doing her best to show "fine" and "experienced" body language, crossing her arms and repeating her mantra in her mind. He hadn't given her a reason to believe he would judge her, but she had to conceal fear. Raised by a perpetual victim, Isadora had learned to appear fine when she wasn't, lest she take attention away from the person it always belonged to. Hiding any emotion was second nature.

Karim didn't speak to her again until the plane landed. She wanted to say something nice to him while collecting her things, but she needed to move with focus to avoid crying out her pent-up fear. His belongings in hand, he stepped into the aisle and smiled.

"Nice meeting you, Isadora."

"You too," she stammered, avoiding eye contact as he left. She let at least ten people get ahead of her and stayed out of his sight at the luggage carousel. In the privacy of her rental car, a good, long cry released the anxiety and adrenaline. Still shaking, she drove to the apartment that would be her home during the legislative session.

That evening, in bed, grocery shopping done and bags unpacked, she had time for regret. Karim was nice, attentive, and damn sexy. Flirting with him made her want more.

Nice job, Isa. You could have at least gotten his number. But it's probably for the best. This session is crucial, you must remain focused. No sense in letting a pretty face distract you.

CHAPTER TWO

Karim

Karim waited in the conference room of the Sacramento office of State Senator Julian Brown. His potential new boss was in the hallway with Christina, the legislative director he would be replacing during her maternity leave. This second interview had gone even better than the Zoom call while Karim was still in Michigan. The only hitch was the length of the position. Covering for a maternity leave wasn't ideal; he was looking for something long-term to start his new life.

You're in a rebuilding stage. It's okay. Just get your foot in the door and see what permanent opportunities present themselves.

Once he'd been admitted to the California State Bar, and with his experience as a senior aide, something would come together. The conference room door snapped open, and Senator Brown walked back in, Christina following with a small stack of papers.

"Well, young man, welcome to the team." He offered his hand. Karim stood to accept it.

"Thank you," he said. "Can't wait to get started."

"Excellent, because we need you here tomorrow, bright and early. There's no time to waste, with Christina leaving us who knows when. That's women for you, right? They keep you waiting or guessing, or they walk out on you in your time of need."

The remark was a double slap to Karim, despite the senator's chuckle. It was both inappropriate for work and hitting too close to home.

"Very funny, Julian," Christina said, stapling some papers and handing the stack to Karim. "You know I'll be here as long as possible, and back as soon as possible. Karim, I already took care of your pre-screening. Just fill these forms out, and the secretary will get them to Senate Administration so that you'll be clear to start tomorrow."

"Will do," he said. "Thanks again, and I look forward to seeing you tomorrow."

"I won't be here," Julian said at the door. "Gotta head back to the district office in San Diego for a couple days. Christina will get you set up. There's one bill I want you to focus on: cosponsoring a freeway project with our dear majority leader. It's very important I show my constituents who really cares about them."

"Got it," Karim said.

"Karim, will you join me in my office?" Christina asked, rising from her seat.

"Sure thing."

Down the hall, Christina closed the door behind her after Karim took the seat she indicated in front of her desk. She took her seat facing him.

She wove her fingers together and rested them on her crossed knee, leaning back into her seat.

"This is going to sound silly, but since you need to be up and running quickly, I need for things to be clear."

Karim raised an eyebrow.

"Okay," he said slowly.

"Julian just mentioned our majority leader. His name is Daniel Etcheverri. He also represents part of San Diego."

"Yes." Karim nodded. He was well accustomed to cities with populations large enough to require more than one state senator.

"And yeah, we're members of the same party," Christina continued. "So, we work together in public. We ultimately have to be on the same page, especially in the face of the minority party. But we do *not* get along. We *never* have. We never will."

Christina's face was hard. Her jaw looked like it could cut diamonds. Karim had come across his fair share of intractable-seeming positions in his years in politics, but the idea that there could be no hope of cooperation in the future was new to him, especially from people within the same party.

"Never will?" he asked.

"Never," she said. "Let's just say that the Capulets"—she pointed at herself—"and the Montagues"—she jerked a thumb toward the window—"have to work together."

"The Capulets and the Montagues?"

She wove her fingers together again and rested her hands on her knee.

"And San Diego is 'fair Verona.'" She shrugged. "Everything in the district is a competition. Anything they bring home for their constituents, you'd better believe we're bringing home the same for ours. Daniel's aides are always on the lookout for ways to make him look better than Julian, so it's our job to make sure Julian looks even better. And that's amplified at the state level. Anything Daniel does, we do better. Always."

What have I gotten myself into? There's always some degree of ego in politics, but come on, it's supposed to be about the people.

He cleared his throat.

"Okay," he said.

"You need to be careful who you associate with, who you are seen with," Christina said. "*Very careful.* You never know who is really on Daniel's team and is looking for a way to stab you, and by extension Julian, in the back. I imagine that the last thing you want is to ruin your new start in California by becoming an Achilles' heel for your new boss?"

Christina's tone chafed. A lot. But he *was* brand spanking new. He wasn't going to create problems by reciprocating her attitude.

"Of course not," he said.

She nodded, then continued. "It will take a little time for you to get to know everyone, but here are the people you can count on." She leaned over, opening a drawer to her right, brought out a file folder, and placed it on her desk. Flipping it open, she took out two stapled front-and-back pages with two columns of ID badge photos and lists of names. "These are the aides." She handed him the pages. "And these are the members." She handed him a second, similar page, titled Senators and Assembly Members. "Naturally, we don't expect you to memorize everyone's name right away. But knowing friendly faces is important."

Karim took a moment to scan the pages. That they would have the "family" printed up and ready made it clear just how serious these allegiances were.

"Obviously, that's for your eyes only," Christina said.

"Yeah," he said. "I got—" Karim had continued scanning the list while she'd been speaking and had just reached the bottom, where he'd found his own photo.

Guess that makes me a Capulet.

He walked through the glass doors of the senate office building, squinting into the sunlight as he loosened his tie. Taking a deep breath, he felt some of the weight lifting from his shoulders. As he walked down the street, more than one woman's head turned. It was something he appreciated, though he always had to mask a wave of shyness when it happened.

Reaching his rental car, he tossed his jacket on the passenger seat and called his brother back.

"Hey, man, what's the word?" Khalil asked as soon as he answered.

"Hey. I got the job. Start tomorrow."

"Excellent! Not a surprise, though."

Karim shook his head. "You never know. Will you pass the word around? Don't need Mom to keep worrying." Though maybe she would if she knew about this Capulet-Montague stuff. Maybe he should. He decided to look on the bright side and focus on the fact that he had landed the position.

"Like it's possible to stop her," Khalil said. "But yeah, I'll let everyone know. So, I'll see you in San Diego on Saturday?"

"You know you don't have to come all this way. I can move in on my own."

"I'm overdue for a vacation. Never been to California. It's the perfect excuse."

"Uh-huh." Khalil wouldn't admit to being worried about him, so Karim wouldn't push. But he could give him a hard time. "One thing," Karim said, admiring the palm trees swaying in the breeze. "You might wanna ease up on the food, man. I didn't wanna say anything before, but you're getting a little soft."

"Hey," Khalil said. Karim could tell he was trying to hold in a laugh. "Don't hate 'cause my girl can throw down. And don't act like you didn't enjoy it when you were here."

"You're right. And I shouldn't complain. It's probably for the best."

"Why's that?"

"People can finally tell us apart."

"Ouch!" Khalil laughed. "I'm glad for you, bro. New city, new start."

"Yeah."

"Now all that's missing is a new girl."

Karim hesitated, remembering his flirtation with the woman from the plane. That Isadora who'd almost scalded him, then made up for it by boosting his confidence. But he wasn't ready to share.

"Don't, Khalil. Gotta go. I'll see you Saturday." He hung up, the phone joining his jacket. As he was getting ready to go to the apartment complex Christina had recommended, his phone rang again. Expecting it to be Khalil, he went to send the call to voicemail, but noticed the number. The area code was familiar, but it wasn't anyone in his family.

Who else would be calling from Detroit?

Whatever it was could wait. He needed to get his living situation squared away. Pulling onto the street, he returned to his checklist.

Move to California—check.

Find a job—check.

Place to live in district—check
Place to live at the capital—almost check
Get a life . . .

Two hours later, apartment situated and back at the hotel to check out, he was loading his bags into the trunk when his phone rang again. It was on the front seat; he didn't reach it in time. The missed call was the same number from that morning, and again, no message.

If you can't be bothered to leave a message, I'm not calling you back.

That evening, he took a stroll through Midtown Sacramento. He was settled in his new place, fridge stocked, and clothes set aside for the next day. His phone rang again, the same number he didn't recognize.

"Finally," a woman said when he answered.

His vision blurred, and he caught his footing with a brief staccato step. But he kept moving forward. Moving forward down the street, as he was determined to keep moving forward in his life.

"Raniya," he said, his mouth cotton, but his voice strong.

"I was beginning to think you didn't want to talk to your dear sister-in-law." If there was a silver lining to his wife's abandoning him, it was that he didn't have to deal with her smug sister anymore.

"As I'm sure you can understand, certain events led me to delete certain contacts from my phone. Had I known it was you, I would have avoided wasting my time and yours by answering."

"Now, Karim. That's no way to speak to your family."

"We aren't family anymore, Raniya. We haven't been for some time." He stopped at the window of an Italian restaurant. Inside, a man who looked like a younger version of himself sat across a table from a woman with long dark hair and golden skin.

Watch yourself, he wanted to warn the guy.

"I must say, we're rather disappointed in you. Running off like this."

His bark of a laugh ricocheted across the street.

"'Running off,' Raniya? Me? That's rich. We all know exactly who did the running. And the cheating. The raging and the gaslighting. And who remained faithful to his vows until he'd had enough of the abuse. Don't call me again."

Raniya was still talking as he ended the call and put his phone in his pocket. He continued walking, trying to discover the neighborhood, to get his bearings in the new place. But it was impossible. His mind was back in Harrisburg, remembering the zombie he'd become once he understood Laila wasn't coming back. At the gate, he fumbled with the keys. He got to his apartment and stretched out on the couch, returning to the work he'd done with his therapist in Michigan after staying in Pennsylvania became too much.

Laila's personality disorder is not a justification for her cruelty. She knew it was her problem but demanded that I shield her from the consequences of her choices. But you can't set yourself on fire to keep someone else warm. When she left, I made the necessary choice to protect myself by not chasing after her. She abandoned our relationship when I refused to keep abandoning myself. He drew in the needed breath.

In the shower, washing away the contact with Raniya and the accompanying memories of Laila, he remembered something else he'd discussed with his therapist—the idea of moving on, of trusting another woman again. In Harrisburg, it had been impossible. The town wasn't enormous, the dating pool microscopic. Celibacy wasn't a goal, but his commitment to his vows kept him from anything past a first date. Back home in Grosse Pointe, he'd had zero interest. Despite his family's best efforts, he wasn't up to it, and he never knew when he might run into his in-laws or friends of theirs. He hadn't had the slightest desire until yesterday. Until Isadora. She was beautiful, with dark, almond-shaped eyes to go with her glowing almond skin. High cheekbones, an adorable round nose, and full, appetizing lips. Her flash of anger had been sexy. Real sexy. The heat in her cheeks from the shock tinged the rich depth of her skin. He wasn't sure what he'd said to her as she raced away. However, he had a clear memory of checking her out, without hesitation.

Maybe I should have shared with Khalil; he'd be proud. He grinned as he toweled off.

When he'd reached his seat on the plane, he'd asked himself if it was a setup. During the flight, he didn't know what had come over him once he'd had an excuse to get her to take her earbuds out. It had been years since he'd flirted. He wished he'd gotten her number, but he wasn't ready.

Don't beat yourself up. It goes in the "win" column anyway because you sure didn't get onto the plane with the idea that you could flirt. This is a good step—it means you're further along than you thought. It's a shame you won't see her again, though.

CHAPTER THREE
Isadora

Closing the mini fridge in the outer office, Isadora added coffee creamer and green goddess dressing to her mental grocery list as she opened a bottled water.

"Ms. Maris?" A young man she didn't recognize tapped on the open door leading to the hall.

"Yes," she said, smiling as she approached.

He slid two file folders off the stack he was carrying and handed them to her.

"From Senate Administration," he said. "HR stuff, I think."

She thanked him and returned to her office. The job posting for Isadora's new Sacramento assistant had been fruitful. Melissa, Daniel's legislative director back in district, had already narrowed down the pool of applicants from thirty to five and made her suggestions. Isadora trusted her judgment, but when it came to the people she'd have to get up and running quickly, Isadora needed to complete the final interviews herself.

She was pleased with the credentials of the top two candidates, but a quick social media search eliminated them both: far too indiscreet for her taste. The third looked promising and came with a reference from a close colleague. She picked up the phone to call the young woman when a man's face in a thumbnail of one of her photos caught Isadora's eye. Dark hair, olive skin, glasses. She clicked the photo open, then exhaled, shaking her head at herself. It wasn't him.

Like that would happen. Another coincidence to make up for the chance I missed.

Karim hadn't faded from her memory. Which was unusual. She was focused on her professional life and did not have time for a personal one. Men were simply blips on her radar screen. The fact that this one had made an impact was a surprise. Straightening, she returned to her phone and dialed the number.

Let it go. I handled it as well as I could have, and I'm not letting a man distract me anyway.

"So, if I understand correctly," the candidate said, "Majority Leader Etcheverri will become president pro tempore at the end of this session, and then he'll run for Congress in two years?"

"That's the goal," said Isadora. "Although it isn't guaranteed, he already has the appropriate level of support. If we end up working together, it will mean an increase in workload once he's pro tem. Is that something you feel comfortable with?"

"Certainly. But he'll leave the senate to run for Congress?"

"His state senate term will be up then," said Isadora. "And once the current U.S. rep retires, the seat will be vacant."

"Oh. Has she already announced her retirement? I heard she was planning to run again."

Isadora smiled. She liked this girl. She knew to ask questions with diplomacy.

"These things are known in advance," she said. "Within the party."

"Ah. So, what happens then? Are you going to become chief of staff for someone else?"

"No. If things go according to plan, I'll go with Leader Etcheverri to D.C." She wanted to say that it had been her dream ever since a school trip to D.C. in the eighth grade. The day she discovered congressional aides existed she knew what she was going to be when she grew up. Even at that young age, she'd known that she wanted to make big changes in the world through politics, but the idea of being a politician herself turned her stomach. She valued her privacy far too much. Working with someone who didn't mind being in the public eye struck the right balance.

And now, with years of experience under her belt, she'd become invaluable to Daniel in terms of driving his policy and managing his current staff, and they could rely on each other to meet their shared career goals, and most important, their goals for the state of California. In addition to her regular work, Isadora had been studying the trends on Capitol Hill and already had plans to help the nation move in a more progressive direction, just as she and Daniel had already done in California.

"Ah, I see. Sounds like a dream come true," the candidate said, smiling.

Isadora grinned. She'd found her new assistant.

After a working lunch with two other chiefs of staff and a meeting on Daniel's behalf with a reporter, Isadora ducked out early to surprise her best friend and colleague by picking him up from the airport. RJ hadn't sounded very good when they'd spoken the night before. *Though how should he sound? His uncle doesn't have much time left.* She and RJ had been attached at the hip since their master's in public policy days and there was no one else she'd ever been as close to. His uncle had practically raised him, and Isadora had spent a lot of time getting to know him during his visits to see RJ. She knew that the love between the two men was strong and true. She'd lost her own father. Watching RJ be helpless before the decline of his paternal figure had been gutting. She knew what he was going through and wanted to help in any way she could.

Pulling into the airport parking lot, she cut the engine but didn't remove her keys. She prepared herself by thinking of some of the great memories they'd shared, and of the many times he had stepped up to the plate to support her when she'd needed it. He'd told her a thousand times that she was more than returning the favor, and she planned to keep doing it, today in a lighthearted way.

Just outside the arrivals doorway, she adjusted the black chauffeur's hat she'd picked up and smoothed her hands down her suit jacket. The doors flipped open, and she pulled the clipboard out from under her arm and held it up, scanning for her friend. He was kind to be as tall as he was. A shaggy blond lock fell over his brow as he shook his head, smiling. She couldn't return the gesture quite as well: RJ never left the house without his hair perfectly styled. That he'd flown halfway across the country without a lick of gel meant things were probably worse than he'd let on.

"You know," he said as he reached her, the sad smile still in place, "it usually works better if the client's name is right-side up." He flicked the clipboard and Isadora looked down to check. She was holding it upside down.

"Oh, you get the idea," she said. "Come here." She stood on tiptoe to hug him, squeezing tight. The deep sigh he let out only confirmed what she'd thought. "I didn't make you laugh a little?"

He stood up straight and smiled. "You know you did. Thanks."

"Come on, got chocolate in the car."

Had it been any other situation, she would have teased him about his un-styled hair and the bags under his eyes. But her intimate knowledge of what he must be feeling kept her from falling into their usual banter.

"You got something you want to say?" he asked as she pulled out of the garage.

"Why?"

"You're all tense. Giving off that stuck-in-between vibe you have when you're trying to choose." He popped another truffle into his mouth.

She couldn't contain the smirk. He knew her better than anyone.

"I wasn't gonna say anything," she said. "But you look like shit."

His jaw dropped, revealing a chocolate-smudged tooth.

"Eww!" she said, glancing at him. "Un-styled hair, bags under your eyes, and now you look like you're missing a tooth."

"You are such an asshole," he said. He flipped his visor down to assess the damage, running a hand through his bangs and scrubbing at the offending chocolate with the tip of his tongue.

"Willing-to-be-honest-with-you asshole." She shrugged. "That's why you love me."

"Guess I must." He folded the chocolate box shut, then flicked the back of her arm, chuckling at her shriek. "There. Even." She caught his grin before he turned his attention out the passenger-side window.

"Slumber party?" she asked, rubbing the sore spot on her arm once she'd stopped at a red light. "Or home in your own bed?"

"Slumber party," he said, as the light turned green.

An insistent ringtone pulled Isadora awake. A quick glance at the clock confirmed it was far too early for her phone to be ringing. Especially since she'd had to drag herself to bed in the middle of the night, having fallen asleep on the couch with RJ after emptying a bottle of wine between the two of them. The phone ringing again and again could only be one person.

"Hello, Mother," she sighed into the phone.

"Brace yourself, Izzy. I have some news."

"Okay."

"Try not to get too upset."

"'K."

Her mother sighed. "I don't want you to take this too hard being so far away."

Isadora ran a hand down her face. "Take what hard, Mother?"

"It really is a shame you're so far away. I just don't understand why you—"

"Mother," Isadora groaned. "Is someone dead?"

"What? Oh no. Nothing like that. Although, you might feel quite bad when I tell you, but I don't want you to give up hope."

Isadora didn't trust herself to say anything else.

"Sharee is getting married."

"I'm sorry?" She clamped her hand over her mouth. Her voice

had been much louder than she'd intended. RJ groaned in the living room and the couch leather creaked.

"I know, honey, I know. It must be hard for you to hear—"

"In most families, a phone call before five A.M. means someone has died."

"Well, honey, for you it might feel like a death because now Sharee has someone and you are all alone."

That was a backhand Isadora hadn't seen coming, so her mouth was hanging open when RJ appeared in her doorway, half asleep.

"You called this early, woke me up, because a cousin I never talk to is getting married?"

"I just found out. I thought it was important to let you know as soon as possible. Especially since it should have been you walking down the aisle first. Your priorities are all wrong."

Isadora rolled her eyes and sighed. "Getting married was such a mistake for you, why are you so hell-bent on me doing it?" The words had barely passed her lips before she was cursing herself for being too honest.

"How dare you! How could you say such a horrible thing about your father?"

"Mother. I was talking about you. You've spent my whole life complaining about your sacrifice—"

"I *did* sacrifice. First, I sacrificed my dreams for all your father's pretty promises. And for a while, things were good. It was all worth it. Then things changed."

Isadora didn't point out that what had changed was her birth. Her mother continued.

"So, then I had to sacrifice even more, didn't I? And then your dad got traded, and injured, and well . . . Anyway. Maybe if I'd still been 'fun,' he wouldn't have been on that motorcycle in the first place. And I wouldn't have lost everything, and we wouldn't have had to come groveling back to my family."

"And me?" Isadora asked.

"You?"

"Maybe I lost something too?"

"Oh. Yeah. I guess. But you need a man, Isadora."

Then it started. Her mother's script number whatever, that she'd beaten into Isadora's head hundreds of thousands of times since childhood. About how men were simultaneously indispensable, but would ruin your life, all your hopes and dreams. And that it was expected of Isadora that she let them be ruined. Especially if she wanted to remain in her mother's good graces. Isadora knew her mother was being illogical but being woken in the middle of the night meant she simply did not have the capacity to argue.

She zoned out. Was it the early hour, or hearing the long-winded script again? She'd always fought back against internalizing her mother's speeches, but after thousands of repetitions over the years, how could they not sink in? Then her mother's voice was loud in her ear.

"Well?" she shouted.

"Well, what?" Isadora sighed.

"I expect you to bring a date to the wedding," she snapped.

"Of course, Mother," Isadora said. "I'm going to go now."

"Don't you want to hear how he popped the question?"

"No, it's not really any of my business. Goodbye."

"Wait—didn't you go to school with a Bob?" her mother asked. "I think his name is Bob."

"Dunno. Gotta go."

"Hold on—do you remember him? I think he graduated with—"

"Bye, Mother, hanging up now, bye." She slammed the phone down on the nightstand.

Still in the doorway, RJ was awake enough to speak. "So, someone's getting married?"

"Yeah. My cousin Sharee."

"She had to call here before the sun was up to tell you that?" He raised a hand. "Sorry. Forgot who we were talking about."

Isadora flopped back onto her back, rubbing her eyes. RJ sat on the edge of the bed.

"I don't remember a Sharee. Are you close?" he asked.

"Not remotely." She readjusted the scarf protecting her hair, noticing that all her muscles felt achy.

"So why did your mother have to call?"

"She was concerned about how I would take the news."

RJ stretched out next to her. "Hmm?"

"Sharee is younger than I am and is now engaged. I am a poor, lonely, single gal. Naturally the news of her upcoming nuptials would have been so hard for me to take that I might well have become suicidal."

He snorted. "Of course."

They stared at the ceiling a few silent moments, Isadora's chest feeling cold.

"I'll answer next time," RJ said. "She wants a man in your bed so bad, let's give her one."

"Isn't it usually the gay man who needs a beard to introduce to his conservative family?" she asked, winking at him. "I'd love to see her face if you did answer my phone in the middle of the night. But I'd rather save my energy for the inevitable battle over moving to D.C. If she's been this resistant to 'chief of staff,' imagine how fun she'll be about 'congressional aide.'"

RJ snorted.

"Who was the last ex you told her about?" he asked.

"Joel."

"Why so long ago? Wasn't he, like, your first year at the senate?"

"Because they ganged up on me, remember? The whole family pressuring me to quit and start making babies."

"Right. I remember now."

Good ol' Mother. Telling the whole family that my dreams are nothing, don't matter.

"Besides," she said, shuffling deeper into the sheets. "It doesn't matter. Emotions are dangerous. They'll completely derail your dreams if you let them in. I've got more important things to worry about than relationships."

CHAPTER FOUR

Karim

"Good thing I came when I did," Khalil said. "You look like hell."

Karim laughed, shook his head, and hugged his brother back.

"Keep telling yourself that," he said, taking Khalil's bag and leading him into his new, very empty San Diego apartment. His capitol apartment was set up; now it was time to get settled in the district. "Movers will be here in an hour or so. Need to take a little nap first? Don't want you to sprain anything, being so out of shape and all."

Khalil punched him in the shoulder. "What's this? The California air doing you good? You haven't begged me to whip your ass like that in months."

Karim laughed, barely missing Khalil's arm with his punch back.

"Maybe," he said. "Been feeling a little more like myself." Khalil was right, and for a fraction of a second, he wondered if it was the new job, or the new girl haunting his thoughts. Then there was a honk outside: The movers were early.

Four hours later, sore and dusty from rearranging the furniture and unpacking the largest boxes, they stopped for lunch. Karim hadn't had much time to get to know his San Diego neighborhood, but after a little wandering and disagreeing, they settled on a fusion restaurant next door to an organic grocery store.

"Wow, guess you're serious, little bro," Khalil said, studying the folded menu on their table. He'd suggested they sit at one of the small tables in front of the restaurant. Karim wasn't crazy about eating so close to the street, but Khalil had made an excellent point about enjoying the weather.

"Three minutes, Khalil," Karim said, as he always did when Khalil brought up which twin was born first. "Serious about what?"

"Still counts," Khalil said, as always. "Fusion-organic-whatever? I'm not even here a whole day and you're putting me on a diet?"

Karim rolled his eyes. "Maybe everything isn't about you. I find I . . . feel better when I eat better. You could support my efforts to turn over a new leaf," he said, cleaning his glasses with the hem of his shirt.

"You're right," Khalil said. "I should be more supportive. Flying halfway across the country to help you rearrange your furniture. Something like that, huh?" He winked, then looked back at the menu in his hand. "Fine. I'll drink some green juice or eat an alfalfa salad if it helps keep you in this good of a mood. But I'm not eating fake meat. Sorry."

A waitress appeared and did the standard-issue double take the twins had gotten their whole lives. Followed by the requisite blush. She took their order and left, but not before Karim caught her glance at Khalil's ring finger, and at his bare one.

"She was cute," Khalil said.

"She was." Karim shrugged.

"She works here; you live around the corner. Maybe—"

"Maybe nothing," Karim said. "Even if I were interested, like you said. She *works* here, I *live* around the corner. Let's say things don't . . ." Out in the parking lot, Karim caught a glimpse of a woman walking toward the grocery store. Her silhouette reminded him of Isadora-from-the-airplane. His breath caught, and he shifted in his seat, waiting for her to appear again as she passed between the rows of cars.

"Things don't . . . ?" Khalil looked up from his phone and followed Karim's gaze. "What's wrong?"

Karim leaned over in his seat, catching sight of her sandal-wrapped feet as she wove around a large truck. Something clattered to the ground beside her, and she stopped short, then her hand swooped to the ground to retrieve it.

"Bro? You all right?" Khalil's voice registered, but it was distant. What were the odds he'd run into her again? She kept walking, and Karim sat upright, repositioning himself to get a view when she rounded the last two cars.

"Karim?" Khalil shifted into his line of sight, brow furrowed.

"Shhh!" Karim swatted a hand at him but didn't say anything else, too focused on waiting for her to appear. Khalil followed his gaze.

The woman reached the sidewalk. She was very attractive, but not Isadora-from-the-airplane attractive. Karim slumped back into his seat. Then his face caught fire. Khalil's grin was a mile wide.

"Okay, little brother!" he said, nodding. He glanced back at the woman again. "Want me to step inside for a minute? I'll intercept the waitress, can't let her disturb you."

Karim shook his head. "Nah, cut it out. It's nothing."

"Dude. That was *not* nothing. When did you start looking again? Doesn't matter. Go talk to her. It's been way too long."

"No," Karim said. "She just reminded me of someone." The words were barely past his lips before he regretted it. Khalil's face lit up.

"Reminded you of who?"

The waitress brought their food, but there was no distracting Khalil. He wouldn't let up until Karim told him everything. Spilling his guts was a little embarrassing, but he felt lighter once he'd done it. And his guess had been right, Khalil was proud of him, and he encouraged him to see the situation as a positive, not a failure to ask for her number. Halfway through the meal, their mother called Khalil, and he was more than happy to tell her that yes, Karim was eating his vegetables, and he'd met a girl. Khalil and their mom carried on like he was bringing Isadora home to meet her that afternoon.

That night, after dinner with Marcus, an old fraternity brother of Khalil's, and his partner, Gabriel, Karim was organizing his books when Khalil called out to him from the bedroom.

"What is it? Gonna admit you introduced me to Marcus and Gabriel so I won't be all by my lonesome in California?" The look on Khalil's face shut Karim up as he crossed the threshold. "Shit, man. What is it?"

"I'm not trying to tell you how to live your life," Khalil said, waiting for him in front of the dresser, hands on hips. "But I have to say I'm surprised you brought this with you." He gestured to Karim's watch case. "I dumped everything onto your bed to get rid of the last box. Didn't notice it until I tried to find a good spot for your case." Karim's wedding band glinted back at him from the gap between the cushion and the frame of the last compartment. The one he never used.

"I'm surprised too," he said. "Didn't know where it was. Sure didn't mean to bring it with me."

Khalil nodded. "You wanna keep it?"

Karim's "no" rushed out with his next breath.

"You want me to take it back for you?" Khalil asked. He pulled it out of the box, holding it between his thumb and forefinger, keeping the others outstretched, avoiding any unnecessary contact. "I could sell it," he said.

There was a lot locked up in that curved platinum. Karim took a deep breath and Khalil turned his hand, getting the ring out of sight.

"I'm sorry," he said. "I didn't think. Maybe it's still difficult to—"

"Actually . . ." Karim put a hand on Khalil's shoulder. "It's okay. That's the first time I've seen it in at least a year, and . . ." He paused, making a quick assessment of his emotions. "I'm good. Seeing it doesn't bother me like it used to."

Khalil shot him an enthusiastic smile.

"That is some damned good news," he said.

Karim returned to the living room, assessing his feelings again. The hurt was still there. He'd come to terms with the fact that in a way, it always would be. But that pain was growth. When Laila had first left, the pain of abandonment had subsumed him. He'd known things had been *off* for years, but it had taken that break, that time alone, and working with his therapist, to understand that his wife had been actively abusive, not just difficult. He grabbed a handful of books from the box he'd been emptying and tried to focus on where they should go. His mind wasn't in it, though. It was rehashing—but with distance—the fact, the actual *fact* that he'd been an abused man, a victim of domestic violence. She'd never laid a hand on him, though there had been things in the apartment that had made physical contact when she'd thrown them. One of the very books in his hand, he realized. He put them quickly on the shelf and reached for a few more. During his therapy sessions, he'd come to terms with the fact that the emotional abuse had been worse; the emotional blackmail, the gaslighting, the successful attempts at shaming him for being a human with reasonable needs for respect and his own agency. He put some more books on the shelf.

CHAPTER FIVE
Isadora

At a quarter after nine on a Thursday, Isadora hurried to prepare the small meeting room next to her office for a face-to-face over a freeway bill with one of the legislative directors to Senator Julian Brown. The well-earned mistrust between Senator Brown and Majority Leader Etcheverri extended to Christina and Isadora, their respective aides. As members of the same party, both representing parts of San Diego, the senators publicly supported each other. But there was no love lost between the two women. Not after years of behind-the-scenes opposition and what amounted to political violence. On more than one occasion, Julian had been responsible for undermining Daniel's projects and building coalitions against him. As ridiculous as it was in Isadora's eyes, she'd accepted her place as a member of the House of Montague in the rivalry. That morning, she was hosting her counterpart from the House of Capulet. The last time Christina had been in her office, she'd come to tell Isadora that Julian would give Daniel his complete support on a massive project. The next day, Julian had voted against it. The bill had passed anyway, but when Julian voted no, it had caused a significant delay on the senate floor during the vote and almost caused the bill to fail, which would have been a serious blow for Daniel. That moment of drama had been exactly what Julian had wanted. He wasn't the majority leader, but by playing up the divisions within the party,

Julian found a way to make everybody dance from time to time. And he did it just because he could.

Isadora was about to scoop some coffee into the machine when there was a knock at the door.

"Come in," she said.

She raised her head and suddenly she couldn't catch her breath. Christina wasn't alone.

"Hi, Isadora," Christina said, as she turned to the green-eyed demigod following her. "This is Karim. He'll be taking over for me in a few weeks. Karim, this is Isadora, Majority Leader Etcheverri's chief of staff. She's one of the most skilled and knowledgeable people in the senate."

A surge of adrenaline blasted through Isadora's chest as she stuffed down teenage giggles.

"Nice to meet you, Karim. Welcome," she said, offering her hand. "And thank you, Christina. That's very kind." She held Karim's gaze a beat longer than necessary, willing him to act like it was the first time their paths had crossed. He got the message.

"It's nice to meet you too," he said. He might have said something else. The tingles coursing over her skin sent static reverberations through her ears. Christina was saying something about his background, but it didn't register. All her efforts were focused on hiding her excitement.

". . . only been with us a little over a month. But based on his experience and credentials, I think he'll be a great fit, don't you?"

"I'm sure he will be. But I don't understand. He's taking over for you?" She had to pretend he wasn't there in order to hear Christina.

"Honestly?" She captured Isadora's full attention with her tone. "We wanted to keep it a secret until the second trimester, but I've been far too sick already. I want to work for as long as possible, but we thought it best to bring Karim on board quickly."

"Oh." Babies and pregnancy were well outside of Isadora's comfort zone, so she opted for a short but polite reply.

"I'm sorry you're not doing well. Though I doubt anyone can take your place, Christina."

"Thank you. Is it okay if he joins us for this meeting?"

"Of course. The sooner he gets his feet wet, the better." Isadora made the mistake of smiling at him. The tingles returned and her heart took off again.

"We'll be more comfortable here than in my office," she said, indicating the meeting room. "Please, take a seat."

Christina went in first, sitting closest to the door, her back to them.

"Hi," Karim whispered.

"Hi, yourself," she whispered back, cheeks burning. With a hand on the doorframe, she started to cross the threshold, but she'd left her notes beside the coffee maker.

"Oops, forgot something," she said, turning around, bumping into him again. He caught her elbow as she went off balance.

"Are you okay?" he asked.

"Yeah, sorry." She shook her head at herself. "Guess I have a problem running into you," she whispered.

"It's not a problem," he whispered back. "Not at all."

Heat flashed over her scalp. She ducked her face down to pass him and retrieve her notes. Choosing the seat farthest from the door, he chatted with Christina. Isadora seized the moment to study him. His lips were as full as she remembered, cheekbones and jaw sexy and masculine; his nose was straight, but prominent enough not to be perfect. Black hair, styled but not tamed. Same charming glasses.

Joining them, she pulled a third chair to the table.

"Would you all care for anything before we get started? Water, maybe a tea? I haven't made the coffee yet, would—" As soon as she said "coffee," Christina's eyes went wide, and she glanced at Karim. He pointed behind her and she shot up, grabbed the trash can he'd indicated, and stepped through the doorway, retching into it out of sight.

"Don't say 'coffee,'" he mouthed at Isadora.

"No?" she mouthed back.

"No. Bad word."

Once the retching stopped, he spoke at a normal volume. "Christina, are you okay?"

"I think—" She was cut off by another retch.

Wow.

"I'll be back in a few minutes," Christina coughed. "Isadora, if you don't mind, I'll need to take this with me." She kept the trash can close to her chest.

"Not a problem, Christina. Take all the time you need."

"Thanks. Will you start, Karim? My notes are in that folder."

"Sure thing," he said.

Isadora chanced a look at him once Christina was gone.

"This is a surprise," she said.

"It is." He let out a long breath. "Not an unpleasant one, I hope."

"No," she smiled, thumbing an imaginary cardigan cuff. "It's nice to see you again."

"You too."

A faint charge crinkled the air between them, his eye contact as hesitant as hers.

"Just . . . so improbable, huh?" she asked.

"Yeah." He rolled his shoulders. "What are the odds?"

"Yeah."

Each tick of the clock in the outer office clacked in Isadora's ears, matching the thump of her heart.

"I, uh, didn't guess right about your job, huh?" he asked.

"No." Isadora chuckled. "Would have been funny if you had."

"Yeah."

"Yeah."

He glanced around the room, looking just as nervous as she felt. She searched for something else to say.

"Poor Christina. And poor you."

He brightened. "Why poor me?"

My god, he's got a sexy smile.

She refocused on the words, not the lips. "It must be some

experience to land a new job and learn that one of your first tasks is to have a trash can at the ready in case someone needs to vomit."

He laughed, warm and rich, sending shivers down her back.

"It has been . . . unique," he said, taking off his glasses to clean the lenses. He glanced up at her through dark, lush lashes, and she had to squeeze her crossed ankles together as the room wobbled.

"I . . . I bet it has." Maintaining eye contact got difficult again. "I'd die of embarrassment if I got sick at work," she whispered.

"Me too. She's fighting hard to do her regular work and show me the ropes." He was also avoiding her gaze.

"Has Julian said anything?" *If you can tell me.*

"I . . . doubt he understands how serious it is. She said she was a little sick in the district, but it's ramped up here. And she isn't telling him how bad things are. Part of me wants to, but . . ."

"You don't feel like it's your place," Isadora said.

"Exactly."

She couldn't imagine joining a team and finding herself in the position of going to a boss she didn't yet know about the health issues of a coworker. Too personal, too private.

"It's a difficult position to be in," she said.

"It is. She's put a lot of pressure on herself."

"No, I meant for you."

"Oh. Well. Yes, it is." The color that bloomed up his cheeks made her melt. Karim, the demigod, *was* shy. "Thank you for noticing," he said.

She'd been here before. An awkward crush on the cutest boy in the entire freshman class, the one *all* the girls giggled about. He'd paired with her on a science presentation. Heart hammering in her chest every time he spoke to her, she'd stammered and stuttered through three study sessions, her hands trembling, like they were right then. High school, undergrad, and a master's in public policy under her belt, and here she was, getting flustered by a boy. Shaking her head at herself, she took a deep breath and pulled her shoulders back.

"I guess we can get started," she said. "Unless you'd like something to drink?"

"Could I have a cup of tea? I stopped drinking coffee so Christina doesn't smell it, and I've been substituting with tea. It's not strong enough, though. I have to drink a lot to get my dose."

"Sure." She left him to make some. While the water was heating, she returned to the doorway.

"That's kind of you."

"What is?" His Adam's apple bobbed.

"Changing your habits so another person feels better. Not much compassion like that around here." She left to pour his tea.

"No big deal," he called out. "I'm sure you'd do the same."

"You are?" She returned, warm cup in hand.

"Of course. You don't look like a monster; I'd be surprised to learn you're not a compassionate person."

"I don't look like a monster?" She laughed. "What *do* I look like, then?"

His lips twitched, attention on his tea.

"Like . . . a very attractive woman." He met her gaze. "And you seem intelligent, kind, and . . . discreet."

Her stomach dropped, and her heart took off.

"Morning!" the delivery man called from the outer office door. He waved the mail in her direction.

"Hello! Please toss it on that desk," she said, pointing to the one beside him.

"Have a good day."

"You too." The interruption allowed her to recover.

She thanked Karim. "Discreet. That's a new one."

"It is?"

"Yes."

"You aren't discreet?"

His reaction nudged her back to herself.

"If I need to be, of course. Depends on the situation, what sort of risk might be worth taking a chance."

Isadora and Christina had planned on minor changes to the bill draft. Karim made several impressive suggestions. There were a few points Isadora needed to clarify with RJ, due to his appropriations experience. She called him from the landline beside the meeting table. As she angled away from Karim, she caught his glance at her chest.

It's about time.

RJ picked up.

"Hey, it's me," Isadora said. "You busy?"

"No, what's up?"

"Julian's new director and I are working on a bill Julian and Daniel are co-sponsoring. We've got a couple appropriations questions."

"Julian's got a new director?"

"Yup."

"And she's there now?"

"Yes, he is." Isadora smiled at Karim. He smiled back.

"A 'he'? Julian couldn't find another woman willing to work for him I guess," RJ said. Isadora inched closer to the phone, pretending to focus on RJ.

"Now would be great," she said. Out of the corner of her eye, she caught Karim's gaze caressing her shoulder and down to her waist. She wondered what it would be like if it was his hand instead. Another rush of heat blossomed, and she swallowed to keep her voice from fluttering. "To get you in the right frame of mind, remember that case study we did as part of our final?"

"You're asking me about some school shit from five years ago?"

"No," she said, laughing. "The other one. With the conflict about zoning laws."

"Seriously, what is the matter with you right now?"

"If I remember correctly, you were *really* into it. You spent a lot of time on it. It was like a *phase* you went through back then. We might come up on some similar issues with this bill."

"Isa. What the hell?" RJ asked. "The *only* thing I was into back then was hot guys with dark hair and light eyes. That was my southern Mediterranean pha— Are you trying to tell me something?"

"Yep."

"Is he hot?"

"That doesn't quite cover it. I'd say more than that."

"For real? I'll be there in five seconds." He hung up.

She put the phone down. "RJ has to make a quick call and he'll be right over," she said to Karim.

"Okay."

"While we're waiting, why don't you tell me a little about yourself? You have some good ideas. Is this your first spin in a legislature?"

"No. I was an aide in Virginia, then legal counsel for several years on committees in Pennsylvania. Christina mentioned it when she introduced us," he said.

"Oh. Guess I was distracted."

"You were?"

"Yeah. You don't think I'm the only attractive person in this room, do you?"

He glanced down at the table, and back at her with a different sort of smile. Shy and seductive, it escaped from him, as though he was flattered and embarrassed at the same time.

"Thank you," he said. "It's good to know your opinion."

Emboldened, she wanted to continue flirting but thought better of it.

"So, legal counsel?" she asked. "Did you become a lawyer so that you could work in politics, or did it go the other way around?"

"I always knew that I wanted to help people," he said. "I just wasn't sure how. My aunt is a lawyer, and she always said that it was a better job than people thought. That if you had the right intention, you could do wonderful things. She's a public defender, and while I always admired what she did, it seemed so frustrating."

"I can get that," Isadora said.

"I figured that you could help more people from a different vantage point, where the laws are made, rather than where they're applied. So, I got my BA in public policy first, then went to law school."

"I got my master's in public policy. With a focus on the health and safety net," she said.

He smiled. "Health and safety net? Looks like we have something in common. The social safety net was my focus." His smile faltered. "I haven't been able to do as much as I'd like to in that area. I think that better healthcare is the best way to improve people's overall quality of life. Not only physically, but financially. If you get sick, it's bad enough. If you're stressed about how much it's going to cost, how can you focus on getting better? Then once the crisis has passed and you're recovering, the bills start rolling in. How can you actually live? Removing that burden is part of what made California attractive to me. It was groundbreaking when you guys passed the Single Payer Act last year."

"Yes, it was," she said. "It wasn't easy. And we've made a lot of enemies with the private insurance companies that work in the other states. Though I imagine you know that."

He smiled again, broadly. "Yeah, I paid close attention. It must have been really rewarding to get a finished product."

"It was."

"If I'd known what you do, I'd have been all over you on the plane." His face flashed red. "I mean with questions. I'd have been all over you with questions."

He shot her another shy smile, and she wasn't sure what to say again, but he spoke first.

"What brought you into politics, Isadora?"

"Well," she said, "there's that desire to help people, like you said. And yes, I feel like where laws are made is the best place that can be done. Plus, I don't know, I just love the process, the way we move from idea to bill to law. Even the formalities of parliamentary procedure." She shrugged. "Guess that kind of makes me a nerd."

He smiled and winked.

"That makes two of us."

RJ arrived, and Karim stood as Isadora introduced them.

"RJ, this is Karim. He's taking over for Christina during her maternity leave. Karim, this is RJ. He's legislative director to Senator Scalzi, who also represents part of San Diego."

Karim was a little slow offering his hand to RJ, studying him.

"You aren't RJ Nichols, are you?"

Isadora and RJ glanced at each other as RJ slowly shook Karim's hand.

"I am . . ."

"RJ Nichols, U.S. rowing team alternate?" Karim asked.

Isadora didn't check her grin. RJ was almost never recognized outside of the rowing community in San Diego. He was playing it cool, but she was sure he was flattered.

"Yeah," he said, a smile breaking through the surprise.

"It's great to meet you," Karim said, heartily shaking RJ's hand between both of his. "One of my brothers rowed for Michigan. He's a big fan of yours. He won't believe it when I tell him I met you."

Isadora ducked her head down, pressing her lips together. Karim couldn't have scored more points with RJ if he'd tried. She returned to her seat, and Karim did as well, while RJ pulled out the third chair and eased into it. He was fighting hard to maintain a professional exterior, but the tips of his ears were bright pink.

"Wow," he said. "Thanks."

Coughing to stifle a giggle, Isadora smiled at both men and started the meeting again. RJ provided several options for the appropriations issue. Karim preferred checking in with Julian before agreeing. Once he and Isadora set the final meeting for the following week, he excused himself to find Christina. Escorting Karim to the door, she closed it behind him and swiveled to face RJ, finally able to let her jaw drop.

"He knows who you are," she singsonged, dancing back to RJ as his ears and his cheeks bloomed pink again.

"Shut up," he said, his tone in contrast to his grin. "That never happens."

Isadora giggled. "I know! I'm so happy for you."

"Should you be? I didn't handle it like a total goober? I barely said anything."

"You played it cool." She shrugged.

Picking up his notepad, he joined her in the outer office.

"Not that cool. But thank you for the heads-up. Otherwise, I'd have walked in here and made a fool of myself before he even said anything."

"I know, right?" She went over to start the coffee. "He is pretty attractive."

RJ stared at her.

"Oh all right! He's sexy, he's sexy, so what?" She faltered, scooping more coffee next to the machine than into the filter. RJ smirked.

"What do you mean 'So what'? If he's not interested in me, he had better be interested in you."

"What good would it do if he's interested in either one of us?"

"I know. He works for Julian. How long has he been there?"

"Not long." Isadora shrugged.

RJ raised an eyebrow. "Maybe we could turn him!"

"You're kidding, right?"

"Not a bit. You are gorgeous. The only person around here more gorgeous than you, is me. Either way, he should be receptive to our charms."

She shook her head. RJ kept smiling.

"Come on. You know you want to."

"RJ."

"It's been a while . . ."

"Don't start."

"Seriously, how long has it been?"

She rolled her eyes and poured herself some coffee.

"That long? God, woman, you should have come with me on vacation this summer. I had my pick."

"Last I checked, we shop in the same store. Just not on the same aisle," she said over the rim of her cup. "And you know I can't be browsing around Julian's staff!"

"So what if he's a Capulet?" RJ asked.

Isadora rolled her eyes.

"You know I think that 'Capulet-Montague' stuff is ridiculous," she said.

RJ shrugged.

"Okay, so it's a little dramatic. But you're gonna tell me it doesn't fit? Julian doesn't 'bite his thumb' at Daniel each and every chance he gets?" RJ asked.

Isadora finished her sip.

"No, I most certainly will not. It's like breathing to him."

"He'd stab Daniel in the middle of the rotunda if he could get away with it," RJ said. He took a step closer to the door, then turned to face her, his smile wicked. "All the more reason this could be fun. This Karim could be a delicious way to end the getting-laid drought."

"No," she said. "No fraternizing with the enemy. We have to be good little soldiers, even if it means some self-deprivation. Besides, remember what happened to the original Capulets and Montagues who tried to get together?"

He rolled his eyes and stood. "Come on. I said have some *fun*. Not fall in eternal love. And can't we just go for 'don't ask, don't tell'?"

"RJ!"

"You know you want to," he whispered, opening the door and stepping into the hallway.

Maybe I do. And that's precisely why I shouldn't.

CHAPTER SIX
Karim

Saturday afternoon, Karim followed Julian's directions, stopping about three miles away to pick up the requested six-pack. Julian and fellow senator Peter Luccini hosted occasional get-togethers at a place called Ike's. As Julian's aide, Karim was expected to put in an appearance.

He'd anticipated a private home. Instead, Ike's was in a semi-commercial part of town. The number of cars surprised him, as did the number of people inside. A large lounge with a back wall of sliding glass doors opened onto a swimming pool flanked by couches and tables. Karim had been disappointed when he learned Sacramento was a good two hours away from the Pacific. But the pool, surrounded by sand, lounge chairs, and a few parasols, brought the ocean inland.

Peter approached him from behind, thumping a hand on his shoulder, a feat due to their difference in height.

"Karim! Good you could make it," he said.

"Thanks for the invite."

"Of course. Thanks for bringing these," he said, taking the beer. "We've got the place to ourselves tonight, but the manager always gets overexcited on the drinks, so we save the taxpayers a couple bucks where we can." He winked and clamped Karim's shoulder again. "Lemme show you around."

Peter introduced him to guest after guest, mostly men surrounded by two or three attractive women. After the seventh or eighth introduction, Karim leaned toward Peter.

"You're gonna have to help me out; there's no way I'll remember everyone."

"Don't worry about it. There are only a couple senators and assemblymen here. The rest are members of the Third House. They will make it a point to remember you."

Karim nodded, pleased to learn that the lobbying corps had the same nickname on both coasts.

"Listen," Peter said. "I gotta take a leak. You're a big boy, you can make friends on your own?"

"Of course, Peter. And thanks again for inviting me."

"Oh, don't thank me yet. You'll be far more appreciative by the end of the evening." He winked and walked away. Karim gave him a tight-lipped smile, tipping his chosen beer in Peter's direction. He took a swig and as soon as he lowered his gaze, made eye contact with two women sitting on one of the poolside couches. They waved him over. One shifted and patted the empty place between them. The invitation wasn't that appealing, but he didn't know who they were and couldn't risk offending anyone.

"Hi," said the short-haired blonde as he sat. "You're new here."

"I am," he said, committing himself to polite conversation.

An hour later, confident he'd never been hit on as much in his entire life, Karim was making his escape from a conversation when the other host of the party found him.

"Karim! There you are." Julian's robe matched the exterior furniture and he still had steam coming off him from the jacuzzi. "Peter forgot to tell you to bring a bathing suit? You're welcome to borrow one of mine and swim if the mood strikes." He nodded toward three women at the far end of the pool, wriggling out of their dresses. "Though suit, no suit, that rarely stops the girls," he slurred.

Karim provided the expected chuckle.

"Come," he said. "I try not to talk shop here, it's supposed to be for fun, but I head back home tomorrow so now's what we've got." He approached two chairs under a parasol at the edge of the pool. They were occupied, but the man engaged in an in-depth conversation with a young lady's cleavage stood up and took her elsewhere as Julian arrived, swatting a hand at them. He caught the woman's wrist as she walked away.

"Tell someone to bring me two rum and cokes, huh?"

"Sure, Julian," she said, following her friend.

Karim spoke up, "I'm good." He lifted his second beer in her direction. She nodded.

"Who said one was for you?" Julian winked, settling into his seat. "How's it going? First month, a lot to learn."

"I've had a good start. Thanks again for the opportunity."

Julian waved his hand again. "Don't mention it. You were a good candidate on paper. Christina tells me you're better in action. You handled the freeway bill meeting?"

Karim nodded. "She wasn't feeling her best."

"Yeah, yeah." His drinks arrived, and he leaned back in his chair. After a sip, his body language shifted. He wasn't as drunk as he wanted to appear. "Listen, I'm gonna be straight with you because we need to be on the same page."

Karim nodded and leaned toward Julian as he lowered his voice. He began with his doubts—Christina had been with him for years, and she said she'd be back after giving birth, but his gut told him otherwise. He wanted Karim to be ready for the possibility of staying long-term if this session went well. Karim nodded again but kept his expression neutral. His instincts told him to remain noncommittal. Julian switched to history and his goals. He was sick of Daniel Etcheverri. His status as majority leader had been difficult for Julian to swallow. It was a role he'd yearned for. Daniel had always found a way to outshine him, and Julian had had enough. While the freeway bill was a good opportunity for them both, he was certain Daniel would find a way to carve out a better deal for himself. Isadora made things more complicated.

"I have to admit she's good. Always three steps ahead when it comes to anticipating Daniel's best interest and finding a way to achieve it. I need you to be on your guard."

"Okay."

"You also have to be careful because I'm sure she uses all of her attributes to her advantage. Never had any proof; she's got this damn impeccable reputation. But the number of times she's managed to get someone I was sure I had on my team to switch sides? There's no other explanation."

Julian's jaw tightened each time he referred to Isadora. It was a surprising amount of aggression. Then it clicked for Karim. Julian had wanted her, and she'd sent him packing. If Julian was accustomed to women throwing themselves at him or his friends, her refusal must have been an insult. Karim had to smother his smirk. It made him respect her even more. However, this was his boss, and he'd just dangled the possibility of something long-term.

"I hear what you're saying, Julian," he said. "I understand."

Julian started to say something, but then a young woman approached. She bent over to whisper something in his ear, and he chuckled.

"What an *excellent* idea," he said to her. "I'll meet you upstairs in two minutes." He ran a hand down her back, cupping her bottom and squeezing hard. "Naughty," he said as she giggled and walked away. He turned back to Karim.

"Glad we're on the same page. I need to count on you. Now, go have some fun." His gesture encompassed the room. "Trust me, you have your pick. You're in Capulet territory here." He winked at Karim and left to catch up with his friend.

Capulet territory? Even he's into it? Karim sat for a moment with his beer. It was his second and it was still full. He turned the bottle in his hands. Splashes and giggles caught his attention. He raised his head, noting the couples and triples forming. This wasn't his scene.

He ducked out after going to the men's room. Peter's voice

echoed in the darkened hall as he escorted two women toward a stairwell. Karim got to his car and headed home.

If Julian was right, and Christina didn't come back, the permanent opportunity Karim needed was there for the taking. If he and Julian were a good fit. He'd researched Julian Brown while he was back in Michigan. An average state-level politician: city councilman, then assemblyman, then senator; nothing stood out. Experience and leadership of the same sort of committees Karim had worked with—Rules, Judiciary, Public Safety. A scandal early in his career about a child out of wedlock. The young mother later retracted her claim. Other than that, he hadn't found anything on the man's character despite several days' research. Now, after a month at work and the envy and hypocrisy Julian had just shown, Karim began to wonder if he wanted a permanent opportunity with Julian Brown.

His thoughts returned to Isadora. He told himself it was for professional reasons. Julian said she was always a few steps ahead. If Karim was going to shine on this freeway bill he needed to be at his best as well.

He picked apart their meeting. She *had* flirted with him. Maybe Julian was right, maybe she did use her charms. But in all fairness, he had tested the waters too. And she hadn't known who he was on the flight.

Those first few minutes at the meeting had been beyond challenging. When he crossed the threshold behind Christina, he'd almost plowed into her. The moment on the plane was just that, a moment. And then, there Isadora was, right in front of him—no longer just the star of his fantasies.

She'd kept his full attention while she spoke with Christina. Her voice had a luxurious, feminine depth he'd missed before. Her hair was up, away from her face. She was even sexier, more confident, in her element. And when she'd smiled at him and shook his hand, he was thirteen years old again.

Bumping into him wasn't some ploy. The professional mask she'd worn with Christina wasn't there when they were alone.

He'd encountered the real Isadora, twice. Did Christina know that Isadora? Did Julian? He smiled as he unlocked the door to his apartment. In a parallel universe, he would have caught her in his arms when she lost her balance. His fingertips still held the warmth of that unexpected introduction to her skin.

Fear popped up. A tiny light warning of the danger of being hurt. He didn't want to go there, so he stretched out on the couch and flicked on the TV. But Isadora haunted him. While waiting for the water for his tea, she'd returned to talk with him, leaning against the doorjamb. The curve of her hips had seared into his memory. Her light blue sweater had been fitted enough to make his mouth dry.

After the two hours he'd wasted at Ike's, he wanted some way to reach out, some excuse to contact her before their meeting the coming week. Her work email had to be available in the internal database. He put down the remote and picked up his work phone, rolling it in his hands.

CHAPTER SEVEN
Isadora

Saturday evening, RJ dragged Isadora to the movies. Finding themselves in a sea of teenagers, she'd balked at the choice and tried to leave. But she'd gotten sucked into the film, laughing enough to wipe away the occasional tear.

"Okay," she said, stepping into the Sacramento evening. "It was funny. The premise was stupid, but it was funny."

RJ linked his arm in hers. "Exactly. Pointless, improbable, and I nearly wet myself. What's next? Drinks or straight to dinner?" She tried to pull away, but he snapped her back against him. "Which?"

"Drinks sound good, but I need to at least look over—"

RJ smashed his index finger to her lips. "No."

"But—"

"No. No work. This is what is colloquially known as a week-end," he said, gesturing with his free hand. "It is the end of the week, one of two days people do not go to work, or do work-related things. You know I love you, and we both love what we do. And not to get all heavy, but you are not avoiding your mother's mistakes by being a workaholic and not taking a break from work on the *week-end*. You know this. You cannot live your entire life trying not to be your mother."

She chewed on her lip. The criticism was fair, and his point completely correct, but she couldn't go there right now.

"Fine. You're right. But it couldn't hurt to take a look at—"

"No." He kept striding forward, pulling her along.

"Fine. Dinner. I wanna choose to sleep in tomorrow, not do it because I'm hungover."

Settling in at a Chinese restaurant, she put her work phone beside her plate on autopilot.

"I said—" RJ began.

"Sorry!" She picked it up to put it away, jumping as it buzzed in her hand. A gasp escaped at the notification.

"What?" RJ asked.

"It's from Karim. An email."

"What's it about?"

"I have permission to check?" she asked.

"If it's from Mr. Sexy Pants, of course."

She rolled her eyes at RJ as she opened the email. "It's about the freeway bill."

"He's working on that? On a Saturday night? Gah. He's even worse than you."

The waiter took their order and Isadora bunched her lips at her phone.

"Remorse about your choice?"

"No," she said. "Weird question from Karim. He asked if we have to go through the Environmental Quality committee. And if so, why not do that as a separate bill? Revamping large parts of the freeway system is obviously going to impact the environment. There shouldn't be anything for him to be confused about."

"Is he a beautiful idiot? I brought the last one home. Maybe it's your turn."

She shook her head. "He isn't an idiot. It's just . . . strange. Do you mind if I answer?"

"Go for it." He sipped his water.

She answered what he asked but didn't tell him that a second bill was out of the question in case it embarrassed him. The waiter appeared with their appetizers, and a few bites in, her phone buzzed again. Karim thanked her and asked another question, confirming which cities would be the first to get the HOV lanes. She read it again and frowned at RJ.

"What?" he asked.

"I don't get it. What's this game? Is he trying to get written proof of parts of our meeting?"

RJ chewed, considering along with her. "Did you indicate flexibility on anything he's asking you about?"

"No. This is stuff I established with Christina. The order of the cities was on the first page of her notes. He'd have to understand that San Diego is the top priority for both Daniel and Julian. They have to start with their own districts."

She continued chewing and frowning. The phone buzzed again. She slid it across the table, letting RJ read for himself.

"No. I remember that," he said, wiping his mouth. "Maybe it's not his background, but it's obvious that a project this extensive has funds appropriated over . . ." He stopped and beamed.

"What?"

"He isn't asking you about work," RJ said.

"Umm . . . ?"

"He isn't asking about *work*. He is asking *you* . . . about work." She squinted at him.

"Oh, my clueless darling." He slipped his hand over hers and squeezed. "He just wants to talk to you."

"What?" Her growled whisper didn't tamp down his enthusiasm. He squealed and did a jig in his chair.

"If this isn't the cutest thing ever—he wants to talk to you so much he doesn't care if he looks like an idiot doing it."

"That doesn't make any sense. If he wanted to talk to me, he knows where my office is."

"It makes all the sense in the world. The meeting was days ago. If he really had questions, he would have brought them up already. But it's Saturday. No work keeping him busy. His mind can wander to more *enticing* subjects."

"Or his shithead boss can have him play mind games with me. And you know full well that if there's anything Julian loves to do, it's playing mind games and roping his staff in to play along," she said. "We've all been back for a couple weeks, it's about time for those sketch parties at Ike's to start up."

"That's true." He shrugged.

"Those parties start early in the evening. How much do you want to bet Julian took Karim to one?"

He retreated into his seat. "Okay."

"So," Isadora said, leaning forward. "How difficult is it to imagine that Julian told Karim to get in touch with me and play all nice? Try to get my guard down and soften me up for the future?"

RJ sipped some tea. She sipped along with him, ignoring a shiver of disappointment.

"Wait," he said. Teacup to the side, he scrolled through the conversation again. "Maybe I'm wrong, but there isn't anything here that gives Julian an advantage. Karim's asking things he should already know. And if he doesn't, he certainly shouldn't ask you, the chief of staff to his boss's nemesis. These would be questions for Christina." He slid the phone back across the table.

Isadora crossed her hands in her lap, still focused on the phone.

"So why?"

"'Cause he likes you."

"Please, RJ."

"And more important, you like him." He raised a hand to her protest. "You don't want to, but you do. You got all giggly the second you saw his name."

"I did n—" His glare silenced her denial. She considered tossing the rest of her tea in his face to rinse away the smug.

"Let's say, for argument's sake, that perhaps, *maybe* I do find him attractive," she said.

"And you have a crush on him."

"I do not! I barely even know him."

"So. Get to know him. In the biblical sense."

"RJ! He works for *Julian*. We've watched Julian step on anyone he can, because he can. His last mistress decides it's over, and before you know it, she's let go from her lobbying firm and can't get picked up by anyone else. How many bills has he voted against just to spite the sponsor? You're right. Karim is sexy as hell and in any other situation, I would love to find out more about him. Especially in the biblical sense. But I don't know a damn thing about his character. I *do* know a lot about the character of the guy who has power over him."

RJ sighed, shoulders slumping.

"Such a shame. Cause you are so much easier to deal with when you're getting some on the regular," he said.

She balled up her napkin and threw it in his face.

Dropping her off at home, RJ made her promise not to do any work. She relented and chose to pamper herself before going to bed. Hair reconstructor under a hot towel, purifying mask in place, she flipped through the TV channels. Her work phone was on the valet table beside the door. She glanced at the TV, then back at her phone.

She found a historical documentary.

Why would Karim send me such bizarre emails? Either Julian has him up to something or RJ's right. She wouldn't allow herself to recognize how much she hoped RJ was right. The phone beckoned again. She hadn't answered his last two emails.

No reason to be rude.

She was back on the couch with her phone in a flash.

Hi Karim, she wrote. *Sorry for the delay in responding. To be honest, I'm a bit lost. We spent a lot of time on both issues during our meeting. Christina and I already established the order of the cities, and you and I double-checked the projected dates together. For such a massive project, I'm sure you can understand that multiple rounds of appropriations will be needed over several years. But perhaps appropriations work differently in Virginia and Pennsylvania? It's easy to get tripped up, especially being thrown into things so quickly. I'm happy to help you if I can. I'd have just guessed that Christina would be a more confidential resource for you. Best regards, Isadora.*

She hesitated to click "send." Although she'd struck the appropriate tone between helpful and professional, the contact itself made her pause. She *did* want a connection with him, an excuse to talk to him. She had since their flight. But Julian excelled at setting traps. And giving in to her attraction to Karim was a bad idea. As she put the phone down on the coffee table, her finger slipped and off the email went.

Can't take it back now.

His reply was waiting when she returned to the living room after rinsing her hair and washing her face.

> *Hello again, Isadora,*
>
> *I am sorry, you're right. Christina is the best person for me to turn to, but she's become so ill that I hesitate to contact her at all. I appreciate your patience with a new guy who is probably making mistakes left, right, and sideways. I hope I haven't offended you.*
>
> > *Have a good evening,*
> > *Karim*

His email reminded her of his shyness with a tug at her heart. It must have been difficult for him to reach out at all.

> *Dear Karim,*
>
> *Don't worry, and please don't apologize. You haven't offended me in any way. Why don't we take it down to brass tacks on Tuesday? We'll take our time and I'll answer any questions you have—please don't hesitate, even if it's minor. There are no stupid questions! I'll be happy to help you.*
>
> > *Best,*
> > *Isadora*

She smiled as she hit Send, imagining him at that moment, perhaps lounging at home as well. Prickles shot through her as she caught the first word of her reply. She'd called him "Dear." Hand clamped over her mouth, she recoiled from the phone. She never used "Dear" with anyone at work. Sure, it was acceptable. She knew that. But it was the way she'd opened the letters her mother had forced her to write to her grandmother when she was a child. It was the way she'd addressed notes to her first crush when she was in middle school, so for her the familial or romantic tinge was still there. Maybe those sorts of connotations existed for Karim, and he'd think she was a weirdo or inappropriate for using it with him.

She scrolled back through the emails. He'd said "Hello," she'd said "Hi," then he'd said "Hello again." *Why didn't I just say "Hi again"? Why did I have to make it weird? Wait. Am I overthinking this?* She looked at her phone again, scrolling through the emails. *Nope. Weird. I totally made it weird.* Mortified, her stomach prickly with anxiety, she returned the phone to its spot, clicked the TV and lights off, and marched herself straight to bed.

CHAPTER EIGHT
Karim

On Monday night, Karim ironed his moss green dress shirt, lips in a tight, painful line. Julian had set him up for a shitty morning.

Across a table from Isadora in less than twelve hours, he had to try to convince her to reorganize the freeway bill into something that would make her boss look like a weakling and his, a power broker. He hadn't asked Julian why he wanted the changes he'd sent Sunday morning, but Karim was sure he'd had more than his ego stroked at Ike's. The lithe representatives of several lobbying firms had probably jammed his head full of the ways their clients might benefit and how eager they would be to show their appreciation. It would have lowered Karim's opinion of Julian to know for sure that he was unfaithful, but as the practice was so common, and Julian didn't seem the type to restrain himself from any sort of pleasure . . . Julian's fun over the weekend meant Karim got stuck dealing with the fallout.

Thanks a lot, boss.

Christina was back in the district, so Karim would be alone with Isadora. He should have been thrilled. Instead, he was angry, his emotions still running high from trying to convince Julian to be more reasonable, without pushing too hard. Desperate for anything that might help Isadora hate him less, Karim chose the shirt she'd complimented him on. At a fine foods shop, he'd purchased the nicest coffee available to brew for her tomorrow. He'd considered stopping for pastries on his way to the office, but he didn't want to go overboard.

The knot in his stomach grew tighter as the evening progressed. The contractors Julian had already spoken with had difficult histories with Daniel according to some articles Karim had found. And as he expected, it was illegal in California to promise state work to anyone before the bidding process. He'd checked detailed maps of San Diego, and of course Julian's desired changes also meant work in his district would begin months before Daniel's.

Either he's completely out of his mind, or he's doing everything possible to force Daniel to kill this bill.

The next morning at the office, Karim had trouble keeping still. The coffee was made, and his laptop was open on the meeting table, along with two copies of Julian's suggestions. He'd considered making only one copy so that he'd have an excuse to lean over the list with her, but he didn't want to be a creep.

He went back to his office and double-checked that he hadn't forgotten anything useful; back to the coffeepot to ensure he had creamer and sugar and stirrers. And then back into Julian's personal office, the only space large enough for the separate table for the meeting. He was getting on his own nerves.

Returning from the men's room, a woman's laughter floated down the hall. He turned the corner, and there was Isadora, her back to him, in an indigo blouse and a fitted cream skirt. He wanted to fall into the depth of that blue, but the curves under the cream snapped him to attention. She was chatting with a man he didn't recognize. He was shorter than Karim, blond and built like a linebacker. The man's face switched from flirty to serious but polite as he and Karim nodded a hello. Isadora followed the linebacker's attention, greeting Karim as well. He returned the gesture and continued on his way.

Of course. He'd been so mesmerized by her that he hadn't thought about competition from men who'd already gained her trust. *Maybe they're just friends. Then again, Laila had lots of "just friends" over the years.* He shook his head, clearing bad memories. *No. It's for the best. Starting over starts with work.* He would focus on his job— trying to satisfy as many of Julian's demands as possible. Begin building his reputation as professional in any circumstance.

Isadora knocked on the open outer office door. He invited her in, stepping out of his office to her right and smiling.

"How are you today?" he asked, offering his hand.

"I'm well, and you?" She returned his handshake, her smile heating his cheeks.

"Good, thank you. Christina's back home, so it's just us. Shall we get started?" He gestured toward Julian's office.

"Sure."

"Coffee?" he asked, after inviting her to sit.

"It smells delicious. I'd love some."

At least he'd scored one point. He asked her how she took it and returned to the outer office to pour her a cup.

"Nice shirt," she called out. A smile tugged at his lips.

"Thanks. A smart woman with good taste complimented me on it once. I decided to wear it more often." He returned to her side with the coffee. "Let me know if it isn't to your liking. Be careful, though," he said as he took his seat. "Might still be a little hot."

She leaned closer to the cup. "I'll give it a minute, but it's tough to be patient. Smells awesome. Not your run-of-the-mill supermarket coffee, I imagine?"

He shook his head, willing himself not to blush. He wanted to chat with her, but he was too tense.

Might as well get it over with.

"So," he began. "Julian asked me for some changes in the draft. I'm concerned they . . . might prevent us from filing it as soon as we'd hoped."

"Oh?" She accepted the two stapled pages. Her eyes narrowed, and she pursed her lips as she read. By the time she'd placed the pages on the table and turned to the window, she was like a tiny sun, emanating anger instead of light. When she faced him again, his stomach dropped. She wore the mask of professionalism she'd worn with Christina. The mask he hoped she'd never use with him.

"So, it was a ruse?" she asked.

He didn't follow.

"All your polite little questions on Saturday night. You were trying to soften me up, so I would be more amenable to changes today."

Scanning the list, his blood went cold. More than half of the items touched on his questions from Saturday night. It hadn't occurred to him. Glancing back up at her, he caught a shimmer in one eye. He wanted to crawl under a rock.

"No, Isadora, please. There was no ruse. Julian sent me a list on Sunday morning and by yesterday evening, we reached this. My questions were . . . I wanted to . . . they had nothing to do with these suggestions."

"So, it's a coincidence that you weren't sure about the timing of the project, and now Julian would like Daniel to accept a significant delay for our district, but an immediate start for yours and several others?"

"Yes," he said. "It is a coincidence." *Gotta be professional. Do your job.*

"I explained how important the Environmental Quality committee is—in terms of its status, and to Daniel himself—and now, oddly enough, Julian wants us to commit to things that will cause controversy with multiple environmental protection groups?"

Karim pressed his lips together and nodded. It was the best reaction given the circumstances. She stopped speaking and scrutinized him. A sparkle of desire burned his insides as he maintained eye contact, but its flame didn't catch.

"If the shoe were on the other foot, I would be suspicious as well," he said. "This bill is an excellent idea and would certainly benefit our constituents and the state as a whole. Even though we are further apart on our goals than we were at our last meeting, I'm confident we can still find a way to make this work." *And I'm sorry and I hate that this situation has made you think I'm playing a game.*

She raised an eyebrow but remained silent. Other than looking at the list again, she did not move. Her phone buzzed.

"Will you give me a moment?" she asked, glancing at it. "It's Daniel, I have to reply."

"Of course," he said. "I'll give you some privacy." He returned to the outer office and poured himself a half-cup of coffee. Isadora was still within earshot, so he pulled out his phone to text Christina. After a quick back-and-forth, he got what he needed to know: points five, eight, and fourteen were the least likely to force Isadora to refuse. And his hunch was right. Julian usually left Ike's with a long list of bad ideas.

A sigh escaped him as he slid his phone back into his pocket. Three options were much more attainable than eighteen. Two of the three were related to the bogus questions he'd sent her on Saturday night, so she might remain suspicious. But there was nothing else to do except move forward. He'd find a way to earn her trust, to get her to be as relaxed with him as she was with that guy in the hallway. Reasoning with himself, he went over yet again why this attraction to Isadora was such a bad idea. But it was getting pointless. He envied that guy. He wanted her to laugh with him like that. And when she'd asked him if his emails had been a ruse and he saw what might have been the glimmer of a tear in her eye?

It was too late. He was smitten.

CHAPTER NINE
Isadora

Rage and disappointment battled inside Isadora when Karim stepped out of the room. She went back to the start of her morning, dreaming of him in a large, luxurious bed with gleaming white sheets. His smile, licking his lips as she approached. Then she was on top of him, riding him. His hands on her hips, moving up her back, his face buried between her breasts. He rocked up hard into her, she was so, so close.

Then her alarm had gone off and ruined everything. Perhaps it was an omen for her day. He'd made her pulse skitter in the hallway. He was polite and attentive when she'd first arrived. And now Julian and his list of impossible demands had come blaring in and destroyed it all. If there was one positive thing, it proved her hunch had been correct—Julian had been behind Karim's oh-so-charming emails on Saturday. She wanted to believe his denial, but it all fit together too well. He was gorgeous and loyal—to his boss. *Should I have expected anything else?* She'd almost lost her temper when he said he was "confident" about making the bill work. Good that Daniel had texted her when he did. She shifted in her chair, making sure her body concealed the screen of the phone from the doorway and checked what he had to say.

Daniel: Morning. You in with Christina on the freeway bill yet?

Isadora: In the mtg, but with the new aide.

Daniel: Julian's already promising contracts and rates.

Isadora: Before we even have the bill in committee?

Daniel: Heard from 3 contractors who wanted to know why
   they hadn't had the chance to bid.

Isadora: Wow. OK.

She paused a moment, glancing out the window, weighing options.

Isadora: When did the contractors find out about the project?

Daniel: Lunch yesterday. Julian told some Labor Fed reps the
   deal was already sealed.

Isadora: Did they ask about what cities and when?

Daniel: No. They already knew the first few—SD, SJ & SF. Why?

Isadora: Wanna know if something the new aide said is legit.
   Let's let it die in committee. Julian can't blame you.

Daniel: Perfect.

Isadora: Gonna stay. "Negotiate." Throw them off.

Daniel: And that's why you're the chief.

Isadora: Thx, Boss Man.

She locked her phone and slid it back onto the table. If the union reps already knew the correct cities and dates, why had Karim asked her about incorrect ones? Had he just made up the question? He'd also asked about environmental issues and funding. Those were general subjects. Anyone who'd heard a transportation bill was in the works could have made up similar questions. Karim was probably telling her the truth. If Julian hadn't sent him this list until Sunday morning, Karim's questions on Saturday night weren't really him talking about work. They were him trying to talk to *her*.

No. You're imagining things because he's hot, and the idea is flattering. You can't go there. Just focus on the part to be played today and get out of here. The longer you're alone with him, the more tempting things are going to get.

"Karim?" she called out.

"Yes?" He appeared in the doorway.

"Thank you. I'm ready to get back to work on this bill, are you?"

He smiled as he returned, triggering a kaleidoscope of butterflies in her stomach. She smiled back.

"Your coffee has probably gone cold," he said. "Would you like a fresh cup?"

"Yes, please."

She checked him out as he walked away. His deep gray pants fit like they'd been tailored for him, outlining his tight, sexy little butt.

"Isadora," he began, the warmth in his voice sending delicious shivers over her skin as he returned with the cup. "I want to apologize for the last-minute changes."

"It's okay. These things hap—" Their fingers brushed as she accepted the cup. It slid from her grasp, spilling the contents on the edge of her skirt, down her calf and onto the carpet.

"Oh! I'm sorry!" She searched for something to blot the floor.

"Don't worry, I'll be right back." He grabbed some paper towels from the outer office. Giving her a few, he knelt to clean the carpet. She squatted down to help.

"Are you all right?" he asked. "Please, don't worry about the floor, I'll take care of it. Did you burn yourself?"

"No, I'm okay. I'll do it, it was my clumsiness." She moved closer to him, trying to absorb as much as possible.

"Really, don't worry. I think you got some on your skirt. Are you sure you're okay?"

There was a small stain on the hem, but she hadn't burned herself.

"I'll put some water on the skirt. And my leg's a little warm, that's all." He was pressing some towels into the carpet, but his attention wasn't on his hands. He might have been looking at her leg out of the corner of his eye. She followed his gaze and saw that the top of her stocking and a bit of the garter she'd worn for a confidence boost was visible.

"I'm really sorry," she said, returning to her seat. "Please get up. I'll call Senate Services and ask them to send someone to steam clean the spot. The smell will probably be awful for Christina when she gets back."

"Okay. I didn't know there was someone to call."

"Do you mind if I use this phone?" She pointed to the one on a small table nearby.

"No, go ahead." He left to toss the stained towels in the trash in the outer office.

"You didn't know about Senate Services?" she asked while waiting for someone to pick up.

"No." He returned. "Learning something new every day," he said with a smile.

She smiled back, but her attention was drawn to the person on the other end of the line. He left again while she asked for someone to come clean the carpet. When she hung up, he was back with a small bottle of club soda and clean paper towels.

"For your skirt," he said, handing them to her.

"Thanks." She sat, opening the bottle to dab at the stain on the fabric.

"It's been a bit of a crash course for you, hasn't it?" she asked.

He smiled again, adjusted his nerdy-cute glasses, and returned to his seat. The relaxed way he crossed his arms made his shoulders even broader, sexier. "There's a lot to learn," he said.

"And a lot to watch out for, apparently. Morning sickness, clumsy coffee drinkers. I don't think it's safe for me to be around you with a cup of coffee."

He blushed and laughed, glancing at the table.

God, even his laugh is sexy.

"You do . . . keep me on my toes a bit. And a new job wouldn't be much fun without a few surprises, I guess."

"I guess not." She shrugged, closing the bottle. There was a draft—one of the buttons on her blouse had come undone in the commotion over the coffee. She often had problems with it, the second to last one she buttoned. If it was open, the middle of her bra might appear depending on the way she moved. She was wearing the bra that matched the garter. If they were back to the flirting they'd started in their first meeting, no reason he shouldn't get a peek to feed his imagination.

He smiled, tucking his fists deeper into the crook of each

elbow. Then he uncrossed his arms and reached for his pen. He was delicious to look at, but she wanted to know more about him.

"Tell me," she said. "What's the craziest bill you've worked on?"

"The craziest?" he asked, rolling the pen between his fingers.

"Yeah. Or the weirdest. One that sticks out in your mind."

He chuckled.

"Clowns."

"Clowns?" she asked.

"Yeah. Regulating the number of clowns a circus can have," he said.

She leaned back in her seat.

"I've worked on a variety of subjects over the years," she said. "But I can't say that clowns have ever crossed my desk."

"It was a surprise for me too," he said, glancing down at the table. "I didn't have to do much work on it personally, but I did have to give advice on a few legal arguments a senator wanted to make against the bill. He felt very strongly that circuses should have an unlimited number of clowns."

The image of a circus tent with masses of clowns spilling out popped into Isadora's head, and she tilted her head back to laugh. Karim joined her, but when she looked at him again, she caught his gaze dart up from the collar of her blouse.

Gotcha. My collar is close enough for your peripheral vision to catch that open button, isn't it? She tried to keep her smile closer to "tickled" than "victorious."

"How did it work out?" she asked.

"The bill failed. They kept their unlimited clowns," he said, smiling. "What about you? One that sticks out?"

She thought a moment. It was tough to choose just one.

"Matchmaking agencies," she finally said.

He raised his eyebrows.

"I ended up learning a lot about them. Including the fact that sometimes lines can get blurred between legitimate agencies, dating websites, and escorting services."

"Ah. Well, the escorting is a completely irrelevant issue, but I'm certain you wouldn't ever need those other two services personally," he said, leaning closer. She maintained eye contact with him but didn't speak. An ember expanded in her chest, and she wondered if he could hear her heart beating.

"I don't think you would either, Karim."

Okay. This is bad. I'm sitting here flirting with this man, and we are supposed to be enemies. Get it together, Isadora. A gorgeous man isn't any reason to lose your head. She cleared her throat.

"You mentioned something in our last meeting," she said. "When we were getting to know each other."

"Yes?"

"I believe we share the goal of using politics to help people. But our bosses' goals usually originate from different perspectives. So, I think you understand we have a little problem here." She crossed her palms at the edge of the table and leaned forward.

"I do."

"I don't see how I can go to Daniel with these . . . suggestions."

"I'm not surprised." He met her gaze. "Would you do me a favor?"

"Maybe, what is it?"

"Do you think Daniel might be willing to negotiate on points five, eight, and fourteen?"

She reviewed her copy of the list. They were bulleted, not numbered.

"Here," he said, reaching for her page. "I'll show you."

She turned it so he could read as he scooted his chair closer to hers.

"Point five," he underlined it. "About the contractors eligible for the work. Point eight refers to private funding. And point fourteen concerns the environmental impact assessments."

Isadora studied each point. A touch of the lace along the edge of her bra was visible, so she took her time.

"And Julian won't push hard for point sixteen?" She caught his gaze flash back up to her face when she looked up.

"Julian is going to push hard for all eighteen. But, faced with the prospect of Daniel refusing these changes or scrapping the entire project, I think I can convince him to be more reasonable."

She leaned back into her seat. "You're that sure I'd advise Daniel to scrap the entire project?"

Karim leaned back as well.

"You're brilliant and skilled at what you do, Isadora, but not impossible to read." His voice was soft, a deep, masculine rumble. "And nothing on this list is in Daniel's interest. You and I both know that. Julian does too—he just doesn't care."

She was speechless for a moment. That was a lot of information at once. And his tone sent a wave of heat through her that made her breath catch.

"Well." She cleared her throat. "Thank you. And thank you for understanding our position."

"I'd like to understand *everything* about you, Isadora," he said, his voice warmer. The phone rang in the outer office. "If you'll excuse me, I'd better get that."

She needed a deep breath to get herself under control.

It's time to get out of here.

Then he was back.

"I'm sorry, I'm afraid this call is going to take a while. Could you speak with Daniel and get back to us?"

"Certainly," she said, gathering her things. She was about to step into the hallway when he called out to her.

"Are you headed back to the district this weekend?"

"No," she said. "I'm staying here."

"If our paths don't cross before the end of the week, I wish you a good weekend, Isadora."

CHAPTER TEN

Isadora

The next day, Isadora was returning to her office after lunch when her nose started itching. She sneezed as she crossed the threshold, and her assistant excitedly stopped her at the door.

"Something came for you while you were gone," she said, smiling broadly.

"Oh?" Isadora followed her around the entryway desk. Her assistant turned to face her with a large bouquet of magnolias in a glass vase. Isadora took a giant step back.

"I thought they were for the office from a lobbying firm, but the card is addressed directly to you," she said.

"Ah," Isadora said. "Well, could you hand me the card?" She didn't step forward to take the vase. Her assistant looked puzzled but put the vase down and pulled out the card to hand to her.

Dear Izzy, the card read. *Mommy was just thinking about you and wanted to send a little something. Love you bunches! —Mom*

Isadora sneezed again as she looked back up at her assistant. Her throat was starting to get scratchy.

"Do you have a secret admirer?" the young woman asked.

As if.

"Nope, just my mother," Isadora said.

"Oh! That's so sweet! My mom and I are best friends too. Isn't it great?"

Isadora didn't let her shoulders slump with her sigh. She hated lying to people, but anytime she'd let on to anyone that she and her mother didn't get along, the response had always been something that minimized Isadora's feelings or experience. No point in putting her hand on a hot stove again.

"That is nice," she said to her assistant.

"Do you want me to put them in your office?" she asked.

Isadora shook her head and sneezed again.

"Unfortunately, I am quite allergic to magnolias." *Which my mother should know.* "Why don't you put them on your desk? That way the whole office can enjoy them?"

"Oh? Okay," she said.

Sneezing again, Isadora turned to go into her office when there was a knock on the door behind her.

"Hey," RJ said when she turned around. He nodded a hello to her assistant. "You busy?" he asked Isadora. "Just wanted to stop by and say hi."

"Not busy right now," she said. "Come on down."

He frowned at the flowers as he passed them.

"Were those magnolias?" he asked, closing her office door behind him and taking a seat.

"Yep," she said.

"Ugh. Bad luck for you. Though the firm that sent them couldn't know how allergic you are. Maybe it'll be okay if they stay in the outer office."

"Hope so," Isadora said. "But they aren't from a firm." She unlocked the drawer for her purse and slid it in, clearing her throat.

RJ tilted his head to the side.

"Are they for *you*?"

"Yep."

His eyes went wide. "Did Mr. Sexy Pants send you flowers at work?"

"He has no reason to," Isadora said. "They're from my mother."

"Your mother? Why?"

"No idea. Another one of her games, I imagine."

"Your mother sent you flowers you're allergic to?"

"Yep," Isadora said, opening the folder of news articles mentioning Daniel that her assistant had left on her laptop. The phone on her desk rang. "Yes?" she answered.

"Hey," said her assistant. "I've got your mom on the line."

Isadora gritted her teeth. "Did you say that I was in?" she asked.

"Um . . . yeah? I shouldn't have?"

How to draw boundaries without spreading my business? If she told her assistant to always screen her mother's calls, that would show that she and her mother had a difficult relationship, which was none of the assistant's business. If she didn't ask her to do that, her mother would have yet another way to intrude into her life. *I just don't have the bandwidth to figure it out right now.*

"It's okay. You can put her through," Isadora said. "Hel—"

"Did you get the flowers?" her mother asked before Isadora could greet her. "I got a notification that the delivery had been made, but you can never trust those things."

"Yes, Mother, I got the flowers," Isadora said, looking at RJ, who rolled his eyes.

"Aren't they beautiful? Don't you have something to say?"

"Just hang up the phone," RJ mouthed.

Isadora sighed.

"While I appreciate the gesture, did you choose magnolias or was that the florist's decision?" she asked.

"I chose them because they're your favorite. A mama always looks out for her baby."

Isadora didn't know what to say for a few seconds. RJ mouthed for her to hang up again, but she knew how that would work out later.

"Mother," she said. "I am allergic to magnolias. I always have been."

"No, you're not," she said.

"What do you mean 'No, I'm not'?"

RJ's eyebrows shot up.

"You're not allergic to magnolias," her mother said. "You love magnolias. I know my child. I know what she likes."

Isadora sighed again.

"When I was eight, we went to Aunt Gloria's house to help her with her garden. I picked up some magnolia clippings and broke out in head-to-toe hives. When I was twelve, we went to the Mother's Day luncheon at church and the table centerpieces had magnolias. The side of my face swelled up and a deacon and one of the members of the mother's board told you to take me to the emergency room, which you didn't, of course."

"Oh, you were overreacting. You just didn't want to stay for the luncheon."

"How does a twelve-year-old make the side of her face swell up on command, Mother?" Isadora asked.

"Hang. Up. The. Phone!" RJ mouthed, leaning toward her.

Her mother didn't say anything. Isadora continued.

"When I was seventeen, my prom date bought me a corsage with magnolias. You insisted that I wear it to be polite, and I did, and I ended up in the emergency room because my throat closed up. So, no. Magnolias are not my favorite flower, Mother."

Her mother huffed. Isadora waited for the click and dial tone from getting hung up on, but it didn't come. Instead, her mother drew in a shaky breath.

"If I say you love magnolias, then you love magnolias. What is wrong with you? Nothing I do is ever good enough," she sobbed. "You never appreciate me, or all that I've sacrificed for you or anything!"

Isadora looked up at the ceiling. RJ tapped on the edge of her desk to get her attention.

"Time for the waterworks?" he whispered.

Isadora nodded.

"No matter what I do, you just push me away!" Her mother began wailing incoherently. Isadora didn't want to be affected. She fought the rising guilt, the impulse to placate her mother. Logically, she knew that her mother was being manipulative, but she couldn't get past her conditioning to put her mother's demands before her own needs.

"Mother," she said. "Mother?"

The sobbing continued but got a little quieter.

"It was a very nice gesture," Isadora said.

RJ cocked his head to the side. "*Do not*," he mouthed. Isadora shrugged.

"I can understand that it's been a while since you saw me react to magnolias, so maybe you might have forgotten. I don't expect you to remember things like my favorite flower or food, because those things change and we haven't lived in the same place for quite some time."

Her mother wailed again. Isadora pulled the phone away from her ear to protect her hearing. RJ threw his hands up in the air.

"Why don't you want to live here? Why don't you want to live near me? Am I that horrible of a person? I don't deserve to be loved?" her mother sobbed.

Isadora sighed. *How many times have we been over this?* Of course, she couldn't be honest and say that there was no way she'd ever live in the same place as her mother. She refused to have her entire life engulfed again the way that proximity would allow. She could only tell part of the truth.

"Mother, my job is out here. My career. My educational and career choices have nothing to do with you. This is not personal."

"Stop doing this!" RJ whispered. "Stop sparing her feelings while minimizing yours. I know that's what you're doing. Just get off the phone!"

Isadora widened her eyes at him and shrugged. What else could she do, though? Suddenly he stood up, turned, and knocked hard on her office door. He widened his eyes at her, then knocked again.

"Oh!" she said. "Mother, I have to go. Someone's at my door, sounds urgent."

"Okay." Her mother sniffled. "I just, I get it. You're working."

Isadora's eyebrows shot up. That was the first time she could remember her mother acknowledging that in a way that wasn't heartily negative.

"Isadora!" RJ said loudly, but with a forced depth in his voice. "I need you in my office immediately!"

"Oh, Isadora?" her mother asked. "Is that your boss?"

"Um . . ." She looked up at RJ, trying to stifle a laugh. "Yeah, that's my boss. I have to go."

"Okay," her mother said. "I'll let you go." She hung up the phone.

Isadora put the phone down and let herself laugh.

"Dude?" she said to RJ as he sat back down.

"What?" he asked. "I had to get you off the phone. You weren't doing it fast enough."

Her chuckles died down as she looked at him.

"Thank you for being a friend," she said.

"Travel down the road and back again," he answered. "So how did things go with Sexy Pants yesterday? Sorry I couldn't call when I got home last night. I passed out."

Isadora waved away his apology.

"It went well. If a little too flirty for our own good. He asked if I was going to be in the district this weekend."

"Maybe for a little date?"

She rolled her eyes. "Don't be ridiculous, RJ." She turned her attention to the files on her desk, gathering the things she needed for the meeting she had in half an hour. "As much fun as it might be to joke around, and even if we skirt the issue a little when we talk about Capulets and Montagues, at the end of the day, two things remain."

"Um . . . not digging the super serious tone," RJ said. "What are these two things?"

"One: Sex is not how I get my business done. Which I know you know, but it doesn't hurt to repeat because people will always think that sex is somehow involved if a woman is advancing in her career in politics. And two: Straight men ruin everything. Look at the life of the person I just got off the phone with. I—"

"You are not your mother, Isadora," RJ said.

"I know that. But life provides us with cautionary tales. I pay attention." She stopped messing with the things on her desk and sat back in her chair. She made eye contact with her friend, and he raised an eyebrow. She held his gaze.

"Again, you're not your mom. You aren't, I don't know, pre-destined to go through the same shit that she did."

"I know, I know," Isadora said, waving a hand in the air as she rolled her eyes. But did she know? She sighed. "I just want to be careful. Careful here at work with my reputation, and careful in my personal life. Yes, I will definitely enjoy some delicious eye candy, and I can be honest and say that he is interesting and intelligent and skilled and is probably a great legislative director, and it's a shame that we didn't recruit him first. That's as far as it can go, though."

"Bullshit. Well. Only half bullshit. Straight men usually do ruin everything. But there are some unicorns out there, and this Karim might be one of them. The only way to find out is to get to know him better." He stood and returned to the door. "I'm taking those magnolias with me. God only knows how much worse your reaction could get if you're near them for an extended period of time. Besides, Helena will like them." He opened her door.

Isadora nodded. "Tell Senator Scalzi I said hi. And Daniel may call her this evening. Thinking of having a couple off-campus meetings in the coming weeks."

"Will do," RJ said, winked at her, and left.

Thursday, Daniel called to ask about her weekend plans.

"Nothing in particular, why?"

"Melissa won't be able to come with us, so I need you to head back." The San Diego senators and assembly members were guests of honor at the inauguration of a new stadium complex. Melissa, Daniel's in-district legislative director, was supposed to go to answer any reporter's questions, and to reiterate Daniel's appreciation of the support he'd received while promoting the project.

"Can you be here for Saturday night?" he asked.

"Sure," Isadora said, already tasting the metallic anxiety of the flight.

"It's supposed to be a fun time. We get to listen to a bunch of pompous windbags—yours truly included—and then dinner and dancing. Come on, it'll be a blast."

"'A bunch of pompous windbags.' That does sound like a blast. Can Melissa send me her notes?"

"On the way now. Would you like to ride with us?"

"If there's enough room."

"No problem."

Isadora hung up, wanting to strangle Daniel. She'd been home the previous weekend, now she had to fly back. While she was at it, she might as well strangle herself too. She should have said no.

CHAPTER ELEVEN
Karim

On the plane back to the district Thursday evening, Karim allowed himself to return to his disappointment that Isadora was staying in Sacramento as he flipped through some journalist information Christina had emailed him. He was going to a stadium inauguration gala to shadow Drew, Julian's in-district legislative director. The event gave Karim the chance to learn the office modus operandi in the face of the press, and to be introduced on the San Diego political scene as a member of Julian's staff.

He also wanted to get to know Drew better, hoping that face-to-face, he wouldn't mind answering a few questions about Julian. When Julian gave him the assignment, Karim had let himself hope Isadora might be there too. He was sad she was staying in Sacramento, but it was for the best.

He left the district office after lunch on Friday.

"Karim!" Julian called out as he was preparing to go.

"Yes?"

"I need you sharp tomorrow night, okay? Drew's going to do the heavy lifting, but we're a team, got it?"

"Yes, sir."

"We should arrive together, but I think separate cars are best—

never know how these evenings may end up." He rubbed his hands together like there was a feast before him. The glint of his wedding band caught Karim's eye.

Really have to ask Drew about that.

"Of course," he answered, hoping his face reflected the appropriate degree of lasciviousness.

"Good." Julian smiled. "Meet you in the lobby at six thirty."

Karim picked up his black suit from the tailor's and took it with him to Marcus and Gabriel's menswear shop to get an appropriate shirt. Although he spent most of his time in Sacramento, the weekends he had been in San Diego, he'd made it a point to catch up with Gabriel for an early run or pick-up basketball. Having gotten to know him, Karim trusted his judgment. But Gabriel still managed to surprise him when he recommended a black shirt.

"Everyone else will be wearing white," he said.

Karim appraised the combination in the triple mirror. He had a point. And while Julian wanted a united front, Karim hesitated about being 100 percent united with him.

"And don't shave," said a young woman in the waiting area.

"Really?" He hadn't shaved that morning; he wasn't sure about skipping another day.

"Trust me," she said. "Don't."

Julian had a different reaction the following evening.

"Who are you supposed to be? Johnny Cash?" He slapped Karim on the back, laughing as Drew approached. Karim took it in stride, laughing along. But the number of appreciative glances he'd gotten in his ten minutes of waiting for Julian had already confirmed Gabriel's suggestion.

"Okay, boys," Julian said. "Let's go."

He barreled to the area reserved for the press. Turning to the first female journalist in his path, Julian smiled and began talking about himself. Drew stayed a step or two behind him, so Karim did the same. After speaking to several newspaper reporters, Julian turned to his aides.

"Listen, I'm gonna handle the TV stations. Why don't you head over to thc cocktail party and do a little reconnaissance? Don't want to waste any time before dinner."

Drew nodded, and Karim followed.

"Reconnaissance?" Karim asked once Julian was out of earshot.

"Julian never spends the evening alone. He wants to have a companion or two lined up," Drew said.

The security guards checked their invitations at the door to the cocktail area.

"Julian is . . ." Drew shoved his hands in his pockets and began a stroll around the room.

A skirt-chaser? A misogynist?

". . . an old-school politician," Drew finished. "As clichéd as it is, I think he really enjoys maintaining his sleezeball image." He eyed Karim. "You won't share this with him?"

"No. In fact, I had hoped to get your read on things."

A passing waiter offered glasses of champagne.

"He seems to revel in it, but deep down, I think he's a sad little kid. A very adulterous one." Drew shrugged and sipped, scanning the room.

"That's another question I have," Karim said. "But first, what are we looking for?"

"Blond, brunette, redhead, Black, white, Latina, Asian, turquoise, tall, short, whatever. Just make sure she's young and not fat. Not very bright is a plus."

"Oh-kay." Karim sipped. "You were going to say something about his marriage?"

"Yeah. He and his wife have an agreement. He brings home power, money, and any prestige he can maintain. She does the photo ops, campaigns, and manages the kids. And they live their separate lives. She would have come tonight, but she's in Barbados with her yoga teacher. Or tennis coach. I forget which." He waved a hand in the air, swatting away the idea that it might have made a difference. "Official line is that she's under the weather."

Karim tried to absorb without judgment, a little sorry for Julian and his wife. Maybe his compassion was misplaced because he understood the pain of an unsuccessful marriage. There was no way for him to know if Julian and his wife were okay with mutual infidelity. That was well beyond an appropriate conversation to have with his boss. But Julian clearly didn't care about appropriateness if he sent his aides out on missions to hunt for women, something Karim wasn't about to do.

Julian spotted them as he entered the cocktail party. He waved them over to join his conversation with a woman in her early fifties.

"Gloria," Julian said. "I'd like to introduce my new legislative director, Karim Sarda. Karim, this is Assemblywoman Hughes."

"Nice to meet you, Assemblywoman," he said, offering his hand.

"Well," she said. "It is very, very nice to meet you, young man." She took her time checking him out. "I see the reality is even better than the rumors."

Karim's throat was sandpaper.

"Um, thank you," he managed.

"Julian," she said, still admiring Karim. "I'm looking forward to supporting your wine bill when it comes over to the assembly. But I have a few questions. I'm sure this charming young man could stop by my office sometime and illuminate me on the merits of supporting it."

"What Madam Assemblywoman wants," Julian said, "Madam Assemblywoman gets."

"If you'll excuse me, gentlemen, I haven't been here long, and you know how sensitive some people get if you don't say hello. I look forward to seeing you soon, Karim." She walked away.

"Well," Julian said, a hand on Karim's shoulder. "Looks like you might bring more to the team than just your mental skill set."

Karim's desire to start over in California did not extend that far. Julian chortled.

"Don't worry. That bill isn't going anywhere, she just doesn't know it yet. You and your considerable attributes are off the hook—for now."

Karim didn't try to keep the bite out of his laughter with Julian and Drew. After a few more introductions and outright pickup attempts, he excused himself to the restroom. Taking his time at the sink, he returned to his checklist.

Move to California—check

Find a job—check

Places to live—check

Ah. I wasn't specific. I didn't say, "Find a job with a normal boss who isn't going to try to pimp me out to advance his agenda." He ripped a paper towel out of the dispenser and returned to the cocktail party.

As he took the scenic route back to Julian, a woman in a vibrant blue dress caught his eye. She was chatting with an older woman in a long yellow dress. The younger one had her back to him, which he greatly appreciated. Her dress was short, but appropriate, revealing sexy legs that went on for days. Her ass was perfect, just the sort Karim never got enough of: a little large, round, and high. He wanted to run over and sink his teeth into it. Narrow waist, one shoulder left bare by her dress. She wore her hair up, a restrained cascade of curls he wanted to take down and run his fingers through.

He was trying to come up with an approach when she and the other woman turned to go into a different section of the room. His heart stopped.

CHAPTER TWELVE
Isadora

Isadora and Daniel's wife, Glenna, strolled through the cocktail party at the stadium inauguration. Although she had to be "on" for work, Isadora enjoyed spending time with Glenna, their relationship more aunt-niece than boss's wife–employee.

Glenna shook her head at Isadora as one of Daniel's biggest detractors walked away from them, at the end of an insincere conversation. She suggested moving into another part of the room when a man approached them from the left.

"Isadora? Is that you?"

"Karim! Hello," she said. Her heart jolted into overdrive. "What a pleasant surprise."

"It is," he said, smiling back. "I thought you were staying at the capitol this weekend."

"I was going to, but Daniel asked that I come. Oh! Excuse me," she'd forgotten Glenna existed. "Karim, allow me to introduce you to Mrs. Etcheverri. Glenna, this is Karim. He's Senator Brown's new legislative director."

"Karim, nice to meet you," Glenna said.

"Mrs. Etcheverri, it's a pleasure. How are you this evening?"

Maintaining a cool exterior consumed every ounce of Isadora's strength. Karim looked incredible. He'd been clean shaven at the capitol, but he'd let his beard grow out, and the stubble made him rugged and sexy. Without his glasses, his eyes were so exquisite she was almost afraid to meet them. His hair was less tamed

than she was used to, and she had to hold on to her empty glass
to keep herself from running her fingers through it. She stared at
him, her lips parted. He finished whatever it was he'd been saying
to Glenna and turned to her, stepping close.

"I, um, hope you don't mind my saying so, Isadora, but you are
breathtaking," he said softly.

"Thank you, Karim." Her voice had to work its way out of her
throat.

"I see both of your glasses are empty, ladies." He smiled at
Glenna and then back at Isadora. "May I get you a drink?"

"That's very kind of you," Glenna said. Isadora nodded, not
ready to use words.

"Champagne?"

"Yes, please. For both of us," Glenna said. As he walked away,
she grabbed Isadora's hand and squeezed it. "*He* works for Julian?
How long has he been there? How did Julian find someone so
attractive? Why on earth am I married?" Her last question broke
the spell and Isadora laughed.

"He is good-looking. He's been with Julian since the start of
session, I think. I have no idea how he ended up there. He's
worked in other state legislatures, so he has some experience and
good ideas."

"He is beautiful." Glenna studied Isadora. "Please tell me
you're interested in him."

"I . . ."

"Isadora. You would have to be in a coma not to find him attractive."

"Oh, I do. But he works for Julian."

"What does that have to do with anything?"

"Fraternizing at work is already a dangerous idea. You never
know how someone might react if things don't work out. And he
works for *Julian*. Any slip-up or oversharing, and Julian could
manufacture some sort of scandal. I'd like to trust Karim, but . . ."
She shrugged.

"I see," said Glenna.

Oh my God, he's here. Isadora let out a shaky breath. The same terrified charge she felt before takeoff crinkled over her skin.

"I have to go powder my nose, Glenna," she said.

"What? He'll be back any moment."

"I know. But I need to get myself together before I talk to him again."

Glenna grinned. "Is that so?"

"What's wrong?" Isadora asked.

"Nothing. I'll be right here. *We'll* be right here. Don't take too long."

Isadora wove her way through the crowd, scanning the walls for the ladies' room. Reaching the safety and privacy of a stall, she locked herself in and leaned against the door to breathe.

What on earth is the matter with you? This is exactly what you wanted. He's here, you look awesome, and . . . She vacillated, chewing on her lip, her heel bouncing up and down. This was a bad idea. A very bad idea. If she went down this path, it could turn Karim into more than a colleague. It could hurt her career. And potentially her heart.

Glenna's canary yellow dress was easy to spot when she rejoined the party. She and Karim were still chatting. The moment she caught his eye and before Glenna saw her, Isadora shot him a once-over and bit her bottom lip. He froze.

"Hello again," she said, returning to her spot next to Glenna.

"There you are!" Glenna said.

"Is that for me?" Isadora asked, nodding to the second glass of champagne in Karim's hand.

"Yes, it is."

"Thank you for getting it for me. And sorry to have left you two." She took a sip.

"No problem at all, my dear." Glenna's grin tipped Isadora off: She'd been the topic of conversation.

Karim started to say something, but the background music faded, and a woman's voice invited the guests to move into the adjoining room for dinner.

"Mrs. Etcheverri, it's been a pleasure getting to know you a little," he said. "I imagine we're at different tables, so I'd better go find Julian. Enjoy your meal, ladies."

"Thank you, Karim. Hope to speak with you again soon," Glenna said.

"Isadora." He nodded to her.

"Karim." She smiled and nodded back.

Finding their table, Glenna seized on the privacy she and Isadora had before Daniel joined them.

"It doesn't matter who he works for," she said.

"I'm sorry, I don't follow."

"It does not matter who Karim works for, you need to get to know him better."

Glenna put her glass down next to her plate and turned so she and Isadora were face-to-face. "I don't want to meddle. But I'm pretty sure you'll regret it if you don't give him a chance."

"I'm not sure he wants a *real* chance," Isadora said, fidgeting with the hem of her dress.

Glenna leaned down, placing herself in Isadora's line of sight, taking her hands. "He does."

"Is that speculation, or . . ."

"He asked me if you were seeing anyone."

Isadora's breath caught and then stuttered, out of rhythm with her heart. "He did?"

"Yes. He asked me if I thought it was inappropriate for you two to get to know each other."

"He did?" She sat up straighter, breath faster, searching Glenna's eyes.

"Yes."

Isadora furrowed her brow. "What did you say?"

"I said no."

"Really? Are you sure—"

"He also asked me if I knew what sort of man you were usually interested in."

He wants to know my type! "He did?"

"You're starting to sound like a parrot, honey."

The sparkle of the fairy lights on the table left spots in her eyes.

"He just asked you all these things about me? Point blank?"

"No, no, dear. He was far more subtle. But you were the only thing that interested him. He tried to make polite conversation, but everything came right back to you."

Isadora was flattered, but . . . She raised an eyebrow.

"Are you sure everything came back to me, or did you steer everything back to me?"

"Okay, I can admit it. I may have answered him in a way that made him comfortable enough to ask more questions."

This is dangerous. He is dangerous. Flirting is one thing, but I can't risk this.

"I . . . I didn't expect to see him tonight." Isadora's voice didn't carry far. She fiddled with her bracelet. "Figured Julian would bring Drew."

"Are you happy he's here?"

Isadora wouldn't let herself answer. She was thrilled, but saying it out loud, sharing her feelings, even with someone she trusted . . . she shrugged and had to turn her attention to the plates, the utensils on the table. They began to shimmer as her eyes watered.

Glenna scooted closer and squeezed her hands.

"What's wrong?"

Isadora shook her head, her gaze dropping to her lap.

"Honey," Glenna continued. "You know we think of you as a second daughter, right? For us, you're like Josie's older sister. Please tell me what's wrong?"

Isadora had to gulp back a sob.

"I . . . I can't. I can't let myself go there. I can't . . . feel."

Glenna sat up straight.

"Why not?"

Either tears or words were about to come out in a rush. Isadora opted for the latter.

"I've been careful for so long, Glenna. Careful to stay on track. Emotions make you weak, well, romantic ones. They'll hurt you and make you bitter if you don't let them in at the right place and the right time. And this is most, most definitely not the right time. The steps on my path are clear. Daniel becoming pro tem. Him going to Washington. Me going with him. If I . . . This is a crucial moment in my life, for my goals. If I let someone in, let myself feel anything serious for them, it could break it all apart."

Glenna sighed. Then she leaned closer and rubbed Isadora's forearms.

"You've been carrying so much, sweetie. And I don't want to add more weight, but there's something very important you should know."

Isadora looked up at her.

"There is no right time to let your feelings in, Isadora."

Glenna's tone cut deep. She let go of Isadora's hands to fish a pack of tissues out of her purse.

"Your feelings are just as important as your work, Isadora. As your goals. It might seem like they can get in the way of what you want, what you have planned for yourself. But trust someone who knows from experience, letting them in can bring you joys that make you wonder what you were fighting so hard for in the first place. If I hadn't let mine in, I'd have missed out on so much, including the pleasure of knowing you."

Isadora smiled, accepting the offered tissue and dabbing at a tear that had escaped. "I'm sorry. Excuse me for crying."

"Don't. Don't you dare apologize for letting me see how you feel. Let me thank you for sharing."

Isadora had to stare at her lap and take several deep breaths. Her surrogate mother was flipping her world upside down. The idea that she could trust her feelings, share them, follow them . . . Her mother had done that, had given up her dreams for love and then he'd "abandoned" her by dying. The years upon years of her mother complaining, blaming Isadora and her father for "taking" what could have been away from her . . . She took a deep, shuddering breath.

And now Glenna was articulating something RJ had said multiple times—the idea that Isadora could get romantically attached to someone and maybe not turn into a miserable, bitter person was too foreign to accept.

"Let go, honey. Tonight, just be Isadora. Don't think about work, don't think about politics. You work too hard as it is, all the time. It's not good for you. You can allow yourself one night to truly enjoy your youth and beauty. Trust me, they're more powerful and more fleeting than you realize."

Isadora dabbed at her eyes and got herself under control, giving Glenna an appreciative smile. Sharing her true emotions with her own mother had always ended in shame and regret. The fact that Glenna wasn't making her feel that way warmed her from the inside out. Maybe Isadora could trust her judgment.

"Okay," she breathed. "I'll give Karim half an hour. But it's hard because there are other people from work here. I don't want them to see . . . you know . . ."

"Fuck them, Isadora." It was the first time she'd heard Glenna use anything close to profanity. "Yes, that's right. I said 'fuck them.' Fuck 'em all. You deserve this."

She stared at Glenna, shocked away from tears.

"And half an hour isn't sufficient. You give him at least an hour, okay?"

"Umm, okay."

"Promise me?"

"I promise."

"Now shhh . . . here comes my husband. Can't have him hear me whispering about a younger man!"

CHAPTER THIRTEEN
Isadora

An hour later, at the end of the last speech, Glenna gave Isadora a final encouragement and nudged her to follow the other guests making their way to the adjoining room. Checking the crowd on and around the dance floor, she didn't see Karim. She continued along one side of the room and found open doors leading to a balcony. There were people outside, in groups of twos and threes. There was only one person at the railing with his back to the party.

He raised his head when she was a few feet away. Slowing down, she made the most of her stride, her hips, the way her dress moved. There was a glimmer of fear in his eyes as he glanced away and then back at her.

Please don't be afraid of me. I'm already afraid enough for us both.

"There you are," she said, reaching him.

He raised his eyebrows, a smile pulling his lips to one side. "Here I am."

"Thought I'd come by and say hello again."

He nodded, turning to the view. "Before you go?"

"I . . . I doubt Daniel and Glenna are ready to go so soon. I rode with them."

"You aren't leaving now?"

"Um . . . no. I hadn't planned on it. Should I?" *Okay, I read this wrong, let me get out of here before I make a total fool of myself.* She started to head back to the party.

"No, wait. I'm sorry," he said. "I misunderstood."

"Oh." She returned close to him, standing side by side, their backs to everyone else. She wasn't sure what to say. The fear she'd discussed with Glenna was still there. But another primal emotion was taking its place. His cologne wafted by, and she wanted to plunge her face into his neck and gorge herself on it. His proximity doubled her desire for him, tripled it. She gripped her little clutch hard, rather than give in to the need to caress his jacketed arm, or to acquaint herself with the golden skin of his wrist.

"I know I said so before, but you're beautiful tonight," he said, his tone heating up the cool evening.

"Thank you again," she managed. "Um . . . you said I was breathtaking earlier. I have to admit you've taken my breath away as well."

"I have?"

"Yes. I really like this." She slid the back of one finger down her cheek to indicate his stubble.

"You do?" He rubbed his chin. "I was worried it looked too unkempt. Almost shaved this afternoon."

"Well, I'm very glad you didn't." She hadn't meant to whisper, but she was happy he had to come closer to understand.

"Thanks, I'm glad you like it."

"And contacts tonight?"

"Yes," he said. "Just to change things up. Sometimes I feel like the glasses aren't formal enough."

"I like your glasses. They give you a rather . . . endearing quality. But the contacts are good too."

"Why's that?"

"It's nice to really see your eyes. The color, the shape. You have beautiful eyes."

He glanced at the railing, and she saw a flash of that shy-boy smile he'd given her during their first meeting. "You keep talking like this and my head's going to get so big it won't fit in my car."

She laughed.

He rolled his lips and tapped his fingers once on the railing. "I'd like to invite you to dance. But . . ."

A tingling wave shifted up from her lower back and over her shoulders. It took her breath away for a moment. "But?"

"Montagues," he said.

She nodded. "Capulets," she said.

He glanced toward the open doors leading back inside.

"Maybe the very edge of the dance floor?" he asked.

"We can try."

He turned to go back inside, then stopped. "We're alone out here," he said.

She looked around. He was right. They'd been alone for a while. Her heart rate kicked up again. "That's true."

"Wanna risk it?" he asked, reaching for her.

She swallowed against the lump in her throat and let him lead her to a corner of the balcony that was out of the direct light coming from the party inside. The music was still loud enough to dance to. She tried to calm the tremble in her arms as he took her in his.

"What's the deal with the Capulets and the Montagues thing?" he asked.

"Ha." Her chuckle felt forced. "It's weird, right? I don't know who came up with it or when. But it kind of stuck." She hesitated to say more. She thought she'd read him right, he seemed like his own man, not the type to run to his boss and tell him every word she'd said. After all, he'd just asked her to dance. It would be safer to consider him an enemy. But God if he wasn't making her absolutely weak in the knees. And Glenna had told her to give him a chance. Her brain was buzzing. She needed to find something to say.

"I like your outfit."

"You do? I hesitated about the shirt. I didn't want to look too gloomy. And Julian asked if I decided to come as Johnny Cash."

"He was probably just jealous," she said.

"Jealous? Why?"

"He believes he's a ladies' man. I'm sure he sees you as direct competition. Especially tonight."

"Competition? I didn't think our interests intersected." He

surprised her by spinning her away from him, then pulling her back closer. "And why tonight in particular?"

"Karim, you look incredibly sexy. Far from gloomy. The 'Johnny Cash' look makes your eyes stand out more. And this"—she rocked onto her toes and brushed her cheek against his stubble—"makes you look wild, manly, dangerous."

His eyes fluttered closed at her touch.

"Be careful," he whispered.

"Why?" she whispered back. The thudding of her heart clipped at her vocal chords.

His gaze fell to her lips, as he wet his own. "Because I really, really want to kiss you right now."

"I really, really want you to kiss me," she whispered. "But . . ."

"Yes?"

"I don't feel comfortable here. I promised Glenna I'd stay, get to know you."

He smiled. "She asked you to promise that?"

Isadora rolled her eyes. "More like made me promise. She told me I need to relax. Stop working. Have fun."

"I could help you with that . . . if you'd like."

"I would."

"Let's get out of here?"

"Yes."

"Meet you downstairs at the valet? I'll have to come up with something to tell Julian," he said.

She nodded. "I came with Glenna and Daniel. I should let them know I won't need a ride back."

He smiled at her before walking away. "See you in a minute, beautiful."

CHAPTER FOURTEEN
Karim

Karim returned to the last place he'd seen Julian. There was no sign of him. He started to look further, but he didn't want to keep Isadora waiting. Then he bumped into Drew.

"Hey, I'm out," Karim said.

"So soon? This is when things start to get interesting."

Karim hid his smile. "Nah, I'm good. Let Julian know if you see him."

"Sure."

He hurried to the exit. He wanted to run but held himself back. Reaching the valet stand, he was relieved she hadn't beaten him there. The valet took his ticket stub, and he waited a moment, hands in his pockets, trying to tamp down his excitement and shy, nervous grin. A worry cropped up. One he didn't want to acknowledge but that refused to remain silent. Isadora was not part of his starting-over plan. He didn't remember how to see someone, how to date. It had been nearly a decade since he had. But the flirting had come back on its own. Maybe it was like riding a bike? He glanced over his shoulder and an electric blast shot through his chest.

Isadora had stopped partway down the stairs. She was speaking with a woman on her way up, smiling. As Isadora continued down, she moved in her usual, graceful manner, made even more enticing by the way the left side of her dress was floating behind her. She was a seductive sea goddess. A goddess headed straight for him.

Holy shit. This is happening. This . . . um, date? Whatever. Doesn't matter. Just me and Isadora, no one else. He gulped and went back inside to wait for her at the foot of the stairs.

"Wow," he said, offering her his arm.

"Thank you," she giggled, accepting it.

His car was waiting at the curb.

"Where to?" he asked, changing gears, pulling onto the street.

"Somewhere small. Far. Far away from everyone."

"I know just the place."

He changed lanes, taking the direction of the freeway.

"AC, windows, or top down?" he asked.

"AC, please," she said.

He flicked on both the AC and the radio. The road connected with the freeway and he accelerated to merge. He was paying attention to the traffic but had to fight another moment of doubt. The push-pull was intense. This was what he'd wanted for weeks. But it was the exact opposite of what he'd done for years.

This is skipping at least eight steps on my plan. If things get weird, she's got enough clout to make a new professional start very difficult. If Julian finds out, I could lose my job. And I'm not . . . totally back to me yet.

She sighed, drawing his attention. She'd closed her eyes and settled into the passenger seat.

If she's that relaxed, she must trust me, at least a little. If she's willing to trust me, I should try to trust her in return.

"Too chilly?" he asked.

"No," Isadora said, smiling at him. "Don't worry, everything's perfect."

"I couldn't agree more."

———

After a few miles, he took an exit, taking them closer to the ocean. He turned onto a side street and pulled the car up in front of a jazz club.

"I'd heard about this place, but I've never been here before," she said as he held the club's door open for her. "Do you come often?"

"Been here a few times. Haven't ever seen anyone from work."

"Good."

The club was small, with live music, a dance floor, and a few tables and booths on a higher platform. It was busy but not packed.

"Would you like to take a seat?" He motioned toward the tables at the edge of the dance floor.

"Yes, but . . . Not over there. Somewhere more private?"

He wanted to put his hand on her cheek, to smooth away the nervousness written all over her face. A clap of cold thunder exploded inside him. The last woman he'd wanted to comfort that way had cast him aside. His therapist's words came back to him:

Laila's choices were hers alone.

Karim chose to stay in the present. "Over there?" He pointed to the booths along the wall. She nodded, and he led her over to one that gave them a good view of the stage and the dance floor. There was a small candle on the table, but other than that, the little corner was dark.

"Is this okay?"

"Perfect," she said.

As they slid into the booth, a waitress appeared. Isadora hesitated.

"Wine?" he asked.

"Okay."

"Two glasses of Riesling, please," he said to the waitress. She nodded and walked away.

"I'm not familiar with Riesling," Isadora said. "Is it red or white?"

"White."

"Oh." He caught the flash of a side-frown she tried to hide.

"You don't like white? I'm sorry, I should have asked. I'll get something else." He slid to the edge of the booth, headed to the bar.

"No, it's okay. I'm up for trying something new." She smiled.

He had trouble believing his eyes. Isadora, this sensual, beautiful creature sitting at a table with him, alone.

"It's dangerous when you do that," he said.

"When I smile at you?"

"Yes."

"Why?" she laughed, breathy, sexy. "I've smiled at you before."

"You have, but not like that. And we've never really been alone before."

The waitress returned, placing two glasses of chilled white wine on the table.

"Willing to give it a shot?" he asked, raising his glass.

"Here's to new experiences," she said, tapping her glass to his.

Maintaining eye contact with her as he sipped, he was curious to know if she liked it, but his heart started pounding too quickly for him to speak. Thankfully she spoke first.

"It's really good," she said, smiling broadly.

He relaxed, letting out a chuckle.

"I'm glad you like it."

"I do," she said, nodding. She took another sip, then scooted a little closer to him. "Back to what you were saying before. About being alone—we were alone just the other day, in Julian's office."

"You're right. But we were at work, could have been interrupted any time."

She shrugged and nodded, her gaze flitting from the table, to the dance floor, to the hem of her dress, until she risked a glance at him again. *She is nervous. Maybe if I'm open with her . . .*

"Can I be honest?" he asked.

"Sure."

"I'm nervous. It's not the work thing. I think we're safe here." He waved a hand at the rest of the club. "I've been through some . . . stuff lately and when it comes to women, I'm kind of out of the habit."

She chuckled. "I haven't been through any *stuff* in a while, and I'm definitely out of the habit. I kind of make it a point not to be in the habit. But . . ."

"But?" he asked.

She slid closer to him on the seat. Crossed her legs under the table and tucked her shin behind his calf. She leaned toward him, sliding the tip of her finger down the lapel of his jacket. He was afraid his heart was going to shoot out of his chest.

"In the weeks after the flight, I couldn't stop thinking about you," she said.

He was parched. A gulp of wine would have helped, but he couldn't move.

"You couldn't?"

"No," she whispered.

She moved closer still, the underside of her breasts grazing the arm he'd rested on the table. When she inhaled to speak again, they pressed against it, he couldn't doubt she was doing it on purpose, couldn't fight the want coursing through him. She caressed his cheek.

"Me either," he whispered back.

She smiled, trailing her fingers along his jaw, over his lips. Then she bit her lip.

Doubt and hesitation evaporated. He gave in to the desire he'd been fighting for weeks.

"Isadora," he whispered, wetting his lips.

"Yes?" she whispered back.

"I need to kiss you now."

"I need you to kiss me, Karim."

For a moment, their kiss was gentle. Then he angled himself toward her, pulled her closer to consume her. She opened her mouth to his, sliding her tongue against his, devouring him in turn. He groaned, one hand caressing the silken skin of her arm, the other cupping her cheek, his fingertips sliding into the hair at the nape of her neck. She pulled back to let them both breathe and then came at him again. He wanted to put his arms around her, to tear off her clothes. But the table was in the way, and he remembered it was a public place. She broke the kiss, staying close enough to whisper to him.

"Stop," she panted.

"What's wrong?" He was out of breath too.

"Dance with me. I need your body against mine . . . now . . ."

Out of the booth in a flash, he offered her his hand. She took it and followed him onto the dance floor. He pulled her close, crushing her body against his. The music had a Latin feel to it but was slow enough to dance to; they clung to each other, and no one noticed.

Several hours later, the club closed, and Isadora was quiet as he drove her back to her condo. He wasn't going to mess things up by pushing too hard, but he didn't want the night to end as he walked her to her door. He brushed his lips across the spot where her neck met her bare shoulder as she stepped onto her doormat. Her shiver and giggle were going to haunt his dreams that night.

"Back to the capitol tomorrow," he said, leaning against her door, stroking the back of her hand with his thumb.

"Yeah . . ." she whispered. "I have an early flight."

"Too bad," he said. *Dammit. Why not just say outright that you want her to invite you in, idiot? Slow down, no reason to rush.*

"What time is yours?" she asked.

"I'm driving back tomorrow. Need to have my car up there."

Her brow knitted together. "That's a long drive. You'd better get some rest." The worry in her tone touched him, that she would be concerned about him like that.

"Yeah, I should."

"Please be careful," she said.

"I will. Unless . . ."

"Unless?"

His shyness surged forward, but he didn't let it win.

"Would you like to ride with me?"

She smiled with more excitement than he'd hoped for. *She wants to be stuck in a car with me for eight hours? Excellent.*

"That's a good idea," she said. "We could take turns driving."

"You know how to drive stick?"

"Yes."

"Of course you do," he said, nodding, letting two fingertips glide down her bare arm.

"What's that supposed to mean?" She sighed.

"I'm pretty sure you can do just about anything, Isadora." He nuzzled her neck again, her gasp giving him goosebumps.

"Thank you? I guess," she whispered.

"I meant it as a compliment."

"You keep complimenting me and *my* head's going to get too big."

He stood straight, smiling. "What time should I pick you up?"

"When had you planned on leaving?"

"Well, early. I didn't think I'd have such an interesting evening." He lifted the hand he'd been caressing and linked his fingers through hers. "Thought I'd have been in bed by now."

Her sigh set off a shiver that made him wriggle.

"Me too," she said.

"Maybe ten? That should give us both time to get a little sleep."

"Okay, ten it is."

She pulled her fingers from his and lined their fingertips up. He smiled, and she giggled.

Don't think she wants to say goodbye either. He smiled at her toe on the doormat, her ankles crossed, the side of her foot against his. *But one of us has to go first. Sooner I say goodbye, the sooner I can say hello again.*

He leaned forward, caressing her cheek with his, bringing his lips to her ear.

"Good night, Isadora," he whispered.

"Good night, Karim." She smiled at him again, stroked his stubble one last time, unlocked her door, and went inside.

CHAPTER FIFTEEN
Isadora

"Listen. We do not have time for this." Glaring at her hair in the mirror, Isadora shook the bottle of heat-protection spray again, pressing the trigger repeatedly in rapid succession, to get the remaining drops onto the last section of her hair. She kicked herself. It would have been wiser to start on the left. She'd be in the passenger seat; she should have made sure she was at her best from that side.

After two more passes with the flat iron, her hair was as straight as it was going to get. It was a ponytail day, and at least her edges were in order and the top of her head wasn't puffy. She misted herself with a final layer of holding spray, unplugged the iron, and put everything else away at lightning speed. Karim was due any minute, and she wasn't going to make him wait.

She'd put the iron on the stovetop to cool when she heard a car pull up. Taking a deep breath and calming her giddiness, she reminded herself of her goal.

Okay. Last night was . . . wonderful. But it wasn't reality. Evenings like that, unusual things happen. If RJ and Glenna are right, and this . . . what if this isn't okay? I shouldn't even be allowing myself to be attracted to someone. She placed her hands on the kitchen counter and leaned into them, trying to gather her thoughts. *I can't help that I'm attracted to him. There's nothing wrong with being attracted to someone. And yes, I did have fun last night. But even beyond a threat to my plans to go to D.C., this is dangerous. Romantic emotions are a threat. They are dangerous.* She focused on the backs of her hands. *But that doesn't make any sense.*

That's another one of my mother's lies. RJ and Glenna are right. I'll choose to believe them, even if I don't fully understand them right now. She blew out a shaky breath, surprised at the need to wipe at a tear escaping. *There's no danger in getting to know a man I'm attracted to. And God, am I attracted to him.*

She jumped at his knock at the door. More anxiety cropped up, and she shook out her hands and rolled her shoulders, approaching the door.

She swung the door open and had to squeeze the knob hard. His fitted dark green T-shirt accentuated the V formed from his broad shoulders to his narrow waist. He hadn't shaved, but he was wearing his glasses again, and the contrast between rugged-sexy and nerdy-cute made her knees weak.

"Good morning, beautiful." He smiled.

Good morning, you sexy motherfucker.

"Hi there," she said. His appraisal made her hope he had a similar thought. He tipped his gorgeous head to the side.

"Do you mind if I kiss you?"

A chill went down her spine.

I want you to do a whole lot more than kiss me. I gotta slow this down, though.

She offered him her cheek. He raised his eyebrows but accepted it, giving her a light peck. Her nostrils filled with cool and woodsy and male. All those delicious man smells she wanted in her bedsheets.

"Ready to roll?" he asked.

"Yep." She grabbed her bag and locked the door. He led the way down the stairs.

The back was as good as the front. She shook her head and touched her fingertips to her lips. She wanted to slide a hand into his back pocket so she could feel if his butt was tight and hot up close. Then it wasn't moving anymore. He'd caught her staring and his lips were twitching, holding back a laugh.

"See something you like?" he teased.

She ducked her head and shrugged her shoulders. "Guilty," she said.

He opened the passenger door for her.

"It's okay," he said, getting into the car. "I like what I see too." He glanced down at her legs, up to her breasts. The heat that bloomed up her neck forced her to let out a sigh.

He started the car and was about to unlock the emergency brake, when she changed her mind.

"Wait," she said. She leaned over and kissed him, properly this time, teasing his mouth open, sliding her tongue along his, caressing his jaw and neck. He smiled against her lips, letting her lead. When he reached for her cheek, she released him with a satisfied moan, and returned to her seat. Flipping the visor down, she pretended to check her lipstick in the mirror, savoring the dazed expression on his face.

"Okay," she said. "I'm ready to go."

"What was that?" He was even sexier, happy and confused, but the drive hadn't started, and she'd let her desire leapfrog her logic.

"A little much? Sorry. You said you wanted a kiss before . . ." She smoothed her skirt down her thighs, fiddling with the hem.

"Uh no, no. I am not complaining. Not at all. Feel free to surprise me like that any time you want." He laughed. She joined him, her cheeks warming.

"Cool," she said.

He backed out of the space and drove out of her neighborhood, headed toward the freeway.

"Just one thing," he said. "Didn't have time to fill up. Need to stop and get some gas."

"Okay."

"AC, windows, or top down?" he asked.

"AC, please." She ran a hand down the leather of her seat. There was a hint of new car smell, but not much.

"You said this is your car?" she asked. "I mean, I can tell it isn't a rental, but I didn't realize convertibles were popular in Pennsylvania."

He ran a hand down his face and shot her a glance.

"Promise not to make fun?" he asked.

"Of course. Why would I?"

His squeeze and release of the steering wheel was a surprise. She'd have to get to know him better to be sure, but it seemed like he was nervous all of a sudden.

"Karim?" She modulated her tone, going for light but honest. "I'm . . . uh . . . not a car person. I hope you don't think I'd judge you because of the type of car you drive."

"No! No," he said. "I don't . . ." Tapering off, he chanced a longer look at her. She wasn't a fan of the insecurity she caught in his eyes.

"Do you think I would make fun of you?" she asked.

He'd returned his gaze to the road and kept it there, shaking his head.

"No," he said, sounding more confident. "*You* aren't like that, are you?"

Surprised by the emphasis he'd put on "you," she shook her head. "I'm not."

He gripped and released the wheel again.

"I bought it as soon as I got here."

She checked out the dash, the seats, the gear shift. She was lost.

"Not too much of a cliché? Guy moves to California and the first thing he does is buy a convertible?" He pulled up to a pump at an older gas station.

"Oh. It seems like a nice car. Do you like it?"

"Yeah." He unbuckled his seat belt.

She shrugged. "Well, there you go, that's all that matters."

"Thanks," he said, giving her his shy-boy smile. His back-and-forth between sexy and shy was beyond unfair.

"Sit tight, beautiful. I gotta go inside to pay."

"Why don't you let me pump?" she asked. "And would you mind grabbing a bottle of water for me?"

"Okay. No problem."

She got out and removed the nozzle, sliding it into the opening for the gas tank. The weather was excellent, and on any other day she would have relaxed into it, but her nerves were getting in the way. It was a good nervousness, though. A curiosity. She fidgeted, rocking on the balls of her feet. The pump clicked, and the gas started flowing. A large pickup pulled up to a pump behind her. There was a whistle behind her and even though she doubted that was Karim's style, she turned with a smile in her eyes. It was one of the guys in the pickup.

"Hey, pretty lady," he said, closing the driver's-side door. She ignored him, facing the street again.

"That is one nice piece of ass," he said to his friend in the truck. "Where you going this fine morning?" He stepped over to her side of the pump.

"Nowhere," she said, straightening her spine.

"Now, there's no reason to be like that," he said. "Me and my boy over here were headed out to the state park. Why don't you join us?" His friend got out and joined the man speaking to her. And, as bad luck would have it, the light breeze she'd been enjoying a few moments earlier made her skirt billow up, showing the two cretins too much of her thighs. She took a calming breath, gritting her teeth.

"Morning, gentlemen." Karim appeared behind her. He fixed the first man in a cold stare, not enough to provoke, but enough to be clear. He slid his hand down Isadora's back. "Ready to go, baby?" he asked, studying the two men. She didn't want to go all damsel-in-distress, but she could have fallen into his arms from relief.

"Almost." The pump clicked. The tank was full.

"Uh, morning, dude," the first man said as the other scampered back into the truck. Isadora returned the nozzle to the pump. Karim moved around her and toward the driver's door, studying the first man.

"Hey, uh, no harm, no foul?" The man backed up, tripping over his own feet.

"No harm? You called her a 'nice piece of ass.'" Karim didn't open his door. Isadora walked around the back of the car to the passenger side. "An apology is in order."

"Look, I didn't mean anything by that." He turned to Isadora. "You understand?"

She paused, opening her door.

"Didn't mean anything by it when you thought I was alone, but another man calls you on it and suddenly it's an inappropriate thing to say?"

The man peered at Karim, who'd raised his eyebrows.

"I . . . I don't . . ."

"Have anything useful to add," Karim finished for him, opening his door. "Good day to you. And your *boy*." He nodded at Isadora, and they got into the car. About to drive away, the man delivered a parting shot.

"Fucking towel head! You can keep your little black bitch!" He gunned his engine and sped off. Karim's jaw visibly clenched as he turned on the engine and headed toward the freeway.

"And here I thought moving to California meant I didn't have to deal with that anymore," he said.

Isadora shook her head, looking out her window. "Nah, it's here too. Doesn't make it to the travel brochures, but it's here."

"I'm sorry," he said after a mile or two.

"Why are you sorry?" she asked. "You came to my rescue." *And I liked it when you called me "baby."*

His jaw relaxed. "You think?"

"Yes. It felt good. Especially because there were two of them."

"I didn't like that either," he said. His face got tight again. Stopped at the light before the on-ramp, he focused straight ahead, lips pressed together.

"Look at me, please," she said. "I think you handled it splendidly." She stroked his cheek. The light changed, and she noticed first, flitting her gaze toward it. He followed the van in front of them, onto the on-ramp.

"You do?" he asked.

"I do. You made me feel all warm and fuzzy. Protected. I liked it."

"Yeah?" His blush through the sexy scruff made her heart skip a beat.

"I did. Now let's forget about them. We have the whole day together. How about some music?" She settled into her seat as the car sped up.

He relaxed, flicking the radio on as he merged onto the wide stretch of road. Cruising along at a good speed, he picked up her hand and swept his delicious lips across the back.

Another urge to stroke his cheek in response renewed her concerns. She returned to her goal, angling herself toward him in the seat and tucking her hands into her elbows to keep them off him.

"You were in Pennsylvania before you moved here. Is that where you're originally from?" she asked.

"No." He glanced at her with a cute bend to his lips. "I'm from Michigan. Grosse Pointe. Near Detroit."

"Oh," she said. "Never been. I . . . um . . . I guess it gets cold there?"

He chuckled. "You could say that. Growing up there, then living in Virginia and Pennsylvania, made California even more attractive."

"I bet." She nodded. "Pennsylvania to California. That's really far. Not too drastic of a change?" Her gaze slid to his arm, trickling over the ridge of his deltoid, down to the cuff of his T-shirt, taut over a golden biceps.

"Uh, no," he said. "What about you? California native?" He glanced at her before she anticipated it and caught her ogling him again.

Heat flashed into her cheeks and she hid her face in her hands as he chuckled.

"Sorry! Oh God, sorry." She shook her head, turning away from him. "I'm a transplant too. Undergrad and master's at Berkeley. Then I stayed."

"You don't have to apologize," he laughed, glancing at her again.

"Yes, I do! Excuse me." She covered her eyes. "I'm so embarrassed."

"Don't be," he said. "I'd be checking you out too, if it wouldn't get us both killed." He winked at her.

"Yeah?"

"Yeah."

She observed him another moment, her lips bunched to one side.

"You have created a conundrum, Mr. Sarda."

"Have I? How so?"

She racked her brain to find a cool, yet diplomatic, yet sexy and not desperate-sounding way to explain. A pinball in a machine, bouncing and zooming from one point to another, would have had more clarity about its situation than she did. She gritted her teeth.

"Can I be blunt with you? Honest?"

He glanced at her, like he was afraid he was in trouble.

"Please do."

"I had a *very* naughty dream about you last night."

He laughed. "Really?" The visible half of his face turned wicked. A wicked that sent a sizzle over her breasts, down her stomach, and forced her to readjust herself in her seat.

"Can you tell me about it?" he asked.

"Are you sure that's a good idea? Don't you need to concentrate on driving?"

"Good point, Isadora. But . . . uh . . . I'll tell you about mine if you tell me about yours."

"You had one too?" The idea sent a cool tingle all through her. She became more glowing orb than zooming pinball.

"I did. Well, when I got home, I was rather tense. So, I needed to *relax* a bit before I went to sleep." He released and re-gripped the steering wheel, readjusted himself in the seat. She couldn't believe he was admitting to thinking about her that way. "That little exercise set me up for a couple of explicit dreams."

"I see."

He glanced at her, his smile dimming. "Did I offend you?"

"What do you mean?"

"Telling you I . . . um . . ."

"No," she said. *You said be blunt. Be. Blunt.* "I'm surprised how much that . . . turned me on." She focused on the scenery. The glow abated but lit right back up when she peeked at him.

"Turned you on?"

"Yes," she said, nervous. But the truth tasted good.

"I see." His wicked smile flashed again. "So?"

"So?"

"You gotta tell me about this dream."

She fidgeted, holding her breath a moment. "Okay, fine," she sighed. "We were at your place. Well, it wasn't mine."

He changed his grip on the wheel and nodded.

"We were in your bedroom. My dress from last night was on the floor."

He switched the radio off.

"I was in your bed, you were stalking toward me, undoing—" She froze. "No, this is wrong . . . it's embarrassing."

"You aren't gonna stop now?"

"Well, it's . . . I don't *do this,* Karim. Flings, or even relationships. I don't know how. This is why you are a conundrum. This is something I don't do, but all of a sudden, I really, really want to."

The hum of the car on the freeway filled the empty space. Mortified at what she'd let slip, she was also nauseated from the attraction. The violent pull, the running away, the release from the previous night. She was a pinball again and even the machine was shaking.

"You're right," he said. "It is a conundrum. I'm sorry, I . . . I don't want to make you uncomfortable."

Her reply lodged in her throat. She'd messed everything up and now there were hours of awkward ahead of them. He tapped the radio, turning a podcast on. And then the smallest movement registered in the corner of her eye. He swiped the pad of his thumb at the base of his left ring finger.

CHAPTER SIXTEEN
Karim

A second podcast ended, and he suggested lunch.

"Have you tried Roy's? The burger joint up ahead?" he asked.

"Nope. Seen it a few times, but I haven't tried it." She gave him a tight smile. "Guess you heard my stomach growling?"

"No. Just felt mine. Does it sound good to you?"

"Perfect," she said.

After picking up their order, they went outside to eat in the fresh air. The large trees protecting the picnic benches didn't block out the freeway noise, but the patrons were spared the view. It had gotten much warmer, allowing Karim to enjoy the graceful slope of Isadora's shoulders in her tank top.

Their first meal together gave him a lot of details to study about the alluring woman across the table from him. She half rolled her French fries in her ketchup—only one or two at a time. After each bite, she centered her hamburger on its paper and in the basket on her tray. Both her lips and her fingers remained pristine, despite the messy meal. She did it all with grace and femininity.

Who knew it was possible to eat a hamburger with femininity? Then he realized she'd asked him a question.

"I'm sorry?"

"You seem tense," she said. "What's on your mind?"

About a billion things, he wanted to say.

He vacillated long enough that he sensed her sliding into uncomfortable. He caught himself bouncing his leg, the desire to be honest with her pushing hard against the fear.

"It's about earlier, isn't it?" she asked. "That was too much. I'm sorry." She squinted, avoiding eye contact.

"Sorry? For what?"

"Maybe I went too far. Shouldn't have said anything about my dream." She shrugged and looked away, rubbing the outside of one arm.

"Please don't apologize," he said. "This has been one of the best Sundays I can remember." Heat crept into his face, he rubbed the back of his neck, sighing. "And all I want is more. But I'm afraid."

If he hadn't been so nervous, the scrunch of her brow would have been adorable.

"Of me?"

He slid a hand across his forehead, massaging above his brows. "Of what you'll think of me."

"Have you murdered someone, Karim?"

He chuckled. "No. Can I be blunt with you? Honest?"

"Please." She nodded.

Taking a deep breath, he leaned forward and gripped the edge of the table with both hands. "I moved here because my wife left me, and I wanted to start over in a completely new place. I wanted to rebuild professionally and intended to avoid any sort of sexual or romantic connection for the foreseeable future. It is clearly unwise, considering who we both work for; and beyond that, the timing might not be the best. But, from this side of the table, it looks like we could be heading in a very specific direction, and I don't want to fight it anymore, even though every bit of logic is telling me that I should."

She'd glanced at his bare ring finger at the word "wife" but said nothing. He'd purposely given her the bare bones of the story, still ashamed of having put up with an abusive relationship for years. He gave her a few moments to absorb everything, willing her to say something, anything. So, there he sat, in a temperate, blue-skied purgatory that was getting harder and harder to bear.

She got up from her side of the table, joining him on his. The breeze wafted her perfume around him. He wanted to hold her as he had the night before. Instead, he held his breath as she studied her hands folded in her lap.

"Are you still married?" she asked.

"Technically, yes."

"Why didn't you say anything before?"

"I . . . I didn't think I was important enough to you for it to matter. I didn't think anything could happen between us."

"And now you do?" she asked her hands.

His sigh came up from his diaphragm. "I'd like to hope," he said, studying the table.

"Blunt? Honest?" she asked.

He swallowed hard. "Yes."

"I can't be the other woman."

"I wouldn't ask you to be."

She took a deep breath, her focus steadfast on her hands. "Do you have kids?"

"No. She really wasn't ready. Worked out for the best." He had to study his own hands. Starting a family had been a point of contention. Another sting.

Isadora nodded and then looked at him. "It's . . ." She sighed. "I'm curious, Karim."

"Me too."

Her smile was close-lipped, though for a moment her eyes beamed at him. She leaned in, giving his shoulder the sweetest caress with her cheek. He wanted to lean in to her, stroke the top of her head with his chin and fill his lungs with her sweet fragrance. And just like that, he was stone. Another instinct he hadn't had since Laila. And even then, well before she left. He was still recovering from the surprise when Isadora stood.

"Walk with me? It's my turn to drive, but I'd like to stretch my legs," she said. He stood too, collecting their trash and putting it in a nearby bin. He was grateful for something to do, so he could also collect himself.

"I can keep driving, you know," he said. "Your company is helping me stay alert."

"Don't want a girl driving your car?" she teased, starting to walk down one of the paths in the small grove of trees behind the restaurant.

"No, that's not it," he said, following. "I'd love for you to . . . drive . . . my car."

She tucked her head and grinned, continuing along the path. He moved next to her, keeping his hands behind his back.

"You know," she said. "I had a really good time last night."

"You did?"

"Mm-hmm. I didn't think I was going to. I was really annoyed when Daniel called."

"Why?"

"Hobnobbing, or whatever. It's not my thing. And I didn't think there was going to be anyone there I wanted to see." She winked at him.

He swallowed, his cheeks warm. "Well, you are quite good."

"What do you mean?"

"It didn't show at all."

"No? My irritation is always seething below the surface in those moments. But it's part of the job. I wish I were more like RJ; he revels in those situations."

"You two are good friends, aren't you?"

"We are. Since we got our master's together. You're not jealous of him, are you?" Her crinkled nose was even cuter than her crinkled brow.

"No. I could tell he wasn't competition." He laughed.

She laughed along. "He's not. But I'm sure he's a little disappointed you're straight."

Karim laughed louder. "Is that a fact?"

"Yes. But don't tell him I told you."

"My lips are sealed."

The end of the path brought them back to the parking lot.

"Would you unlock the door, please?" Isadora asked. "I'm gonna grab my purse, go powder my nose. Then I'll be ready to be your chauffeur."

"How lucky am I?" he said. "To have such a beautiful chauffeur."

After another thirty minutes in the car, she reached over and stopped the podcast. She'd been quiet since lunch, and he thought it best to follow her lead.

"You said your wife left you?"

A strained "yes" slid from his lips.

"I'm sorry, I should have asked first; is it painful to talk about?" She glanced at him.

He sighed. "It still hurts but being honest with you is worth it."

"Thank you," she said, her voice lighter. "When did she leave?"

"Two years ago."

Her eyebrow shot up.

"But the divorce isn't final?" she asked.

"I filed last month."

She kept her attention on the road, but her eyes narrowed.

"What took so long?"

His sigh was much heavier than the last. "A lot of things." He studied the passing cars. "Shame. Embarrassment. I fail— I *felt like* I'd failed." He needed a moment. He felt her glance at him, but he couldn't make eye contact. Facing it all inside of himself was tough. The first few appointments with his therapist had been worse. Now, with her, it was taking all his strength.

"We lived in Harrisburg, in Pennsylvania. I was at the senate. I thought things were fine. Until one day I came home from work and she was gone." He took a breath. "At first I lost it. I thought she'd been kidnapped, or worse. Then it turned out to be the last of her games, her tests of my love that I'd somehow failed. I waited. For months. Like a fool. Then I went home to Michigan.

But I'd made a commitment. My vows were serious to me. It took a solid year for my parents to convince me to file. Even though . . ." He sighed, then swallowed against a dry throat. "The relationship was abusive—had always been abusive. I just didn't understand it at the time."

He flinched at her hand on the back of his, resting on his knee. She squeezed.

"I'm so sorry, Karim," she said.

"Thanks," he said, squeezing back. She returned her hand to the wheel.

"It's strange," she said. "Cruel, almost."

"What's that?"

"She left you but didn't file herself?"

Karim chuckled. "It's not strange at all if you know anything about Laila. She would expect me to wait for her indefinitely. Like a good little puppy. I was always a *thing* that belonged to her. I had to act the way she wanted, think the way she wanted, express the feelings that she wanted me to express. Not be a real human being with my own mind. If I were, it was some sort of attack against her."

Her visible eyebrow shot up again.

"It was like that?" she asked.

"Yeah. Of course it wasn't like that at first. It . . . It wasn't until she was diagnosed after our first few years of marriage that I understood the magnitude of what we were dealing with. I was ready to support her; she was my wife, after all. But when she rejected the diagnosis, refused to follow her therapy plan and stay on her medications, things got a lot harder."

"Her diagnosis?" Isadora asked. "I mean, maybe you don't want to go into all of that with me. I don't mean to overstep."

"It's okay," he said. "She has borderline personality disorder. "It's . . . a lot of things, a big diagnosis. But what it meant for us, for me, was an abusive relationship that couldn't work."

"Oh," she said.

They were quiet a moment, the hum of the car on the road filling the space.

"What did she have to say about it?" Isadora asked when she broke the silence. "About leaving?"

"I haven't heard a word from her since the day before she left."

Isadora shook her head, then glanced at him again.

"I'm sorry, Karim," she said.

"Thanks." He reached over to turn the podcast back on.

"That's really powerful, you know," she said.

"Powerful?"

"Yeah. Recognizing the situation for what it was and getting yourself out of it."

He shook his head.

"I don't know about powerful. I waited in Harrisburg for a long time. My brother, Khalil, had to kind of come rescue me, get me to come home. It took therapy for me to really see that the situation had been abusive."

"Well, I'm glad for you that you're out of it now," she said, her voice bright. "You seem to be healing."

"Yeah, I'm getting there. And maybe . . ."

"Maybe?" she asked.

"Maybe it's time for something new to happen." He glanced at her. "I liked last night."

"I loved it."

"I'd like to do it again. But we can't, can we?" he asked.

"Leader Etcheverri's chief of staff and Senator Brown's legislative director?" She glanced at him. "What would people think?"

"That Brown's director is one lucky SOB." He appreciated her shy smile in response.

"Or," she began, that smile wiped away, "that Etcheverri's aide isn't all that clever and has to use sex to advance her boss's goals. Maybe she's been doing this all along. That's how she's gotten to where she is, using her attributes to get men to give her what she wants."

"Do you really believe people think that?" *My boss does, but that's about his ego, not about you.*

"No one's said anything to my face. But there will always be someone ready to believe that about any woman. At this point though, I have enough credibility that any gossip that might start wouldn't get much traction."

"So, it's not them you're worried about. It's me," he said.

She opened her mouth to answer and then closed it.

Too direct . . . talking about this stuff is hard. What are we both comfortable with?

"You remember before, in our first meeting, we talked about how we both got into politics to help people, to find ways to make things better."

"Yeah," she said.

"Well, I kind of see it like solving a puzzle. And I've loved solving puzzles since I was a kid. I love what I do now because I have to make a way for a situation to fit within the complex framework of existing laws or precedent. The bills I like working on most are the ones where we carve out something new. Those are the most challenging, and the ones I find most rewarding."

She kept her focus on the road but nodded.

"Sometimes, the most interesting puzzles aren't about legislation. Finding a way to make a complicated situation work." His gaze went back out the window. "Those are the puzzles that can have very enticing rewards, I think." He took a breath. "Is . . . this, whatever it may be . . . really more difficult than the things we have to figure out every day at work?"

Silence reigned for a few moments. He softened his voice when he broke it.

"You have a small birthmark on your neck, a little below and behind your left earlobe."

Her breath hitched.

"You made this sound last night, when I let my lips brush across it . . ." He needed to pause. The memory had him too excited. He adjusted his pants and reminded himself to refill the windshield wiper fluid, check the oil level, mundane thoughts to get that excitement to die down. "It was the slightest, softest little gasp."

She shivered.

"I am very interested in hearing that sound again—in being responsible for you making it."

She was quiet at first, but he caught her smile.

"The hollow of your throat," she said. "Usually you're all buttoned up, collared shirt and tie. But last night, I got to see the skin there, got close enough to . . . I wish I'd kissed you . . . tasted you there."

Glancing down, he was glad she was focused on the road and missed the full blush that warmed his cheeks. Laila had never made him too shy to look at her, but Isadora kept provoking that response. "Sounds like we both have challenges we'd like to address," he said.

"Yeah." She sighed, shooting him a look that was sweet but made him readjust his pants again. She bit her lip as she refocused on the road.

"Now you're just tempting me," he said, tapping the bridge of his glasses back into place.

"What?"

"That lip-biting move. You're playing dirty; that could get you in trouble."

She giggled. "Oh really? That's Karim's little button?"

"I'm not responsible for my reaction when you do that. I almost caught fire when you did it last night."

"Hmmm . . . You did catch that signal, didn't you? Wasn't sure how else to get your attention."

"Maybe it's another cliché, but it flips a switch that can be very . . . *hard* . . . to un-flip."

"Hmm," she murmured. "That's good to know."

"Careful, beautiful." He picked up her hand, praying she didn't feel his nervous tremble. He brought the inside of her wrist to his lips, softening his voice. "We still have a long way to go." He teased her skin with his stubble and caressed it with gentle parted-lip kisses. She gasped.

"Oh, really?" he said, flashing her an impish grin. "I wonder what happens when the kisses become more intimate?" He made sure she caught his glance at her skirt.

Then her hand was gone from his and back on the steering wheel.

"I potentially crash your car." She took a deep breath, straightening her shoulders.

He chuckled, tapping the Play button to return to the podcast. The narrator said "run" and something clicked. She hadn't run. He'd told her the truth, and she hadn't assumed that his wife's departure meant something was wrong with him, hadn't shied away. She'd done the opposite—wanted to know more. About him. He swallowed hard. His therapist had said he'd know when he was ready. Was he?

CHAPTER SEVENTEEN
Isadora

As she took the exit for Sacramento, Isadora's mood dipped. She weighed the pros and cons of inviting him in. She would have loved spending the night with him. But the reality of their situation became harder to ignore the closer they got to the capitol. She agreed with him, wanted to see where whatever this was might be going. Even though they were technically enemies, her gut was telling her that he was genuinely interested in her as a person and not getting her to let her guard down to help his boss.

Karim made her wonder if he was savoring their last moments together as well. At a red light, he leaned over and asked if he could kiss her. She tucked her chin but nodded and gasped as he nuzzled into her neck, mouthing from shoulder to ear. Her eyes fluttered. The honk from behind them forced her back into the present.

As they reached her complex, the warm cocoon melted away when she pulled up to her building. Her door was ajar.

"Well, beautiful, let me help . . . What's wrong?" he asked, following her gaze.

"I think . . ." She squinted. "I think my apartment door is open."

"Which one is it?"

"It's 3C."

The door swung wide, and a man in dirty overalls stepped outside. He wiped his hands on a rag, pulled a phone out of his pocket, and started dialing.

"Do you know him?" Karim asked.

"Not at all."

"Wait here?" He hopped out of the car before she answered and took the stairs two at a time. She stood and closed her door as the two men spoke. Karim's body language softened.

"Bad news, beautiful," he said, returning to her. "There's been a big leak."

"The pipe burst at the joint leading to the kitchen," the maintenance man explained once they'd joined him in the apartment. "Sorry we had to come in without your permission. I guess I have the wrong number for you. But as you can see, it was an emergency."

The kitchen, dining area, and half of the carpet were damp. Her laptop, sitting at the other end of the dining table had been spared, but not the presentation and documents she and her assistant had prepared for the healthcare bill working group the following morning.

"How much longer do you need?" Karim asked him.

"Oh, not even fifteen minutes. I was finishing the final seals on the new tube. Then I'll turn the water back on and be out of your hair."

"That's good news," Karim said, turning to Isadora. She didn't notice, still dumbstruck. She would need several hours to get even close to being prepared, and she was already tired.

"Well, we appreciate it," Karim said. "We'll let you finish." He guided Isadora by the arm into the only other room in the apartment. She sagged onto the edge of her bed.

This is not what I wanted to deal with this evening.

"Isadora? You haven't said a word. Are you okay?"

"Oh, yeah, sorry."

"Good thing your computer wasn't damaged."

"Yeah."

"What's wrong?" He sat next to her.

"I have this stupid working group with these asshole people from the Department of Health at eight A.M. about this supplemental insurance bill Peter's filed. Have you seen it?"

Karim shook his head.

"It's—" She slammed her mouth shut. Still in the romantic haze of the previous evening and the time they'd spent in the car, she'd almost forgotten that Karim was a Capulet and on Peter's side. The bill Senator Luccini had filed would allow some private entities the ability to provide supplemental coverage under single-payer. On its face it *seemed* innocuous, but Daniel had doubts. It looked like Peter was setting up a Trojan horse. Daniel wanted the staff at the Department of Health on his side as he tried to dissuade the other senators from supporting it. The absolute last thing Isadora should do was *tell* Karim what Daniel's arguments against the bill would be. Even though she was sure Julian and Peter were already trying to guess. She took a deep breath and smiled at him.

"We're workshopping the bill. We want to get the department's input just so things flow smoothly." She felt bad lying, but he was a Capulet; his boss was his boss. "My notes, handouts, and copies of Daniel's priorities are the pile of disintegrated papers you saw at the wet end of the table. My laptop was being weird last week. One of the IT guys is going to switch it out for me tomorrow afternoon. To be on the safe side, I wrote out most of my presentation. I'd planned to come home, take a hot shower, read through everything, and go to bed. But now . . . I see that I have several hours of work ahead of me, unless I want to go in there and look completely unprofessional in front of the working group tomorrow."

"Can your assistant help you? It is Sunday, but maybe?" Karim asked.

"Nah. I'm sure she'd be willing to, but she's out of town until Tuesday. Plus, this is my baby."

"What about your legislative director?" he asked.

She checked her watch and sighed. "Good idea, but it would take more time getting her up to speed enough to help restructure than it will if I just do it myself."

"What about this legislative director?" he asked, pointing at himself.

She smiled and shook her head.

"I know you said you paid attention to what we did with single-payer, but did you follow the minutiae of it?" *Please say no, please say no.*

"I can't say that I did," he said.

"I'll handle it," she said.

He gave her a sad shrug. "I'm sorry. I wish I could be more helpful."

"There's nothing for you to apologize for. I'll get it together." She rested her head on his shoulder.

"Well," he said. "You have to eat, right?"

"Crap . . ."

"No, wait. I'll go get some dinner. And you mentioned handouts and Daniel's priorities. Do you have those on a USB key? Maybe I can go print some more copies. That way you can focus on rebuilding your notes. Would that help you get ready faster?"

She paused. Could she trust him with the handouts? Relying on others was always a struggle for her. The skitter of her heartbeat and shakiness in her hands made it difficult to just say yes. And then there was the content. Was there anything in there she couldn't let a Capulet see? She'd had her assistant make the handouts as neutral as possible. She'd just have to trust her work.

"You'd run around and do all that for me?" she asked.

"It would be my pleasure, beautiful." He kissed her on the cheek. "But first we'll wait for the maintenance guy to head out."

"Why?"

"Feeling rather protective of you today. Not leaving you alone with a strange man in your apartment. Even if he seems nice."

Isadora hid her smile, playing with the hem of her skirt. "Aren't you sweet?"

He smiled, kissed her on the cheek again, and then hopped off the bed, headed for the door.

"Where are you going?"

"To get my stuff out of the car."

"Why?"

"Because I would prefer it if he thinks I live here."

She raised an eyebrow. "Is that the only reason?"

"Maybe, maybe not." He winked at her and strode into the living room, chatting with the man a moment before going back downstairs.

The maintenance man finished and wished them a good evening. She tried to fight down her stress as she got started on her notes and Karim left to do the running around.

An hour and a half later, he was back.

"Hi, beautiful," he said, kissing her on the cheek when she opened the door. She was so disheartened, she didn't even get excited about his kiss.

"Hey."

"I'm sure you're going to get everything ready in time."

"I'm glad one of us is sure." She went back to the couch, tucked her legs underneath her, and picked up her legal pad again. He rustled bags, opened and closed cabinet doors in the kitchen. Despite her need to focus, she did notice that the presence of someone else, the sounds in the background, reduced her tension.

"Dinner's ready, beautiful," he said. "Come eat with me."

Smiling, she put everything down and turned to the table. She'd expected some plastic take-out boxes and utensils, but he'd set the table with glasses and real plates. A small but beautiful bouquet of white roses was on hers.

"Karim!" She gasped.

"Surprise." The shy boy was back. "I thought a nice break was in order."

"Oh." She sat down in front of the flowers. "Thank you." She leaned over to kiss him on the cheek and stroke his stubble. "I'm going to miss that when it's gone."

"Is that so?" he asked, grinning.

"It is."

He went into the kitchen. "I bought two salads; I don't know what you prefer. And I also bought a bottle of Riesling. Would you like some?"

"Hmm. I would, but I'm afraid it will make me too relaxed to work. Maybe we'll save it for the next time you come over?"

"I like that idea."

They ate, and talked about the process of bringing single-payer to California. Isadora felt much better. She wanted to linger at the table with him, but there was still so much to do. When they finished, he cleaned up, took his things back down to his car and returned to say good night.

"Thank you so much for today. For this whole weekend, really," she said.

"Why are you thanking me? I should be thanking you. I was absolutely blown away when I saw you in that blue dress. I'd been sad thinking that you weren't going to be there, then there you were, a vision in front of me. I had to blink a couple of times to be sure."

She giggled. "I felt the same way. When I saw Drew, my heart sank. I figured, 'Okay, if he's here, Karim won't be,' so I thought I was going to have a crap evening. I'm glad I was wrong."

He bent to kiss her cheek, nuzzle her neck. "Will you do me a favor?"

She nodded.

"Will you call me when you've finished? I'd like to hear your voice one more time before going to sleep."

Her heart fluttered. "Sure, but I don't have your number."

"Yes, you do." He grinned. "It's on the card with the flowers." She turned back to the bouquet lying on the table.

"Aren't you smooth?" Before he spoke, she went up on tiptoe to kiss him. It was a long kiss, a deep kiss. Like their kisses from the previous night. He pulled her close, she slid her hands into his hair. They kissed for a long time, savoring each other. Moaning, he released her lips, resting his forehead against hers.

"We'd better stop." He sighed, his eyes closed.

"Yeah?"

"Yeah. Or you won't be able to finish your work. I won't let you," he whispered.

"Mmm . . . okay, Karim."

"Talk to you later, beautiful?" He turned to take the stairs, with reluctant steps.

She nodded. Words were complicated for her.

A few minutes before eleven, she rearranged the last stack of handouts and closed her laptop. After taking a quick shower and getting into her pajamas, she picked up the card with Karim's number and read it again.

Missing you already, beautiful. Thank you for spending the day with me. —K

She giggled, picking up her phone.

"Hello?"

"Hi," she said.

"Mmm, I hoped that was you. All done for the night?"

The sleepy timbre of his voice sent shivers over her skin.

"I am. Thank you again. You didn't have to do all that, I'm sure you were tired already."

"What was I going to do, beautiful? Let you struggle by yourself? I wouldn't have been able to come home and relax knowing you were stressing out and I could have done something to help."

"Guess I'm accustomed to being responsible for it all myself."

He didn't say anything at first.

She hesitated too, thinking she might have made a misstep, sounded egotistical or bossy somehow.

"That's a lot to bear," he finally said. "Why do you think that is?"

"Why do I think what is?" she asked.

"That you feel you have to do everything yourself? I mean, you don't do it all the time; you have your staff. But in a crunch you wouldn't reach out to them. And I'm not trying to get all psychiatrist-y on you or anything. It's just, you know. Something to think about. I really appreciate you letting me help you if it's hard for you to do that."

She swallowed around a lump in her throat. How many times had RJ held up a mirror to the fact that she struggled with asking for help, had made life much harder on herself than she needed to because she just could not do it. Hell, he'd even printed out article after article, showing her that she'd arguably had something called an adverse childhood experience, having a mother who expected Isadora to have as few needs as possible. As a result, Isadora learned to be as perfect as possible, as self-reliant as possible. And now she couldn't stop.

"I . . . um . . . yeah, sure," she said, her voice unsteady. "I appreciate your help."

She needed to change the subject. Get the focus off her.

"There's something I wanted to ask you about," she said, her voice evening out. "Though it's about your divorce, your, um, wife. I don't want to upset you."

"It's okay," he said. "I don't mind, it means . . . I'll take it to mean that you're curious about me, about what's going on in my life."

Isadora smiled. How could she not be curious?

"I am," she said. "But, um. Earlier, you mentioned that your wife expected you to only think and feel the way she wanted you to. Is that a trait of people with her disorder?" Isadora asked.

"I'm not an expert," Karim said. "But I think that's one way it can express itself. Why do you ask?"

Isadora hesitated. What he'd described sounded so, so very familiar. What if Karim could get what dealing with her mother was like because he'd been there with his wife? But what if she opened up and he didn't understand? Or worse, found a way to use it against her. Indecision zinged across her skin. She bit her lip hard, squeezed her eyes tight, and decided to leap.

"I have a family member. Who I think might be . . . like that," she said. "So I was just curious."

"It's really hard to live with," he said. "Because she was always expecting some sort of perfection that was rarely articulated. I mean, sometimes she'd say what she wanted me to do, but more often than not, I was just supposed to *know* what she wanted from me without her having to say it."

A chill went down Isadora's spine. That was *exactly* like her mother.

"And when I failed to meet her expectations, there was always some punishment. Either toward me or herself."

"Um . . . punishment like what?"

"Could have been something minor, like embarrassing me in public, or something major, like self-harm," he said.

How many times had her mother humiliated her in front of family members? Though she was too vain to injure herself.

"That's intense," Isadora said. "I'm sorry you went through all that."

"I'm just glad it's behind me now."

"I bet."

"Your family member," he asked. "Have they ever gotten help?"

"What? Ha. Oh no, they never would. They don't think anything is wrong with them. Everyone else is the problem."

"Yeah, that's pretty common thinking in personality disordered people. The joke is that it's the rest of the family that ends up in therapy."

"Oh," she said. *Maybe I need therapy.* "I appreciate you being willing to talk about all of this with me, Karim."

"It's cool," he said.

"But I imagine you don't want to dwell on the past."

"No," he said. "I've got more enticing things to think about now. Like smart, intimidating chiefs of staff to the majority leader of the California State Senate."

She could hear the smile in his voice.

"Aww. What a sweet thing to say."

"I'm just being honest, beautiful."

Karim

On Monday, Karim was just getting situated in his office when Julian appeared in his doorway.

"So," he said. "I see you took advantage of the . . . social lubricating effects of the inauguration."

Karim paused. Had Julian seen him with Isadora? He thought they'd been careful by leaving early. And Drew hadn't seen him with Isadora, but someone else may have. Karim kicked himself internally.

"What do you mean?" he asked.

"You disappeared early. Found a friend and took the party elsewhere?" Julian's grin soured Karim's stomach. He decided to remain discreet.

"The meal was good and I did enjoy chatting with my colleagues. But I drove back here. Had to get to bed early enough for a good night's sleep."

"Did you? Guess the Johnny Cash look wasn't as successful as you'd hoped." Julian sidled in and took one of the seats across from Karim's desk.

Discretion.

"Guess not," Karim said.

Julian smirked. "Well," he said. "Back to business. SB 317. Have you seen it?"

"No, I haven't," Karim said, turning a little in his chair to wake his laptop. "What's it about?" He went into the bill search system and typed in 317. The summary indicated that it would create an obligation for each voter in the state to have a new identification card in order to participate in any election.

Julian grinned when Karim looked up from the screen.

"New voter ID? That's quite an ambitious undertaking," Karim said. "Why not just ask people to use their driver's licenses? If any identification is necessary at all?"

Julian's eyes narrowed.

"Don't tell me you're one of those social justice warriors who wants a free-for-all when it comes to voting. Of course we need identification. We've been too lax. Shouldn't have just anyone doing it. Should be the right people. And *our people* know that. Senators May and Davis. They represent the more conservative parts of the state; they already have support for the bill in terms of votes and donors. It's the bit about requiring a new identification card that will bring the money in for us. Think of all the private vendors who will be thrilled at the opportunity to get a piece of the action."

Karim was a bit lost.

"But if it's a state-issued ID . . ."

Julian smiled.

"That's not what the bill requires," he said.

So it was about money. Money and making sure only the *right* people could vote. Karim's skin was crawling. Julian stood up.

"Get familiar with the bill," he said. "Then go have a chat with May and Davis's directors. They need to be on board. This will be a fight. Senators Douglas and Knight have already been very vocal in opposition. But they're from San Francisco. You know how *those people* are."

Uh, no. How?

Karim cleared his throat.

"But, um, Julian. How do you plan for this sort of a measure to hold up? Voter identification attempts are frequently struck down in court. If you're making everyone use a new form of identification, you're creating a new cost burden on every single voter in the state. Voting ID is already an inflammatory issue. Why make it worse? And set up a legal battle?"

Julian waved his hand in the air.

"It will all come together. And the money will be rolling in before anyone goes to court. Just get the bill going, Karim."

He turned and left.

Karim sat a moment. His boss was disgusting. He'd guessed Julian was two-faced at Ike's that night; Julian had shown him that he was socially inappropriate at the stadium. And now he'd put the nail in the coffin in terms of Karim's opinion of him on political issues. Karim didn't have anything lined up yet, though. He'd never expected to be 100 percent in alignment with a boss, but this was going too far. So he'd go talk to May and Davis, these Capulets. Make notes to show Julian that he was doing his job. And he'd start making friends with the other side.

There was only one Montague who truly interested him, though. He wondered what Isadora was up to that morning. Their offices weren't on the same floor, so he rarely had a chance to run into her in the hallways. There was the occasional possibility to cross paths with her when he was on his way to a committee meeting. He'd been holding his breath for those chances just to see her, but now . . . He smiled. Now he could reach out any time he wanted to. Even though she had to know who his boss really was. Could she be playing him? Trying to get an ally inside of Julian's team? She'd certainly been there long enough to know who was who and what was what. But her interest in him seemed genuine. And there was most certainly a risk for her too. She'd referred to it on the drive. He wanted to reach out again. But he didn't want to annoy her. Though she'd said she wanted to learn more about him. He wished they could go out together and get to know each other. But their bosses were outright enemies. No way they could be seen in public together, especially if their mutual interest was visible.

As Karim stepped out of the elevator and headed toward Senator May's office, his personal phone started ringing. He fished it out of his pocket, letting himself hope it was Isadora, even though he knew it wouldn't be. The caller ID flashed a Harrisburg, Pennsylvania, number.

"Hello," he answered.

"Mr. Sarda?" a young woman's voice said. "Attorney Sanders calling for you. Is now a good time?"

"Oh, yeah, now's good," he said. He looked around and ducked into a darkened committee meeting room. There wasn't an agenda posted on the panel by the door, so he figured he'd have some privacy.

"Karim, how's it going?" his attorney said when he got on the line.

"Just fine, Mart, but get to the point, I know you're gonna bill me for every second," Karim said with a smile.

Martin laughed.

"All right, all right. I'll get to it. Things just got tricky."

"Why's that?" Karim asked.

"Laila's fired her attorney again."

Karim slumped back against the wall, rolling his eyes, then let them shut.

"Again, Mart? Again? This is the second time."

"Yeah, yeah, I know," Martin said.

"Why would she even— Never mind. I don't care. What the hell does it matter?"

"It just means we have to start all over. Wait for the new guy to get up to speed. Once we find out who the new guy is."

"They haven't even approached you yet?"

"Nope. I have no idea who it is. Although, it would appear that things did not end well with previous counsel because he may or may not have informed me of her latest um . . . tactic."

Karim raised an eyebrow.

"And what is that?" he asked.

"You're not going to like it."

"Mart. Give it to me straight."

"Apparently, her assertion is that she did not abandon the marital home, thus we cannot argue a no-fault divorce."

Karim didn't understand. She just disappeared. How was that not abandoning the marital home?

"Go on, Mart."

"I suspect that she is seeking counsel to argue that she *fled* the marital home, for her safety."

Karim's head got woozy. The only good thing about the time he'd spent confused, hurt, and grieving as he'd waited around for Laila to come back was that one year just happened to be the necessary separation time to qualify for a no-fault divorce in

Pennsylvania. But if Laila was saying she had no choice but to leave . . .

"So, wait, Mart. Wait. You're telling me that I don't have grounds for a no-fault divorce based on a year's worth of abandonment because she's getting a new attorney to argue that *I* was a danger to *her*?"

"Uh, yep, you got it."

Karim ground his teeth so hard his molars locked together. The room he was in was dark, but he squeezed his eyes shut tight enough that flashes of rage danced behind his eyelids. What was the point of this game? He wrenched his jaw apart.

"What the fuck, Mart?"

"Well . . ." He sighed. "Based on what you've told me, and past experience, it looks like a double stalling tactic. New attorney that has to get up to speed, plus an allegation that knocks the legs out of no-fault. Looks to me like she doesn't want to get divorced, man."

Karim slumped back against the wall. Of course Martin was right. If she'd been willing to let him go, she'd have just agreed to it after having left him. But no, this was par for the course. This was Laila being Laila.

"What's the plan?" he asked Martin.

"I'm working on it. Just make sure to let me know if she contacts you at all. Her or any of her family members. Do not communicate with them at all. No emails, no phone calls, no text messages, nothing. Let me handle it."

"No problem with that," Karim said. He figured that if he spoke to her now, he'd start shouting.

"Okay, I'll be in touch."

"All right."

Martin hung up. Karim stayed in the dark for a few moments. He preferred keeping his anger and frustration there, rather than in the busy hallway. It wasn't a surprise that Laila would start playing games with the divorce. The greater surprise would have been if she'd gone along with it peacefully.

CHAPTER EIGHTEEN
Isadora

"Majority Leader Etcheverri sees his colleagues across the aisle as partners, not competition," Isadora said on the phone the following Thursday, letting her irritation coat her voice. "I can't imagine you'd expect us to be amenable to your client's goals after such a threat."

The lobbyist on the other end of the line hemmed and hawed. He was too new to have known how his attempt to force Daniel's hand by asserting that an ancient allegation of bribery was really evidence of ongoing corruption would backfire, but Isadora had no qualms about teaching him. She wasn't surprised that the old story had come up again, but she had expected it in two years' time, when Daniel would be running for U.S. representative. And she hadn't expected the creative new spin. She rolled her eyes at the time she was wasting on this phone call. Although she could have left it to her staff, every now and then opportunities popped up that her skill and experience were uniquely honed to deal with. Sometimes shit just required her to take off the gloves and be a boss bitch. Particularly when it involved snot-nosed little lobbyists trying to get Daniel to support their client's agendas by threatening to go public with shiny new exaggerations. She cleared her throat.

"I'd strongly suggest you let your boss know about the little stunt you just tried to pull, before she finds out from someone else. The senate is much smaller than you think. Particularly as a quick Google search would have told you that Kim and I debated together for Berkeley."

She caught his sharp intake of breath at the sound of his boss's name. He didn't need to know that she wasn't going to get in touch with Kim; she had enough on her plate.

"I'll um . . . I'll let her know," he said.

"Wise choice. I trust the subject is closed?" Isadora asked.

"Yes, ma'am."

Leaning over to put the phone back on its base, a wisp of hair tickled the back of her neck and she stood to check in the mirror next to her office door. A section of her crown braid had fallen out of place. She slipped the pin out and into the corner of her mouth while she got the hair back into position. There was a knock at the outer office door. Her ten thirty appointment was early.

"Anybody home?"

She jumped at Karim's voice and gasped, the pin falling out of her mouth.

"Be right there!" Holding her hair in place, she searched the floor, then the narrow entry table below the mirror for the pin. His steps got closer. She didn't want him to see her, elbows in the air, but the whole thing would come undone if she let go.

"Hi," he said, in the doorway of her office. He cocked his head at her bizarre position.

"Hi, yourself?" Heat flooded her cheeks as she resigned herself to being embarrassed. He glanced down at her jacket.

"Looking for something?"

She followed his gaze, and there it was, the errant black hairpin as clear as day dangling from the edge of her tan lapel. She chuckled.

"Yes, I was. Thank you." She reached for it, but another bit of hair fell.

"May I help?" he asked. His voice was warm and deep and honeyed.

"Um, yeah. Thanks," she managed. He took the pin, careful to touch only that, and stepped behind her. He put the documents in his hand on the edge of her desk and studied the disobedient section of hair. Every inch of her body began to hum. Time slowed down. Air became difficult to find. His body heat seared her through her clothes, drawing her to him like a magnet. She wanted to fall into his reflection in the mirror.

"I . . ." He paused to lick his lips, meeting her gaze. "I don't really know what I'm doing here."

She smiled, rolled her hair into place and tapped a spot with her finger. "Can you slide it in right there?"

He followed her instructions and then lowered his hands. She lowered hers. He met her gaze in the mirror.

"I . . . I came by because I wanted to see you. I know it's risky." Things had been getting spicier, more interesting with their phone calls every night. They'd managed two Zoom dates where they'd shared dinner, but the second had been cut short by Julian calling Karim. His voice was soft, his breath caressing her neck. Her attention fell to her fingertips on the table.

"Um, okay. But I have an appointment. They'll be here soon," she whispered.

"Oh. Won't take long. It's just that . . ." He took a deep breath. "I wanted to—" He closed the remaining space between them and kissed her nape, just below her hairline. Fire and ice radiated from his lips, scalding and freezing every bit of her. A high-pitched sigh fell out of her mouth. He sighed and caressed her skin with his prickly cheek, brushing his lips across the birthmark he'd mentioned in the car. She gasped. Their eyes met in the mirror again, both breathing fast.

"I hate that we're in Sacramento," she whispered.

"Me too. I feel like the whole world is in our business even if nobody knows. I waited until the hallway was clear before I ducked into your office."

She nodded.

"Because what if it gets back to Julian that you came here without an official purpose?" she said.

"Exactly."

"It's not fair."

"It isn't."

"I wish we could just decide it didn't matter and take the risk," she said. "I wish—"

She turned to the outer office and tilted her head. Then she stepped through the doorway and motioned for him to follow. He collected his documents from her desk and went after her. She turned to offer him her hand.

"That's good," she said, voice confident. "I look forward to Senator Brown's response."

Looking confused, he returned her handshake and started to answer but was cut off by two people knocking on the open door. He nodded them a quick hello and thanked Isadora before he left.

Forty minutes later, Isadora let herself smile as she closed the door behind the departing reporters, twirling one of their business cards in her hand. Her assistant handed her a small stack of notes indicating the phone messages she'd missed during her meeting. But Isadora wasn't in the mood to look at them all yet. She returned to her office and slid the business card into a box on her desk when two of the photos next to her computer screen caught her eye: RJ giving her a bouquet of flowers at the end of a salsa competition. She, RJ, and some of their San Diego friends at a paint and sip party. Picking it up, she smiled again. The party had been her idea. She'd stopped painting after graduation; it hadn't seemed like the most judicious use of her time. Especially for something that was just for fun. But if it was okay to let her feelings in, it would be okay to let some fun in again, wouldn't it? The blast of a siren coming from her desk wiped the smile off her face. The new ringtone she'd chosen for her mother's calls did its job of warning her, but it also set her teeth on edge. Though the previous ringtone, a melody with chirping birds, had the exact same effect. She returned the photo to its spot.

"Hello, Mother," she answered, pushing her office door closed most of the way.

"Isadora. What is the point of giving me your work phone number if you do not answer when I call? I had to leave five messages with that secretary. She knew it was important. She should have interrupted whatever nonsense you were doing and put you on the phone." Her mother's tone mixed condescension and pleasantness. That meant she wasn't alone.

"I was in a meeting, Mother. She did exactly what she was supposed to do."

Her mother huffed. "Your silly meeting couldn't have been as important as my phone call. Anyway, I am calling to express my disappointment. I can't believe I raised a child who goes back on her promises."

"What promises?"

"To call your Uncle Ray and help him plan his Hollywood vacation. He's right here and said he hasn't heard from you at all. You should be ashamed. Only terrible people break promises to family."

Isadora closed her eyes against the insult, massaging the bridge of her nose. She willed her jaw to unclench.

"What . . . on earth are you talking about, Mother?"

"Don't play games with me, young lady. You will help your uncle because I say you will."

The rapid shift from content and relaxed after the meeting to fight-or-flight mode made Isadora's stomach burn and her head spin. Anyone else and she would have fought back. But direct confrontation was not only the best way to stoke her mother's anger, it was the best way to guarantee Isadora being subsumed by her own emotions once the call came to an end.

"When did I make this promise?"

"Just the other day!" The pitch shift in her mother's voice made it difficult for Isadora to think straight. She took a deep breath and returned to a system she'd used in the past to verify discussions her mother said had taken place.

"Where were we for this conversation?" Isadora sat back in her seat, chest out, shoulders back, hoping to counter her distress by getting her body into a more confident position.

"At the store."

"What store?"

"Just the other day at the grocery store. I was on my way to the office and ran in to get something for lunch."

Isadora sighed. She wasn't crazy. There was no way this discussion had ever taken place.

"It was before you went to work, Mother?"

"Yes."

"So, if it was around seven A.M. for you, it would have been four A.M. for me. I couldn't have been on the phone with you, it would have been too early in the morning."

"Whatever," her mother said. "Don't try to weasel out of it; you promised."

Isadora wasn't letting go. But as this was far from the first time she'd confronted her mother with logic proving that something did not happen, it was a surprise that she didn't know what Isadora planned to say next.

"So, we weren't on the phone," Isadora said. "I was with you."

"Of course," her mother said.

Isadora's throat went tight, fighting against the building rage. But long-honed skill kept her voice polite and respectful. "I was with you in the store?" she asked.

"Of *course* you were! Now are you going to keep your promise and actually help your uncle, or did I raise a terrible, self-centered human being?"

"*How* could I have promised anything standing in a grocery store with you? I haven't been home in over a year!"

The sound of liquid pouring into something was the only proof Isadora had that the line hadn't gone dead. She remained silent, waiting for her mother to come to the obvious conclusion.

"I guess you weren't with me," she said.

"Nope. We never had that conversation."

"Oh. Yeah. Guess not."

Met with more silence, Isadora stifled the urge to defend herself further. Her mother would make herself out to be the victim.

"So," her mother began, her voice light, pleasant. "How are things with you? Did I tell you about my promotion?"

Isadora didn't answer. And her mother filled the space, talking about herself. Making the occasional sound to show she hadn't hung up, Isadora double-clicked her mouse and scrolled through the emails she'd received during the meeting. Her temples burned, and she reconsidered her lunch with RJ. Digesting well would be a pipe dream once the conversation was finished.

"Well," her mother said. "I have to run. It's been so good catching up. You should call more, Isadora. We never girl-talk."

"Girl-talk"? Open myself up to you? Share things just so you can use them to attack me later? Isadora rolled her eyes and forced herself to take a silent deep breath. She made a noncommittal grunt.

"Okay, sweetie, talk soon!" her mother said.

"Guess I'm not such a terrible person, after all?" Isadora said.

"What are you talking about?"

"You started this conversation by calling me a terrible person."

"I did no such thing, Isadora. You're always blowing things out of proportion."

Her mother hung up. Isadora placed the phone on its base, momentarily numb. Then feeling came rushing back. Her hands started shaking and prickly waves charged her skin. She swallowed against a dry throat, noticing that her breathing was shallow. She tried to get it under control. It was just as bad as the last time she'd been on a plane and there'd been a lot of turbulence. Her heart felt like it was going to shoot out of her chest. She forced herself to take a deep breath. Then another. *You're safe. You're in Sacramento, and she can't do anything to you.* She laughed internally at that thought. Her mother was far away, but look what she'd done to her. Isadora was on the verge of a panic attack and was in precisely the wrong place to succumb to it. On shaky legs, she got up to close her office door. She locked it, resting her head on the cool wood. *Breathe, just breathe. You're not a terrible person. You are a good and kind person, excellent at what you do. And it is important work, no matter what she says. You're going to keep working hard, and Daniel is going to become pro tem and then U.S. representative, and then you're going to D.C. to become a congressional aide.* Her hands were still shaking, her heart thumping, but not as hard or as fast. *It's all a lie. You are not a terrible person. You are not.*

CHAPTER NINETEEN
Karim

*S*uch *bullshit*. Karim swirled his cocktail, the best part of his evening, at the edge of the circular booth where Julian had set up camp for dinner at a restaurant called Gordito's. At the end of a long, stressful week, here he was again, a cast member in his boss's entourage. It had been an eternity, first at the bar, now at a table, though they had yet to order. Julian, Peter, and Peter's aide hit on every woman in sight. Karim recognized a few from Ike's and caught on that Gordito's was yet another spot for the youngest and prettiest lobbyists to make friends. All he wanted to do was drag his ass home, take a shower, and stretch out on the couch. Catch up on some ESPN, check in with Gabriel for their next jogging session and, in all likelihood, reach out to Isadora.

The memory from earlier that day, being so close to Isadora, touching her hair, tasting her skin right before her appointment showed up . . . He took another sip of his cocktail to hide his grin.

He tried to make polite conversation. He needed to keep Julian satisfied, to play the part, not arouse suspicion. He'd begun making contacts, getting to know committee staff in both the senate and the assembly. Julian was still dangling the carrot of Christina's position in front of him, but Karim was already sure that a long-term relationship wouldn't work out. He worried that the time they'd already spent together was tainting his own reputation.

"So serious, always so serious," Julian said, drawing Karim's attention. "You've been here for months and haven't taken advantage of that pretty face of yours!" He laughed, and his sycophant joined in. "Seen women practically throwing themselves at him," he said to Peter. "And nothing . . . it's like he's not even interested." Julian studied Karim over the edge of his glass as he took a sip. Karim heard the implication loud and clear. He took a sip as well.

"What can I say? I've always been very picky." He maintained eye contact with Julian.

"Quality over quantity, is it?"

Karim shrugged.

"Dunno. Variety is the spice of life," said Peter, laughing. Julian joined in, and Karim followed suit. But Julian was still sizing him up. If Karim wanted to make sure that Julian didn't blackball him in the entire California legislature before he'd had a chance to find a permanent position, Karim would have to make Julian comfortable by reflecting an image of himself.

All right. If that's the game tonight. Another unanticipated part of starting over—put boss at ease by hitting on women. He cast a gaze around the room, taking his time checking the bar. There were two unfamiliar faces. Both brunettes—one adorable and petite, the other pretty and curvaceous. They were sipping glasses of wine, people-watching, and giggling. After watching them a few moments, the shorter one met his gaze. He smiled, looked away, then looked back at her again. She flushed and elbowed her friend. Julian and Peter were talking, but Julian was watching, so Karim went in for the kill. The curvaceous one darted a glance at him and he smiled again. Her cheeks got blotchy, and she raised her eyebrows at her friend. Karim stood, picking up his glass.

"Peter," he said. "Can I ask a favor?"

"Uh, yeah?"

"Order me the chicken quesadilla if the waitress gets back before I do?"

Peter followed Karim's gaze, focused on the two women.

"Heh, heh. Not a problem, Karim," he laughed.

Okay, ladies, he thought as he strode across the room toward them. *Help me out here.*

Twenty minutes later, Karim returned to the table, conspicuously sliding his phone back into his pocket as though he'd gotten some new numbers.

"Ah, there he is," said Julian. Two women had joined him and Peter. Their faces were familiar. One snuggled between Julian and Peter, the other between Peter and Karim's empty seat.

"Karim allow me to introduce you to Daria and Sarah. Daria is a lobbyist for the chamber of commerce, and Sarah is with Darwin and Coates."

"Ah, yes," Karim said, sitting next to Sarah. "You came by about the gaming bill last week, right?"

"I did, in fact. Sweet of you to remember."

Pretty amazed I did. The intensity of her makeup was much stronger and the plunge of her neckline much, much deeper than when she'd visited the office. She shifted away from Peter and closer to Karim. Peter started to protest, but Daria drew his attention. Karim had to respect her ability to entertain both Julian and Peter while Sarah turned the heat up on him.

"So," she said, leaning closer. "Tell me all about yourself. We didn't get to chat much the other day." She crossed her leg toward him and let it rest against his. His instinct was to move away, but Julian was watching. So Karim rested his arm behind Sarah on the back of the seat.

"You don't mind, do you?" he asked.

"Not one bit," she said, getting even closer.

Other senators and young women joined them. Appetizers came and went. Along with more drinks. Karim was careful. He'd had one cocktail and hard liquor was not his friend. He maintained his flirtation with Sarah, joked with Peter, and threw the occasional line at Daria. Julian's wariness had gone; he was happy in his element surrounded by bootlickers and scantily clad women.

The group was boisterous, and Karim played his part. He was confident he'd accomplished his goal for the evening.

Another thirty to forty-five minutes and you can go home. You've done your job. Make something up; pretend you have someone to meet and get out of here.

He excused himself to the men's room to avoid another round of shots. Sarah made a joke of not letting him leave, catching his hand to pull him back. Playing along, he brought her hand to his lips and kissed the back, placing his other hand on his heart, promising to return. As he straightened, laughing, his body temperature plunged. His eyes locked with Isadora's across the room. He staggered as he stepped away from the booth; a chorus of laughter bubbled from the group around him, drawing his attention to the role he had to play. He laughed too, pretending his misstep had been from too much to drink. He kept his gaze on the floor until he'd passed Julian, then tried to make eye contact with Isadora again. She was deep in conversation with RJ and didn't look up.

His phone was in his hand before he'd locked the door of the stall.

Karim: Isadora, please. It's not what it looks like.

He waited, tapping his toes as he leaned against the wall.

Karim: Isadora?

Isadora: ?

He paused. She'd made eye contact, so she'd seen him flirting. Why reply with a question mark? He'd expected anger; he wasn't sure how to answer.

Karim: I'm just playing along.

He couldn't stay much longer. He was about to give up when he had another response.

Isadora: K

"K"? Just "K"? Does that mean she's mad? Does that mean she doesn't care? Does that mean she's okay with me flirting with someone else?

Dazed, he left the restroom. He had the presence of mind not to look at her as he passed but couldn't wrap his mind around her reaction. Maybe she was a silent angry. Cold. He had years of experience dealing with silent angry. Well, initially silent. He made a detour at the bar before returning to Julian and the rest.

Screw another forty-five minutes. Twenty more and I'm out of here. He slid back in next to Sarah, draped his arm behind her like before, and joined in the joking. He felt like a buffoon, a court jester. Daria was taking up more and more of Julian's attention, so Karim's departure might be easier than anticipated. A slight shift in position gave him a clear view of Isadora. Her waiter arrived with the glass of Riesling Karim had sent. She looked up, surprised, and then shook her head as they exchanged a few words. But then Sarah leaned into him, hard, too friendly, whispering an invitation into his ear. And he pulled his attention back to the lie he'd gotten himself into.

"I'm sorry, what?" he had to ask Sarah. He hoped he'd added enough of a slur. Julian was watching again, so he paid closer attention.

"I said, this is getting a little boring, isn't it? I bet we could find more interesting things to do." She was too close, her breast pressing into his side.

He nodded. "I'm sure we could, but I'm gonna have to call it a night pretty soon." Sarah pouted, and Daria leaned toward him.

She looked him up and down and bit her lip. "Oh, come on, I'm sure we can make it worth missing a little sleep."

He sighed inside. His reaction to that lip bite was one hundred eighty degrees from his reaction to Isadora's. Searching for a reply, he caught the waiter returning to the bar with the full glass of Riesling on his tray.

He got home. Sliding his phone out of his pocket, he hesitated before placing it next to his keys on the counter. Then he scooped it up again, to reread her last messages, as though they might have changed.

One question mark, one "K," and that acidic ache was back, the one he'd hoped had gotten lost somewhere over Nebraska. Two characters and he was waiting for the other shoe to drop like a hundred times before, when his best efforts to quickly make up for whatever slight Laila had identified resulted in silence followed by her rage.

Changed, brushing his teeth, he glanced at his phone again. Isadora wasn't like Laila. And even before he'd met her, he'd been over this a thousand times with his therapist. Laila's stuff was her own. Another woman wouldn't necessarily behave the same way. Sluggish, he got into bed. He knew it was best to lie down and let his heavy lids close. Sleep would help him order his thoughts the next day, keep exhaustion from letting irrational ideas shove their way to the forefront in moments of doubt. It would be the wisest thing. Instead, he propped himself up against his pillows. The remote was on the nightstand, beside the book he'd started a few days earlier. He picked up his phone again, read her replies, and scrolled up through all their previous conversations. They were essentially dating, at least as much as they could. She was into him, seemed to want more. She'd even said as much in her office before her appointment had arrived. But now, she'd seen him flirting with another woman and she didn't even care?

Grunting, he switched the phone for the book and turned on the lamp on his nightstand. After reading the same page for the third time, he shoved his glasses up to rub his eyes. But maybe he was wrong. He didn't know how long she'd been there, what she'd seen. *The fake swagger? The two girls at the bar? The other on the way back?* In his haste, he'd risen to Julian's bait. And yeah, his self-esteem had grown since his arrival in California; yeah, it made him confident enough to approach those women, to flirt. But how much of that strength had come from Isadora? The way she looked at him, spoke to him? The electricity that crackled between them, making him risk kissing her when they were going to be interrupted at any moment?

Nah, it wasn't even a risk. I had to kiss her. I couldn't have stopped myself if I'd wanted to. Now, how can she think I'm anything other than some pitiful skirt-chaser, out for conquest after conquest? No wonder she sent the Riesling back.

He needed help. It was midnight, so three in the morning on Friday in Detroit. He wouldn't wake Khalil for this, but if there was ever a time he needed his twin, it was then. He picked up his phone again and began to type.

Late Friday morning, Karim waited for the elevator in the legislative office building. The doors opened and there Isadora was, with RJ. They shared muted greetings as Karim stepped in.

"Oops!" RJ said. "I need this floor." He leaned across Isadora to push the Door Open button, avoiding her surprised glare.

"I thought you were going with me to Judiciary," she said. Karim couldn't tell if the sharpness in her tone was surprise or irritation at RJ for trying to leave them on their own.

"Yeah, sorry. Forgot something." The elevator doors opened again and RJ scooted out. "Later!"

Isadora looked as lost as Karim was uncertain. He took a deep breath.

"Listen, I get that you're disappointed," he said.

"Disappointed?"

"Yeah, in me. From last night."

Her silence wasn't helping. In spite of his best efforts and Khalil's advice, he couldn't stop himself from filling it.

"I just . . ." He stopped for another quick breath. "Blunt, honest?"

"Um . . . yeah?"

"If you're gonna get angry, can you just go ahead and do it? Let's have the blow up, get it over with, and I can do what you want to fix it."

She shook her head, blinking.

"What?" she asked.

"Will you just get angry, so I can fix it?"

"Why should I be angry?"

"So you just don't care?" His tone had been much sharper than he'd intended, and he immediately regretted it. Along with the fact that the elevator was slowing down. Isadora's lips were still parted in confusion when they came to a stop. Then she sucked in a breath and that professional mask appeared as she stepped as far away from him as possible before the doors opened. He was almost hurt until he remembered who they both worked for. He locked his attention on the opening doors.

Two women got on. People he didn't know. They both smiled at Isadora and continued their conversation. He stared at the doors to avoid glaring at the women for the interruption. They got off two floors later.

"This isn't the wisest place for this conversation," Isadora said as the doors came together again. She touched the button for the first floor, and just as the doors were almost closed, a suit-jacketed arm poked through.

"Hey there, good-looking," the blond-haired, linebacker guy crammed into his suit said to Isadora before he noticed Karim in the back corner and turned red. "Um, hello." He pressed the button for the second floor.

Karim nodded. The closing doors deserved his attention. Or the files tucked against his side. Or his watch or his cell. His attention should have been anywhere but where it got stuck, on Isadora and this guy, making small talk. Flirty small talk. *Who is this guy?* Karim's skin was prickling all over. Was he jealous? Embarrassingly, yes. *What the hell is wrong with me? I'm losing my mind.* His torture continued for the short ride that lasted three days. When the guy left, Karim took a breath to speak, but Isadora raised her hand and shook her head.

"Follow me once we get out," she said. "But not too closely, please."

He nodded and obeyed, letting her get well ahead of him as she left the legislative office building, got into the main capitol building, and ducked through a doorway in the rotunda. She went down a flight of stairs into a basement and stopped, waiting for him in front of a door marked B23, her arms crossed.

"So, let me see if I've got this straight," she asked. He searched her tone but only came up with confusion, not anger. "If I care,

I'll get angry with you and punish you? Or demand that you do 'X' to make me happy with you again?"

He wasn't in love with the exact phrasing, but she had the idea.

"Yeah," he said, arms also crossed, crushing his files against his chest.

"Okay. So, if I'm not angry with you, that means I don't care at all?"

He really didn't need the heat burning his cheeks and neck. The toes of his shoes were suddenly very interesting, but he forced himself to look her in the eye.

"Uh . . . yeah," he said.

"Okay. Where's the benefit of the doubt option?"

He was too confused to speak.

"You were with Julian, right?"

He nodded.

"When Julian goes out, he wants people to envy him, he wants to look important. So he surrounds himself with women and followers and noise."

Karim nodded again.

"You're the new guy, gotta go along to get along."

"Yeah."

"I've known Julian long enough to recognize his game. And that's all it is, a game. I know you have to play in order to keep him happy with you. I also know the rules and the habitual playing field: RJ and I only went to Gordito's because we thought most of the members would have already left for the weekend. I can admit, I wasn't thrilled by what I saw. But we were in public, and I wanted to give you the benefit of the doubt."

She got closer, and that electric pull sparked between them. There was no anger at all.

"Your messages and the wine told me all I needed to know." He had to suppress a wriggle. *Does she know it makes my skin tingle when she warms her voice like that? But* . . .

"Why did you send the wine back?" he asked.

She took another step, resting against the doorframe. "The waiter didn't tell you?"

He took a half-step, to lean against the other side. "No."

She moistened her lips. "I was the DD last night. And I'd already pushed my luck by having a cocktail before we ate. The waiter was supposed to bring you another of your drink and thank you for me."

Another reality began to form in his mind. A possibility he hadn't conceived of.

"You're sure you aren't mad at me?" he whispered.

She frowned a little, readjusting her crossed arms. "Do you want me to be mad at you? If I storm off somewhere and slam a door, will it help?"

"Blunt, honest?" he asked.

She nodded.

"It might." He shrugged, looking down. "Guess old expectations die hard." He looked back up into her deep brown eyes and his heart stuttered.

She stepped in close, placing a hand on his cheek. *Are her fingers trembling?*

"Gotta say, I don't like what I just saw," she said.

Shit. She saw what a mess I am and doesn't want anything to do with me.

Her brow knitted. "Uh-oh. I said the wrong thing. You just got all mopey. We've spent at least three nights a week on the phone or a video date. Why would I do that with someone I don't trust?"

"I . . . I guess you wouldn't," he said.

"I think we should change the subject," she whispered, leaning in as close as possible without touching him. He followed the pull, falling forward to kiss her; then she pulled back.

"Can we?" she asked, still so close he could feel the heat of her words.

The air vibrated, stealing his breath, restricting his ability to hear anything, be aware of anything, other than her. Her lips, her eyes, the rise and fall of her breasts as her breath quickened along with his.

"We can," he whispered, and let himself fall. She caught him.

Groaning deep, he kissed her back, crushing her to him. They wavered, then she pulled away, grabbing his hand and dragging him deeper into the basement.

Tucked in a niche, she attacked him, moaning as he devoured her. Dropping his files and holding her close, he turned them so that her back was against the wall, her surprised cry, muffled by his mouth. He released her lips and breathed into her ear.

"I'm sorry I freaked out," he breathed, before kissing her again, then mouthing his way along her jaw, reaching her neck.

"Don't be . . ." She sighed. He pulled back to look her in the eye. "Don't apologize, we've all got baggage." She slid a hand over his shoulder, to his chest as she licked her lips. "And yours comes in a very nice package." She looked back up at him and bit her lip. Kissing her again, he shuddered as her nails scratched down his chest, leaving a trail of sparks. Her mouth left his as her head tilted back to let out a high-pitched sigh. He'd slid his hand to her breast. Cupping it, he pushed upward a tiny bit, measuring its weight. He let out a stream of air through pursed lips.

"Tell me to stop, Isadora," he breathed, still focused on his hand. "Tell me to stop . . ." He tried to clutch the fullness of her breast, but there was too much. She cooed at his harder touch. He groaned and bent to kiss her collarbone, her chest. He scraped his thumb over the center of her breast, her breath hitched deep.

"Please don't," she sighed. "Don't stop."

He groaned again, louder, taking her in his arms, gorging himself on her. She clung to him, the heat of her body against his from chest to thigh made him curse the existence of clothing.

"Come over?" he murmured, his lips still entangled with hers.

"What?" she whimpered as he mouthed along her jawline and down to the birthmark below her ear. He grazed it with his stubble and then sucked, eliciting a sound he'd only imagined hearing if he were inside her.

"Come over. Tonight." He hoped she took the tremble of his entire body for lust, not the trepidation he had to force away.

Her hand in his hair brought his ear to her lips.

"No," she whispered, dragging his earlobe through her teeth.

He died inside at the same time as he had to claw the wall and let out an open-mouthed groan. "Not tonight," she panted. "Tomorrow."

He pulled back to meet her gaze, sliding his hand down her side to grasp her hip. Her eyes widened.

"Tomorrow?" he breathed.

"Yes."

"Seven? You promise?"

His heart was in his throat as she cradled his cheeks. "I promise," she said, yanking his lips back to hers. He surrendered himself to being consumed, groaning when she tugged at his belt with both hands.

He pulled away, bracing his palms against the wall on either side of her head. Placing his cheek against hers, he panted into her ear.

"There's something I need from you, Isadora. Something I've been dying for." Her chest heaved, and she searched his eyes, her perfect brows asking her question.

"I need to taste you," he said. Her eyes went wide, and he dropped to one knee, gliding his hands down the sides of her thighs to the hem of her skirt.

"Please?" he whispered, his gaze still locked on hers.

His hands below the hem, he began to push back up, inching her skirt up along with them.

"We should stop," she whispered, her breasts rising and falling.

"We should," he sighed back, still pushing up.

"Anyone could catch us."

"Anyone could," he whispered, nodding. "But . . ."

"But?"

He shoved, forcing her skirt up over her hips, pressing his face hard against the ecru lace of her thong. His eyes fluttered closed as he inhaled deep.

"You smell too good for me to care," he groaned. He looked up at her again. "Please."

Begging for her permission was much more of a turn-on than he'd ever imagined.

She ran a hand through his hair, panting.

"Yes, Karim," she groaned. "God, yes." Those four words made him feel safer than he had in years.

Growling, he moved lower to drag his tongue along her lips, from bottom to top over her panties. Her hand shot up to her mouth as she watched. He did it again and she whimpered, her hips bucking forward to follow his tongue. A hand between her thighs, he tapped them apart to hook a finger into her panties. Then there was a new sound. Someone was coming down the stairs.

He froze and registered the panic in her eyes. She ripped her skirt down as he scrambled for his files. Then she grabbed his hand and pulled him farther still, through a large, darkened space, then back up another hallway as a familiar voice reached his ears.

"Here we are, Daria," Julian said. "Just you and me."

CHAPTER TWENTY
Isadora

Isadora snapped her shaking finger from Karim's doorbell less than an inch away from making contact. She'd been having trouble with buttons and keys over the past thirty-two hours. First, there were all the times she'd picked up her phone, pressed the button to call him, then pressed the button to end the call before it went through. She searched for excuses, reasons not to go, in spite of how much she wanted him, of how much she needed to go.

They're exactly that, excuses. Stop trying to make something up, some lie that isn't supposed to hurt him but will because you're scared. . . . But this is dangerous; letting myself follow my feelings about him is dangerous. This step could lead to something, anything, and that could get in the way of . . . She'd pick up her phone, resolute, only to put it down again.

She'd had trouble with the buttons on her favorite jeans, the ones that hugged her curves just right. After missing one button and then bending a nail back as she tried to button up again, she'd gotten mad and ditched them for her second-favorite pair. She'd misplaced her keys and dumped out the contents of her purse in a minor explosion of anxiety that she was going to be late and make him believe that his fears were well founded. Then she'd dropped the damn things while locking her door, and again beside her car.

And now, standing on his doormat, she couldn't press the button, to ring the damn bell.

What are you so afraid of? He didn't plan for this, and you didn't either. No one is going into anything with big expectations. There's work, but that's dumb too. Are you gonna let Julian's jealousy of Daniel keep you from getting some smoking-hot sex from a smoking-hot guy? Julian's childish games are gonna keep you from getting laid?

Fuck them, Isadora! Now ring the goddamned bell! She punched her finger into it and threw her shoulders back.

He opened the door and his smile disintegrated.

"What's wrong?" she asked.

"Noth-nothing," he said. "You . . . I think this is the first time I've seen you with your hair down."

"It is?" She'd straightened her hair, twisted two small sections on each side and pinned them down.

"I think so." He blinked twice.

"You don't like it."

"No, no, I do. I really . . . Sorry, would you please come in?"

"Thanks." She ducked down as she stepped inside, tucking a bit of hair behind her ear.

"Isadora, I'm sorry. You surprised me, that's all."

"You look like it's a bad surprise."

He closed the door. "It's certainly not. You're, well, I keep using the same word, but it fits. You're beautiful tonight."

"Thank you," she said, the uncertainty she'd tried to leave on his doorstep wrapping itself around her again.

"Please, come in." He led her through the short entry and into his living room. He kept glancing at her as though he wasn't sure who she was. "Would you like something to drink? I have some Riesling."

She smiled. "Sounds good."

He went into the kitchen and poured two glasses. She tucked her purse behind her on the couch and slid her hands over her knees, calming their tremble. His session-only apartment was pretty much as decorated as her own. But where she'd taken the cheapest furniture package, his was all masculine brown leather.

"Opted for the leather package?" she asked as he joined her on the couch.

"I was surprised you hadn't."

"Why?"

He handed her a glass, and they both took a sip.

"I'd imagined you were into leather." He smiled.

She rolled her eyes and shook her head. His gaze got too intense.

"I'm sorry, but you are gorgeous. I don't mean to stare."

"Thank you, Karim. I had no idea it would throw you for such a loop."

His lips bent up, an attempt at a smile that didn't succeed. He focused on his glass, rolling it in his palms. "I wanted to make you dinner," he said.

"Oh?" Food hadn't occurred to her. Fighting between her want and her nerves, she hadn't had any available mental space.

"But then," he said, voice low, gaze still on his glass, "I didn't know what you would like . . . and I couldn't decide, and . . ." He sighed, meeting her eyes. "Blunt, honest?"

"Yes."

"I have . . . a *really* hard time thinking straight when it comes to you."

He'd set off that delicious kaleidoscope of butterflies again, and she was terrified. But she refused to leave him vulnerable.

"Blunt, honest?" she asked.

"Yeah."

"Same for me. About you." She let out a heavy breath. "Maybe . . ." She put her glass on the coffee table and then reached for his and did the same. "Maybe we should just stop thinking?"

She put a hand on his knee and slid it up his thigh. "Is that okay?" she whispered, leaning into him.

He nodded, breathing a "yeah" as he cupped her nape, bringing her to his lips like she was his oxygen. He fell back onto the seat, pulling her on top of him. The melding of lust and relief flipped her world upside down. Desperate want and reassurance weren't feelings she'd ever had to manage at the same time. She wanted to examine this, to understand how it was possible to feel both ways at once. But that analytical part of herself was slipping away; he was overwhelming her senses, obliterating her ability to do anything other than feel.

Their kiss dove into something potent, all consuming. She drew his fragrance in deep, as she clung to him, one hand on his cheek stroking his stubble, the other on his chest feeling his heart pound. His hands slid around her waist, up her back, gripping her shoulders.

She pulled away for a moment, to catch her breath and study his eyes, flushed cheeks, reddened lips. *What am I so afraid of?*

He smiled, spreading a hand wide on her scalp, massaging. His touch sent cool, sparkling tingles down her back and into her breasts.

"What is it, beautiful?" Even his tone made her feel safe, valued. She leaned into his caress, letting her eyes flutter closed for a moment as she sighed. "Mmmmm," he groaned. Feeling that through his chest was light-years better than hearing it.

"Call me 'Isa'?" she whispered.

He groaned deeper, warmer. "Thank you." He sighed, still massaging her scalp.

"For what?" Her eyelids were too heavy to open.

"I've wanted to for a while," he whispered, sliding his other hand into her hair. "Was too nervous to ask."

She smiled, then her mouth fell open in a moan. At his sharp inhale, she opened her eyes.

"Take me to bed, Karim?" she asked. The look in his eyes erased the final doubt. This man was worth the risk.

"Your wish is my command, Isa." He pulled her back in for another kiss. She giggled and tried to sit up, but he wanted another. Satisfied and smiling, he let her sit up, got to his own feet, and she took his hand to pull him toward the hallway leading out of the living room.

"Come here." He brought her back to him again, claiming yet another kiss. She laughed against his lips as he scooped her up and carried her into his room.

He lowered her onto his bed and took off his glasses. Her legs still around him, he explored her neck with his lips. Another wave of fear and safety rolled through her. Beyond kissing her, arousing her, he was studying her, learning what to touch and how. When she gasped and squirmed as he grazed his lips from collarbone to chest, he stopped, stroking the same spot with his cheek, then with his breath. Her whole body tingled, goosebumps covering every inch of skin. When he kissed hard again, sucking, a high-pitched moan fluttered from her mouth and she arched up, pressing herself against him. He moaned and smiled against her. His observation was so intense, she was at a level of need she didn't know existed. She wanted to run away as much as she needed more.

"Karim?"

"Yes?" He nuzzled the top of one breast.

"I think we're both wearing too many clothes."

He grinned, straightened, and pulled his own shirt off. Shifting up onto her elbows, she took in every inch of him.

My God . . .

His body was flawless. His pectoral muscles were perfect—large but not too much. There was dark hair in the middle of his chest, wiry, black. But not enough to hide the detail of his chest, or to reach his dark nipples. For the first time in her life, she wanted to take a man's nipples into her mouth, bite and tease them the way she liked hers to be. His abs were beautiful, each muscle detailed, outlined. She wanted to lick every single line. The dusting of hair started again beneath his navel, darkening and drawing her eyes down to the waist of the jeans she'd begun to hate. They covered the rest of him, and she wanted nothing more than for them to disappear.

His grin turned wicked and he leaned back over her, kissing her, then lapping at her parted lips with the tip of his tongue. His hands were on her sides, pulling on the bottom of her shirt. She followed his motion, letting him pull it off over her head.

As soon as it was gone, his gaze slid to her breasts. She'd been stressed but had chosen her undies with care. The lace bra was structured to give her ample breasts deep cleavage.

He stared at her, wetting his lips.

"*Shit,* Isadora."

She sighed, shaking with want for him. As he skated his hands up her sides, an instant of hesitation cropped up. But then she focused on him, on the way he was looking at her, watching his fingertips as they grazed the tops of her breasts and caressed the straps on her shoulders. He looked like he couldn't believe it, like he needed to see his fingers in contact with her skin to know that what was happening was real. Taking one of his hands, she kissed the palm as she got to her knees. He raised his eyebrows, cocked his head to one side.

Sliding the straps off her shoulders, she bit her lip and unhooked the clasp in the middle, tossing the bra away. He pulled in a jagged breath.

"I'm real, Karim," she said. "This is real."

"Is it?" His Adam's apple bobbed. "I'm having trouble believing it."

She kept her gaze locked on his as she got out of her jeans and knelt on the edge of the bed.

"Touch me, then. See for yourself." She put his hand between her breasts, and he let out a yearning moan, bending to kiss her skin, to cup each breast in his hands. She sighed, running her hands through his hair as he stroked and caressed her, kissing all over each one. She wanted him to take her nipples into his mouth, to touch them at least, but he didn't. He stood straight, his breath ragged, eyes piercing.

"You know what I want, Isa. Desperately. We were interrupted the last time." He pulled her to him, his naked chest on hers making her gasp into his kiss. He wrapped her legs around his waist and they fell into the bed. He ground the thick bulge in his jeans against her and she cried out.

"May I—"

"Yes, Karim, please." He knelt on the floor. His thumbs in the waist of her panties, he pulled them off. His gaze was fixed between her legs. She held them together, shyness surpassing desire. He looked into her eyes.

"Please don't keep yourself from me anymore."

She took a deep breath, and slid her legs apart, no more hiding.

"My God . . ." He groaned. He inched forward and kissed her outer lips. She shivered, the air moving across her skin as he inhaled, his nose above her mound.

"Mmm . . ." His eyelids fluttered as he lapped the skin between her thigh and her lip, once, then twice. She shuddered as his lips grazed hers, and she was surprised when he licked her other lip. His head moved down, tongue gliding along her opening, as he groaned again. Her thigh twitched, and she couldn't breathe. He paused, moved back a second, and sighed.

"You taste so good, Isadora."

He caressed her inner thighs to coax her legs farther apart. The heat from his breath was there again, making her yearn for his touch. When their gazes locked, he flashed her a wicked smile before dragging his tongue between her inner and outer lips up one side, down the other. Over and over, laving her hood at each pass. She sighed his name, clutching the comforter. He released her thighs to slide his hands up her body, stroking the sides of her breasts with his thumbs.

"Touch me, Isa." His breath was its own caress. "Put your hands in my hair." She did, and he groaned as she ran her fingers through it. He brought his mouth down, tonguing inside of her, with increasing force. She shuddered again and looked down at him.

She caught the reflection in the mirrored door of his closet, off to one side. Her breath stuttered at his golden, muscular back, his dark hair, his head between her thighs. He moved back up, massaging her tightest bundle of nerves with the side of his tongue. She gasped and her hips bucked, but she stiffened, nervous. He sensed her tension and stopped.

"Isa," he whispered. He curved his arm around her thigh from underneath. She peeked at him, pulling her hands away. He caught one and brought it to his cheek, kissing her palm.

"Guide me, beautiful. Put your hands on my head and guide me. Teach me what you like."

She wet her lips to answer. "I . . . I'm afraid," she breathed.

"Of what?" He turned to kiss her palm again, nuzzling it.

"Moving too much, hurting you?" Oral sex had always made her self-conscious. Her nervousness and history with partners who hadn't had much interest in oral sex, had left her in the dark. His intensity, and his demonstrated desire to please her made her afraid of losing control.

"Don't worry, beautiful. You won't hurt me." He mouthed her lips again and smiled. "And even if you did, I couldn't dream of a better way of getting hurt."

A naughty smile glowed in his eyes as he started again. She slid her hand into his hair, telling herself to relax, to let go of her worry, and she guided him as he licked and sucked at her. He did something, and a bolt of pleasure went through her. Her fingers clenched in his hair and her hips jerked up as she cried out. He growled against her and did it again. And again, and again. Her back arched and her shriek filled the room. He did it again and she shouted his name.

Her skin melted away, an explosive scream building inside. He did it again, strumming her clit and sucking harder, gripping both of her thighs to follow the bucking of her hips. She locked onto his eyes, begging, even though she was well past the ability to formulate a thought. He reached up for her breast, catching her nipple. Tugging on it, he did it again.

Her thighs quaking, she clung to his hair and the orgasm ripped through her, forcing the scream out as she lost herself.

Her heart still racing, struggling to catch her breath, she was aware of him kissing his way back up her body. He hovered over her, breathing hard himself, and kissed up the side of her neck to her ear.

"You're like a delicious, exotic fruit, Isadora," he whispered, nipping at her earlobe. Supporting himself with his forearms, hands on either side of her head, he stroked her hairline, her temples. His lips grazed her forehead as he moved to whisper in her other ear. "I could eat you for days."

She smiled and moaned, turning her head against his to fall into those green eyes.

"What about you?" she breathed.

"Me?" He kissed her lips.

"I want to taste you, Karim."

"Not now . . . not a good idea . . ."

"Why not?" She writhed under him, unable to think as he mouthed her neck again.

"Too exciting . . ." he whispered. "Won't last very long. I want to last as long as possible for you." He'd moved back down to her breast. Taking it in his hand, he squeezed and pushed up, forcing her nipple into his open mouth. He sucked it hard and flicked it back and forth with his tongue. Crying out again, she clung to him, her hands returning to his hair. She searched his eyes, mouth open, shocked to be getting close again. He released her.

"That sensitive?"

She nodded.

"Mmm," he growled, taking her nipple back in his mouth and playing with it while he got rid of his jeans.

She didn't know where she was anymore, couldn't breathe, dying for the comfort of him inside her. A crackle and a whiff of the inorganic smell of latex registered in the cloud of his scent mixed with hers. His hand dipped back down between her legs. *Is he . . . he's making sure I'm still wet? Yes, I'm ready for you. I don't know if I've ever been this ready for anything in my entire life.*

She strained for his touch, for him. His hand gone, he moved back over her, his face inches away. He locked his gaze with hers, his lips parted. His burning cock slid up from the bottom of her lips to the top, the head pushing up over her clit, as he ground his shaft hard against her. She bucked into him. His eyes fluttered for a moment as he groaned, then his hands slid up her arms, pinning hers above her head.

"Isadora . . ." She'd never heard her name said with reverence. The entire world ceased to exist apart from his eyes, his face, his body. He shifted, and he was inside her.

Her body arched, and she let out a cry. She couldn't think, she couldn't breathe. She gasped for air, but there was none to be found.

He was so large, so thick. She'd never felt so full. When she opened her eyes again, his were crushed tight, his lips parted. His fingers laced themselves with hers, and he squeezed her hands hard.

"You're so tight, Isa," he whispered. Opening his eyes, his gaze locked with hers as he rocked in deep, then started his retreat. She understood that he was taking care not to hurt her, but her body was responding too fast for her to even smile at the idea.

"Oh . . . God, Karim . . . yes . . ." She sighed as his thrusts became regular. "Yes . . . that's good." She wanted to encourage him more, but she was losing the ability to speak. He pulled out farther, and then went in deeper, her hips rising to meet his. He let go of her hands and tucked his face into the side of her neck.

"Isa . . ." he breathed.

She pulled at his shoulders, clinging to him, bringing him closer to her. He crushed into her. She welcomed his heat, wanted his sweat to leave his scent on her skin. Each advance grew stronger, and his arms slid around her as she arched into his embrace.

"More," she managed to whisper into his ear between sighs and moans. He groaned and obeyed, moving deeper, quicker.

"More!" she cried out. He let go of her, moved up to brace himself with one arm, holding on to one of her thighs as he thrust harder into her. She was close, panting, mouth open. Rocking up to meet him, she clung to his arm, her eyes closed, her lips against his skin.

"Yes, Karim! Yes," she moaned.

He accelerated, his body arching over hers.

"Look at me, Isadora," he breathed. "Look at me."

She opened her eyes and plunged into his. Her body seized, her back arched, and her voice broke as she came. She felt like she'd shot out of herself, dissolving out of consciousness.

CHAPTER TWENTY-ONE

Karim

He was working hard not to follow her into his own explosion. Watching her reach that point, feeling her release, and knowing he had caused it were almost enough to make him tumble with her. He had to tilt his head back, turn away to maintain control.

"Karim . . ." She sighed. "There's something I want too."

She pulled him to her by the back of his neck. He slowed, wanting to listen but unable to ignore his need to move deep inside her. She slid the tip of her tongue along his lip.

"Let me ride you," she whispered. He groaned and rolled onto his back. He still couldn't believe where he was. She'd read him well as things began to heat up—her, topless, on his bed. It had been a fantasy so many times and now the reality was right in front of him. Even sitting beside her on his couch, he'd been lost. When he'd asked her the day before, in that fury of desire in the basement, he'd been shocked that the words had come out of his mouth, and that she'd agreed.

And now, as this exquisite goddess straddled him, he was confident that he must be dead. She leaned forward, her breasts crushing into his chest.

"Bear with me, gorgeous," she breathed into his ear. "I'm a little out of practice." She grasped the base of his cock, sheathing him inside her.

"Fuck!" he shouted. Her heat and tightness from that angle was almost too much. She sat up, licking her open lips. He was prey to be devoured. The thought made him even harder. She reached for his hands to support herself and began to move.

"Karim!" she cried out, rocking her hips, finding her rhythm.

The dark brown eyes boring into him had gone black. Her lips, her skin, the depth of color suffused with pink as another orgasm approached. He wanted to hold on, to watch her explode again. She swiveled her hips and he cried out, his back arching, teeth clenched hard, his nostrils flaring and filling with her scent. The scent that was on his lips, that she'd let him taste.

How . . . does she . . . want me? A growl burned the back of his throat.

She pushed his arms down, pinning them above his head and leaned over to pant into his ear.

"Come, Karim. Let me feel you."

Two hard thrusts meeting hers and he was done, her almond-shaped eyes the last thing he saw as he shattered.

He came back to himself in another fantasy: Isadora lying on top of him, wrapped in his arms, the heat of their lovemaking a halo around them. Her head resting on his chest, her breathing returning to normal. He stroked his chin across the top of her head, the way he'd wanted to on the way back from San Diego. This time, there was no hesitation.

Hesitation . . . it had been in her eyes on the couch. A flash of timidity, of fear. He squeezed her tighter. She sighed and snuggled in deeper. The last thing he wanted was for her to fear him. She was so fearless at work, but with him, she'd been afraid. Even said so in her office.

Is it just work? Julian and Daniel? What people might think of her if they find out? No . . . it's more than that. . . . Maybe she'll tell me one day.

She shifted, and he softened his grip in case she wanted to move.

"You okay, beautiful?" he whispered.

The sexy moan he got in reply could cause some trouble. It made him lick his lips, savoring her taste that was still there.

"I am much better than okay, gorgeous," she sighed.

" 'Gorgeous'? Careful, I could get used to that."

"You should," she said, the post-sex satisfaction in her voice doing wonders for his ego. "It's the truth."

He ran a hand over her head, smoothing her hair into place. "I'll let you be the judge," he said.

She sighed, rolled off him, and then snuggled close, her head on his shoulder. "Do you mind?" If her voice sounded like that all the time, he'd never be able to leave the house.

"God, no," he said. "Been hoping for this from the first time I set foot in your office."

"Really?" She giggled. He caught her shiver as he snatched a tissue off his nightstand and got rid of the condom. He reached for the sheets, covering them both. He smoothed her hair some more, while she slid soft fingertips across his chest.

Yep. I'm definitely dead. I did at least one really great thing in my life that I can't remember, and this is my reward. Or . . . He made the conscious choice to ignore the past. He was in bed with a goddess who'd wanted him, taken him, and given him so much pleasure he'd thought he was going to die from it. He was going to stay in the present. Until the goddess decided otherwise.

"If you don't want to talk about this, please say so," she said. She continued stroking his chest, playing with his hair.

He gulped. "Okay. What is it?"

"You know sometimes, when we talk, you seem surprised."

"Surprised?"

"Yeah. Or confused that I'm interested in you. At first I chalked it up to our bosses, you worrying about people finding out. But I have a feeling it's deeper than that. Once you even said, 'Why me, Isadora?' I didn't get to ask why because Julian called and interrupted." She lifted her head, her eye contact direct but gentle. "Why *not* you, Karim? What's so wrong with you?"

His instinct was to turn away, to hide. But he did *not* want to hide from her. He drew in a long breath.

Her eyes widened. "I'm sorry." She put her head back on his chest. "I shouldn't have—"

He grazed his free hand along her cheek, down to her chin, to tilt her face toward his. "No, Isadora," he said, warming his tone, to make sure she understood that he was telling her the truth. "Don't apologize. I told you that it helps that you have questions about me, that you want to understand who I am." He caught a flash of shyness in her eyes. And her resolve when she looked back at him. "I had to work through a lot of negative feelings when my ex left. A *lot*. And the hardest ones to shake are the ones about myself. She cast me aside. Threw me away, like a piece of trash. That sticks. Even when you try to put yourself a thousand miles away from it." He stroked her cheek again and traced her eyebrow. "So, when someone else comes along and shows . . . an interest in that piece of trash, is curious about it, it's a little confusing." He grazed his thumb over her lips. Her face remained neutral. He wasn't sure he'd managed to explain well. *Maybe I read things wrong, maybe—*

"I can't do anything about what goes on in your head." Her face had gotten tight and her voice sharp. "But you will never refer to yourself as a piece of trash in my presence again, Karim Sarda. Are we clear?"

"Um . . . okay."

"No," she said. "No 'Um . . . okay.' You will not do it anymore. Period."

"Yes, ma'am."

She narrowed her eyes. "No trash, no garbage, not anything even remotely close to an inference." She rested her head back on his chest, taking a deep breath as she tightened the arm she had around him. Then came the sting of tears in the back of his eyes.

After a few minutes, their breathing was in sync. A smile tugged at the corner of his mouth. He had the thought to start playing with her hair again, when she rolled away from him and stretched.

"I think . . ." She chuckled. His last bits of intimidation evaporated. "I was right about being out of practice." She giggled. "My back is killing me. I may need a hot shower and a Tylenol." She scooted away from him to get into child's pose and stretched her lower back.

"I can help you with that if you'd like," he said.

She raised an eyebrow.

He turned to his nightstand, opened a drawer, and took out a small tube.

"What's that?"

"A little something I use to grease the wheels when I need to relax." He winked at her.

"Really?"

"Mm-hmm." He pulled the sheet to her waist and moved up onto his knees.

After warming the oil in his hands, he massaged her arms and shoulders. Her sighs of contentment encouraged him along. He took his time, enjoying the trip down her back, until something stopped him.

"And what do we have here?" He'd found a tattoo on her upper hip.

"You sound surprised," she murmured, eyes closed.

"I am." He changed position to take a closer look.

"Why's that?"

"Dunno. Hadn't imagined that the serious, professional Isadora had a tat."

She giggled, turning to look back at him. "Listen to you, Mr. Traditional. Does it shock you?"

"A little. But in a very good way."

"Mmm. Good, I'm glad."

"Is it . . . It looks like an eagle. Had no idea you were *that* patriotic."

"Not quite," she smiled. "It's a swallow-tailed kite. A little raptor. Same family as eagles, but smaller."

He traced a half-circle around it, captivated by the detail.

"Why a kite?" he asked. She didn't answer. When he looked up, her chin was resting on her fist, as she passed the pad of her thumb back and forth over her lips. Her eyes met his.

"You don't have to tell me if you don't want to, beautiful," he said, moving his hand away.

"A kite is one of the representations of the goddess Isis," she said.

"Ah." He nodded. "You are quite the gift."

Bunching the pillow, she turned to face him better, with a multi-watt smile.

"You know what my name means?"

He shrugged, his shyness washing over him. "It's pretty unique. I was curious."

"Oh, Karim." She sighed, smiling, but he caught a hint of sadness in her eyes.

"She was a major deity, right?" He began to massage her again. There was new tension in her back. "The pharaoh's power came from her? Makes sense for you, such a politically powerful woman."

"Yeah." She faced the headboard again. "She's also the protector of the dead."

The weight in her tone told him not to ask any more questions. He pressed his palms into her lower back and ran them up to her shoulders, slow and deep.

"Thank you for sharing that with me," he whispered. Her eyes were closed, but a real smile tugged at her lips.

"You're welcome, gorgeous. Keep it to yourself, though? Can't have word getting out that the serious Isadora has ink."

"Oh, I will. I find it really sexy knowing a secret about you."

Sunday afternoon arrived well before he was ready. Stretched out on the couch watching TV, Isadora said she had to go home. He was lying on his back, head propped up on a pillow against the armrest. After their last tryst, he'd taken a shower but had only put on a clean pair of boxer briefs and his glasses. She stretched out on top of him, her head on his shoulder. She'd stolen one of his dress shirts after her shower.

"Are you sure?" he asked, caressing her back. "Ready to leave so soon?"

"Soon?" She laughed, looking up at him. "I've been here since yesterday."

"You say that like it's a long time ago. It's only been five minutes." He wrapped his arms around her and she rested her head on his shoulder again. He pulled in a chestful of air, gorging himself on her perfume, on the scent of her shampoo.

"What do you suggest? I stay tonight and just go straight to work tomorrow?" She brushed her fingers across his chest, along his shoulder and down his arm. He could get used to the way she touched him.

"Sounds good to me," he said. "I liked waking up next to you this morning."

She giggled. "You mean you liked waking me up."

"No, I'm pretty sure you were awake. You rubbed your perfect ass against me on purpose." He slid his hands down her back, cupping both naked cheeks.

"Karim!" She swatted at his hands. "Stop. And I did not. I was asleep. You rubbed against me first."

He grunted. "Did not. And why do I have to stop?"

"Because you're going to start something and then I won't be able to leave." Her words were telling him she wanted to go, but her voice was getting sexier, warmer.

"Maybe that's the idea, Little Kite," he whispered, grazing open fingers into the base of her scalp. Her gasp and shudder quickened his pulse. Then her palms were flat on his chest and she sat up, straddling him.

"Aww. 'Little Kite'?"

"Yeah." He nodded, stroking her thighs.

"Naughty." She shook her head and squeezed his hands, stopping their progress. "I have to go. What am I supposed to wear to work tomorrow?"

"What's wrong with what you have on now?" He rolled his hips, testing the waters.

She gasped again and side-eyed him. "You know, you're right. I'm sure everyone will think it's perfectly normal when I show up wearing no bra, no panties and just your dress shirt."

"I think you look great." He licked his lips, holding her gaze. "Good enough to eat." His reward was another sexy gasp and a lip tremble.

"Karim!"

"I can't even talk about it?"

"No," she said, scooting farther down his thighs.

"Why not?"

She got up from the couch and headed for the bedroom, snagging her bag off the dining table. "Because it gets me wet," she said over her shoulder.

He grunted, proud, smiling at her as she walked away.

CHAPTER TWENTY-TWO
Isadora

The dull grate of cement on her bumper stopped Isadora short. In the three years she'd been assigned the spot, she'd never overshot her parking space. Exhaling the adrenaline spike, she put the car in reverse and eased back. It wasn't until she'd shut the car off and checked for damage that the giggles began—replaying her weekend with Karim had her so out of it that she had zero idea how she'd driven to the office. The scratches on her bumper, plus her achy muscles, made her blush and bite her lip.

Get it together. Can't start your week all sex-hungover. Giggling again alone in the elevator, she took a deep breath to get her game face on as she reached her floor. She was in full work mode as she turned the corner, until she bumped into RJ.

"Morning, sunshine," he said.

"Hey, you got a minute?"

"Sure, lemme lock up and I'll be right over."

Daniel had planned a meeting the following week with all the members of the majority. It was her primary focus that morning; bouncing ideas off RJ would help. Dishing about her weekend might help too. But she didn't want to get herself all wound up. Giggling inside yet again, she slipped out of her suit jacket as RJ started the coffee. It wouldn't be a problem to start her day in a camisole with him.

He offered her a full cup and froze. "Isa! What the hell is that?"

"What?"

"That!" he said, pointing to her shoulder. "What did you do to yourself? It doesn't hurt?" He stepped close, squinting at a spot between her shoulder and collarbone. "How did you do that?"

"How did I do what? You're freaking me out." She pushed past him to check in the mirror in her office. There was a bruise in the triangle between her neck, shoulder, and collarbone. Her eyes went wide as RJ gasped.

"Isadora!" He was next to her in a flash. "It's a hickey. It's a hickey, isn't it?" His eyes went bright as if he'd gotten one. She pressed her hands to her cheeks as they caught fire.

Oh my God! I have a hickey like I'm fourteen years old!

RJ ran to lock the outer office door.

"Talk." He perched himself on the arm of the couch.

Her neck muscles burned as she strained to see the mark.

"*Talk,* Isadora." RJ spoke through clenched teeth, smacking a hand on his thigh.

"I . . ." She didn't know what to say first. *How did I miss this? Was I that out of it this morning?*

"It was Karim, wasn't it?" RJ asked. She opened her mouth and then closed it. Shocked she had a mark that visible, she couldn't even answer. RJ tipped his head down, like a ram getting ready to head-butt her. "It had *better* have been Karim. You haven't said a word about anyone else."

"Yes." *Did I just squeak?*

RJ clapped his hands, laughing. "Oh, thank God. This session is going to be so much better!"

She raised an eyebrow.

"I wasn't kidding the other day. You are *much* easier to live *and work* with when you're getting laid."

She swatted at him. He caught her wrist and pulled her closer.

"How was it? I want details."

She glanced at the door. She knew the click of that lock, knew that no one would be interrupting them. Anyone who came by could assume she wasn't in yet.

"I am sore all over," she whispered, leaning into him. "He can do things with his lips and tongue . . ." She shivered and grabbed RJ's arm with both hands, rolling her forehead on his shoulder. "I don't know exactly what he was doing down there, or even how. All I know is he is spectacular at it. And he *loves* doing it. I had to make him stop." She lifted her head and let out a breath, her unfocused gaze sweeping over a bare section of wall. She sighed. "Wouldn't be surprised if he has a bald spot from me latching onto his hair every time I lost control."

"You do know I'm hating you right now, don't you? Well, I'm happy for you, because I love you, but I hate you." He smiled.

She sighed again.

"When was this?" he asked.

"Saturday night. His place. I think I slept at some point. . . . We ordered dinner in. Wasn't much point in getting dressed."

RJ started to speak, but she caught her mistake.

"No. *Technically* things started Friday in the basement."

RJ raised an eyebrow. "You didn't."

"No. Just a little making out before we were interrupted. No one saw us. Then Saturday night, then most of the day on Sunday."

Eyes widening, RJ tilted his head to one side. "Well. Sounds like our boy has some stamina."

"You have *no* idea."

"So?"

"So?"

"What does this mean? Are you guys like a thing?"

"Mean?" She lifted her head off his shoulder. "It means I spent the night with Karim; that's what it means. It means he's good in bed and I have the aches and pains—and apparently at least one hickey—to prove it."

"Do you want to do it again?"

"Hell yes. But . . ."

"But?"

She shrugged and pushed away, to pick up her cup. "There's a lot, you know?"

He narrowed his eyes at her. "What, exactly? Tell me."

She didn't want to do this. To enumerate all the wise, logical, responsible reasons why sleeping with Karim again, really starting something with him, was a bad idea. She'd avoided all of that, shoved it from her mind the moment she asked him to take her to bed. But now she was back at work. And all of *that* was staring her in the face. She took a deep breath to answer, but RJ spoke first.

"If Daniel finds out, do you think he will doubt your loyalty?"

"No."

"If Julian finds out, do you think he'll try to get Karim to spy on you or something?" He went back to his cup, stirring in some sugar.

"Maybe."

"Do you think Karim would do that?"

"No, never." Her certainty came as a surprise. RJ's expression reflected it back. "Sorry," she said. "Kinda snapped at you there."

"No, it's fine." He covered his smirk by taking a sip. "Are you worried about what other people might think, that you're letting yourself be used? Or betraying Daniel?"

"Yes."

"Since when have you worried about what other people think?" he asked.

"Since I came to work today? I can opt not to care what people think in San Diego, but I certainly can't here, can I?"

RJ sighed. "Can you all be discreet?"

That was the word Karim had used during their first meeting. And Glenna had implied it. Isadora ran a fingertip around the lip of her cup. Karim was new to California but not to this field.

"Of course we can." She met RJ's gaze.

He shrugged. "Well, there you go."

"What if this becomes a thing?"

"It better," he said, blowing to cool the coffee.

"Okay. It can be a fun thing. It can be a temporary thing. But you and I both know it cannot become a serious thing. I can't let myself be distracted this close to Daniel becoming pro tem. And I will not set myself up for the slightest hesitation if I get an opportunity in D.C. I will not sacrifice my dreams for a man."

He swallowed. "Please, let this be a fun thing. Fun is safe. Fun is not sacrificing anything. You are not your mother; you're not bound to repeat her mistakes. Right now, we're in Sacramento, not D.C. Please just be in Sacramento and let him do every dirty thing he can imagine to you."

Her lips bent up, against her better judgment.

"You want him, right?" RJ asked.

"Yeah."

"Then have him." He put his coffee down and went into her office for her suit jacket. "Put this on." He slid it onto her shoulders, and she faced him. "Perfect. Can't see it. Just don't take it off unless you're alone."

"Thanks, babe," she said, kissing his cheek.

"Now . . ." He unlocked the outer office door and opened it. "About this meeting."

Mid-morning, she had to run up to the president's office. Waiting for the private elevator, she fiddled with her phone, wanting to reach out to Karim.

"You gave me a hickey!" she typed, then erased it. "I'm still sore." *No, not that either. Keep it simple?* "Morning, gorgeous" she typed as the elevator door opened. She stepped inside, and her knees almost gave out. The elevator smelled cool, woodsy, with a hint of sandalwood. Karim's cologne. She leaned back against the wall, drawing in every molecule of air. Her eyes fluttered shut and she was back in bed with him. On her back, him above her, the sheet up over them both, a tent, while they laughed like children. She exhaled, then took another deep breath, fast, too fast. Her head spun, and it was the moment he'd been behind her, they'd been on their knees and she'd clung to the headboard as he'd driven her out of her mind.

The door slid open. The narrow hallway was empty. She stayed up against the wall, panting for a moment. She glanced at the control panel. *I have time for another ride.* She pushed the button for the basement, closing her eyes again as the door slid shut.

At lunch, her phone buzzed. She squealed, and RJ rolled his eyes but smiled.

> Karim: (insert witty greeting with light sexual innuendo here)

She giggled. He wanted to reach out but couldn't find the words either. A hand to her lips, she tapped her fingers against them as she tried to come up with a response.

> Isadora: (insert equally witty greeting with mid-level sexual innuendo here)
>
> Karim: Been thinking about you all morning, beautiful.
>
> Isadora: Ditto, gorgeous. You left marks.
>
> Karim: You did too. My back stings every time my shirt brushes my skin. I love it.

She fanned herself. RJ raised an eyebrow from the other side of the table. She hesitated but went for it.

> Isadora: Gonna need the name of your cologne. So I can have you on my skin anytime I want.
>
> Karim: Trying to get me stuck behind my desk?
>
> Isadora: Wasn't really that naughty, was it?
>
> Karim: Now that I know what that skin tastes like, it was. Especially that most forbidden skin. That gets so warm and slick and mouth-watering.

She gasped, putting the phone down on the table. Her jacket suffocated her. She waved it open and closed to cool down.

"Really?" asked RJ, nodding toward the hickey. Lunch in the capitol cafeteria meant that there were eyes everywhere.

"Yeah," she puffed. "Don't even care right now."

"Wow," RJ mouthed, spearing another forkful of salad.

> Karim: Oops. Got myself stuck behind my desk. When can I taste—I mean see—you again?

She had half a mind to tell him to meet her in the basement in thirty minutes. Instead she paused. Setting another date was making it a thing. *"Date,"* she thought. *That's not even the word. We can't be seen in public together. We meet up, there's no doubt where it's headed. Then again, that keeps it fun. Fun in Sacramento. I'm down for that.*

Isadora: Friday, 7, my place.

Karim: Hmm. Tough to be patient. But worth it. Gotta go. Will
  be thinking of you, Little Kite.

Sharp tingles sparkled over her skin as her heart dropped.

Isadora: Will be thinking of you, Karim. Every bit of you.

It's official. It's a thing. She ran her fingertips down her throat and exhaled through pursed lips.

"Well," said RJ. "Well, well, well."

As Session revved up, she didn't have to try hard not to think of Karim all the time. Her schedule was packed, and she had to focus on setting the agenda and Daniel's strategy for the majority meeting the following week. The nights got steamy with sexy texts, but they didn't sleep together because they wouldn't have slept.

On Wednesday, in the rotunda, she ran into a committee staff member who'd returned from a long illness. Happy to catch up, she'd put her hand on his arm, laughing at a joke, when she felt eyes on her.

Karim, stalking toward them. She couldn't stop the sharp intake of breath. His face was hard, in spite of the nerdy-cute, as though someone was stroking something that belonged to him. She tingled all over and had to shift her focus to the floor. Her friend asked if she was okay.

"Yes, fine, sorry." She smiled at him. Karim's stride slowed, and her memory shot back to his thighs—hot, hard, powerful. She exhaled, lips open, doing her best to remain in her conversation. Out of the corner of her eye, she saw Karim's lips shift into a quick grin as he continued on his way.

After wrapping up her conversation, she pulled her phone out

of her pocket. Seeing him for the first time since Sunday lit a fire
that was too much to bear.

Isadora: Do you have ten minutes?

Karim: Yes.

Isadora: There's a supply closet in the third-floor copy room.

Karim: I'll beat you to it.

CHAPTER TWENTY-THREE
Karim

The notepad paper was a poor substitute for her skin. But it was all he had to glide his fingers across right then. It was his memento of the stolen moments from the previous week in the supply closet; those few, hot minutes had tided him over until the weekend. And what a weekend it had been.

He loved that she wanted to wear her hair down for him. She was beautiful however she styled it, but knowing it was only for him . . . He tucked his chin as the thought heated his cheeks. When she'd opened her door Friday night she apologized for not being ready as she undid her bun. He'd almost died when she explained that she'd wanted her hair already down when he got there because of how much he liked it.

A signature guffaw knocked the smile off his face, calling his attention back to his boss. Again, he was at the small table in Julian's office. Again, forced to sit in on Julian's phone conversations. On rare occasions, there was some substance, but often, it was blather. He was pretty sure Julian needed someone—anyone—to think what he was saying or doing was important. It made Karim hate him as much as he felt sorry for him.

I get it, Julian, trust me, I do. How desperate you get when your wife doesn't pay attention to you anymore. Been there, done that. But come on, you know I have a thousand other things to do.

Julian's conversation hinted at this personal project. He hadn't chosen to share any details, and direct questioning had been met with indirect answers and smarmy grins Karim wanted to smack off his face. He was on the phone with another senator, bragging about how his new strategy would change a lot of minds during the full majority meeting the next day.

"Trust me. The tide is turning . . . Yes, you're right, I have said that in the past. But if I'm saying it again, it's because I know I'm right. Just do us both a favor and pay close attention tomorrow," Julian said.

Karim rolled his eyes. He'd gotten the same line earlier in the day. Seeking more pleasant thoughts, he returned to Isadora, to the second passionate weekend he'd enjoyed, where there had been little rest. The sex was amazing, but the sharing, the understanding about what he did and what it meant to him, the interest in who he was as a person, was so much more. A lot more than he'd expected when he'd stuffed the last duffel bag into the trunk of his car back home.

Smart, funny, beautiful. And sexy as hell . . . I could fall hard— Everything stopped. His breath, his fingers, his mind. *"Fall"? No. There's no falling. I'm nowhere near ready.*

It was standing-room only when Karim walked into the War Room Tuesday morning. He'd had to stifle a laugh when he'd learned the dramatic nickname of the large conference room behind the senate chamber. But entering, with it as full and buzzing as it was, he got it.

The enormous table in the middle of the room was the same deep burgundy as the wainscoting. Contrasted with the plush navy carpeting and the solemn paintings of previous presidents pro tempore, there was a seriousness about the room that was absent everywhere else except the senate chamber itself.

The seat reserved for his boss was empty, of course. His ego required making an entrance. Karim leaned against the wall, between two other aides, typing away on their phones. Peter had also yet to arrive, along with two other senators who spent time with Julian, his "crew."

Guess they're all gonna "roll up" together. He flipped open the file he'd brought with him. The most important thing on his agenda for that day, an amendment to be tacked on to Peter's supplemental health insurance bill. It would codify habits that had already been taken concerning timelines for committee planning and extraordinary meetings like the one that day. It had full support, but Julian had insisted that all his colleagues sign off on it; Karim was to take care of it that afternoon. As it was the first document he'd prepared since being admitted to the California State Bar, he wanted to be sure it was perfect.

He was halfway through when one of his new favorite sounds reached his ears. Isadora was coming down the hall, laughing. He ducked his head down into the file, in case the heat creeping up his neck was bringing blotches too. She crossed the threshold, and his nostrils flared, his anticipation shifting into hostility. She was laughing with another aide, a guy, one who Karim thought was nice and had no problems with.

You're being ridiculous; she has to talk to other men. Stifling the same reaction he'd had in the rotunda the previous week, he glared at the paper in his hands. *She does not belong to you, and even if she was your girlfriend or something, what the hell kind of antiquated caveman shit is this?* He reminded himself of what had happened after the flash of jealousy in the rotunda. She'd reached out, wanting him. He hid behind the file again, to cover a wicked smile.

Julian and his posse arrived with dopey grins, making too much noise. Karim shifted his facial expression into neutral, scanning the room for Isadora out of the corner of his eye. She was near the refreshment table, prepared with coffee and pastries.

Excellent. Please stay there, beautiful. Need an excuse to get closer to you.

Daniel called the meeting to order and reminded everyone why they were there. They had all worked hard the previous session, and even the years before, at crafting the legislation that eventually became California's single-payer health insurance program. He thanked everyone again for their hard work and reminded them of how much had also been done by their colleagues in the assembly and in the executive branch. He then expressed his surprise at the impetus to make any changes so quickly to what they had crafted concerning the delivery of healthcare to Californians, but he gave the floor to Peter to explain. It was no surprise that Peter had agreed to sponsor the bill; the insurance lobby had been bankrolling his campaigns for years. Daniel was opposed, and as leader, would steer the other party members in his direction.

Time for a cup of coffee.

As Peter made the case for the bill, Karim pushed himself off the wall and made his way to the refreshment table. His change in position was unremarkable, aides were coming and going, getting coffee or something to eat. A shudder of pleasure went through him when he caught Isadora in his peripheral vision as he passed. She'd been typing on her phone, but her fingers stopped moving as he got close. He took his time, pondering the pastries, whispering a hello to one of the two aides who stood between him and his destination. Deciding on coffee, he had to inch behind the first aide and grab a cup. Realizing he was blocking part of the table, the aide left to lean against the wall across the room.

Okay, just one more person between me and where I want to be.

He happened to meet RJ's eyes across the room. His smirk made it clear that he knew what Karim was up to. He slid his phone out of his pocket. The aide between Karim and Isadora was much shorter than he was, the entire screen of her phone was visible as she scrolled through her emails. She got a text message and tapped it open.

RJ: You got a second for a quick chat?

Karim took a sip and rolled his lips. He'd suspected that RJ knew what was up but had not anticipated having him as a wingman. He lifted his cup in thanks, remaining discreet. RJ nodded, fighting down his smile. He stepped to the doorway and waited to let the short aide pass, as she'd left Isadora's side to see what RJ wanted.

Karim slid in next to Isadora, as close as possible without

touching her. She nodded a professional hello. He returned the
gesture, breathing deep to keep the smile off his face. His nostrils
filled with her fragrance—the almond notes of her perfume, but
also the warmer, deeper smell of her skin. He leaned back toward
the refreshment table to toss his cup in the trash, and when he
returned, she surprised him, shifting her weight so that her hip
brushed against his thigh. He froze, and she took it further, turning so that the curve of one cheek caressed his leg for the briefest
instant. Her arms were folded, her focus on the discussion at the
table.

So, you wanna play, beautiful? He stifled a smirk and shifted the
file to his left hand. He dropped his right to his side and ran the
back of his fingers along the bottom curve of her cheek. Her
gasp was the tiniest sound, under the noise of the discussion, but
he heard it loud and clear. It resonated into his memory, launch-
ing a replay of much louder sighs and moans—the ones he focused on as he feasted on her, his head between her thighs.

He needed to clear his throat. She slid a hand up to rub her
neck, stretching her head away from him, caressing her skin with
splayed fingers. Her birthmark beckoned. So close, he felt his
mouth water.

*How did I get here? She is beyond sexy. And she's into me? I am seconds
away from an embarrassing situation in a room full of people, and I don't
even care.*

He pulled out his phone.

Karim: You're playing dirty again.

Isadora: I thought you liked it when I played dirty.

Karim: Adore it.

Isadora: Shame. Everyone here for the meeting. No one on
    the 3rd floor, near the supply closet.

Karim: It is a shame. Wouldn't have to cover your mouth with
    my hand this time.

She squirmed, a full-body wriggle betraying her. He smirked,
his head ducked, waiting for her reply.

"Oh, come on, Daniel!" Another senator had been speaking,

but Julian cut her off mid-sentence. "Just because you're interested in completely snuffing out the healthcare industry in this state doesn't mean we all are."

That came out of nowhere, and the room fell silent.

Daniel leaned back in his chair and crossed his arms. "Snuffing out the healthcare industry? That's not even close to what I'm suggesting, Julian. You know that."

"Yeah, right." Julian leaned forward. "First of all, it's bad enough that you aren't supporting a majority member. That's *supposed* to be your job, right?"

There were several audible gasps but not from Isadora. She had gone still, the set of her shoulders reminding Karim of their first night together when she'd forbidden him from referring to himself as trash.

"Secondly," Julian said, "we already did enough damage last session. If we don't give the private insurers at least this, we're going to lose them completely. And all their support."

Daniel took a moment before he replied. "We've been over this, Julian. Multiple times. I really don't think—"

"That's exactly the problem, Daniel. You don't think!"

Has my boss lost his mind?

Julian turned to another member. "Rex, I'm sure you can see my point? If we continue like this, Daniel's going to make sure that our constituents can't add on the care they want." Julian stifled a grin. "Rex?"

"Well, um . . . you do have a point," Senator Roberson said, more to the empty coffee cup on the table in front of him than to Julian.

Thirty minutes later, the meeting came to an end. Everyone except for Julian and his posse left surprised and confused. Low murmurs continued from the War Room, down the stairs and through the hallways. Going into the meeting, more than three-fourths of the majority members had been against the bill. Leaving, two-thirds were for it. Julian wasn't that good at negotiation. And a lot of them had switched with minimal argument. Something else was going on.

Isadora had slipped into the back elevator with Daniel. Karim saw them go into the majority office followed by RJ's boss and two other senators as he turned the corner on her floor. Isadora's body language said "determined," "efficient." She'd left Karim's side to lean against the wall behind Daniel as the tide began to turn.

Julian said that would happen. Didn't expect a tsunami. Karim returned to his own office, closing the door behind him. *If Julian wants to start an open war with Daniel, it's only going to make things more complicated with Isa. If she's willing to continue seeing me and someone finds out, she'll look like a traitor. Dammit, Julian, you have to mess up my personal life too?*

At the beginning of the afternoon, Karim began his rounds for the signatures he needed on the amendment. He'd sent a group email to the aides informing them of the final changes to the draft. After the meeting, he needed to make sure Isadora was okay. She was signing off on the final document in Daniel's place, so he began with her.

Tapping on the outer office door, he waited for her to acknowledge him. At her desk, on the phone, she'd cupped her forehead in her hand and didn't hear him at first. He tapped louder, and she waved him in.

"Listen, Mother . . . Listen . . . No, I know, I know, but look, I have to go. Someone's just come into my office and I . . . Mother! Mother. I have to get back to work. We can talk later. We can . . . we . . . No, I'm not disrespecting you . . . Look . . . Listen. No, I don't hate you . . . I am not abandoning you. Will you listen to me? I cannot talk right now. I am at work. I have to go . . . I have to go. I'm hanging up the phone now. I'm hanging up. Hang-ing up. Goodbye. Goodbye." The receiver clicked into place as her forehead returned to her hands and she sighed, eyes closed.

A bitter taste stung his mouth. He was angry that just because someone might come into her office and see them, he couldn't go around her desk and take her in his arms to comfort her. He wanted to speak but couldn't, fighting to stay in the present, to be there for her. Instead, he was suddenly back in Harrisburg, back with Laila, enduring one of her rages when he tried to get a word in edgewise, tried in vain to defend himself. He'd been unable to help himself then, maybe he could help Isadora now. He dragged his knuckles down the edge of the door to ground himself in the present. She looked up, and her eyes were brimming with tears that sucked the breath out of him.

"I didn't mean to interrupt," he said.

"It's okay. That's just the way she is. Is that the copy?"

"Yes. If now's not a good time, it can wait."

"No, no, now's fine." She reached out for the file, opened it, signed at the bottom without checking what had changed, and handed it back to him.

"Thanks." He hesitated to leave her. "Do you want to talk about it?"

Her head was back in her hands, elbows on her desk. When she looked up again, a tear slipped out. His shoulders ached, furious at his uselessness to stop her tears.

Why am I so angry? Wouldn't want to see anyone hurt, but this? Isadora's vulnerability had become more important to him than his own fears. He scanned his emotions again. He wasn't afraid of her hurting him, but he was enraged at the thought of someone else hurting her. *What does that me—*

"No, it's okay." She broke his train of thought, flashing him an attempt at a smile. "I'd feel I was burdening you."

He stepped closer to her desk and lowered his voice.

"Little Kite?"

Her eyebrows came together, and she wiped fast at another tear.

"I would like to help if I can," he said.

She didn't move.

"Pizza?" he asked.

She was still wavering.

"I promise, just pizza. Pizza and beer. We both have an early start tomorrow."

"Okay," she said. "Just pizza and beer. Seven?"

"I'll be there."

"Thank you."

CHAPTER TWENTY-FOUR
Isadora

Her breakfast dishes were *still* in the sink.

Shit, shit, shit! Her purse thudded to the floor, missing its hook. She nipped the dirty pajama top and yoga pants off the back of the couch and flew with them to the hamper. It was already overflowing, she had to jam everything in. *Why did I say seven? I should have said seven thirty. I should have gotten out of the office on time!*

She grabbed the Windex and paper towels, cleaning the bathroom in less than three minutes. The doorbell rang once she was back in the kitchen, rinsing the last dish. She'd taken two calming breaths and put her hand on the doorknob when she felt moisture on her stomach. A glance down revealed a dollop of soapy water on her blouse. *Of course.*

"Hi," she said, opening the door. He smiled and kissed her on the cheek as he walked in, hands full. "I'm sorry it's such a mess in here. I—"

"Don't apologize for anything. You're here. You're beautiful. I'm in heaven," he said. He put the pizza down in the kitchen and came back into the living room, putting two bottles of beer on the coffee table. She tried to smile, still bothered about not being ready.

"Can I really kiss you?" he asked.

"Of co—" He cut her off, taking her face in his hands and pressing his lips to hers. He stroked her cheek with his thumb and she relaxed, opening her mouth to his. He threaded a hand into her hair, fingers spread wide across her scalp. Her sigh tumbled into his mouth as he massaged her. He kissed her so lovingly that all her stress and worry disappeared. All she wanted was to kiss him back, relax into the feeling of his body against hers, drown in his smell. He broke the kiss but continued holding her close against him.

"Hi," he whispered.

"Hi."

"I missed you."

"Mmm, but you saw me at work today," she breathed, eyes still closed.

"Not like this. Not the way I want to every time I look at you."

"Ah . . . Then maybe this isn't such a good idea." She let her internal tug of war show. He tried to keep her close, and she did want to stay. But the habit of standing on her own pulled her out of his arms.

"I appreciate what you said this afternoon," she said. "I was upset, and it wouldn't hurt to talk about it, but the last thing I want is to ruin this. I am enjoying you. Very, very much. You're like a wonderfully delicious playground I want to explore and explore." She hoped that if she voiced the idea that this was nothing more than casual sex, it might stay that way. She'd even put the couch between them, walking around to the back of it.

She didn't let her gaze stray from his. The scared little girl inside wanted to hide. She didn't want another person to sum her up again and decide that she wasn't enough. But there was a tiny spark—a spark of hope that this man in front of her already thought that she was enough. A ragged breath pulled itself in.

"Please tell me," he said. "I want to understand."

"My cousin is getting married. And I . . ." Another ragged breath came out. She swallowed hard. "I am a disappointment."

"I'm sorry, what?"

She shrugged. "I'm a disappointment. That's the message every time. Every phone call, every visit. Every Christmas, Thanksgiving, wedding, what have you. And Mother's Day. Especially Mother's Day." He reached for her hand across the couch and brought her around to the front, next to him. They sat together. He didn't let go.

"I should have been married by now; I should have had my *first* baby by now. I should be done 'playing around in California already' and have come home to do what I'm supposed to."

His eyebrows crowded together. "And what's that?"

She sniffled. "It's never really been articulated. Beyond married and grandchildren. When I can't talk, she'll call repeatedly until I answer. And when I do, I never know what to expect. Sometimes she says nice things, like she's proud of me, then in the next breath she's telling me I'm a failure and I should just give up. For a long time, I thought if I could just be perfect, the perfect daughter, she'd be happy. But what that concretely means is that I can't follow my dreams, the things I want for myself in life."

"Perfectionism is anxiety in disguise," Karim said.

She looked up at him, raising an eyebrow.

"That's what my therapist back in Michigan told me. I tried to be the perfect husband because I was anxious about my marriage failing. Anxious about being rejected. There's no way to be perfect. Not for anyone, not even for yourself. If you're trying to force yourself to be perfect, you're anxious about something."

She sat back against the couch, chewing over that idea.

"A lot of the time, she'll tell me I *have* to do something. Something I have no desire to do and doesn't even make sense. Especially with the level of urgency that she's pushing it. Then, once I do whatever it is, she's happy with me again. Will even brag that I'm the perfect daughter. I wonder if she's feeling some anxiety about something and pushing it off onto me to fix."

"That could very well be the case," he said. "Maybe she's anxious about you not being under her control anymore and that's why she doesn't want you to follow your dreams. That's what it really came down to with my ex. She had a deep, deep need to control me. But—" He looked down at his lap, as if he was mulling something over. "What I really mean is your own perfectionism." He looked back up at her. "Sure, it's gotten you really far, but the anxiety behind it may be harming you."

"Maybe," she said. She wasn't sure what else to say. She'd thought that her only anxiety came with flying. He might have a point that there was more to it. She took a deep breath.

"What I don't understand is how my mother thinks the things she says would make me want to be around her. I'm 'a terrible daughter.' I'm 'perverse and devious.' I'm supposed to be 'where I belong,' 'taking good care of my mother and making her happy.'"

Karim leaned into the couch and put his arm around her.

"What does that mean? 'Taking care' of her?" he asked.

"It could be anything. Calling me in the middle of the night— early morning for her—because she's having a problem with her computer and wants me to fix it. For a while she would get angry with me if I didn't file her taxes for her. Even when I was in college. I'm supposed to come up with things she can do on the weekend, and I'm supposed to be setting aside money for her retirement."

Karim rumpled his brow again and tilted his head to the side. "Uh, all those things are her responsibility."

"According to her, they're mine. I'm pretty sure she feels like I owe her for raising me on her own."

"Your parents split up?"

"My dad died when I was little."

He pulled her into his arms. "Oh, Little Kite. I understand better now."

"Hmm?"

"Your tattoo. When you told me that Isis was the—*is* the protector of the dead. You chose the symbol for him?"

"He chose my name." She snuggled in deeper, head under his chin. "Seemed fitting."

Karim sighed, holding her tighter.

"It is fitting. I'm so sorry."

"It's okay. Well, I mean . . . it's not like we were totally alone. I have two aunts and three uncles and spent just as much time at their houses as I did at ours growing up. I guess she's angry because we were such a close-knit family that me being here and not doing the same things as my cousins makes us the odd ones again?" She took several deep breaths as he rubbed her back. "But it's not true. We aren't that close. There's a lot of backstabbing and criticism. That's why I'm happy to be so far away."

He leaned back to meet her gaze. "You know you aren't 'perverse and devious,' right? That's a horrible thing to say to anyone and especially to you. You're kind and giving. Look at your relationship with RJ. The way you've treated me. And you aren't a disappointment. Look at everything you've done. There are very few women in positions of responsibility like yours, and even fewer your age. Doesn't that count for something with your mother?"

She snuggled back into his chest, hiding her tears.

"No. It doesn't."

He sighed. "So today when I came into your office?"

"She was at me again because I haven't RSVP'd for the wedding yet. She'll probably start calling me again in a little while. If I don't go with a date, she'll have an assortment of guys who are single—for a reason—at the ready to shove me in front of. She's probably already got her sisters on the hunt. I'd thought to take RJ, but I have several uncles who are homophobic. I can't expose him to that sort of nonsense, even though I know he's heard it all before. And then I'd just end up in a fight with one of them, and that would only make things worse."

He squeezed her tight again, tucking her head under his chin. Closing her eyes, she slid deep into his smell, the rhythm of his breathing.

"Isadora?"

"Hmm?"

"I'm not an expert, just someone on the outside looking in. There's something not quite right in the dynamic with your mother. No healthy parent would ever call their child perverse and devious," he said.

"I'd hope not."

"And I need to make sure you understand, that you *know* you aren't a disappointment. You could *never be* a disappointment. Even if you weren't the most skilled and intimidating and beautiful chief of staff at the California State Senate, even if you hadn't accomplished all the things that you have, you could *never* be a disappointment."

She wanted to answer, but the words refused to come. The sobs were at the ready, one slipping out.

"Isa." He pulled away again, wiping her tears and tilting her chin up. "I can't do anything about what goes on in your head, or what anyone else says. But I need you to know that no matter what, you could never be a disappointment to me. Do you understand?"

She nodded, smiling at him reflecting her words back to her.

"If you're a disappointment, I'm a piece of trash, okay?"

"Thank you, Karim," she whispered.

He held her a few more minutes, stroking her back.

"Are you hungry, Little Kite?"

She excused herself to the bathroom, checking that her makeup hadn't run all over the place. Karim was the second person she'd shared that with, the only person other than RJ who really knew how bad things were with her mother. And he hadn't judged her or implied that her feelings were wrong. Another tear escaped. Maybe he did think that she was enough. She changed her clothes and returned to him. There was a white rose lying on her plate.

"Karim!"

"Couldn't help myself." He shrugged, giving her that shy-boy flattered and embarrassed smile. She put the rose in some water; he put a slice on her plate. After a few bites, he reached for her hand, gliding his fingertip over her knuckles as they talked. When she wanted to switch from beer to water, he insisted that she not move, and went into the kitchen to get it for her. Returning to the table, he laced his fingers with hers.

"Karim," she said. "Don't get me wrong, I love touching you. But you're right-handed. It can't be easy eating with your left hand so you can hold on to mine."

"I just need to hold your hand tonight, Little Kite," he said.

She squeezed. She loved their fingers like that, adored it when he held her hand like that while they were making love. Heat rose into her cheeks, remembering the last time he'd done it, his mouth and the fingers of his right hand occupied with driving her over the edge, his left hand reaching out for her right.

They talked about his family. He was describing all the joys of being the second-youngest of five. She wanted to pay close attention but kept getting distracted by his neck—the line she liked to nibble down, from the end of his jaw to his collarbone. And farther back, the spot where it met his shoulder.

"Isa?" He'd said her name twice. "Are you okay, beautiful?"

She smiled, tugging at her napkin on her lap. "Yeah," she said.

"I'm sorry, maybe it's too difficult?"

"What is?" *Get it together, we said tonight would only be pizza and beer.*

He tilted his head to the side. "I asked you what they'd think, the rest of your family. Would they approve if . . . if you were with someone who isn't black?" His nervousness made her want to wrap her arms around him and cover him with kisses. She slipped her hand out of his to wipe her lips with her napkin.

"Honestly? It's not pretty, but it's the truth: My mother would be far, far more interested in the JD beside your name than anything else. The rest of my family? I don't know. The uncles I mentioned before would probably have a problem with it. But they can take a long walk on a short pier for all I care. What about yours?"

His eyebrows came together. "Guess I lost you there for a little bit, beautiful. I mentioned that one of my sisters-in-law is black. My brothers and I have dated pretty much everyone. And my parents wouldn't say much anyway. My dad is French, and my mother is Berber, from Algeria. They had a lot of difficulty at first, because of the history between the two countries. They'd never put anyone else through that."

"That's good," she said.

"So, you think—"

She'd linked her fingers with his again, then she brought his hand to her lips, brushing them across his knuckles.

"I'm sorry, Karim," she whispered.

"For what?" His lips had fallen open, his question soft.

"It's not going to be enough." She turned their hands, placing the tip of his thumb onto her lower lip. She held his gaze as she sucked the fleshy part into her mouth.

He gasped.

"Pizza and beer," she whispered against his thumb. "It won't be enough for me."

"No?" His gaze homed in on her lips. He still hadn't let her taste him; she wasn't playing fair.

"No," she said, sucking more, pulling him in deeper, then out, letting the tip rest on her bottom lip again. "I need you, Karim. Come with me?"

She led him to her bedroom. At the side of the bed, she removed his glasses and pulled his sweater off over his head. He took off her cardigan and reached for her neck. She stopped him.

"Let me," she whispered. In accepting her vulnerability, he'd made her yearn for him to accept her power—the power to take him over the edge the way she wanted.

"Sit for me, gorgeous?"

Standing between his knees, both hands sliding into his hair, she smiled as he tucked his face between her breasts and molded his hands to her hips.

"There's something I want from you, Karim. Something I've been very patient for, but you still haven't let me enjoy."

"What's that, beautiful?"

She luxuriated in the depth of his voice, its warmth. Sighing, she rocked a hip forward, nudging his hand onto her ass. Chills greeted his pursed exhale as he cupped it.

"I need to taste you, Karim. Every inch."

Shyness skittered through the arousal written all over him. "You don't have to."

She shoved his shoulders hard, crashing onto the bed with him.

"I know I don't," she breathed against his neck. Then she attacked him—kissing, nipping at the tendon she'd gotten hung up on at the table. His gasp and shudder strengthened her resolve to do this the way she wanted. Working her way down, she varied her attention. The beginning of a protest died on his lips when she reached down and caressed the bulge straining against his jeans.

"It's hard," he groaned.

"That's what I like about it."

A chuckle bubbled up, but it morphed into a sharp gasp when she took one of his nipples between her teeth.

"I mean—" He groaned deep as she sucked hard, plucking at the other. "It's . . . it can be difficult, and I don't want you to feel like you have—"

"Are you saying that you're too well-endowed for me to take you into my mouth?" He writhed under her tongue circling a pad of muscle beneath his navel. If she looked and sounded the way he did right now, she understood why he loved going down on her. Creating that response was its own turn-on.

"No," he breathed. "I just . . . it's a lot of work."

She giggled. "I'll be the judge of that."

An hour later, legs still entwined, sweaty and exhausted, they lay naked next to each other trying to catch their breath. Isadora felt a chill first and pulled the sheet over them both. Karim broke the afterglow.

"Why don't you want me to go with you?"

"I didn't think it was a possibility," she said.

He swallowed hard.

"Not because I wouldn't like that. We're *supposed to be* enemies, remember? Something . . . like this, you helping me this way . . ." She fiddled with the sheet, smoothing it over herself with open palms. "It would mean we're on the same team." She kept her gaze downcast, away from him. His hand came to her cheek, fingertips grazing her jawline. She looked up at him.

"I've been on Team Isadora for quite some time now," he said. The timbre of his voice and his caress quieted all the anxious thoughts, all the fears. *He makes it so easy to imagine that really letting him in won't tear everything down. Could it be true?* She made eye contact with him again.

"Would you like it if I came with you?" he asked.

She nodded because she was afraid to open her mouth and have a sob come out. A hot tear trailed to her temple.

"Shhh . . ." He wiped the tear. "Don't. Please don't."

"But . . ." Things were too hot, too sharp. She couldn't tell him that she was also afraid of sacrificing her dreams if she fell for him. The easiest concern was the most public. "If Julian finds out about you helping me, about . . . all of this, you could lose your job."

He smoothed her hair down, tucking some behind her ear. "It's just a job, Isadora. I'll find another if I have to. What about you? Do you think Daniel would be upset if he found out?"

She sniffed, but a smile tugged at her lips. "Glenna gave . . ." She wasn't sure what to say next. *Me? Us? If I say "us," does that mean an "us" already exists?*

"Isa? What did Glenna give?" He stroked her hair again, her cheek.

He is so sweet. And so perfect. If he's willing to be there for me like this, if he's on "Team Isadora" . . . She took a deep breath.

"Glenna gave *us* her blessing. Daniel wouldn't dare contradict her," she said. His smile made her feel warm, safe. But she had trouble letting go of all her worries.

"But what about your new start, Karim? If Julian finds out, he'll do everything he can to destroy it. He'll use all his connections to blackball you. I won't be responsible for—"

He put his finger to her lips. "Shhh . . . my choice, my responsibility. You're worth it, beautiful."

"It seems unfair to you, though," she whispered.

"If I want to help, how is it unfair?" He picked up her hand, curling it into his and kissing the back. He nuzzled their joined hands into his chest. "Isa. I want to help."

She didn't say anything.

"Will you let me?"

CHAPTER TWENTY-FIVE

Karim

Khalil answered after the first ring.

"Hey bro, what's up?"

Even though he knew Julian wouldn't get to the office for another thirty minutes, Karim locked his door and went to the window at the other end of the room. "Hey, doing good. You?"

"Not bad. How's your lady friend?"

Karim rolled his eyes. "She's good, she's the reason I'm calling, actually."

Karim told him about the wedding. He knew that, as the confirmed ladies' man of the family, Khalil would help him sweep her off her feet. Karim wanted to, but he'd avoided examining why.

"You gonna tell her how you feel?" Khalil asked.

Karim squirmed. "What do you mean?"

"What do you mean, 'what do I mean'? Are you going to tell Isadora that you love her?"

"I . . . don't know that I love her."

Karim braced himself to be teased when Khalil hesitated before answering. But his brother's usual joking tone wasn't there.

"It's not for me to tell you how you feel. But, I know you better than anyone on the planet. I've never heard you sound the way you do when you talk about her. Never. And that's when I can even get you to talk. We used to share everything. You don't volunteer anything about this girl. I have to pump you for information like I'm drilling for oil." They both chuckled, but Khalil wasn't finished.

"I know it's been a difficult couple of years. And the last thing I want is for you to open yourself up and get hurt again. But I can tell you something else: The way you talk about *yourself* has changed. You sound as excited about the future and as confident as you did when you first moved to Harrisburg.

"Maybe it's the new job, maybe it's being in a new place where difficult memories aren't around every corner. Or, maybe it's because Isadora has brought *you* back. Maybe there's something in her that clicks with something in you just the right way. All I know is that I'm not worried about you anymore." He chuckled again. "Haven't met this girl, but I like her already. She gave me my little brother back."

Karim was grateful for the work of the capitol landscapers. They'd given him something to look at as he tried to get the lump out of his throat and fight the tears away. He swallowed hard, taking a deep breath. "Three minutes, Khalil. Three minutes," he managed to say, as always.

"Still counts," Khalil answered, as always.

He's right, I love her. Since she stopped me from talking bad about myself our very first night together. She's been building me up this whole time.

"What if she doesn't love me?" His voice cracked. *What if she turns her back on me, like Laila did? The pain would be a thousand times worse.*

"Is she worth the risk of finding out?"

"Yes." Karim sighed.

"All right," Khalil said. "Sounds to me like you've got your answer." He waited another moment, then went back to his usual, joking tone. "So. Let's get started. Gotta come up with a surefire get-Isadora-to-fall-madly-in-love-with-Karim plan."

Two hours later, Karim was on the audience side at the Judiciary committee meeting, waiting to present one of Julian's bills. It had taken a good twenty minutes to recover from his conversation with Khalil, and with a task to complete, he felt his emotions were under control.

Then they weren't anymore. Isadora walked up to the dais, squatting next to a senator to say something. Both women's expressions were measured. Karim might have been concerned about why Isadora looked stressed, if he could have gotten past her lips. Time slowed, everything else fell away. All he could see was the way they curved and pursed, pressed together and opened. He could feel them on his own again. Their silken heat on his throat, across his chest. The way they curled when she fought to hold on, keeping an orgasm at bay while he drove her toward it.

He didn't know he was rapid-fire clicking his pen until the woman a seat away from him huffed and gave him a dirty look. He exhaled, long and low, and tucked the pen into the top of his bill folder with shaking hands.

Back in the office, Julian and Peter's laughter resonated from behind Julian's closed door. Karim went to his own office to type up his notes from the discussion on the bill.

While copy-pasting the relevant statutes he'd referenced in answer to a question, his imagination took a break. He hadn't dealt with his anger from the previous day, seeing Isadora in tears because of the coldness of the person who should have held her the most dear. There had been a moment, when she'd gone to the other side of the couch, putting up a barrier. She'd been almost like a child, hiding. The strong, powerful woman he'd been getting to know replaced by a little girl. *She was probably so cute, so spunky.* He smiled at this imaginary little Isadora. *Wonder what she would look like with green eyes? With skin somewhere between mine and Isadora's? Hair with—*

"Hello! Earth to Karim!" Peter was next to his desk, waving a hand in his face.

"Whoa, sorry. What can I do for you, Peter?" Karim shook his head to get back to the present.

Peter laughed. "It must have been good for you to be that hung up on it! Anyone I know?"

Karim's face heated, and he searched for a comeback, but Julian spoke first.

"Don't waste your energy, Pete. Our boy here is far too private to share the interesting bits," he said from Karim's doorway.

"Maybe he'll trade?" Peter said.

What could you possibly have that I would be interested in?

"No, no. I don't think he's ready yet," Julian said.

"What is going on, Julian?" Karim took the risk of being direct. "Maybe I'm off. I haven't been here very long, but that was quite the performance in the War Room yesterday. I've never seen so many members flip sides on a subject so fast."

Julian slid into Karim's office, leaning against the wall across from his desk. He brushed imaginary lint off his lapel. "That was impressive, wasn't it? My powers of persuasion not what you expected?"

You didn't persuade, you jackass. You bullied.

"No," Karim said. "They were not. Odd though, most of the members who flipped seemed afraid. Don't know how you did it, and maybe it's best if I don't. I'm just surprised that a senator with your experience would use such scorched-earth practices on his colleagues. You still have to work with them, even Daniel. Why not compromise? Why make it difficult for them to save face?"

Julian's jaw clenched. "Compromise doesn't interest me. There's been too much compromise, for too many years. Enough is enough." His lips curled into the smarmy grin Karim hated. "Daniel is, has always been . . . a special case. Are you a fan of his? I hope I don't have to worry about a traitor among my staff."

Julian *was* up to something. Karim needed to stay close to him if he was going to have any hope of figuring out what it was, and if it might be a danger to Isadora. But, given how smug Julian was, and how aggressive, Karim needed to tread with care. He sighed.

"Julian, I believe that my work up to this point has proven my professionalism and loyalty." Pushing past the nausea of using that word, he tried to be precise with his next statement. "If it has not, I hope that you'd let me know, rather than jump to conclusions. I don't know Daniel at all, haven't been here long enough to form an opinion. I'm simply respecting the office that he holds."

"It is a nice office, Majority Leader," Julian said, picking up the glass paperweight on Karim's desk and holding it up to the light. "Who knows, in an alternate universe, it could have been mine." He returned the paperweight to its place. "But what's most important is the future. And, if things continue progressing as I predict, there may be even greater opportunities in store."

Peter's sycophantic laugh bubbled up. He slithered to Julian's side. "You think Karim will make a—"

Julian raised a hand, silencing Peter. "Shhh . . . not yet. Let's not get ahead of ourselves." He stepped to the door. "Everything good for the rest of the week?"

Karim appreciated the change in tone from "trying-to-be-mysterious" to "habitual jackass."

"A few loose ends to tie up, but nothing major," Karim said.

"Excellent. You do excellent work, Karim. Please don't think I haven't noticed."

"Thank you."

"We're headed to Ike's. I imagine you won't join us?"

Karim shook his head. "Thanks, but I'd like to get a little more work done."

"Such dedication. I won't forget that," he said, following Peter out the door.

CHAPTER TWENTY-SIX
Isadora

A few weeks later, Isadora yanked her carry-on down the aisle, her phone to her ear, completely lost.

"What do you mean the amendment changes the rules about electing officers?" she asked RJ.

"I was trying to get out of here fast and I needed to check a couple things before the insurance bill and its amendment get voted out of committee next week," he said. "It looks like the cited statutes *include* the ones about electing officers."

"But that's not what it's supposed to do at all," she said, getting to her row, jamming the carry-on into the overhead, and plopping into her seat with her purse on her lap, then digging for her work phone.

"I didn't think it was supposed to," he said. "That's why I called you to check."

The amendment she'd signed before anyone else, the one that Karim had brought to her, potentially touched on officers, including the president pro tempore. She might have signed something that would change the means or dates for electing Daniel president. An unguarded switch of her pen, and she might have undone years of hard work. She could wait to ask Karim once he joined her on the flight, but she wasn't capable of being that patient.

"Did you check the email Karim sent? I'm almost one hundred percent sure he said the officers were not included," she said.

RJ was quiet, and Isadora got her work phone open and began scrolling back through emails. Each keyword she chose brought up a thousand similar emails, so she had to rack her brain for the approximate date.

"Got it," RJ said. "You're right. He said it doesn't cover officers, so there's nothing for Daniel to be concerned about. How did I mix that up?"

Relief, quickly followed by guilt, crashed Isadora against her seat. RJ had been a zombie since his uncle had passed away earlier in the week. He kept forcing himself to work, and even though she understood his drive, she was afraid he was pushing himself too hard.

"Sweetie, it's normal. Maybe it's time to put work aside? Go home and pack? I should be going with you to the funeral."

"Isa. Don't you dare get off that plane. You aren't *leaving* me. The timing just sucks. But I will be fine. I'm not on my own."

"I can still cancel." She wrestled her work phone back into her purse, scooping the straps to shove back on her shoulder.

"Isadora. Think for a second, please. Your mother will make your life miserable if you don't go."

She sighed. "Maybe I'll be a better friend if I'm there for you in the next couple of weeks rather than fighting off her rage, huh?"

"Exactly."

The tears welling up caught her off guard.

"I'm sorry," she said, sniffing. "For all of it."

"I know. Me too."

"I love you, RJ."

"I love you too, babe. Have a good flight and say hello to Sexy Pants for me."

She shook her head through a sad chuckle. "Bye, RJ." She hung up and took a deep breath. Karim arrived at the seat next to her, his smile fading when he saw her face.

"Hey. You okay, beautiful?"

"Hey. The amendment you drafted didn't impact the dates to vote for senate officers, right?" she asked.

"Not at all. I took a lot of time with that. I'm sure it doesn't modify those statutes."

"Good," she said. "RJ just freaked me out for a second."

"How is he?" Karim asked, sliding his bag under the seat.

She shrugged. "As well as can be expected."

He nodded, getting buckled in. "Did he get my email about the amendment?"

"He did. He was getting ready for next week, and he thought he might have mixed something up, but he wasn't sure."

The bang of the cargo hold being closed shot Isadora to the side of her seat. Talking to RJ had distracted her from the fact that she was on an airplane. The anxiety that had been at bay came rushing back. When Isadora jumped, Karim did too.

"Is everything all right, Isa?" he whispered.

Okay. Guess I can't hide it anymore. "Well, um . . . there's something I haven't told you." She didn't know what to do with her hands. "I don't like to fly. Like, I seriously don't like to fly. Actually, that's not it. I just get really anxious. It's really only the beginning. And the end. And the middle if there's any turbulence." The words flew out of her mouth as a continuous stream.

"Oh . . . that explains it," he said.

"What?"

"The day we met. When we were on the plane, there was a moment you sort of shut down. I thought things were going well. It was the first time I'd been able to flirt in years. I was really enjoying it, then you stopped everything when we hit turbulence. You were terrified, weren't you, Little Kite?"

She nodded.

"God, you're amazing," he said, taking her shaking hand in both of his.

"Why?"

"I had no idea you were afraid. Is it like this every time you fly?"

She nodded again.

"How—"

"That's not true, I wasn't afraid the whole time." Her cheeks warmed, and she glanced down at their hands. "I wasn't afraid when you were talking to me."

He nodded, his shy-boy smile escaping as his neck got blotchy.

"Guess I'll just have to talk nonstop for the next four and a half hours."

She laughed out loud.

"But if you don't like to fly, what was that about liking the thrust of takeoff?"

She'd forgotten that. Her whole face got hot. "That was a lie. I just wanted to say 'thrust' to you."

A smile crashed across his face.

As the plane moved into position for takeoff, she closed her eyes. Her chest rose and fell as she fought off her panic. He leaned in close.

"It might sound silly," he began, his forehead at her temple, his breath caressing her neck, "but you look the way I felt at the stadium inauguration."

"What do you mean?" she managed, her eyes still shut.

"When I asked you to dance and you said yes, I got so nervous I wanted to run away. I had to keep reminding myself to breathe."

In spite of her fear, she smiled.

"Breathe with me, Isa," he whispered into her neck, before kissing her below the ear. She sighed. He nuzzled her and then drew a deep breath in through his nose and out through his mouth. She followed his lead. Without her sight, other details consumed more and more of her attention: his pressure on her hand, the aroma of his cologne and shampoo, and the underlying smell she adored, him. The engines roared, and he whispered soothing nonsense words to her, giving her a different sound to focus on. Then there was the uncomfortable woozy feeling she always got as the plane climbed higher and higher. *That means we've already taken off—I barely noticed.* The plane banked to the right and she let her head roll with it. Her forehead met Karim's. She opened her eyes, her gaze meeting his. She'd stopped shaking.

"Hello, beautiful," he whispered.

"Thank you, gorgeous," she whispered back.

After an uneventful flight, they stepped outside of the Atlanta airport, waiting for a taxi. He lifted her hand and held the back to his lips while scanning the taxis for an available one. A driver pulled up to the curb, and Isadora slid in while Karim tossed their bags into the trunk and gave the driver the name of their hotel. Once seated, he took her hand in both of his again and stroked it with his thumb.

Despite the buzz of the arrivals area, Isadora wasn't stressed at all. Though headed into a situation that might otherwise have caused her a colossal amount of anxiety, with Karim next to her she felt like everything was going to be fine. There wasn't the habitual fear of entering the arena that came when she had to be face-to-face with her mother. Maybe because she wasn't alone, and she had the impression that Karim wasn't going to put up with much nonsense.

"Thank you." She leaned over and rested her head on his shoulder.

"For what?" he whispered.

"For coming with me. For being here for me. I really appreciate it."

"Thank you for letting me be here for you." He gave her hand a squeeze, and they continued the ride in silence.

Karim had asked if she minded him choosing the hotel. She'd agreed and was impressed when they arrived. Isadora took in the lobby while he checked in, and a beautiful chandelier caught her eye. She was admiring it when she felt his hand on her lower back.

"You ready to get settled in, beautiful?"

"I am," she said with a smile.

"Come on." He led the way to the elevators, keeping her hand snug in his.

"What made you choose this hotel?" she asked on the way up.

"Oh, a Little Kite told me that it might not be a horrible idea to go someplace with a spa. Plus, we're a little farther away from the hotels recommended for guests, so I hope we'll have some privacy. I thought that might be particularly important if your mother really got to you and you needed a break."

Isadora's eyes watered. It had been ages since someone had been so attentive to what might make her comfortable.

"Thank you," she said. He kissed her on the cheek as the porter opened the door.

She thought he'd booked a room, but it was a suite. An enormous bouquet of white roses was waiting for them on the coffee table. She gasped and went over to bury her face in them and absorb their smell. She smiled at Karim over her shoulder, and he smiled back as he took off his jacket and strode over to her.

"Are you surprised?"

"Very! They're beautiful!" She wrapped her arms around his neck and kissed him.

"I'm glad you like them. And now, you should get undressed."

"Already? We've only just arrived." She pressed herself closer to him.

"As much as I'd like to, no. It's for our couples' massage. They'll be here in less than ten minutes."

She froze, an excited buzz growing inside.

"Really?" she whispered.

"Yeah," he smiled.

Her personal phone blared. She didn't need to see the contact name that flashed across the screen for the bubble Karim had created to burst.

"Hello, Mother. How are you?" She stepped close to the window.

"Are you here?" Her mother's voice was even more harried than usual.

"Yes, just getting in. Is everything okay?" Isadora asked.

"Of course it is! Why wouldn't it be?"

"I don't know, you sound really—"

"Is he here?" her mother asked.

"Who?"

"Your date? Kahil or Kamel, whatever."

"Yes, he's here." Karim came up behind her, his arms around her waist, stroking her cheek with his. His chest rose against her back as he took a deep breath and eased it out. She followed his lead, relaxing back into his arms, surprised at how tense she'd gotten so quickly.

"When do I get to meet him?" her mother asked.

"At the rehearsal dinner."

"That's in three hours! Why do I have to wait that long?"

Isadora sighed. *Always the same thing—we agree on something, then she changes her mind, but somehow, it's my fault.* "Isn't that what we said before, that we'd meet up at the dinner?"

"Okay, fine. I've waited this long for you to have a man in your life; another couple of hours won't kill me." Isadora went rigid. Karim moved into her line of sight, his eyebrows furrowed. Those green eyes snapped her out of the automatic submissiveness she slid into with her mother. There was a knock at the door and Karim left to answer it after giving her a prolonged kiss on the temple.

"That was uncalled for, Mother," she said.

"Why's that?"

"First of all, it was just rude. Secondly, I haven't shared all the details of my personal life with you for a long time. Experience taught me it's wiser—"

"You've had other boyfriends and not told me? Isadora, you can't do that!"

Karim was back at her side, cupping her shoulder. She turned and nodded hello to the two massage therapists setting up their tables. *Enough of this. I'm not letting her spoil my time with Karim.*

"I have to go, Mother."

"You always rush me off the phone."

"Okay, see you at dinner. Bye!" She made her voice light and pleasant at the end of the call but knew it wouldn't matter. Her mother would be unhappy no matter what she did. She accepted

Karim's hand and took a step toward the tables. The thought she'd had stopped her dead.

My mother will be unhappy no matter what I do. No matter what . . . Okay. That's it. I'm done trying. I'm here with Karim and he's done so much to make me happy. This weekend is going to be about us.

He'd stopped when she had and was studying her face.

"Everything okay, Little Kite?"

She put her hand on his cheek and kissed him. "Everything is perfect, gorgeous."

The massage was wonderful, but it sent Isadora on an emotional roller coaster that she had to work to keep under control. When they'd begun, face down, she went with it, letting all the stress and worry disappear. But once they'd switched to their backs, and she glanced at Karim, her heart leapt into her throat. *Awesome hotel, flowers, couples' massage. Is he trying to make this more than just dating? . . . No. He's just being sweet. It can't be anything more than that . . . but what if it were? What if there was no Daniel-Julian drama, and we could be together long-term without me giving up on D.C.?* She focused on the ceiling instead of reaching out for his hand like she wanted to. *"I've been on Team Isadora for quite some time now,"* he said. *He also said I could never be a disappointment to him. But what if he's wrong? What if I let myself fall for him, and he changes his mind? He decides that I'm not worth . . . Don't start crying. Get it together, Isadora.*

After the massage and getting dressed, they took the elevator back down to leave for the rehearsal dinner. He'd asked her what she planned to wear and she'd sent him a photo of the demure baby blue dress she knew her mother couldn't criticize. He surprised her by stepping out of the bathroom in a navy suit with a shirt that matched the color of the dress exactly.

"So we make a united front," he said. "Glasses or no glasses?" he asked, smoothing his navy tie.

"Glasses. Let's go for serious but endearing."

In the elevator, she curled into his side, still in a mellow co-coon. She was with him, they didn't have to hide, and she was determined to enjoy every minute. Reaching the lobby, they strode hand in hand to the exit.

"I guess we'll need a taxi, huh? You've got me so relaxed I didn't even think about how to get there and back," she said.

There was a glimmer in his eye. "Don't think we need to worry about that, beautiful."

She squinted at him as they stepped outside. He led her to a black sedan with tinted windows.

"Mr. Sarda?" the driver asked, stepping out.

"That's me," Karim answered.

"I'm Brad. I'll be your driver this weekend."

"Nice to meet you. May I present Isadora Maris?"

"Hello," she said, returning Brad's handshake. He opened the door and they slid inside.

"Are you kidding me? The entire weekend?" she whispered to Karim, trying not to giggle.

"Well, I figured it was the most convenient option. I got a deal through my friend Gabriel's connections so you can come and go in style all weekend long."

She looked out the window, tears welling up.

"Karim . . . what are you doing?" Her voice wavered. "The hotel, the flowers, the massage, and now a driver? This is too much. You didn't have to do all this for me."

He surprised her, solemn as he took her hand. He focused on their joined hands at first, but when he did look into her eyes, she asked herself if there was a tear in his.

"Yeah, I did, Isadora. I needed to do this for you."

Her heart was going to explode. The pain of abandonment was written all over his face. She couldn't imagine the amount of courage it had taken for him to do all of this for her, in spite of the pain or the fear that she might reject him like Laila had. Unless the way that he felt about her made it worth the risk. She gulped down the fear that was lodged in her throat of losing control over her own life. Squeezing his hand, she leaned in close.

"Thank you, Karim," she whispered, then closed the space between them and kissed him deep, not caring that Brad got to witness it all.

CHAPTER TWENTY-SEVEN
Karim

The closer they got to the restaurant, the tighter her grip on his hand became. Her breathing, shallower. He ached to get her out of that stress, back to the sweet, relaxed state she'd been in at the hotel. He'd never seen her so intimidated. Not even in negotiations with the governor's office. It broke his heart that this is what she went through going to a dinner with family.

Brad turned the car into the parking lot.

"Oh God." Isadora sighed. "She's waiting for us out front."

As Brad pulled them up to the entrance, the headlights flashed across a short, round, impatient-looking Black woman standing beside the door with her hands on her hips. She scanned the parking lot but didn't look twice at the car they were in.

"That's your mother?" Karim asked.

"Yep. That's her." Isadora was checking her hair and makeup in a hand mirror.

"You look perfect, Isa," he said as Brad parked and got out to open his door.

"Maybe in your eyes." Everything about her shrank. Her smile was sadder, her shoulders hunched over. Even the light in her eyes diminished.

He stepped out of the car and faced Isadora's mother. She glanced in his direction but looked through him. After buttoning his jacket, he held his hand out to the woman he loved.

"Come on, beautiful," he whispered to her as she stood next to him. "We got this."

Her eyes lit up. "We?"

"Yeah. You and me." He laced his fingers with hers and they approached her mother together. She glanced at them and did a double take, looking at the car, Karim, and then Isadora.

"Hello, Mo—"

"My *baby*!" She threw her arms open wide and closed the distance between them. "My *darling*!" She clasped Isadora in a bear hug, never taking her eyes off Karim. The hug looked uncomfortable for both parties. When her mother ended it, Isadora stood straight again at his side, and he placed his hand on the small of her back.

"Mother, I'd like to introduce Karim." She turned to him. "Karim, this is my mother."

"Mrs. Maris," he said, putting out his hand. "It is so nice to finally meet you."

"It's nice to finally meet you too, Karim. Come on you two. I want to introduce Karim to everyone." Without a second look at Isadora, her mother linked her arm in Karim's and tried to pull him into the restaurant.

"Let me get the door, Mrs. Maris," he said, freeing himself and taking two quick steps to reach the door first. He held it open for her, and for Isadora, taking her hand once they were inside. "You and me," he whispered to her temple. She took a deep breath and squeezed his hand.

"We got this," she whispered back.

Mrs. Maris took great pride in introducing Karim to every family member in the restaurant. He didn't mind being introduced as "Isadora's boyfriend, the lawyer" over and over, but it did bother him that Isadora's mother kept trying to separate them. When a cousin stood up to give Isadora a hug, her mother tried to pull Karim away to meet the next person. When an aunt waved from the other end of the table, she tried to send Isadora over on her own to say hello. He wasn't about to lose physical contact with Isa. Khalil had stressed the importance of touching her, showing her he was with her at all times. A lot of her family was happy to see her, though a few exchanged confused glances, when they looked at her, not at him. But her mother's attitude about Isadora's career irritated him more than he could conceal. When an uncle asked Isadora how work was going, her mother tried to get between Karim and Isadora as she implied Isadora's work wasn't important.

Remembering her tears and the ludicrous idea that she could be a disappointment, he decided to make sure everyone knew she wasn't. Once they'd been seated and the meal began, he cleared his throat.

"Mrs. Maris," he said, making his voice carry. "You must be terribly proud of Isadora."

"Um . . . why yes, of course."

"You know"—he made eye contact with the uncle who'd asked about work—"it's due to Isadora's hard work and strategy that her boss will likely become a U.S. congressman in the next couple of years."

"Is that so?" the uncle said. "Izzy, your mom said you were barely making it as an assistant secretary."

All eyes on their half of the table turned to Isadora's mother. Karim squeezed Isadora's hand under the table, and her lips twitched as though she was fighting back a laugh.

"Maybe she was just being modest," Karim said. "Like Isadora. I bet neither one of them would ever mention that Isadora is the youngest woman to become the chief of staff to the majority leader in the history of the California State Senate. Or that no other aide, male or female, has risen as far as fast. And she's managed to do it maintaining a flawless reputation and the respect of her colleagues."

"Oh, Karim . . ." Isadora said.

"You won't toot your own horn, but I will. I'm proud that such an amazing woman lets me be part of her life." He looked her in the eye for the second sentence, hoping she understood he was serious. Her shy downward glance gave him the confirmation he wanted.

"Of course, we are very proud of her and all her accomplishments," Isadora's mother said. But it was too late. The attention shifted to Isadora, relatives peppering her with questions, and her uncle shook his head at her mother.

The car rolled away from the restaurant, taking the on-ramp headed back to their hotel. Karim didn't take his eyes off Isadora as she looked out the window. After a few moments, she turned to meet his gaze.

"What is it?" she asked.

"I was just sitting here, thinking . . . What is an incredible woman like you doing with a guy like me?"

She smiled, shaking her head. "I'm getting spoiled, but I don't deserve it. You were awesome in there." He started to reply, but her expression made him pause. She reached for his hand, focused on it. "I didn't know that I was *with* you, though," she whispered. "I thought this was sort of an aid mission for you. Thought you came to help me deal with my mother. I didn't realize you wanted us to be . . . an 'us.'" Her eye contact was hesitant, and she was so exquisite in her uncertainty that he couldn't believe she was speaking to him.

"I did come to help," he said. "But how could I not want that?"

"I don't know. I didn't want to make any assumptions." She looked back at their hands again. Her thumb slid back and forth across his index and middle fingers. "And you still seem . . ."

"What?" he asked.

"A little fragile." She shrugged. "I didn't want to ask or let myself hope for too much."

His heart thudded; his throat was dry. He was back at the stadium inauguration, in the seconds before he'd asked her to dance. He'd been terrified, but the leap had been more than worth it. He swallowed. "I would like it very much if we were an 'us,'" he said. "More than I can really say, though I know it's asking a lot in our current situation. The thing is I . . . I don't know if you would want to . . . officially . . . be with me."

Her head snapped up. "Of course I would, Karim. How could you doubt that?"

"Yeah?" Relief cascaded over him, the prickly buzz of adrenaline fading away.

"Yes, are you kidding me? Of course. I want to be with you, officially."

He laughed, squeezing her hand. "You'd like to be my girlfriend, Isadora?"

She laughed too. "Would you like to be my boyfriend, Karim?"

"Hell yeah! Hey, Brad, can I get a fist bump?" Brad laughed with them and obliged.

Back at the hotel, he yearned for her skin. He held her hand as they crossed the lobby, his fingertips grazing the back of her arm in the elevator. They were going up, but he was falling into the depths of those dark eyes, only aware of her hand on his cheek, her thumb grazing his lips. She broke their gaze to study them, and his chest burned at the nip of her teeth on his lower one.

In their room, door bolted, he took a breath to speak.

"Shhh . . ." she whispered, a finger to her lips as she backed away from him, unzipping her dress. He obeyed, following her, leaving his jacket on the back of a chair, his tie on the puddle that was her dress once she'd stepped out of it.

He kept his eyes locked on hers through the spike in his heart rate when she unhooked her bra and let it fall as she reached the side of the bed. Ridding himself of his pants, he accepted her outstretched hand and let her pull him close, so they were chest to chest, skin to skin. He felt her warmth, her breasts rising and falling against him, and he didn't hold back his groan as she wrapped his arms around her. She slid her hands up his shoulders and then into his hair, fingernails sparking shivers that radiated from his scalp. She smiled at his reaction, her parted lips close enough to feel the heat.

He leaned in, caressing her cheek with his.

"Thank you," she whispered. "For taking a chance."

He pulled back to look her in the eye. His heart thudded, then stilled. There were no fears, no thoughts, nothing but Isadora.

"Am I dead?" He grazed his thumb across her lower lip, felt it stretch as she smiled.

"Why?" she asked.

"You're heaven."

She giggled. "Was that a line?"

"No—"

She clutched his hair and brought his lips back to hers, to consume him. She wrenched a groan out of him, and before he anticipated it, turned them both and pushed him to sit on the edge of the bed. Drunk with her, he throbbed, panting as she slipped out of her thong. He leaned to put his glasses on the nightstand and got rid of his last shred of clothing. He stroked himself once, his gaze slipping from hers to the meeting of her thighs. He licked his lips.

"No," she said, a fingertip under his chin, bringing his attention up. "You're turning me into an addict." She smiled. "But not now. Now I need you inside me."

Sliding his hands up her thighs, he guided her onto his lap, her legs on either side. There were condoms in the nightstand drawer, and he thought to reach for one, but she beat him to it. He ran a hand from her chest, between her breasts, and down her abdomen as she stretched in front of him. What started as an exhale deepened into a growl.

"Come here." He pulled her back.

She licked her lips. "I like it when you get greedy."

He got the condom on and looked at her bewitching face again.

"Do you like this?" He tilted his hips, throwing her off balance enough that she crashed against his length.

She gasped, and her eyes narrowed into slits.

"Now, Karim."

He darted a hand between their thighs, and she rocked her

hips to take him inside of her. The high-pitched sigh she made each time he entered her forced him to clench his teeth, letting the sparks flow over him. His face fell into the haven between her breasts, and he groaned deep as she rode him. She cried out, but it didn't register. He could only feel her heat, her constricting tightness, the increasing friction that was going to push him over the edge long before he was ready. He splayed a hand at the base of her spine and stopped her on a downward stroke, holding her in place.

Her shocked gasp wavered, then exploded as she contracted around him, the orgasm breaking before either of them imagined it was close. Swallowing a groan, he stomped a foot to keep from tumbling with her.

"Shit!" he growled, both arms circled around her as she slumped into him.

"Why . . ." She panted. "Why did you . . . stop?" Then he lost her again, her eyes rolling back as an aftershock rumbled through her. He moaned deep, struggling.

"Just . . ." He had to stop to let out a breath. "Just wanted to change position, but we learned something new, huh?" He smiled, still not sure he'd won the fight against a surprise of his own.

"Oh yeah, we did." She sighed.

He loosened his grip, careful not to let her fall.

"Lean back, beautiful," he whispered. Her hands found his knees as he brought her legs around his waist. She let out one of those erotic moans, tensing around him again.

"God, Isa," he groaned. "I'm not gonna make it five minutes."

Glancing up at her was dangerous, with her chest rising and falling, lips open, panting.

"Your fault," she breathed. "You go so deep. . . . Feels too good . . ."

Having this amazing, sexy woman, his *girlfriend*, look at him like that . . . He had to give her more, had to show her how much he loved her.

"Closer," he whispered.

She leaned into him, shuddering as her arms went around his

neck. He held her close with one hand, using the other to bring her face to his, locking his gaze on hers.

"Don't look away," he whispered as he began to move. Her eyes went wide as she sighed, but she didn't blink. The range of motion was limited, and it took a moment to figure out how to rock into her. The work was worth it. He needed her close, face-to-face. He focused on slight movements, trying to put additional pressure on her clit. But gazing into her eyes eroded his ability for analytic thought. Opting for his thumb, he slid one hand down her body to make gentle circles at the meeting of her lips. Her external and internal quivers were his reward.

"Beautiful." He sighed. "So beautiful, so perfect."

Her whimper broke his heart, her fingernails digging into his shoulder, her eyebrows crunching together, her panting growing louder with his. She shook her head.

"Yes . . . yes, you are," he breathed. "Beautiful, perfect . . ." *I love you.*

She picked up the tempo, drawing closer, the mist on her forehead mingling with his.

"Yeah," he sighed. He remembered his thumb.

"Yes," she echoed, eyelids fluttering but snapping open again, not shying away.

He groaned deep, accelerating his hips, circling faster with his thumb.

"Ka . . . I . . . I love . . ."

His heart started racing in a different direction. He rocked faster without intending to.

"Love it . . . feels so good." She groaned. She clung to him, rolling into his thrusts. "You . . . gonna . . . you're gonna make me . . ."

"Sing for me, Little Kite," he breathed. "Sing."

She snapped down hard, her explosion crashing through him. There was a rush of heat, the loudest cry he'd ever wrung from her, then his world went black.

———

When he awoke, years, minutes, eons, or days later, he'd wrapped himself around her, snuggled up, spooning. He rolled away a moment, tossing the condom in the trash by the nightstand. Curling back, he smiled as she pulled one of his arms tighter around her and laced her fingers in his.

"Best orgasm of my life," she sighed.

"Mine too," he whispered, squeezing her back.

The reception was going well, and Isadora's body language was much better than it had been the previous day. He'd reminded himself of Khalil's advice when they arrived, but he didn't need to think about remaining in physical contact with her. He yearned for the warmth and softness of her skin. He felt more confident, more relaxed, with her perfume in the air, her voice in his ear.

But he couldn't take her to the men's room when he needed to go. Returning to the reception hall, he caught her voice from a side hallway. The stress in it set off all his alarm bells.

"Enough is enough. I'm going back to the party," Isadora said.

"Wait a minute," her mother said. "How much does he bring home?"

"Mother!"

"What? It's important to know when you can stop working."

Karim's eyebrows shot up.

"When I stop— Why would I stop working?" Isadora asked.

Her mother sighed. "You've never known how to accept your place."

"My place?"

"A man doesn't like a woman with too much ambition."

Karim had heard enough. He rounded the corner.

"Actually, Mrs. Maris," he said, walking around from behind her to stand beside Isadora. "I don't know how much Isadora earns, but it's likely more than I do." He kept one hand in his pocket and found Isadora's with the other. He loved the way they snapped together immediately, like a pair of magnets.

Her mother huffed a moment, surprised, and stood straight,

trying to make herself taller. A ridiculous attempt, as she was eas-
ily a foot shorter than he was.

"You see," he began again, "Isadora is chief of staff—
something I should not have had to remind you of yesterday—
and I am only a legislative director. Her pay grade is automatically
higher than mine. Plus, she's been at the legislature for five years;
I just arrived. If, for some reason, one of the two of us should
stop working, it would be more logical for me to stop, not her."

"Chief of staff, legislative director, same difference," Isadora's
mother said. "And her job can't be *that* important. She's wasting
the prime years of her life on some silly nonsense she'll just have
to quit anyway once she grows up and does what she's supposed
to do."

"And what's that?" Karim asked.

She huffed again, stamping her foot. "Taking care of me, of
course. I didn't put in all those years of taking care of her not to
get anything out of it. She owes me. She also owes me grandchildren."

"That's ridiculous," Karim said.

She narrowed her eyes at him. "I don't think I appreciate
your—"

"I'm not finished," he said. He had a shimmer of concern that
he was being disrespectful; then he remembered Isadora's tears.
His hesitation evaporated. "She doesn't owe you a damn thing.
You're the parent, she's your daughter. If you weren't so self-
centered, you could see that Isadora is flourishing. She's following
her dreams. And she should continue following them, wherever
they take her. It's your job to support her in that. If you won't, I
sure will. Because I find her ambition inspiring and sexy as hell."

He wanted to look Isadora in the eye, to check on her, but
finishing the showdown was important.

"You should watch your language with me, young man," her
mother said. She stepped a few more feet down the hall. "You
come over here, right this instant, Isadora Maris." She snapped
her fingers, pointing to the floor in front of her feet. She looked

at Karim. "If *you* will excuse us, I need to speak with my child in private."

"I hope you'll excuse me for pointing this out, Mrs. Maris, but I don't see any child, anywhere," he said.

"What did you say to me?"

"I said, 'I don't see any child.' I see your daughter. Your adult daughter. But I don't see a child." He kept his face as pleasant as possible, but his jaw began to ache.

"Fine," she said. "Isadora, come here."

"No, Mother," Isadora said. "Anything you have to say to me, you can say in front of Karim."

"How dare you talk to me like—"

"You'll never be happy with me, Mother," Isadora said, resigned.

"What kind of nonsense is that?"

"It doesn't matter what I do or say." Isadora paused, tightening her grip on Karim's hand. He squeezed back. "What I'm about to say isn't a criticism, Mother. It's a fact. I can't be the daughter you seem to want me to be. And you can't be the parent I need as an adult. This isn't an argument, it's just a fact. I'm tired of hurting all the time. Tired of every contact from you being a criticism that makes me doubt myself and my worth. We need a break. Don't call me. If you do, I'm not going to answer."

Her mother began to huff.

Isadora's eyes met Karim's. "I think we're done here," she said. "You and me?"

"You and me," he repeated. Leaving her slack-jawed mother behind, Isadora led him back to the party.

On the way to the table, Isadora was polite and friendly with the family members who stopped her to talk. But he could feel her fatigue. He let go of her hand to run his down her back, and every muscle was tight. It was her family, and he didn't want to push, but once they'd sat down, he had to ask.

"Beautiful?" She smiled at him, but it didn't reach her defeated eyes. "Maybe we should go to the hotel?"

Her lips parted, about to speak. Instead, she nodded, and he
was sure there was a glint of a tear in her eye. He took her hand.

"Are you okay, Isa?"

"I'm just exhausted. She always wears me out." She looked
around. "Everything's over. No more speeches or anything. It'll
just be dancing from here on out. Let's go."

They said their goodbyes to the bride and groom, along with a
few cousins and the uncle who'd shown interest in her job.

In the car, he didn't let go of her hand. There were a thousand
thoughts swirling through him, but it was hard to get past the
anger at Isadora's mother. That she would hurt her daughter,
again and again, even in front of other people. She reminded him
of Laila. Of course, he didn't know Isadora's mother, but the effect she had on Isadora felt all too familiar.

"I can't believe you did that," Isadora said, drawing his attention from the window.

"Did what?"

"You called her out. I don't even notice anymore that she re-
fuses to see me as an adult, but you saw it right away. And you
called her on it."

"I shouldn't have?"

"No, I'm glad you did. More than glad. I'm not even sure how
to describe how I feel about it. For a couple of seconds, I felt like
I was sliding into some other dimension."

"Why?"

"No one gets it. Literally no one. Except maybe RJ, and it took
him a year to understand the level of crazy. You're the very first
person in my entire life who got it so quickly and refused to act
like it was normal or pretend it wasn't there."

He looked down, a little shy because of the way she was looking at him, a little proud that she felt the way she did.

"You know," he said, "it may not be my place and I'm not a
specialist or anything, but I think your mother is more than just
difficult."

Isadora's response was a relief. Instead of balking, she waited
for him to continue, her expression calm and open.

"Last night, did you notice how she kept trying to separate us at dinner?" he asked.

"Yeah. But I didn't really think anything of it. She's always done that, anytime I've brought someone around. She tries to physically get between us. It's weird, but I feel like she's trying to keep me to herself. Unless it's one of the guys she's tried to set me up with. Then she can't do enough to shove us together."

He nodded, about to speak, but was cut off by the blare of a siren coming from her purse.

"Ah," Isadora said. "Speak of the devil."

"That's her ringtone?"

"Yep."

Isadora rejected the call, continuing the conversation.

"Even before you said anything today, I got the impression that she saw you as a threat. You get in the way of doing what she wants with the thing she owns." Isadora pointed at herself.

He nodded. "Do you remember what I said about Laila? How she saw me as her property? Personality disorders are supposed to be rare, so of course I'm not diagnosing your mother or excusing her behavior. It's just that she reminds me so much of my ex. So much. Maybe look into it? If that's what's wrong, it might help you deal with the aftermath of life with a person like that. It's taken me two years to mostly recover from being married to a toxic person. It sounds like you've been dealing with one your whole life."

"I've been wondering about it. Since you told me about Laila," she said. "The idea that it could be a real thing, that I'm not the source of the problem, or just too weak or broken to handle being loved the way my mother wants to love me seems like too much to hope for."

"It's freeing to discover it's a real thing."

"But what is it? What causes it?"

"I don't remember why some people develop them, but they're beyond needy, clingy. For my ex, she had this massive fear of abandonment that ironically made her do everything possible to push me away. While expecting me to accept what amounted to emotional abuse. And in her case sometimes physical. It's taken time and a lot of therapy for me to understand why she behaved the way that she did, and that in spite of her problems, she was still responsible for her behavior."

Isadora looked out the window. He didn't know if he'd explained things well, if he should say more. But it had taken him a long time to understand what Laila's issues meant; he doubted that those few words would be enough to explain things to Isadora, if he was reading the situation correctly at all.

"It's hard to think of it as abuse," Isadora said, her voice wavering. "Like I said, RJ's been the only person to say it wasn't normal. Deep down, I already knew that it wasn't, but when the feedback from everyone else is that it's just tough love, or worse, 'Your mom is such a great person,' it's . . . it's easy to think there's something wrong with me." The slight sob he heard her swallow broke his heart. He reached out to put an arm around her and hugged her as much as their seat belts would allow.

"That's exactly how it was for me with my ex," he said. "She is intensely charming with other people. Her life looks perfect from the outside. And according to her, it was part of my job to maintain that image. A couple weeks after she left, I heard that her official line was that I'd been cheating on her, abusing her. It stung that our mutual friends cut me out of their lives too, because Laila is very persuasive. And why wouldn't they believe her? She'd had them sure that she was the perfect wife as long as they'd known her. I was the one who worked too much, who didn't pay enough attention to her. But back to your mom. It might be time to get some help."

"She'll never agree to that."

"I meant for you."

"So you think I'm broken too?"

He squeezed her tighter. "Not at all. I think you've been through years of traumatic experiences and anyone would need help to begin addressing that. You might even have CPTSD."

"CPTSD?"

"Complex Post Traumatic Stress Disorder. It's common—" The siren started again. She rejected it again, keeping the phone in her lap.

"Didn't you tell her you wouldn't answer if she called?"

She shrugged. "That's exactly why she is. I don't have the right to decide not to talk to her. I need to take a break from her, but . . ."

"But?"

"The last time I tried to cut contact she wore me down. Calls, emails, family members harassing me, asking how I dared be so ungrateful and cut my mother out of my life."

"There's no shame in protecting yourself from a toxic person, even if it is your mother." He rubbed her shoulder. "And now you've got two people in your corner to help you push back. Can you turn off your phone?"

She shook her head. "Been keeping tabs on RJ. Don't want to miss it if he calls."

He caught himself tapping his foot, wanting to help but not cross any lines. "I could screen the calls if you'd like? Put it on silent in my pocket and if it buzzes, I'll check to see if it's RJ so you can take it?" The siren started yet again, and she immediately rejected the call, put it on silent and handed it to him.

"Thank you, Karim," she said.

He pulled her closer and stroked his chin across the crown of her head.

"It's my pleasure, Isadora."

Early Sunday, Karim went to reception to check out while Isadora chatted with Brad as he loaded their bags into the trunk. Karim needed to take care of one final detail before she caught on.

"What's my half of the damage?" she asked, arriving before he was ready.

He looked past her, toward the car. "I think Brad just dropped your bag."

She checked but turned back to Karim as he signed the bottom of a page and passed it to the man behind the desk.

"What was that?" she asked.

"What was what?" He accepted a folded piece of paper in return, nodded his thanks, and slid his wallet into his jacket, taking Isadora's hand.

"Karim," she said, letting him pull her toward the exit.

"Yes?"

"You did not just pay for the entire weekend."

"I didn't. You paid for the plane tickets."

"Uh, technically, I did not. I bought them, and you already paid me back for yours. I thought we agreed to split the expenses for this little adventure fifty-fifty."

They'd reached the car, and Brad closed the door behind them.

"Actually," he said, buckling himself in, "you suggested splitting everything and I said, 'That's a good idea.' At no point did I agree to do it."

She squinted at him, her arms crossed.

Please Isa, I can't let you pay for a romantic weekend I planned.

"Okay, fine, Mr. Lawyer-man. You're right. You did not explicitly agree. But I'd feel like I was taking advantage if I didn't cover half of the cost."

He thumbed his chin, searching for a way to explain that wouldn't anger her.

"No, Isadora. I can't. You're my girlfriend, right? We're together now?"

"Yes."

"Then please, don't press me on this," he said.

"I don't need a man to—"

"Oh, I know. I'm fully aware you don't. You don't *need* anyone to. That's why I'm asking you to let me."

She wrinkled her nose. "I feel guilty, Karim. It's not fair."

"I don't want to make you feel guilty. I want to make you feel cared for."

She looked out her window. Her sigh was heavy, and her hand darted to her cheek.

"Okay. Thank you, Karim," she said, her voice soft. She reached for his hand.

"You're welcome, beautiful."

He'd left his phone on silent the entire weekend. The only people he'd wanted to speak to were Gabriel and Khalil, his support team. And he'd stolen a few moments to keep them in the loop. When he pulled his phone out to turn it off before takeoff, he had a new message.

Julian: Excellent work again, Karim. Getting Isadora to sign the amendment first was a stroke of genius. Don't know how you did it, but I think it made the others follow suit. Everything is coming together. Great job.

What the hell is he talking about? Why would it be a stroke of genius? That's twice in three days this amendment has come up. I was careful, but something is wrong.

CHAPTER TWENTY-EIGHT
Isadora

"I'm with Diane," RJ said.

Isadora's goals for the first day back had been to check on RJ and get a copy of the amendment to see for herself that Daniel's presidency wasn't in danger. But the second she'd seen him, RJ dragged her into her office and demanded all the details about her weekend, preferring to talk about his when they weren't at work. She tried to temper her excitement out of respect for his loss, but she couldn't avoid including a moment when her cousin Diane had pulled her aside to say that Karim was in love with her.

"It's as plain as day every time he looks at you," she'd said. Isadora had been stuck for a reply, much to Diane's delight.

"But . . . RJ, how? He can't be in love with me."

"Why not? If some guy did all that stuff for me, I'd take it as a pretty big sign."

She groaned, putting her head on her desk. "I don't know how to *do this,* RJ. I don't know how to . . ."

He sighed. "Believe someone cares about you? Loves you?"

A vacuum replaced her lungs. Grateful her forehead was still pressed against her desk, she fought the deep black. That cold, crippling emptiness she battled at the end of every contact with her mother, at the fuzzy memories of her father. If she gave into the sobs, the entire senate would hear her. She nodded.

"You know I love you, babe. And maybe this will help," RJ said, sliding a large manila envelope onto the desk next to her head. She curled her arms around herself and sat up, her vision blurry.

"What is it?"

RJ stood, opening the door to her office. "I don't know." He shrugged. "I'm just the messenger." He winked at her and left, closing the door behind him.

She picked up the blank envelope, sifting it back and forth. When she unsealed it, several handfuls of white rose petals tumbled onto her desk, into her lap, and onto the floor. She started crying and put her head on her desk again, the smell of roses filling the air.

She lifted her head, the wave of emotion having run its course. *Why are you crying? There's no denying he makes you happy. He was beyond awesome.* She went back over everything he'd said, defending her, boasting about her. She thought of his excitement at becoming her boyfriend—she pressed her hands into her cheeks at the idea. And there was something she hadn't shared with RJ: The way Karim made love to her had changed. It felt different now. Closer, warmer, more emotional. She looked at the cascade of rose petals around her and picked up her phone.

Isadora: Thank you, baby.

She deleted it. *Can't call him "baby" for the first time by text.*

Isadora: Thank you, Karim. So sweet!

She stared at the screen. *No. That's not enough.* She deleted the new message.

Isadora: Thank you, gorgeous. When can I see you?

She hit Send.

The next evening, she couldn't stop fidgeting after she rang the doorbell at Karim's. He opened the door and before she knew it, he'd zipped her inside and folded her into his arms. His kiss was deep and intense, and it excited her as much as it soothed her. She moaned, his lips, his warmth, and his smell turning off all her thoughts and pushing her toward her needs. She slid her hands to the buttons on his dress shirt, beginning to remove the flimsy barrier. After two buttons, his hand cupped hers, stopping her. He pulled back to whisper.

"No, no baby . . ." He looked her in the eye, his forehead grazing hers. "Let me savor you for a little while."

She smiled up at him. "Baby?" she whispered.

"Yeah." He nodded, his gaze darting back down to her lips.

"Yeah," she echoed, biting her lower one.

He growled and began devouring her again.

He'd been wise to leave a blanket on the couch. She appreciated the intent behind his desire to enjoy each other little by little, but they'd failed. They hadn't even made it to his bedroom. He pulled the blanket over them, lying naked in a post-sex cocoon on the soft leather. After taking time to come back to themselves, he began gliding his fingertips over her skin. She loved the way he caressed her after sex. It wasn't to arouse, but to appreciate, to have another way of connecting with her. She was in a perfect state, listening to his heartbeat.

"I'm sorry I was MIA this week," he said.

She didn't open her eyes. "It's okay, baby." She smiled, using that word for him. "RJ had to talk me down a bit, but it was a crazy busy week for us all."

"Remind me to thank him. To be honest, though, I did use work as a bit of an excuse."

She lifted her head, resting her chin on his chest. "An excuse for what?"

He shrugged, not looking at her. "Got a little freaked out. Still can't believe you really want to be with me. Wanted to give you a chance to reconsider, maybe change your mind if you wanted." He focused on playing with her hair.

She stilled his hand. "Why would I change my mind? Have you?"

"No, of course not," he said, eyes wide. "I just . . . I don't want to be the cause of any problems for you."

"It'll cause me more problems if you disappear on me."

He smiled. "Not a chance. Just need some time to believe this is actually happening to me."

"I wish I could take that away from you," she said, running a hand down his face. "I wish I could make that pain and doubt disappear."

"You know I feel the same way about you, right? I'm still so angry at the idea of you thinking you could be a disappointment to anyone."

She chuckled. "That's what RJ had to talk me down about. I decided I'd done something to disappoint you this week. He kinda got in my face about it."

"Isadora." He took her face in his hands. "You will *never, ever* be a disappointment to me. It's impossible. Odds are much greater that I'll be a disappointment to you somehow."

"No, gorgeous. I'm pretty sure that's impossible too." She put her head back on his chest.

"I'm serious. I'm sorry to talk about work right now, but things are weird. People are looking at me differently. And the amendment I drafted is not the one available for review online."

She raised her head. "It's not?"

"No. Not at all. I don't understand what happened. It's like . . . like a different document was put in place of the one I worked on. With different statute numbers. But somehow everyone's signature is on the new version."

Mine right at the top, she thought.

"And I'm worried that if I missed something there, I missed other things. And I don't want any mistakes I've made to have a negative impact on you. I spent each evening this week double-checking everything I could, and that seems to be the only weird thing."

"What's different?" she asked.

"The statute concerning the dates to elect officers is included. It was *not* on the version I drafted."

She had a spark of adrenaline but breathed through it.

"We'll get to the bottom of it, but Daniel still has enough pledges," she said.

"Pledges?"

"Promises to vote. Three-fourths of the majority have already pledged to vote for Daniel to become pro tem. He only needs half plus one. He hasn't done anything to lose that support, so I don't think it's anything to really worry about. Let's not let it spoil our time together, okay, baby?"

CHAPTER TWENTY-NINE
Karim

Grazing her cheek, Karim asked her how she wanted her eggs when he came back into the bedroom after taking his shower Saturday morning. She bewitched him—dark, bare shoulders contrasted with his cream-colored sheets, her curves creating undulating waves beneath them. He wanted to climb back into bed with her, but he also wanted to make her breakfast. She smiled and stretched.

"Over easy, or scrambled, or whatever's easiest, gorgeous."

"Toast?" he asked.

"Sure."

"Juice?"

"Silly. Whatever you make for me will be wonderful. You don't have to take a breakfast order."

"Okay, Isa. It won't take long," he said. "Do you want it in here, or at the table?"

"At the table, after my shower?"

"Okay. Take your time. No stress today."

"I like that. No stress today."

He kissed her cheek again and went to get dressed. His back was to her when he dropped the towel around his waist, but he peeked at her over his shoulder.

"Careful, beautiful. You keep looking at me like that and we won't make it out of this room."

"Would that really be so awful?" she asked, gliding one leg out from under the sheet. Her skin beckoned from ankle to hip.

"No, it wouldn't. But I think you should eat so you have enough energy for what I plan to do to you later." He'd slid on a pair of black boxer briefs and turned to face her. She licked her lips.

"If you insist." She sighed, slurping him up with her eyes.

He smiled again, threw on a black T-shirt and headed for the kitchen. Humming, he took the eggs and bacon out of the fridge, grabbed some juice, and set the table with dishes from the machine. He tossed the dishtowel over his shoulder. Once the shower went off, he started the bacon. His personal phone rang. A Harrisburg number. He asked himself why his lawyer was calling on a Saturday.

"Hello?"

"Hey there, sexy."

His vision narrowed. The sizzle of bacon faded away. He stumbled back from the stove. At least instinct saved him from flipping the pan and burning himself.

"Laila?"

"Of course. How are you, sweetie?" The syrupy "sweetie" clicked him back to himself. And the stored-up rage. He stalked to the patio and once outside, hastily jerked the door back along its track, worried that Isadora might hear if things got as messy as he anticipated. He turned to face the parking lot.

"'Sweetie'? Are you serious?"

"You aren't my sweetie anymore?" The memory of the pout that went with that tone set his teeth on edge.

"What do you want?" he asked. "I've been satisfied communicating with your lawyer through mine, there's no reason for us to speak directly."

"You know, I've been thinking about that. I'm not really sure this whole divorce thing is such a good idea."

There was a nerve under his right eye that had only twitched on a few occasions in his life. All those occasions had to do with

Laila. The nerve fluttered with an electric buzz as he tried to form an answer without shouting. He failed.

"You've got an awful lot of—"

"Hey! Watch it!" she said. "Who do you think you're talking to like—"

"I'll talk to you however I want. You're lucky I'm speaking to you at all."

A brief clatter drew him out of the call and back to Sacramento. Isadora was in the kitchen, moving the bacon from the hot burner to a cool one. Laila's voice faded away. Isadora, graceful as always and dead sexy in one of his dress shirts, went up on tiptoe to leave the kitchen. She had to walk past the patio door he'd failed to close. *Is she trying not to disturb me? She's thoughtful even—*

"You don't expect me to just let my husband—" Laila's voice broke back into his consciousness.

"Your husband? Your *husband*? You mean the husband you walked out on? The husband you've ignored for the past two years?"

Isadora jumped when he raised his voice and her eyes met his.

"I'm sorry," he mouthed at her.

She shook her head. "Don't be," she mouthed back.

"Don't go?" he mouthed. He didn't try to hide the emotions that were bubbling up. He knew his anger was going to burn itself out soon, and it would help to have her nearby. She nodded, curling her legs under herself as she sat on the couch. Laila's background blather faded. He let himself fall into Isadora's eyes, that deep, dark brown abyss he'd fallen into so many times as she brought him to another mind-bending climax, or in moments like this one, where he felt safe and important and . . . loved? He'd barely recognized the thought when Laila intruded again.

". . . you're seeing someone. Who is she? *You* belong to *me*, Karim. How do you think it makes me look—"

"This conversation is over," he snapped. "There is nothing for us to discuss anymore. You call me again—you, or anyone else in your family—and I will have my lawyer request alimony. I'll demand half of *everything*. The townhouse in Harrisburg, the condo in Barbados—*our* wedding present. All the assets I was just going to let slide so I could be done."

"You wouldn't dare."

"Don't tempt me," he said. "This conversation is finished. *We* are finished. Do not contact me again." He hung up, exhaled, and stepped back into the apartment, sliding the door closed. Isadora reached out to him. He put his phone down on the table and went over to sit next to her on the couch.

"I'm sorry you had to—"

She cut him off, shaking her head. "Don't apologize for anything. Are you okay?"

He shrugged.

"Come here," she said, pulling him to her. He put his head in her lap, shuffling a little because of his glasses. "What did she want?" she asked, running her fingers through his hair.

"I don't really know. She asked about you, though."

"She knows about me?" she asked.

"Not your name. Just that I'm seeing someone. She doesn't like it."

"But . . . how?"

He shrugged again, snuggling closer, his eyes closed.

"If I had to guess, my mom. I told her about you. She's probably been shouting it from the rooftops, or at least said something to her hairdresser, who knows everyone back home."

"You told your mom about me?" Her voice was frail. He peeked an eye open to smile up at her.

"Of course I did, beautiful."

Her blush warmed his cheeks, and he closed his eyes again.

They sat together a long while. Isadora stroked Karim's hair, the side of his face. He let himself relax. He'd been right, he did need her touch after the burst of anger passed. He'd returned to the impression he'd had, that she might . . . really care for him, when she spoke.

"She seems to still have a lot of power over you," she said.

"Do you think?" He didn't open his eyes.

"You seem really upset."

"I'm not so upset now." He smiled, facing her.

"But after you hung up . . ."

He sat up, tapping his glasses back into place. "Exhausted, I guess. And it brought up a lot of old pain. It took a long time, but I finally realized that I was grieving the idea of being a married man, more so than the loss of the person. We got married too young, because everyone else thought we should. Remember how I told you that I had to help her maintain the facade of us being a perfect couple? We were good on paper, but in real life . . ." He shrugged.

"If she's been gone so long, with no contact . . ."

"Why now? Because of you, I think," he said.

"I see," she said, quiet tension in her voice.

"Everything okay? You look uncomfortable."

"Well, it feels kind of weird."

"What does?" he asked.

"Up until now, your wife has just been this mysterious ghost. But now, she's a lot more real to me. I feel kind of . . . wrong."

"Why wrong?"

"Because you're married, silly," she said.

"Well, not for much longer. And I doubt we were *that* married before. I took the commitment pretty seriously, but she didn't."

Her quick exhale and rigid shoulders made it clear he'd said the wrong thing.

"So, am I like . . . revenge, or something?"

"What? God, no. I'm sorry. That's not what I meant at all. You're a whole nother story. You don't have anything to do with my past." He took her hands in his, looking her in the eye. "Isadora. I have never thought of you in reference to her. The way I feel about you is only about you."

He needed to be honest and tell her he loved her, but he still wasn't ready. Her face softened into a slight smile.

"Okay," she said.

"Okay?"

She nodded, but her discomfort was still palpable. He thought it best to give her time to process everything.

"Breakfast, beautiful?" he asked.

"Breakfast." She nodded.

As promised, Karim spent the time after breakfast doing his best to bring as much pleasure to his girlfriend as possible. He'd gotten her to a point where he felt like their connection was as deep as it had been before Laila burst in, when his work phone rang.

"Do you want some privacy?" Isadora asked, lifting her head from his chest.

"Please don't go," he whispered, nestling her back into him. "It'll only take a minute.

"Yes, Julian," he answered. As usual, he tipped the phone away from his ear to protect his hearing.

"Ah, there you are. Listen, wanted to give you a heads-up: The next few weeks are going to be a whirlwind, and I need you ready."

"Okay," Karim said, rolling his eyes.

"If the insurance bill passes this week, it means I have enough influence within the majority to cut Daniel's legs out from under him. And I have you to thank. You and some welcome help from our young woman with the bird tattoo. See you—"

Isadora shot off his chest like a rocket. "What?" she mouthed.

Karim shrugged. "I don't know what he's talking about," he mouthed back. Julian hung up, so he put the phone back on his nightstand. Isadora was out of the bed and flying to the bathroom.

"Isa, wait!" He snatched his glasses back on.

"'*Our* young woman with the bird tattoo'? Karim! How could he know that? There are only two people in the entire legislature who know about that, and only one works for Julian!"

She was grabbing her stuff and jamming it into her bag.

"Baby, stop! I don't know—"

"Don't you dare 'baby' me!" Tears streamed down her face. She jerked her bra back on and tossed through the disturbed comforter. She got into her panties as soon as they tumbled out. "How could you do this, Karim? 'Welcome help.'" She stopped to sniffle. "It's the amendment, isn't it? You brought it up all casually last night. 'I don't understand what happened.' You knew *exactly* what, didn't you? That's why you had me sign it first, so everyone else would go along."

"No, please, I seriously have *no idea* what he's up to. I tried to figure out what was going on all week, but I didn't want to say anything to you until I had something useful."

She stopped dead. "You knew something was wrong *all week* and you didn't say anything to me until *last night*?"

It wasn't until he'd voiced it that he saw how it might look from her perspective.

"Isa, please. I . . . I didn't think of it that way."

She stood in the middle of the bedroom, facing the door, her bag in one hand, jeans in the other. "I'm sorry, Karim, but this is just too much."

Terror sent ice down his spine. It was happening. The woman he loved was about to leave him, and he didn't know what to say, how to stop her.

She hiccup-sobbed and wiped the back of her hand across her cheek. "Has this been some sort of game all along? I wouldn't put it past Julian." She hiccupped again. "But you?" She turned to look at him, tears streaming down her cheeks. "We're done." Then she was moving, yanking her jeans on and running out of his bedroom, his apartment, and in all likelihood, his life. He'd followed her into the living room and stood there, stark naked in the silence after she'd slammed the door. A chill slithered over his skin, but rather than coming from outside, the cold came from within.

CHAPTER THIRTY
Isadora

Isadora gave up after the third try. She was just going to have to feel her way to the bathroom. Her eyes were too swollen from crying to get them open. In spite of her stubbing her toe on the way, keeping her eyes shut was a blessing. The cool, white bulbs over the bathroom sink flooded pain through her closed lids and into her temples as soon as she flipped the switch. Leaning over sent an ocean of pain washing through her head, but it was no match for the explosion of grief in her chest.

Don't.

She'd cried enough the previous night. She splashed cold water on her face, cupped some in each palm and held her palms to her eyes. She'd check the time eventually, to see if it was as close to lunchtime as she thought. Maybe she could convince RJ to come by. She'd need to tell him what happened, but she preferred doing it in private in case she fell apart again.

Her phone was nowhere to be found. She gave up looking for it, then heard a distant buzzing. She had been a mess the night before—it was in the hamper under the clothes she'd stripped off the second she'd locked the door.

Two missed calls from a 404 number. Could have been anyone in her family, but the next part, the 778 was familiar, though she couldn't remember why. She googled, panicked when the results brought up a hospital near her mother's house, and called the number back.

"Hi, this is Isadora Maris," she said, before the person could speak. "Someone called—"

She was cut off by a sharp laugh in the background and someone demanding the phone.

"Gotcha!" her mother said. "Good to know there's a chance you'll answer if I'm hospitalized again."

Isadora simply did not have the emotional reserves to deal with her mother's games.

"You . . . aren't in the hospital?" she asked.

"I am, sort of. Came to visit someone and asked the nurse if I could make a call, let my daughter know everything's fine."

"Because you knew I wouldn't answer the phone if I saw your number," Isadora said.

"I don't know why you have to make things so difficult, Isadora. I am your mother. You are to answer the phone when I call."

Tears were back. Rage, fear, nausea. A panoply of emotions she should have been able to control.

"Izzy? Is something wrong?"

Isadora fought not to fall for the concern in her mother's tone. She reminded herself that the woman on the other end could not be trusted, even though she desperately needed the sort of mother she'd always wished she'd had.

"I'm fine," she forced out through a sob.

"No, you aren't," her mother said. "I can tell when my child is upset. What's wrong? Did that nice boy dump you?"

Isadora held in her shudder. Any hint of vulnerability would be blood in the water as her mother circled.

"Everything is fine," Isadora said as pleasantly as possible.

"If that's what happened, I'm not surprised," her mother said. "That's what you get for siding with someone against me."

Isadora had to get to the bathroom. She hadn't eaten yet, but it felt like something was on its way up.

"I'm gonna be sick, Mother. Gotta go, bye," she said, hanging up and throwing herself down the hallway.

The hard, cold edge of the bathtub felt good against her temple. Exhausted, she leaned against it, waiting for her head to stop spinning. She didn't think a person could throw up on an empty stomach. But with the right encouragement, it seemed anything was possible. She rolled back, resting her nape on the cool porcelain.

This is what I get for choosing someone over my mother? She let out a sharp laugh. *No. This is what I get for letting myself feel. Letting myself imagine that I could have a relationship and my career.*

Isadora found her way to the office early on Monday. She wasn't emotionally ready, but she had her job to think about. She'd failed to protect her heart; she couldn't fail when it came to her career.

The first order of business was to get to the bottom of the amendment situation. She pulled up the online version. Attached to the insurance bill in committee, it didn't make any waves. The goal was to codify current practices. No reason not to vote in favor of the idea. The statute concerning the dates to elect senate officers *was* included. *"I'm sure it doesn't modify those statutes,"* he'd said. *Liar. I can't believe I fell for that. All of that . . . It's what I get for forgetting that romance is dangerous.* Her screen became blurry. *Isadora. Not now. You can cry when you get home.* Two deep breaths and she was back where she needed to be.

She scrolled farther down to the original form of the bill, checking the history of modifications. There was the link to the initial draft of the amendment, two committees back. Then the link to the version Karim drafted, with the date and time stamp. She clicked on it, and an error message popped up: *File not found. What do you mean, 'File not found'?* She backed out and then clicked again. Same result. *That's never happened before.* She picked up her phone.

"Hello?" RJ answered.

"Hey, you at your desk?"

"Yep."

"Can you pull up the draft amendment? I'm trying to get the

one *he* had us sign, the latest version, but I keep getting an error message." She'd managed to speak with RJ on Sunday night; he knew what Karim had done, that not only had he betrayed Isadora by presumably telling Julian any information she'd accidentally let slip when she'd had her guard down, but he'd done it in the most humiliating way possible, even sharing the most intimate details, including her tattoo. If Julian knew details about her body, it made Isadora burn with shame to wonder what else he might know about her.

"Okay," he said.

She waited while RJ tried.

"Me too," he said. "That's weird. Never had that problem before."

"Me either. I'll get in touch with the Office of Legislative Counsel."

"Wait—did you notice the time it was filed? Weren't you on the plane then?"

She took a second look. It was the Friday they'd left for Atlanta, an hour after they'd taken off.

"Oh," she said.

"Listen, this may not be the best time, but I have back-to-back meetings the rest of the day."

"What is it?" *No discussions about* him, *RJ.*

"Is it possible that *he* was set up somehow?"

She gave the idea a few seconds, but her pride was still too bruised to consider it.

"There could have been a backup at Legislative Counsel," she said. "He could have dropped it off right after we all signed it, and they just didn't get to it until after we'd left." She leaned back in her seat, crossing her free arm over her chest.

"That's a long back up, Isadora. And time stamp aside, he wants to start over here, right? He's working toward something permanent. Why would he let himself look like an idiot? Or worse, underhanded? He sent us all an email detailing what had changed. And what didn't. He explicitly said this statute was not affected."

RJ had a point. Why would he be so meticulous in his email and then change something?

"Maybe he has something permanent and we just don't know it yet," she said. "Perhaps Julian found the right carrot to dangle."

RJ sighed. "That is also a possibility. But does it fit in with what you know about him?"

"RJ, stop! Whose side are you on?" Her nose prickled.

"Yours, babe. You know that. It's been forever since I saw you as happy."

"Lemme call Legislative Counsel."

"You know it's okay, babe," he said.

"What's okay?"

"That you let him into your life. You didn't make a mistake."

Her office got blurry.

"Do we have to do this now, RJ?"

"I have the feeling we're gonna have to do this all the time," he said. "Don't you see what's happening here? This is beyond Karim. This goes back to your mom. Everything she's put you through has led to this. She's made it so you can't believe that anyone can have pure motives when it comes to you. You're accustomed to there always being something behind everything, something you have to watch out for. And with her, you're right. But it's not like that with normal, healthy people. That expectation of ulterior motives has destroyed a great relationship because of what might be a simple mistake."

She rolled her eyes, sniffing back a tear.

"You don't think so?" he asked.

"If I address that right now, I'll break down," she whispered.

"Okay," RJ said. "But back to Karim. Maybe I'm completely wrong, but I don't think he betrayed you. I think something else is going on. Either way, you did nothing wrong by letting him into your life."

"RJ. Julian Brown knows I have a bird tattooed on my *ass*. Amendment notwithstanding, that is reason enough not to have let Karim into my life," Isadora said flatly.

RJ grunted. "Finally, you admit it's on your ass, not your *upper hip*. I guess now's not the time to gloat. I am going to say it again, though. You made the right choice by letting him in. You even told me he was helping you see things differently with your mom. Think about how important that is."

She rested her elbows on her desk, rubbing her temple with her free hand. RJ wasn't wrong, she just wasn't in a place to admit it. She sighed.

"Okay, babe, I'm getting all heavy and we both have work to do," RJ said. "I'll let you go. But seriously. You made the right choice by letting him in. Love you."

"Love you too," Isadora said. She hung up.

She squeezed the bridge of her nose hard and continued her research. After an hour, she had to concede that there was no way around allowing a much earlier vote on senate officers once the amended bill passed. Daniel's presidency might be at risk.

We keep it from coming up for a vote just in case. We should have the votes against the bill, but . . . A shiver went through her. The War Room meeting had been surreal. *The way the members flipped was so uncharacteristic. Something is going on. We have to hold our position until we know what.*

She had a post-lunch face-to-face scheduled with Daniel, but she wasn't ready to face him. She checked that the box of Kleenex on her desk wasn't empty, confident she'd need some. Her personal phone chirped with a text. Her heart skipped a beat when she saw who it was from, but her pride told her not to open it. She put the phone down and turned away. Then she swiveled back and tapped it open.

> Karim: Senator Roberson is in with Julian. Loud argument about the insurance bill and demanding that Julian promise he'll delete "it." Unsure what "it" is.

She squinted at the message. *Is this another trick? He can't believe I'll trust anything he says.* She put her phone away and tried to figure out a lunch that would stay down in case she got too emotional with Daniel.

"No, Isadora. You have not let me down."

Isadora had given up holding back, and her tears were dripping onto the table in the meeting room next to her office. The level of shame she felt was so high, she thought she might suffocate from it.

"Yes, I have, Daniel. I can't believe I signed the amendment without double-checking. The years of hard work, trying to get to the presidency, and now it all may be compromised because I got careless?" *And distracted. And stupid enough to believe that I could let my guard down.*

"Since when do we double-check everything, Isa? Unless you've been hiding some sort of superpower from me all these years." He paused. "Actually, that may be possible, with all of the things you've caught well before I did."

She managed a tiny laugh through her sniffles.

"I don't expect you to be perfect," he said. "I'm sorry if I've put that pressure on you."

What was it that Karim said about my perfectionism? It's my anxiety in disguise?

Daniel got up from his seat and slid into the one next to hers. He took her free hand. "Isa, please. You don't have anything to be this upset over. Like you said, I'll delay the bill as long as possible. So what if it was on the agenda for this week? There are other bills I can call for a vote on. I'll just keep delaying it and try to get some answers while you try to figure things out on your end. I'm confident you'll get to the bottom of this before I do. And if worse comes to worst, and it passes and goes into effect, I still have the support of the majority of the party. I haven't done anything to piss off enough people for them to change their minds."

She hiccupped and sniffled. "You're sure?"

"Of course I am. I'm beginning to think I have more faith in you than you do in yourself. That's an idea I *don't* like."

"Okay." She began dabbing away the moisture under her eyes.

He studied her a moment. "Is it only the amendment that has you this upset? Or is something else wrong?"

She panicked. He was right, but she'd die of mortification if he knew she couldn't keep her heart under control. And that her mother was right, she wasn't worth this career.

"I'll get it together, Daniel. It's just the threat to your presidency." Dabbing at her eyes again, she peeked at him, hoping that explanation had been sufficient. She added an awkward smile.

"Why don't you take the rest of the day off?" he asked.

"I can't. You guys are back in session, there's like a thousand—"

"I can handle anything that happens on the floor. We're probably going to finish early anyway. And for everything else, is anyone going to die if it doesn't get dealt with today?"

"But—"

"Okay, fine," he said. "You forced my hand. I'm ordering you to go home, Isa. As your boss, I am sending you home for the rest of the day."

She smiled, shaking her head. "Okay, boss man. I'm going."

He smiled back, standing and buttoning his jacket as he went around the table toward the door. "Didn't Julian's aide send an email about the amendment? His new aide, Karim?"

"He did."

"Seems strange to do that then make a change unless he wanted to look like an asshole."

Isadora had to concede.

"Maybe he just made an honest mistake," he said.

"I guess that's possible."

"Focus on that, please. Glenna will be really disappointed if things don't work out between you two." He winked at her and left.

He knew? This whole time?

After giving herself a few minutes to calm down, she returned to her office to follow Daniel's orders. The chimes began ringing, calling the members back to the floor after their recess for lunch.

Leaving the office while they were in session felt like slipping into
an alternate reality, but she was going to do as Daniel asked. She'd
log into the internal channel from her laptop and listen in while
she prepared for the next day. *Could be fun in my pajamas.* She
paused a moment. *Okay, maybe RJ's right, I work too much.*

Grabbing her phones to slide them into her pocket, she took a
quick glance at both screens. Nothing on her work phone, but her
personal phone indicated five messages from Karim. She took a
deep breath through her nose, scrunching her lips together. *Julian
knows about my tattoo. I'm not reading these, answering and giving him the
chance to learn anything else.* She jammed the phone in her purse,
messages unread. Walking around her desk to grab a couple of
files from Daniel's office, a worry cropped up. What if he sent
something she'd regret not knowing about? She returned to her
chair and checked. Three of the messages weren't much help, but
two set off her antennae. Two more senators had gone to Julian's
office, wanting him to delete something, or talking about privacy
violations, getting attorneys involved. *What could be so serious that
one senator threatens another with legal action?* The idea brought back
the shivers from earlier in the day. She scrolled down to the last
message and her heart broke.

> Karim: I need you to know that I would never try to deceive
> you, never try to hide something from you. If I were in your
> shoes, I'd be wary right now, especially of anything I have
> to say. So instead, I'll show you. I'll keep telling you what's
> going on, even things I think are unimportant, and even if
> Julian finds out and I lose my job. I don't care. I'm on Team
> Isadora and your happiness is what matters most to me. If I
> can't make you happy by being with you, I'll do my best to
> help you be happy reaching your goals. You don't have to
> reply.

Don't start crying again, don't start, she told herself. *Go get the files
from Daniel's office and get out of here.*

She locked the legislative office door and went into his separate majority office. She and her tears were at a stalemate, so she

hurried to reach his desk. Daniel always left the door ajar; she put it back the same way once she was inside. His desk looked tidy, but that was a disguise. The file folders in his drawer were never in order because Daniel had a bad habit of refiling things in front. Back hurting, Isadora got down on her knees to flip through, trying to keep her thoughts at bay. But they didn't want to stay put. . . . *"Never try to hide something from you . . ."* Why did he ask me to *stay when Julian called if he had something to hide?* She paused and reconsidered. It made no sense for him to ask her to stay and hold her as close as he did, knowing how loud Julian talks, if he had something to hide. *Is Daniel right? Did he just make a mistake? Or is RJ right? Could Karim have been set up?* A familiar voice reached her from the hallway.

". . . waiting for my insurance bill to pass," Peter said.

Why isn't he on the floor? They're in session right now. There shouldn't be any members up here. There was a pause; he was on the phone.

"No, the amendment is on the bill. Once it passes, we can call for a vote on the senate officers twenty-four hours later," he said.

He was silent a moment, then cleared his throat before continuing.

"Oh, it'll pass, no problem. It's guaranteed with our intel."

Intel? Isadora crouched all the way down behind Daniel's desk.

"Yeah, we were concerned about drawing too much attention after Julian's aide—"

After Julian's aide, what? Dammit Peter. You always say too much, why are you stopping now?

"Exactly," Peter said. "Then I'll call for a vote and Julian becomes pro tem."

Isadora was afraid her heart was going to shoot out of her chest.

"React? He won't be able to do anything but sit there and take it. I cannot wait. It'll be so good to see him get taken down a few notches. Him and that haughty bitch. She is going to have a *lot* of groveling—"

This haughty bitch will do no such thing. Isadora tried to take a silent deep breath. All she wanted to do was launch herself into the hallway and tear Peter to pieces. That would be satisfying but wouldn't get her the result she needed.

"Oh? Okay. I'll keep you in the loop." His voice disappeared, though the swish of his pant legs remained audible as he walked down the hall. Her calves ached, but she waited before leaving the office. She slipped her phone out of her pocket to text Daniel.

> Isadora: Can you come back to the office?
>
> Daniel: Not the best time. You're still here?
>
> Isadora: Peter and Julian have something on the others. To force a vote on Julian as pro tem.
>
> Daniel: You sure?
>
> Isadora: Positive. Let me look at some things. Text me when you can leave the Floor?
>
> Daniel: K

She waited, straining to hear anyone else in the hallway. It was quiet, so she slipped from behind the desk and tiptoed to the door. She left his office, went past the Majority offices, and returned to her own without being seen.

Her mind was whirring away.

I was right. The flips on Peter's insurance bill had been a sign that something was going on.

She sat in front of her computer, trying to remember the specific rules about pro tem nominations, beyond the general rules for voting on officers.

I cannot believe that asshole is planning a coup.

A "coup." The word brought up a faint memory. Her first year in the Assembly, a coup had failed in the senate. She didn't remember who had been involved, but she had the year. If she had the year, she could find the story. Her phone chirped.

> Daniel: Any developments?
>
> Isadora: Maybe.
>
> Daniel: Maybe good? Maybe bad?
>
> Isadora: Maybe good. Working on it. For now, hold off on Peter's ins bill.
>
> Daniel: Got it.

Within an hour, she'd made some headway. Peter's insurance bill was the end of the line for Daniel's pro tem hopes and a humiliating defeat for Isadora. The reputation she'd counted on getting her to D.C. was in serious jeopardy. If the senators who had flipped in the War Room voted for Julian to become pro tem, they might not have enough other senators to vote for Daniel.

Voting against the majority leader on major legislation like the insurance bill, plus breaking a pledge, were two massive no-no's in a senator's life. Whatever this "intel" was had to be huge for multiple members to break those unwritten rules.

Where and how could Julian have gotten some sort of serious information about enough members for them to flip as they had in the War Room? What could he possibly have on so many people to stop Daniel from becoming president?

CHAPTER THIRTY-ONE
Karim

Karim's week really wasn't going well. He'd thrown himself into work and gone back to San Diego for the weekend. He met up with Gabriel, who'd become close enough to ask Karim what was wrong, but not close enough for him to feel comfortable sharing. He'd been disappointed with his sluggishness during their jog on Sunday, then realized why on Monday when he'd gone to put on his belt: He had to tighten it by two holes so his pants wouldn't sag below his waist.

Then on Wednesday night, he noticed something positive in his personal inbox, though at first it threw him for a loop.

From: Sanders Esq., Martin
Subj: Sarda v. Sarda Resolution

Hi Karim, Good news. Laila's accepted. Your divorce is final.

"Upon consideration of this case, upon evidence submitted as provided by law, it is the judgment of this court that a total divorce be granted between the parties to the above stated case upon . . ."

Karim read the email again. Then a third time. The living room got quiet, though he hadn't turned the TV on in days, so there hadn't been any noise before. Suddenly his pulse was loud. Not fast, just loud and steady. He was extremely aware of the beating of his own heart. He was divorced. Free. Some small part of him was waiting, anticipating the shouts, the joy, the triumph he should be feeling. But . . . there was just silence. He looked around the room. It was the same as it had been a moment ago. Nothing had changed, even though his entire world had shifted. He should be happy. Instead, he felt . . . empty? Before he could avoid it, he glanced down at his hand, at his ring finger. It was as bare as it had been for the past year. And suddenly he felt sad about that. Why? What on earth was the matter with him? He picked up his phone.

Normally, Khalil would be the one to call. Without hesitation. But now he *was* hesitating. This was divorce, the end of something. And Khalil was so happy with Vanessa right now, Karim didn't want to bring him down. He rested the phone on the coffee table. An itchy jumpiness pushed him to his feet, to the sliding glass door that led to the patio. He should be happy. His next reflex was to reach out to Isadora, to let her know that he was well and truly single. But he was dead to her now, and rightfully so. He gazed out the door, rubbing his head, then pushed his glasses up so he could rub his eyes. Who would understand? He went back to his phone and opened a messaging app.

> Karim: Hey, Mo. I'm officially divorced. Should be happy. And I am. But not 100%. Weird?

Mo's divorce had been finalized years ago and was pretty amicable, so maybe he wasn't the right person to reach out to. Karim put the phone down and turned to the kitchen for some water. *Who am I kidding? Mo? Talk? About feelings? That'll be a cold day in he*— Karim nearly jumped out of his skin as his phone started ringing. He went back to pick it up, staring at the caller ID. It said "Mo." He read it again. Mo was *calling* him? Mo had never called him in reply to a text. Had Mo ever called him at all? Other than when their grandfather had died? Karim answered.

"Hello?" he asked.

"Hey," grunted Mo.

"Hey."

There was an awkward silence. Karim glanced at the phone to be sure it did say "Mo."

"It's over, huh?" Mo asked.

"Yeah."

There was some background noise on Mo's end, like a TV with a game on.

"Did I . . . um . . . text you at a bad time?" Karim asked.

Mo cleared his throat.

"No. 'S okay. Sounded important." The TV went off.

Karim wasn't sure what to say and thought to just thank Mo for calling at all, but then Mo cleared his throat again and spoke.

"She ask for anything?"

"No, I got everything I wanted, don't have to do anything. I'm totally free."

"Good."

"But I'm not happy. I feel . . ." Karim swallowed hard. "Like I failed."

"Normal."

"That's normal?" Karim asked.

"Yep."

Karim waited for him to elaborate, then remembered who he was talking to. Mo was never one to elaborate. He took a breath.

"So you're telling me it's normal to feel bad after getting divorced, even if I really, really wanted—well, needed to get divorced?"

"Yep," Mo said.

"But I am happy. Well, relieved. I just didn't think I'd feel this . . ."

"Empty?" Mo asked.

"Yeah," Karim said.

They sat in silence another moment, and Karim realized that was fine, good actually. He didn't need his eldest brother to say anything. He sighed. Mo grunted. It made Karim smile.

"How's Maddie?" he asked.

Mo grunted again, and Karim could tell it was a different grunt, a happy one.

"First place. Science fair," Mo said.

"Excellent," Karim said. "Tell her Uncle Karim's proud of her."

"Will do."

"Thanks for the call."

Mo grunted again and hung up.

Karim put the phone down on the coffee table and returned to the sliding glass door. Only then did he notice how dark it was outside. The twinkling of the city lights made Midtown Sacramento brighter, prettier than it had been in days. But if the night was coming to life around him, that meant it was much later back in Detroit. He hadn't meant to reach out to Mo so late. But his big brother had called when he'd needed him. Karim caught his own lopsided smile in his reflection in the door. It was definitely the first time he'd smiled in the past two weeks.

The next day Peter and Julian cackled in the outer office around nine thirty. Karim was stuck on the subject of his boss. He wanted to kill him for destroying things with Isadora, but he was also the key to fixing them. Julian could harm Daniel, and that would harm Isadora. Karim's only hope for redemption in her eyes was to stop that from happening. He'd keep biding his time, keep sending her messages about what was going on, until one of them figured out what Julian planned to do and how to stop it from happening. She hadn't responded to any of his messages the previous days, but he hadn't expected her to. *She didn't tell me to stop sending them. Maybe her silence isn't so bad.* As soon as he'd finished his thought, his boss's sidekick was at his door.

"Hey, Julian's got something he wants to show you," Peter said.

Karim followed him into Julian's office, surprised when Julian asked him to close the door. His self-aggrandizement wouldn't echo down the hall with the door closed. He motioned for Karim to join him behind his desk, all three of them facing Julian's laptop.

"Show him—"

"Nope. No clues, Peter. Let's see if our straight-laced attorney can figure things out on his own."

Julian double-clicked, and a video opened. It was black and white, the edges of everything blurred. It came from a security camera. A door opened on the other side of the room and a smiling woman entered, followed by an older man. Karim glanced at Peter, who was grinning like an idiot. *Seriously, guys? You brought me in here to watch a hidden-camera sex tape?*

"So, tell me, Rex . . . or do you prefer Rexie?" the woman asked, out of the frame.

Okay, so there's audio too. Awesome. I am not sitting here watching amateur porn—

"Whatever Mistress prefers," the man replied, also off camera. Karim's blood went cold as he recognized Senator Rex Roberson's voice.

"Kneel," the woman said, the camera panning to the right.

And there, in the middle of the screen, knelt Senator Roberson, naked except for a dog collar and his underpants, putting a gag in his mouth. Julian and Peter exploded with laughter at Karim's slack-jawed shock.

"What the hell?" he asked.

"You didn't wonder why Rex switched sides on the insurance bill?" Julian asked, pausing the video. He pointed at the screen. "That's why."

"But how—"

"Wait, Karim, we're just getting started," Peter said.

Julian clicked on another file, video from a different room, another senator enjoying the charms of another young woman.

"That's not his wife," Peter whispered in Karim's ear. Karim jerked back; Peter's breath was too close to his skin. He stepped away from the desk.

"Julian? What's going on? How did you get—" Then he remembered. One of the many times he'd been stuck in Julian's office, he'd heard him say that a new security system was being installed at Ike's.

"You bugged Ike's?" Karim asked.

Julian smiled. "Very good, young Padawan," he said. "Figured out 'where' much quicker than I'd anticipated. But *I* did not bug Ike's. Ike's updated its cameras and has simply been kind enough to *share* the information they collect with me. A real treasure trove, don't you think?" Julian turned his laptop toward Karim, to show him the folder the videos had come from. There were six files, three with Roberson's name and three named after three other senators.

Karim's mind reeled. He tried to process the legal ramifications. "Julian . . . you can't. You . . . just from a privacy perspective . . ."

"You aren't a fan of Ike's," Julian said. "Which is too bad, because I have to wonder what we might have learned about you. Mr. Goody Two-shoes must need an outlet. I bet you're far kinkier than any of us could imagine."

Karim's face began to ache from the pressure of holding his lips together.

"But if you had swung by lately," Julian continued, "you would have seen that the security policy has changed. It is posted that filming takes place on the premises. So no, you don't have to worry."

"*I* don't have to worry? This has nothing to do with me," Karim said.

"But of course it does. You are *my* aide. Who would believe that you weren't in on this from the beginning?"

A blinding cloud of rage blocked Karim's vision. There was a small question, hovering in the cloud, and he chose to focus on it, in the hope of not going to jail for assaulting his boss.

"Why, Julian?" he asked.

"Why what?" His attention remained on the screen, clicking open another file and grinning.

"You've had these for some period of time. And"—Karim needed a deep breath—"you kept me out of the loop. Why are you sharing with me now?"

Julian leaned back in his seat, studying him. "Let's just say that things are going to get a bit . . . exciting in the coming days. Need to be sure you understand the stakes, so you remember that my best interests are your best interests." Julian's mouth kept pulling to one side, like he was laughing at a secret joke.

"What the hell does that mean, Julian?"

"It means our destinies are linked. You support me or say goodbye to your new life in California," he said.

"Are you going to speak clearly for once, or are we stuck on cryptic again?" Karim asked.

Peter tittered. " 'Cryptic.' I like that."

"Me too," said Julian.

Karim said nothing to either of them, turned on his heel and left. He continued down the hallway and took the back stairs to get to street level.

He crossed the capitol grounds, fisted hands buried in his pockets, his jaw aching. He kept unclenching it, but it would clench right back up again.

All I wanted was a new start, a clean slate. Not to get tainted by a Machiavellian little— He had to pause. Panting through flared nostrils, he found a bush covered in flowers. He took a moment to focus on them, on each detail, trying to calm himself. He'd just been admitted to the California State Bar. And now Julian had set the stage to have him disbarred. He focused on the flowers again. White, tight balls of petals that yawned themselves open into wide, white suns. They weren't white roses. He sighed. Isadora needed to know that there were videos of the goings-on in the back rooms of Ike's. It was no surprise Julian had flipped people on the insurance bill if he had that kind of blackmail material. And why stop there?

Fuck me.

It all became clear. Julian was going after the presidency. He'd had Karim prance around to everyone's office to get the amendment signed, and somehow added the crucial statute changing the rules about president pro tem elections after everyone had signed it. With the videos, he might have just enough leverage to get the amended insurance bill to pass against Daniel's wishes. Then Julian could call for a vote on the presidency the next day.

I came here to cover for a maternity leave and I find myself party to a coup against the boss of the woman I fell in love with?

He almost punted the flower bush across the gardens. Instead, growling deep inside, he let his jaw and fists clench again as he marched back into the capitol and returned to his office.

He didn't have to worry about getting himself fired yet. The chimes calling the members to the floor had sounded twice. Julian had three important bills first thing on the agenda; he would be somewhere on time for once. Karim was supposed to have given him the files he needed, but Julian was going to have to be more self-sufficient going forward. The clock was winding down on Karim's time with him. His new start in California was dead in the water. Now his goal was to make it to the end of the week, or of the session, or whenever necessary to stop Julian from becoming president pro tempore.

He got back to the main office and went into Julian's to flip on the little TV in the corner. Tuned in to the internal channel, he studied the senate floor to verify that his jackass boss was there. The senators hadn't been called to order yet, so they were milling around and talking, some arriving, some already at their desks. The camera paused on the vote board; the square next to Julian's name was green, so he was there somewhere. It panned out and Karim's heart skipped a beat and then took off. The camera zoomed in on Daniel standing inside the doorway, leading to the back hall, talking to Isadora.

The last glimpse he'd had of her had been beyond difficult, standing there lost as she ran away from him. Followed by those painful hours curled up in the bed, his face in the pillow and sheets she'd slept on, surrounding himself with her perfume, the traces of her left behind. She nodded at Daniel and then disappeared through the doorway. In those few brief moments, her face had remained tight—tense brow, worried lips.

No, no, no, Julian. You don't get to hurt her. Or the rest of the senate. I'll figure out a way to stop you.

———

But first he had to eat with the bastard. Julian had scheduled a working lunch with him, and Karim didn't want to arouse suspicion. Once Julian was back on the floor for the afternoon session, Karim would go to Ike's and get the information he suspected was there. Then, he'd go to Isadora's and give her everything. He needed her to evaluate the evidence for herself. If things came together as he hoped, they'd save Daniel's presidency, and maybe Karim could win back her trust. For the moment, he had to make it through lunch.

"Karim, my boy! You're back," Julian said, returning at lunchtime. "Was concerned you might have lost sight of what's important."

"Well, what can I say," said Karim, following him into his office with the documents they needed to review for the afternoon. "The idea of being the chief of staff to the pro tem is rather appealing." He took a seat with Julian in front of the two lunches he'd ordered.

"Ha! Knew you'd figure it out. But chief of staff? If Christina comes back, we'll have to maintain lines of seniority. I'd have to reward her years of loyalty."

"I don't think so, Julian. You had to know I'd have certain requirements after being the patsy for your power grab."

Julian's grin warped his face. "Whatever do you mean?"

"The amendment. Don't know when or how you did it, but you did something. I know I didn't include the statute about senate officers."

"Sorry about that," Julian said. "It was too good an opportunity to pass up."

Karim opened his lunch, doubly nauseated. Julian's table manners left everything to be desired, and Karim hadn't truly eaten since Isadora left. He had no appetite. But he could fake it. "So?" he asked, unwrapping his utensils.

"So? Oh, okay. Chief of staff," Julian said.

"And?"

Julian raised his eyebrows, his mouth full. He'd torn off a large chunk of chicken, so he did need time to chew, but Karim wasn't in the mood for stalling. He needed to reflect the same image and behavior Julian would have in such a situation, to make him believe that Karim was on his side. Karim cocked his head.

"More money?" The question was muffled and came with a tiny piece of chicken that landed less than an inch from Karim's plate. He readjusted the napkin on his lap and nodded.

"The highest level in that pay grade, plus twenty percent," he said. He took a bite, maintaining eye contact with Julian.

"Plus twenty? No way—"

"I could get disbarred for the fraud you've made it look like I'm party to. Twenty percent or I talk."

Julian squinted at him. "To who?"

"To anyone. To everyone. I don't get what I want, you don't either." Karim took another bite, posing his utensils on the table and wiping his fingers on his napkin.

Julian huffed, but he didn't have a way out.

"Fine. Fine. You drive a hard bargain, Karim." He laughed. "I like it! I think we'll enjoy working together." Karim offered his hand and Julian shook it, leaving some oil from the chicken skin behind. A tap at the outer office door had Julian on his feet and into the room before Karim could finish wiping his hand.

"It'll be best if we talk in here, Daria," Julian said as he returned to his office. Karim looked up as Julian ushered her in.

"Daria, hello," Karim said.

"Oh, Karim, hi." She darted a glance at Julian's back as she walked in, clutching a file folder tightly to her chest. Her knuckles looked strained. "It's been a while; how are you?" Her voice and smile were sharper, more forced than the last time Karim had seen her.

"I'm good, and you?" He stood and began gathering the rest of his lunch, having already caught the glare from Julian and his light nod toward the door.

"Oh! I didn't mean to interrupt your lunch," Daria said. "Please, don't leave on my account."

"Not a problem," Karim said. "I can finish in my office."

"No, *really*," Daria said. Her tone stopped Karim short. "You don't have to go." Every other time she'd come to the office, she'd barely given him a second glance. Now she wanted him to stay?

"Yes, he does," Julian said, taking Daria's elbow and guiding her to the seat facing his desk. "Karim's got to get back to work, has a lot of things to prepare for the coming days. He's an excellent little worker."

Karim forced himself to stop gritting his teeth. He lifted an eyebrow at Julian, lips straight, then bent them into a polite smile for Daria.

"Julian does have a point. Busy week coming up," he said. "I should get back to work. Good seeing you again, Daria."

"Um, okay. You too," she said.

Karim had barely crossed the threshold before Julian closed the door. He paused a moment, listening. Though he couldn't make out words, he caught the rise and fall of both their voices, Daria's voice only a murmur, Julian's loud and direct. Karim returned to his own office and shut the door.

Once the afternoon session started and Julian was back on the floor, Karim went into his office and tried to copy the videos from Julian's flash drive onto a blue USB key to show Isadora. But the videos wouldn't copy. He tried emailing them to himself, but the files wouldn't attach. He hesitated about taking the drive; Julian might return before he did. He locked the outer office and hurried down the hall. He ran into RJ as he rounded the corner.

"RJ! Hey! Listen—" He paused, unsure of how RJ felt about him.

"Were you set up?" RJ whispered.

"Yes."

"Come with me." RJ unlocked his office, let Karim in, and locked it behind him. "What's going on?"

"Julian's planning to take the presidency. He has sex tapes he's been using to blackmail at least four members. And he changed the amendment. If the bill passes, he's going to call for a vote on the presidency the next day."

"*Shit*," RJ said. "Sex tapes? He has enough sex tapes to do that?"

"There's a file with six different videos. I've only seen a few seconds of two. Two senators who flipped in the War Room."

"*That's* what happened? Have you told Isa?"

"Not yet," Karim said. "Thought it was too big to just drop on her. I have to run by IT, then I'm on my way to see if there's more info at Ike's. I thought I'd take it to her tonight."

"Okay. Good. What can I do?" RJ asked.

Karim's breath caught. He hadn't thought he'd have help.

"If I go by her house, you think she'll slam the door in my face?" he asked.

"She might. Let me work on that."

Karim sighed. "Thank you, RJ."

"Forget about it. You're good for her. She's just a little freaked out right now, but I don't think it's a lost cause." RJ shrugged.

"It isn't?" The question grated itself out over broken vocal cords.

"When I talk to her or see her, it's like she's grieving inside. You don't grieve like that unless you've lost something big," RJ said.

Could I still be something big for her?

"She hasn't lost anything, RJ. And she's not going to. Tell her what Julian's plan is, please? And can you call or text me if the insurance bill comes up for a vote? They're going to try to pass it this afternoon."

"Got it." They exchanged personal numbers and RJ unlocked the door. "Don't worry, I'll get that door open tonight."

He squeezed RJ's shoulder. "Thank you." Then he opened the door and headed downstairs.

"Bullshit," Karim said as he towered over the owner of Ike's, arms folded. Karim understood how he and Julian had been able to work together; they were cut from the same cloth. Both sneaky, plotting little toads.

"You expect me to believe you cut this sort of deal with Julian without setting up an insurance policy for yourself?" Karim asked.

"I don't care what you believe," the little man said. "I'm telling you, there are no videos of either Julian or Peter. That was the agreement. They only spent time in the rooms with no cameras."

Karim nodded, scanning the dingy office. There were two flat-screen TVs in one corner, each with four images from security cameras within the establishment. The man's gaze darted over his shoulder to the flat screens. His eyebrows shifted up for a second. Then he licked his lips and peeked back at Karim.

"You're telling me there are ten rooms here?" Karim asked.

"Uh . . . those other two are on the pool area and the parking lot." The man's forehead started to glisten. Karim went over his mental images of the place. It wasn't that big. He leaned farther over the desk.

"There are no more than six 'special' rooms here. Structurally, you just don't have the space." The little man began to shake. "If memory serves, it's closer to four," Karim said. He pulled the blue USB key from his pocket. "Did Julian tell you about that statute you reference on the new signs? The ones saying that the premises are being recorded?"

The toad gulped. "Yes, why?"

"That's too bad," Karim said. "'Cause it's a bogus statute. It doesn't exist. You have no legal standing to film all the things you do. Now, I could mention that to one of my colleagues. Perhaps one of the stars of your jerk-fests. Or . . ." He tossed the blue USB key to the toad, who sighed and made copies of the files of Julian and Peter.

"Thank you," Karim said, returning the key to his pocket. Then he pulled out a black one. The one he'd picked up from one of the guys in IT who had a *unique* habit of collecting viruses. "Now this one," he said. "I need two copies."

The toad groaned a complaint but obliged, unknowingly infecting his system with a virus that corrupted video files.

"Tell me something," Karim began. "Did I come by today?"

The toad raised an eyebrow. "No. We've never seen each other before."

"Thanks again. It might not be a bad idea for you to get a lawyer. Gonna need to cover your ass about your surveillance."

As Karim sped back to the office, his phone beeped with a text.

RJ: Insurance bill just passed.

"Fuck!" shouted Karim, punching his fist into the steering wheel.

CHAPTER THIRTY-TWO
Isadora

"Peter may call for a vote on pro tem tomorrow," Isadora said to Daniel when he returned to the office after the senate had adjourned for the day.

"Are you sure, Isa?" Daniel asked. "They just went against me on a bill, nothing else has happened that's drastic enough for them to turn on me like that."

"According to Karim, Julian has sex tapes on the senators who voted for the insurance bill."

"He has what?" Daniel whispered.

"I know, it seems very far-fetched. That's why I said it *may* happen tomorrow. I don't trust the source. However, it lines up with my previous impressions."

"But if it lines up with what you expected, you can trust Karim. That's good news," he said.

"Daniel!" Isadora surprised herself with her tone. "Sorry. You can't seriously put my . . . emotional . . . uh, life on the same level of importance as the presidency?"

"Why can't I, Isa?" he asked. "They're equally important."

Isadora didn't know what planet she was on anymore.

"Daniel. Priorities here. We have to do something to stop this."

"Isadora, if I'm meant to become president pro tempore, I will. If not, it wasn't meant to be. But you . . ." He stepped closer to her, putting a hand on each shoulder. "You need to understand that your happiness is also important, worth fighting for."

At the moment, she was fighting not to cry in front of him again. "Daniel. Letting myself . . . feel something like that for, for a man . . . It's too dangerous. If I hadn't opened myself up, if I hadn't let Karim in—"

"Julian would have still found a way to be Julian. And you wouldn't have been nearly as happy as you've been of late. It's none of my business what happened, but I think it might be worth giving him another chance."

She straightened her posture. "Okay. I will take that under advisement. But about the pledges to vote for you, what do you want to do?"

"Sex tapes?" he said, grimacing and sitting on the couch for visitors.

"Yeah." She leaned against the desk across from it.

"I don't know that there's much we can do. How many are there?"

"According to Karim, at least six files."

"Whew. Okay, then." He stroked his chin, gazing at the floor. "If Julian is threatening to make the videos public, I don't want to do anything. The last thing I'd want is to put anyone on the spot like that. It's bad enough that he's outing them by asking them to go against their pledges."

Isadora tapped her fingertips against the desk. "Why don't you reach out to the members who flipped? Privately. Let them know that if they keep their pledge, you'll find a way to protect them from Julian? Whatever he may have."

"Pretend I don't know exactly what he has on them, huh?"

"Kind of lets them save face," she said.

Daniel shrugged, then nodded.

"You start at the top of the list?" Isadora suggested. "I'll get in touch with the aides starting from the bottom."

"Your assistant could help," he said.

"She could. But I'd be wary if a temporary aide called me about something this scandalous."

"Good point." He stood. "I'm going home."

"But, Daniel . . . we have at least three other bills up tomorrow. Don't you want to—"

"Nope. And you don't either. You have much more pressing business," he said.

"I do?"

"Yep. Talk to him. Hear him out. I promise it'll be worth it."

For the second weekday in a row, Isadora found herself at home much earlier than expected. *Well, tonight it's just six, not four like yesterday.* She reached down the side of her nightstand to retrieve her personal-phone charger. She'd just hung up, having sworn to RJ that she'd let Karim in. At first, she'd been irritated that he wanted to come by without asking, but RJ was right, he wasn't trying to be the hero. He was respecting her autonomy, bringing her what he'd found so that she could decide how to proceed. And to do that, he had to bring it to her place.

She didn't understand her life anymore. Until Karim waltzed into it, things had been clear. The path had been evident. The goal was D.C. by way of Daniel's presidency, and her emotions had stayed well compartmentalized where they didn't cause any trouble. But now, down was up and up was down. Daniel was unconcerned with becoming president. He even put her love life on the same level as a multiyear goal. And her heart was running amok. *This is what I get for letting myself feel. Destroying my dreams and ending up hurt and alone. Just like my mother.* She'd avoided crying over Karim that day because she'd been in a rage, trying to manage her regular work while figuring out how to stop Julian. And now, she was stuck, waiting around for that six-foot-plus, broad-shouldered, green-eyed demigod to show up again. On their first flight together, she'd wondered what his lips tasted like. Now she knew. She'd been jealous of the seat-back tray and his magazine because they knew what his touch felt like. Now she knew.

She fell back on her bed. Daniel, Glenna, and RJ were all pushing her toward him, telling her to give him a chance, that he and her dreams weren't mutually exclusive. And that he loved her. She hoped that they were right, because now she knew: She was in love with him. Her doorbell rang.

I'm not ready to see him. She was on her feet and headed to the door before she'd made the decision. She swallowed hard and wrapped her arms around herself to keep from shaking. At the door, she took a deep breath.

"Hi," he said, barely making eye contact over the rim of his glasses.

"Hi . . . yourself," she managed. "Will you come in?"

A smile crashed across his face, full of relief, as he stepped inside.

"Did you think I wasn't going to let you in?" she asked, closing the door.

He looked down, hands in his pockets.

"I wasn't sure what to think," he said. Then he peeked back up at her.

The shyness he always hid was on full display. The contrast with his virility melted her heart while lighting her body on fire. It got difficult to breathe.

"RJ called," she said, sliding her hands into the back pockets of her jeans. "He cleared you a path."

Karim nodded, smiling. "RJ has been . . . an unexpected friend," he said. His voice was already heating her up.

"Um." She swallowed and rubbed the back of her neck. "Yeah, he's a good guy. He said you went to Ike's? Oh! Sorry! Why don't we sit down?" He nodded and followed her to the couch. She sat first, perched on the edge of the seat. He did the same.

"Do you have your laptop?" he asked.

"Yeah." She got it from her bedroom, opened it, and put it on the table. He pulled a blue USB key out of his pocket and plugged it in.

"I'm sorry it took me so long to get here," he said, focused on what he was doing. "Peter and Julian wanted to celebrate after the insurance bill passed. Had to play along."

"Thank you," she whispered, unable to look at him. "For what you're doing."

"It's my pleasure, Isadora," he said. His voice had that deep, soft tone to it. It was the same right after they'd made love, when he was relaxed, and they were talking about nothing, and he was caressing her skin. She let out a heavy breath, meeting his gaze.

His cheeks tinged pink, and he looked down at his hands. "This morning, Julian brought me into his office to show me what he had on the other senators. After I got over the shock, I realized those might not have been the only videos. So, I went to Ike's while they were in session after lunch and . . . convinced the owner to give me what he had on Julian and Peter." He'd leaned into the couch, sliding his hands under his thighs.

"How did you convince him?" she asked, confused at his position.

"Hmm." He looked at his lap and then back at her. "I told him Julian lied to him. Not far-fetched, so he believed me. And then I gave him a different USB key with a video-eating virus."

"You didn't! Karim, that's awesome. I'd have been so focused on getting the videos I wouldn't have thought of destroying the others," she said.

He blushed. "Thanks, Isadora."

"Why aren't you calling me 'Isa'?" The question was out before she'd recognized that she wanted to know.

"I thought maybe you wouldn't want me to anymore."

She sighed. His eyes were so sad and unsure.

"No, Karim. I think, I owe—"

His phone rang.

"Shit. It's Julian. Gimme a second?" he asked.

"It's okay." She nodded. She got up from the couch and went into the kitchen. Tapping her fingers on the counter, she was close enough to follow their conversation, but didn't, too caught up in the storm roiling inside her. *I want him. So much, so, so much. But even if there was a way to have D.C. and Karim, how could he trust me now? What if I just tell him? Tell him how I feel, spit it out, and whatever happens, happens. He's been so—*

"Isa?" He'd finished his call and joined her in the kitchen.

"Yeah?" She turned. He was two small steps away. He took a half-step forward but stopped. A shiver went through her as she remembered the last time they'd been in her kitchen, in almost the same position, both naked. He'd scooped her up, sat her down on the countertop, and kissed, mouthed, and sucked his way down from her ear to the inside of her opposite thigh. It had taken an eternity. By the time he'd reached his destination, she'd been shaking with want.

He let out a puff of breath and moistened his lips. She asked herself if he was remembering the same thing.

"I, um . . . have to go," he said.

"You do?"

"Yeah, I'll leave the key with you, okay?" He turned to leave.

"Oh, okay. Thanks," she said, following him toward the door. "Peter's going to request a vote on the presidency tomorrow?" she asked.

"Yeah."

"That's what I figured. Did Julian set you up, Karim?" Her question was soft, asked as he stepped through the doorway.

"He did." He nodded. "I think he wanted to force me to get angry and quit or align myself with him for good."

"Oh," she said.

"I lied to him, Isa. I'm playing along until I . . . um . . . we . . . well, you and Daniel find a way to stop him. Then I'm done."

"Are you going to leave?" Hot, acidic fear crackled in her chest.

"I don't know." He shrugged. "If he's managed to damage my reputation as much as I think he has, I'm pretty much done in the California legislature. I may even get disbarred for fraud. Then I'll need a new, new start." He paused, nudging her doormat with the toe of his shoe. "But at least this time I'll really start fresh; Laila signed the divorce papers. Threatening to go after her money was my way out. I'd better go. See you later, beautiful?"

Overwhelmed by all the information, she nodded, closing the door as he walked away. She slid down it, tears threatening. On the edge of a huge crying jag, she stopped short.

No, Isadora. No! You have not come this far and worked this hard to let Julian Brown fuck it all up. She forced herself to her feet, fear and rage swirling into a searing charge. She had to use the energy before it burned her up. The USB key caught her eye.

"It's awfully convenient," Isadora said to Daniel on the phone, twenty minutes later. She'd separated the videos by participant and managed to watch as little as possible to verify that yes, they featured who the file names said they did, and they were compromising. Isadora had to give Julian credit—he'd managed to film the ones least likely to give in to habitual forms of pressure. That fact nagged at her. It had to mean something, having material on people who wouldn't have given in any other way.

"Convenient?" he asked.

"Yeah. That these specific members would find themselves in a compromising position somewhere they could be filmed. Your colleagues aren't novices."

"No, they aren't," Daniel said. "Or they shouldn't be. Ike's has its reputation, but how could Julian have been certain that these members would *do* anything worth filming? Do you think he hired professionals? You watched the videos; did you recognize any of the women?"

"*Yeckh,* no. I didn't *watch*. I played only the first few seconds to be sure of the members' identities." She'd heard a couple voices, which was difficult enough. Those were giggles and laughs she'd never erase from her memory. "It would have made sense for Julian to bring in a prostitute to be certain he'd get useful material. But, correct me if I'm wrong, aren't the parties at Ike's closed? To avoid that sort of thing?"

"I think you're right. Staff, members, and lobbyists only."

Isadora leaned back into the couch, letting her head loll on the armrest.

"Staff, members and lob—" The hairs at her nape stood on end. One woman's voice had been a little familiar, she thought. Then it all clicked.

CHAPTER THIRTY-THREE

Isadora

The grate of cement plus bumper didn't register this time. She only noticed once she was out of the car and headed to the elevator. Her car would be fine parked half on the bumper that day.

She could still save Daniel's presidency and her reputation. And she'd apologize to Karim. She only hoped she could do it without humiliating herself. Fidgeting in the elevator on the way up, she almost lost her temper at having to stop at each floor. But when she glanced up in time to see Karim talking to Daria just inside Julian's office, Isadora shoved her hand against the closing elevator doors and headed straight for them.

Karim jerked his hand off Daria's shoulder as Isadora approached. Isadora flashed him a smile, hoping he'd understand she wasn't upset about him touching Daria, but he'd have to wait for her to say so.

"Daria," Isadora said, trying to make sure to warm her voice as much as possible. "Can I have a minute of your time?"

She glanced up at Karim, then back at Isadora. Her lips opened like she was going to speak, then she closed them and nodded.

"Do you mind coming to my office?" Isadora asked.

"I'll . . . uh, I'm here if you still need to talk, Daria," Karim said, hands in his pockets.

"Please, Karim," Isadora said, heat pricking her neck and cheeks. "If it's okay with Daria, I'd like for you to join us. And bring Julian's drive?"

His surprise was so adorable Isadora would have loved to hug him, but it wasn't the time.

"Sure," he said. "If that's okay?" he asked Daria.

"It is," she said.

Unlocking the outer office door, Isadora had a moment to reassess her plan. Daria might not have been ready to tell Karim everything just then. She'd cross her fingers that Karim could be patient with her for a couple more minutes.

"Karim, sorry to ask this, but would you mind getting the coffee started while Daria and I speak privately in my office?" She hoped her smile didn't look as brittle as it felt.

"No problem." He smiled back and soothed her nerves. She noticed the clock over his shoulder.

"If my assistant arrives, just tell her you have an appointment with me?"

"Sure thing," he said. And his smile was even better, warmer. Made her feel like they were on the same team again.

She relaxed, gave him a real smile back, ushered Daria into her office, and closed the door. Daria started speaking before Isadora got into her seat.

"You know, don't you?" she asked.

"Yeah, I do," Isadora said.

"Do you hate me?"

"Hate you?" Isadora asked. "No. Why would I?"

"Because I helped Julian blackmail those other senators to vote for him to be pro tem," Daria said, voice wavering as she stared at Isadora's desk.

"You mean because Julian forced you to help him? And when you told him you didn't want to do it anymore, he blackmailed you too?"

All the color drained out of Daria's face.

"How did you know?" Her question was so soft Isadora had to lean over to catch it.

"Because all of the rooms at Ike's were bugged. There's a

video of you telling Julian that you wanted to stop, and he said he'd use the videos against you too. He didn't know he was also being filmed."

Daria stammered, her eyes wide. "B-but if he didn't know, how—"

"Karim," Isadora said. "Once he found out about the videos, he guessed that the owner of Ike's might have taped Julian too. Do you mind if Karim joins us? It's perfectly fine if you don't want him to. He's only seen a couple of seconds of the videos. Hasn't seen anything with you, really. But I understand if—"

"It's okay," she said. "I was gonna tell him anyway. Ask him to help me. Julian has no business being pro tem."

"Okay," Isadora said. She reached for Daria's hand. "You let me know if you want Karim to leave, or if you want me to, at any time, okay? And Daniel will be in soon. He and I wanted to talk to you before we confront Julian. We want him to turn himself in, but that means what he did will come out, at least to the police. It's not our place to make that decision by ourselves."

"Oh God. Daniel must be livid," she said.

"He is. At what Julian did to you. It's immoral and a felony."

"But I agreed to, at least at first."

"Did he lay out his whole plan?" Isadora asked. "Ask for your input?"

Daria shook her head.

"Did you know you were being filmed?"

"Not at first."

"And when you told him you wanted to stop, he threatened you. So no, we don't think this is your fault. But it impacts you, so we wanted to talk to you first."

"I'm so sorry, Daria," Karim said, once he'd joined them and Isadora had brought him up to speed.

She dabbed at her eyes with the tissue Isadora had given her.

"You have nothing to apologize for," she said, attempting a smile. "I knew Julian kept you out of it."

He shook his head. "But when you came in while we were having lunch. You seemed uncomfortable. I should have followed my gut."

Daria let out a sad laugh. "And somehow guessed what was going on? You're a good guy, but you aren't a mind reader."

Isadora nodded. "You are a good guy, Karim. I'm sorry I lost sight of that." She breathed through the coldness in her chest. She'd meant to echo Daria's praise, not expose her raw nerves.

"Um, thank you . . . both," Karim said, blushing, his gaze intent on the edge of the folder in his lap.

Daniel arrived. After a brief discussion between Daria, Karim, and Daniel, Isadora laid out her plan.

"Karim, can you bring Julian here once he gets in? We'll confront him with the video where Daria says she wants to stop. Then we'll contact the compromised members and tell them that their videos have been deleted. Next, we call the capitol police and have Julian taken into custody until the local police come for him."

Karim nodded. "I can do that."

"I'd rather ask the other members if they want to come delete the videos themselves. Or see it done. So they're confident it's over," Daniel said.

"Makes sense," Isadora said. "But won't it be weird for them to see each other? Maybe they don't want to be in the same room together."

Daria cleared her throat. "If it's all right with everyone, I'd rather not be in the same room with all of them at once either."

"Yes, of course," Daniel said. "I can speak with them individually. No reason to have a group discussion."

"There's just one thing," Karim said. "I don't think we can delete the videos. There's some sort of formatting that prevents transfer of the videos. I bet it prevents them from being deleted too."

That put a wrench in Isadora's plans. If the videos couldn't be deleted, the situation probably couldn't be handled in-house. Daria spoke up.

"Would the police want them as evidence? As much as I'd like to have those videos wiped off the face of the earth, can we do that?"

"Karim, you're our resident lawyer," Daniel said. "What's your take?"

Focused on Daniel, Isadora hadn't realized that Karim was watching her until she looked at him and caught him glancing. He cleared his throat and answered Daniel's question. Then Isadora noticed he hadn't shaved. What had he said before? He didn't shave because she'd said she'd be sad to see it go. She'd run away from him, turned her back, but . . . Had he intentionally kept his appearance the way she liked it?

". . . what we'll do then," Daniel said. He stood. Isadora blinked. Karim and Daria were also on their feet. She shot to hers too quickly, her chair thudding against the wall behind her. Daniel raised an eyebrow but said nothing as he led their guests to the outer office door.

"Thank you again, Daria," Daniel said, shaking her hand. "I doubt it will be a problem, you taking a couple days off while this explodes, but if your boss gives you any trouble, let me know?"

"Thanks, Senator," she said, slipping into the hallway.

"And we'll see you at nine thirty?" Daniel asked Karim, offering his hand.

"Yes, sir," Karim said. "He was so excited about today, he'll be in the office on time. Might take a strong nudge to get him to come to yours, but he'll be eager to get his drive back."

Isadora followed Karim's nod toward her assistant's desk. She'd forgotten that she'd asked him to bring the drive and had no idea when he'd put it there.

My God. I am messed up. Can I make it through today?

"I don't respond well to threats," Julian growled.

"But you expected everyone else to?" Isadora asked. She

hadn't planned on it, but she'd taken over the showdown. She caught Daniel's lip dance out of the corner of her eye. "And no one is threatening you. Out of courtesy, we're giving you the chance to do the right thing and tell your colleagues you will no longer blackmail them."

"Cute, *Isadora*," Julian said. He turned to Daniel. "I'm here for my drive. Karim said you have it."

"I do," Daniel said.

"And let me guess how you got it," Julian said, looking Isadora up and down. "Sent your little spy to seduce my new aide?"

Karim jerked straight in his seat, but Isadora shot him a glare and shook her head.

"Funny," she said, clicking Daniel's laptop awake. "That you would accuse Daniel of taking a page from your book."

Julian eyed her but didn't say anything.

Daniel leaned against his desk, his hands in his pockets.

"Julian, last chance," he said.

"This is pitiful, Daniel," Julian said. "So scared of losing the presidency that you set up this fake—"

"I don't want to do this anymore." Daria's voice wavered, but the sound was strong from the speakers on Daniel's bookshelf.

The color drained from Julian's face.

"Daria," Julian's voice came from the speakers. "We had a deal. What's a couple more times? Is it more money? Fine. Two hundred for a blowjob, five for the whole thing. Or, I'll make sure everyone finds out just how helpful you've been to me."

Isadora paused the video and folded her hands at the edge of Daniel's desk.

"You were saying?" she asked.

"What the fuck?" Julian huffed. "I . . ." He raised his chin. "That's not me."

Isadora turned the laptop around so Julian could see the still frame. On the screen was Daria, her naked back to the camera. She was facing Julian as he zipped up his pants. Isadora looked over Julian's shoulder at Karim. She watched as he caught sight of the thing that had flooded her with regret when she'd seen it the night before: Daria had a tattoo on her left shoulder. A bird.

The morning turned into a blur. Police officers came, Julian was arrested, statements were taken. Daniel went to the sitting pro tem and suggested a recess for that day. Despite his and Isadora's efforts to keep things quiet, word about blackmail and recordings spread through both the senate and the assembly. Isadora's phones never stopped ringing.

But the one person she needed to talk to was just as besieged as she was. There was only one way to get to talk to him face-to-face.

> Isadora: Can I see you tonight?
>
> Karim: Of course. I'm headed home now, but I can meet you somewhere.
>
> Isadora: Can I come to your place? When things calm down here?
>
> Karim: Of course.
>
> Isadora: Great. Thanks.
>
> Karim: My pleasure, Isadora.

CHAPTER THIRTY-FOUR

Isadora

Isadora caught herself fidgeting on Karim's doorstep again. She'd come straight from work, not wanting to waste any time getting to him after the day they'd had. Wisps of hair tickled her neck and ears. She worried she might have gotten too warm from all the stress, but it didn't matter. She had to try to make things right.

"Coming!" he shouted from deep in his apartment. She was glad he said something; she'd started to worry she might have beaten him there. She glanced to the side, down the hallway of his building. His door swung open.

"Hi," he said, out of breath.

"Hi . . ." she exhaled. He'd been in the shower. His glasses were a little foggy; his hair was wet. There were beads of moisture on his skin. He'd thrown on a white T-shirt, but he hadn't dried himself off well and it stuck to him in various places, outlining the detail of a pectoral muscle here, a biceps there. Isadora's gasp escaped, her whole body exploding with burning tingles. The towel around his waist that he had to hold closed did not help. She clutched her purse strap with both hands to avoid hiding her eyes.

"Sorry," he said. "Wanted to grab a quick shower before you got here."

"My fault," she said. "I should have guessed when you didn't reply to my text."

"No worries. Would you like to come in?"

"Thanks," she said, stepping inside.

He closed the door and led her into the living room. "Gimme a sec?" he asked.

"Sure." She nodded, grateful for a minute to get herself under control.

"Thanks. Make yourself comfy."

She nodded again as he returned to the bathroom. The TV was on, tuned in to ESPN, and there was an almost empty beer bottle on the table. Sitting on the couch, she smiled and rolled her eyes. *ESPN and beer, such a guy. He's one of a kind, but a little predictable. It's cute.* She smiled again. Then her face fell. *And I treated him like . . . trash. Oh my God, I tossed him away just like she did.* She clamped her hand over her mouth to stifle the gasp. *He opened up to me, and I did the exact same thing. I am a horrible person. I can't—*

"Hey," he said as he returned, dry and dressed. He joined her on the couch, sliding his hands under his thighs again.

"Karim, I am so, so sorry. I failed you, I was wrong, I—"

"No! I failed you," he said.

"What? How?" His awkward position caught her eye, but it didn't register. She was too busy trying to corral the scattering marbles of her emotions.

"I endangered your goal." His forearms clenched, like he was repositioning his hands, but he kept them pinned down. *What is he doing?* She wrenched her focus back to his words.

"I drafted that amendment," he said. "But I didn't check it again before it was filed, I—"

"I'm sorry, Karim, but I have to ask. What's with your hands? You seem really uncomfortable."

He looked up at her, wistful.

"Blunt? Honest?" he asked.

"Yes," she said, pressing her palms together between her knees.

"I'm trying not to touch you."

She pulled in a ragged breath, her heart taking off. He didn't hate her. Tears blurred her vision as her lower lip began to tremble.

"Isa?" he asked. "What's wro—"

"Please stop," she said, voice breaking. "Stop trying not to touch me."

Their lips were together before Isadora knew she was moving. She'd been on one end of the couch, but in the next moment she was on the other, kissing him, perched on her knees. He'd turned toward her, pulling her to him.

"I-I'm so . . . so sorry," she stuttered between kisses. "I'm so sorry, Karim."

"No, Isa. Don't—" He stopped speaking to crash his lips back into hers. He slid a hand up the back of her neck, cradling her head. The other spread across her lower back. "Don't cry. It's okay, it's okay."

"No . . ." She couldn't stop kissing him long enough to say what she needed to, but she had to say what needed to be said.

"There's no way you could have known what Julian was going to do. I should have known better, Karim. *I'm* the one who failed. I was just like Laila." She gulped down a sob. "I walked away from you; I didn't listen. I was all 'me me me.' I'm so, so sorry, and I understand if you never forgive me."

He jerked back like she'd slapped him.

"Never forgive you?" he asked.

"You shouldn't." She shrugged. "Not like I deserve you," she whispered.

He cupped her face. "What did you just say?"

She couldn't look at him. She took a breath to speak, but another sob slipped out.

"Isadora, please," he whispered. "Did you just say you don't deserve me?"

She nodded. Hot, fat tears rolled down her cheeks and over his thumbs. The deep breath he took wavered on his exhale.

"Is that what you really think?" he asked. "Or did someone else plant that idea in your head?"

She nodded. "I hurt you, Karim. I assumed the worst. And then last night, when I saw Daria's tattoo? I was mortified. It was all clear, what Julian had done, how he'd set you up. I should have seen it. I should have trusted you. And before that, when I was being horrible and not talking to you, you still supported me, still tried to help me reach my goal. How can I deserve someone who would do all that?"

He wiped her tears away and pulled her into his lap, arms tight around her.

"Please don't *ever* say that again. Hearing that breaks my heart because it's something Laila wanted me to believe. And it wouldn't surprise me one bit if it's something your mother wants you to believe about yourself."

Isadora needed a deep breath. Then another. His beautiful eyes were a little dark, clouded. He gently wiped her new tears.

"Does she know?" he asked.

"About us . . . breaking up?" she asked.

He nodded.

"She guessed. Called me from a landline at a hospital since I'd blocked her numbers. She caught me off guard. Said it's what I get for siding with you over her."

His sharp laugh made her jump. He shook his head.

"I swear, she and Laila have the same script," he said.

"Still, I'm so sorry, Karim," she said into his chest.

"Shhh . . ." He stroked her hair and kissed the top of her head. "It's long forgotten. I'm sorry too."

She pulled back to look him in the eye.

"For what?"

"I should have come to you as soon as things felt weird, not tried to wait around and figure out what Julian was up to."

She shook her head, putting a hand on his cheek.

"No more apologies," she said. "I think you did everything right." She savored the scratch of his stubble.

"Did you keep this for me?" she asked.

"Of course I did, beautiful." His perfect lips beckoned.

"Yeah?" she asked, leaning in.

"Yeah," he whispered.

She was almost ready to let herself fall, but there was a lingering fear. "Wait . . . Are you still planning a new, new start somewhere else?"

He tipped her chin back up to look her in the eye. "I think I might have a pretty good reason to stay here," he whispered.

"You want to stay?" she asked.

"Do you want me to?"

The truth smacked her in the face. And before she could talk herself out of it, she told him exactly what she wanted. "I want us to be together every single day."

"And now we can be," he said.

"We can. Without Julian, we don't have to hide anymore. We'll turn some heads, but Daniel's got more than enough political capital to protect you and get you a position anywhere you want."

He wrapped his arms tighter around her.

"I want to be on Team Isadora," he said as she snuggled in deeper.

"Oh, you're already the captain of Team Isadora." She took a deep breath to muster a little more courage. "But . . . I meant more than that. More than work."

"Hmm?"

She squeezed her eyes tight, glad her head was tucked under his chin so she could hide the nervousness that was pushing against what she wanted.

"We've been cheated out of a lot of time together," she said. "Only relying on video dates or our phones. We have a lot of catching up to do."

"We do," he said.

"So let's make up for lost time."

He leaned back to look at her, raising an eyebrow.

"How?" he asked.

"Pack a bag," she said. "Come move in with me. For a week. Just to see."

The smile that blossomed across his face illuminated the room.

"Move in with you?" he asked.

"Yeah," she said. "For a trial run. Just to see what it would be like to live together. Would you like that?"

"I would love that." He slackened his grip around her, letting his hands slide down her arms. "I'll grab some things; you head home. I have a quick errand to run then I'll meet you there, okay?"

A bouquet of white roses popped up in front of her when she opened her apartment door thirty minutes later.

"Karim! Where did you find a florist open this time of night?" she asked, accepting them as he stepped inside, duffel bag on his shoulder, a suit bag in his other hand.

"Let's just say that I may or may not have mapped out all of the florists near your apartment in case of a flower emergency." His smile sent warm tingles all through her.

"Thank you, baby," she said, stepping aside to let him in.

"Come on," she said, reaching for his suit bag. "Made some room in the closet and the dresser."

He followed, sliding his duffel onto the foot of the bed as she took out his suit. They made quick work of putting his things away. Returning from putting the roses in a vase, she stopped at the closet.

"You know," she said. "I like that. I like that very much."

"What?" He stood behind her, arms around her.

"Your clothes. Hanging next to mine."

"Mmm," he sighed, bending to caress her cheek with his. "Me too. I like that too."

"Do you need anything else, baby?" she asked.

"Yes," he whispered. "You."

She let her head fall back against him as he tightened his arms around her, nuzzling in to kiss a spot below her ear.

"I missed you," he breathed against her skin.

"I missed you." She turned in his arms, their kiss morphing quickly from sweet to passionate. She managed to catch one sharp breath in the moment his lips went from hers to her neck before a high-pitched gasp escaped her. She reached for the hem of his shirt, and he released her to get rid of his glasses before he ripped it off himself. He pulled her shirt over her head and bent to kiss the rise of her breasts. She slid to sit on the edge of the bed. He was on his knees between her legs. His eyes were locked on hers as he pushed her skirt up and slid her panties off. He leaned forward, and she leaned back.

"Karim." She gasped, her hand in his hair. He had her groaning and writhing in a matter of seconds. He was gentle and forceful. She wanted to watch but had to lie back as her body responded and her hips rocked, her thighs spreading wider.

"Karim!"

He grunted and looked up at her. A smile sparkled in his eyes.

"Yes! Yes . . . make me come for you . . ."

He groaned deep and his fingers began to move inside her. His free hand pushed her legs farther apart. She lost all sense of time. The only thing she was aware of was him and what he was stoking inside her.

"Karim!" Her thighs shook; there was no air to be found. He reached up and cupped her breast, pinching her nipple through her bra as he pressed his teeth against her clit. Her orgasm was so intense that she had tears in her eyes when it subsided.

He tugged at the waist of her skirt; she helped by getting rid of her bra. Shuffling herself up to the pillows, she watched as he finished undressing and climbed up the bed toward her on all fours. She gasped again, feeling stalked, hunted. The thought had her chest rising and falling again, something the hunter appeared to enjoy. His wicked smile appeared as he cuffed her ankle with one hand, sliding his parted lips up her calf. She wriggled, panting, and he smiled again as he switched to the other leg, teasing the inside of her thigh with the stubble on his chin.

"Karim." She moaned, reaching for his face to bring him closer, faster. It took little work for him to push her to impatience. He grinned again, wicked, and slowed down. His lips brushed hers, then he pulled away. She tried to follow, to deepen the kiss, but he wouldn't let her. She let out a growl of frustration and he chuckled, moving closer, back over her, his hands cradling her head, fingertips stroking her hairline. He gazed deep into her eyes, surprising her with the heat and pressure of his cock against her labia. She sighed.

"Why, Isadora?" He sighed. "What are you doing with me? You could have anyone. Why me?"

The pain in his voice was much softer than when he'd asked her before. He sounded less hurt than surprised. *Enough is enough,* she thought. *Time to stop being a coward.*

"There's only one man I love, Karim."

CHAPTER THIRTY-FIVE

Karim

He froze. There was no movement; there was no feeling; there were no thoughts. He looked back and forth between her eyes.

"You . . . you love me?" he asked.

"Yes," she whispered.

"You do?"

"I do."

There were still no thoughts. He wasn't sure if he was alive or dead or dreaming. He didn't even remember how to inhale. *She is real, she is here, I am not dead, she just said she loves me. Isadora loves me.*

"Have . . . have I upset you?" she asked.

He had to respond, needed to calm that fear in her voice, but he was struggling to know what to do with himself, how to find words.

"No," he whispered. "No, no." He stroked her hairline, her forehead. *She is real. This is real.* His eyes followed his fingers as he slid them down, caressing her cheek, his thumb grazing her lips. He stared at them as he regained some ability to speak.

"You haven't upset me at all. I just didn't think . . ." His voice trailed off.

Her hands drifted down his arms, part of him caught the tremor in her fingers. *Make a sentence! Tell her!*

"Maybe," she said. "Maybe I've said too much." She wasn't meeting his gaze anymore.

"No, Isadora. No," he said, swallowing. His voice was stronger, he felt more like himself. "You stole my heart the moment I saw you coming down the stairs at the stadium in that blue dress. I knew I was in trouble after Gordito's, when I was terrified it was too late, that I'd lost my chance. And I was certain I loved you by the time we were planning the trip to Atlanta. Then . . . then with everything, and Julian . . ." He stopped. He took a deep breath to steady his voice. "I wanted to tell you a thousand times before, but I was so scared."

She smiled at him and put her hand on his cheek.

"Why were you scared, baby?" she asked.

"What if you didn't love me back?" he whispered.

Her eyebrows came together in that adorable crunch that melted his heart.

"But I do love you," she whispered. "I do."

He had to kiss her. And it felt like a different kiss. He'd never thought that she was holding herself back before, but in this kiss, he felt like she was giving herself to him. She was pouring everything in her into him. He groaned, kissing her back, wanting to give her everything she was giving to him.

"I love you, Isadora." He sighed, pulling his lips away from hers for only a moment. He kissed her with the same intensity, his hand caressing her cheek. Her hands were in his hair.

He began to kiss his way down her neck, whispering "I love you" between each kiss.

"Karim, Karim . . ."

He moved back over her face again. "Yes?"

She smiled at him. A beautiful, enormous smile. "I love you."

"Tell me again?" he asked, his cheeks hurting from his own smile.

She laughed. "I love you. I love you, Karim."

A chill went through him and his shyness came roaring to the surface. He tucked his face into her neck, to hide.

"That's the most wonderful thing I've ever heard," he whispered. "Thank you, Isadora."

"For loving you?" she asked.

"For telling me."

Her arms tightened around him, and he took a deep breath, filling himself with her warmth and her scent. She shifted, and he loosened his grip as she brought her hand back to cup his cheek. "I love you, Karim. And I need you," she breathed.

His heart clenched and fluttered, its rhythm off. Then her racing pulse caught his attention, and he asked himself if he was feeling her heart beat against his.

"You have me, Isadora." Lacing his fingers with hers, he rocked his hips, rubbing his half-hard cock against her. Her breath caught. His face was so close to hers, he could almost catch her lips. "I'm right here. Every inch of me belongs to you," he said, crashing his lips into hers.

The kiss obliterated everything. There was no bed, no room, no building, no world. Only them. Only her heat against him, her skin melding with his own. He stroked himself against her again, he wasn't half anything anymore. She gave a cry at the contact, her pelvis rocking up against his. He groaned, released her lips, and moved down to her breasts. He kissed her nipple and circled it with his tongue, before allowing himself the eye-rolling pleasure of taking it into his mouth. He squeezed the other breast in his hand and reveled in the arch of her back, her sharp clutch on his hair as he sucked. Her high-pitched moan sent sparks down his spine. She sighed his name again, but with much more lust.

He already needed to breathe through parted lips as he left her perfect breasts behind and returned to look her in the eye, face-to-face. Those deep brown eyes were dilated, her lips open, as she let out those sexy breaths that made him feel invincible. He needed to grind himself hard against her. She bucked up, forcing a gasp out of him. He glanced toward her nightstand, but she darted a hand under the pillow and snatched a condom from underneath. Tearing it open with his teeth, he chuckled.

"Prepared before I got here?" he asked.

"Knew what I wanted," she said. "No more wasting time."

He groaned as he reached down to guide himself to the right spot. "No more wasting—"

Words disappeared, and they moaned together as he entered her. The sigh she let out when he completed his thrust forced him to grasp the sheets above her head. He let himself crush into her as her arms and legs pulled him close.

"Baby . . ." He sighed, groaning, and began to move.

Gradually, her breathy sighs got deeper. Her ankle hooked behind his leg and she pulled, setting the rhythm.

"Yes . . ." She moaned. "Yes. You feel so good . . ." She was getting close, fast. He studied her, slowing down, lengthening his strokes, to make it last. The change in rhythm excited her more, her nails digging into his back as she tightened around him.

"Isadora . . ." He groaned deep, his face falling into her neck. She tried to pull him closer and closer to her, even though it was impossible.

"Baby, yes . . . baby, yes . . ." She sighed again.

He lifted his head to look her in the eyes as he slid a hand to her hip. He squeezed hard.

"Baby!" she cried, coming, surprising them both. He didn't stop, and as she was returning to herself, he crushed her lips with another kiss. He moaned into her mouth as she contracted again. Her hand went to his cheek. He pulled away, high off the effort of holding back.

"Karim . . ." she breathed. "I love you; I love you so much."

Oh God, baby. He answered with his body. Kissing her again, he increased the tempo. Her heat intensified, her moans growing louder. She tilted her head back, freeing her lips.

"Yours . . ." she sighed. "I'm all yours."

Her pressure around him was getting stronger, her thrusts up into him harder. He accelerated. She moved up, meeting him, clinging to his shoulders. She murmured "all yours, all yours" over and over. He stopped trying to hold himself back.

"Isa . . ." He grunted, arching farther, pushing deeper.

"Karim!" She threw her head back as she tightened again.

"Isa!" He groaned, his muscles clenching as he exploded.

He pulled her into his chest and turned so they could rest on their sides, but in each other's arms. He was still in a place without time when her finger grazed his bottom lip. Smiling, he opened his eyes.

"Hello, beautiful," he whispered.

"Hello, gorgeous," she whispered back, studying his face, her lips bending to the side. "Do you know that you are *the* sexiest man I have ever seen? Literally, the sexiest one."

He laughed, tucking his chin down as he smiled. The heat in his cheeks didn't have anything to do with what they'd just finished doing.

"And that?" She giggled. "How can you possibly be so shy? You are way, way too hot to be shy."

His face caught fire.

"Dunno," he said. "It's always been there. But never this bad. It's your fault."

"Mine?"

"I don't get shy around anyone like I do around you."

"Aww, baby." She caressed his cheek.

"All this, you, I never had to deal with feeling like this. Honestly, it was scary." He'd started to chuckle, but her forehead crinkle stopped him.

"How can that be? You . . ." Her gaze drifted down his chest, following her fingertips. "You were married." Her voice was soft enough that he had to focus to understand. "You must have—"

"I didn't love her, Isadora." With their arms and legs intertwined, he felt every inch of her stiffen. Her eyebrows got closer together. He'd learned that expression well enough to know she was surprised, not angry.

"Like I told you, being married was important to me. Always has been. And I was infatuated, and she thought I made good arm candy. By the time I knew how I really felt, I'd made a commitment. I wanted to honor that, try to make things work."

Isadora frowned and sat up, hugging her knees to her chest.

"Marriage, family, it's important to you. Really important," she said.

He'd said the wrong thing without knowing it. He moistened his dry lips to speak.

"Yes. It is," he said. "But . . ." He sat up, curling a hand over the top of her foot after removing the condom with a tissue from the nightstand. "Isa? Talk to me, please? What's wrong?"

"I'm afraid you'll hate me. It's the other thing I've been afraid of this whole time, why this might be a bad idea, why I fought so hard against falling for you even when it was pointless."

"I can't hate you, Isa. Just tell me what it is. Blunt, honest."

"I'm not ready. At least not for kids. I have to go to D.C. If I get an opportunity, I have to go. It's what I've always—"

His chuckle cut her off before he could hold it back.

"What's so funny?" she asked.

He took her in his arms and kissed her head.

"Oh, Little Kite." He sighed. "Always so many steps ahead, always so worried. I would never forgive myself if I got in the way of your dreams. The day that opportunity comes I will put your butt on the plane—if I'm not in the seat next to yours. I'm on Team Isadora, remember?"

Her eyes glistened, and he caught the warm tint to her cheeks. "You are. You sure proved it today. But you'd come with me?"

"If you'll have me," he said.

"Really? You'd boomerang across the country? Start all over again?"

"It wouldn't be starting over, Isa. It would be starting our next chapter."

His heart broke as her eyes filled with tears and she snuggled into his chest, a light sob crashing against his throat.

"How do you do that?" she asked.

"Do what?" he whispered, caressing her back.

"Make it go away? My fear, my anxiety? When we're together, all that . . . it just fades so far into the background, it hardly registers anymore. Ever since that very first flight. You make everything okay."

He squeezed her tight, taking a deep breath, willing his own tears down.

"Thank you, beautiful," he sighed. Wrapped together, arms and legs entwined, everything stilled inside of him too. "There is one thing, though. Very important to me." She lifted her head, and he felt her take a breath, steeling herself.

"Okay. What is it?" she asked.

"I need you to meet my family. I want to take you home to meet everyone," he said. The grin he'd been holding back took over. Her shy smile broke across her face.

"You do?" she whispered.

"Yes, I do. If you're ready for that."

She smiled. "I . . . I think I am."

"There's no rush, beautiful." He made sure to soften his voice, running the back of his finger along her jawline. "Everything in its time. Though Khalil might show up any day. He's been dying to meet you."

He grinned at her surprise.

"Why?" she asked.

The emotions were heavy and still difficult to handle. He smoothed a bit of her hair back into place to give himself a second.

"He credits you with bringing the old me back," he said. "From before Laila destroyed my self-esteem."

Her cheeks flushed, and her hand went up to her mouth.

"How could I have done that?"

"Just by being yourself. You started building me back up—" A burst of pain made his eyes sting. He had to stop and find his footing again.

She crinkled her forehead. "Are you okay?"

"Yeah." He sighed. "Still difficult, is all." He took her hand and looked her in the eye. "You started building me back up the minute you forbade me from referring to myself as trash. I didn't realize it at the time, but Khalil said I changed. The way I talked about the future, about myself, began to change. Being with you brought me back to me, to my family."

Her eyes glistened, but before he said anything else, she snuggled herself against him and squeezed tight. He stroked his chin across the top of her head and kissed her hair.

"I love you so much, Isadora," he whispered.

She answered with a tighter squeeze.

He held her close, basking in every detail that came with being with her. He smiled, loving the idea of doing it every day when he came home.

"This is new," Isadora said, smiling at his reflection in the bathroom mirror the next morning. Almost ready to go, she was securing the last hairpins in her bun.

"It is." He smiled back. "Don't know how I feel about it, though." He finished tying his tie. "Don't like waking up next to you and not having enough time to make love." He nuzzled her neck.

She gasped and he smiled, enjoying her shiver.

"Is that the last one?" he asked, nodding at the hairpin in her hand.

"Yes."

"May I?"

She tucked her head and nodded, a shy smile bending her lips.

"Do you know what you're doing now?" She handed him the hairpin as he stepped behind her.

"No," he said. "But I fully intend to learn."

She covered her mouth with her fingertips as he smoothed the side of her bun. He tapped the spot.

"Right here?" he asked, meeting her eyes.

"Yes," she whispered. "That's perfect."

He slid it into place and leaned in close to caress her nape with his lips. She sighed.

"That's the way I want to start my mornings," he whispered. "Come on, beautiful, let's go."

CHAPTER THIRTY-SIX
Isadora

Two Years Later

Isadora shrieked, three snowballs whiffing into her in rapid succession. She ran around the bush she'd been using as a makeshift barrier, scooped up Karim's youngest niece from where she'd stumbled, and rushed to hide again.

"We girls have to stick together." She giggled, setting her down.

"Yeah!" the little girl said, scooping up more snow. "Let's get the boys!"

"Yeah!"

Leaning back around the bush, Isadora helped her throw lopsided snowballs at two of Karim's nephews, who'd been ready to pick up their snowball fight where they'd left off the previous Christmas. Isadora was happy they'd remembered, and eager too. The first time the kids had had the upper hand: Isadora had been nervous about meeting everyone and was a wreck after the flight from San Diego. This year's flight had been much shorter as she and Karim had come directly from their new place in D.C. They'd both been looking forward to Christmas after the whirlwind of Daniel's successful campaign for U.S. representative. Isadora was getting settled into her role as deputy chief of staff, Karim as legislative counsel.

"Children!" Karim's mom called from the deck. "It's getting late, bath time."

"Aww . . . five more minutes, Grandma?" one of the boys called back.

"Now!" she said over her shoulder as she headed back inside.

"Come on." Isadora offered him a hand. "The snow will still be here tomorrow."

Time with the kids made Isadora miss her baby cousins, but by now they were in high school. Though she'd gotten to spend more time with Diane's children because Atlanta was close enough for them to visit. Letting out a puff of breath, she brushed off the remaining snow and turned to follow the children inside. She smiled at the six-foot-plus, green-eyed demigod plodding his way toward her with a thermos and two mugs.

He's even sexy in a beanie. How is that possible?

"Hi, gorgeous," she said as he reached her.

"Hi, beautiful. Wanna join me?" He nodded at the gazebo farther down the lawn. The sun had almost set and the undisturbed snow on the gazebo made it look like an enchanted snowball souvenir.

"Sure," she said, reaching for the mugs.

He shoved an armful of snow off one of the benches, and they snuggled together, facing out into the thick patch of trees behind the house. She shivered.

"Just a second," he said. "Promise it'll be worth it." He opened the thermos and filled their mugs. He was right. Warm and fragrant and delicious, the cider hit the spot after playing in the snow.

"Thank you, baby," she said.

"Kids weren't too crazy?" He sipped.

"Nah," she said. "They were fun. Got a lot more energy than I do, but fun. They've grown so much since last year."

Nodding, he slid an arm around her. His lips bent but didn't make it into a full smile. And his thigh kept tapping against hers. She glanced down at his bouncing foot.

Weird. He never does that. Must be cold too.

She snuggled up tighter, taking a sip, and gasped. It had started snowing again. Everything was quiet and beautiful, even the growing darkness. The glowing lights from the house turned the yard into a postcard. It was so beautiful, she didn't know if she could stand it.

"I can't remember the last time I was in this much snow," she said, reaching past the edge of the gazebo to catch some. She looked back at him, and the tension in his face stopped her dead. She took a breath to ask if he was okay, but he spoke first.

"I hope you'll remember this time."

He slid the cup out of her hands and got down on one knee in front of her, resting his hands on her thighs.

Every bit of her froze. There was a charge of adrenaline, her heart kept beating, but her mind stopped, her lungs failed to do their job.

"Isadora, I tried hard to think of exactly what to say to you, all the things I wanted to tell you in this moment, right before I ask you this question. But I couldn't figure out what to say. There are so many ways you are everything to me, but I couldn't make the words flow like I wanted. I'll probably have to spend the rest of my life showing you how I feel about you, how much I love you, how much I need you. But that would make a really, really long proposal, and we'd never get around to actually being married. So. Will you—"

"Yes!" Air and her voice and her thoughts came back, and there was no slowing them down. "Yes, oh my God, yes of course! Yes!" she screamed.

"Are you sure?" he asked, smiling.

"Yes, I'm sure!" she shouted to the ceiling of the gazebo, tears filling her eyes. She threw herself into his arms, and he laughed again, pushing back to keep from falling.

"Oh my God, Karim. Baby! I love you so much!"

He pulled away, looking her in the eye and kissing her.

"I love you too, beautiful," he said. "Do you want to see the ring?"

"Oh! Right! There's a ring?"

He chuckled, shaking his head as he helped her to stand.

"Yes, baby. There are often rings in this situation." He pulled a box out of his pocket. White gold and delicate, the band was perfect, and the diamond much larger than she'd ever imagined for herself.

"Karim!" She gasped as he slid the ring on. "It's amazing. But it's far too much, it's—"

"Shhh, Isa. It's not enough. If you don't like it, we can exchange it."

"Exchange it? You gave this to me. Anybody wants to touch it, they're gonna have to pry it off my cold, dead hand."

He laughed.

"Are you sure, beautiful?" he asked. "You wanna be my wife?"

She looked up at him and stifled a sob.

"You wanna be my husband?"

"Yeah," he nodded.

She went up on tiptoe to hug him again and jumped as an enormous cry exploded from the house. Cheers and hooting and applause. His entire family was on the deck, hanging out of the windows, or coming toward them down the steps.

"Not too much, beautiful?" He picked up the thermos to go greet their audience.

She grabbed her mug.

"No, baby," she said through a happy sob. Then she tripped, the contents of her cup splashing in his direction. He jumped back just in time.

ACKNOWLEDGMENTS

Is it time to write acknowledgments again? Seems so soon after *Getting His Game Back*. The caring village I had to support me for my first novel has held me close again and allowed *Not the Plan* to make its way into the world.

To my agent, Léonicka Valcius: Your encouragement and guidance has been so important on this journey. Especially since it was Karim and Isadora that brought us together! I would be lost without you.

To my editor, Anne Speyer, and the Penguin Random House publishing team: thank you for your continued confidence in me and your vision in making *Not the Plan* the best it can be. And for giving me a platform to demonstrate the impact of untreated parental mental health on adult children.

I'm forever indebted to the Pitch Wars organization for its mentorship program, and to Diana A. Hicks for mentoring me. My road from a hobby writer to a career-oriented one was greatly shortened by the experience.

My family of choice has done so much to help me understand the truth of what I experienced in the past and has given me the strength to keep moving forward when times got rough. Melissa Scalzi, Toushi Itoka, Bibi Gnagno, Alice Quillet, and Diana Vu (welcome to the fam!), thank you.

To the Coven: Janet Walden-West, Anne Raven, and Megan Starks—keep the snark coming please.

To Nanea, Alex, Rudy, and Ana: Thank you for the inspiration.

À Maryline : Merci pour un autre exemple de « maman ».

To my Dad: I'm writing these acknowledgments at a difficult time. Hopefully by the time you read it, things will be better. But I know you'll be there for me no matter what. This time around, just don't read any of the book, please.

To Gabrielle and Marc: Did you catch your namesakes? I had to put you both in because you are so very important to me. No matter what happens, no matter the twists and turns of life, always know that. And you're not allowed to read this one until you're twenty-one.

NOT THE PLAN

GIA DE CADENET

Random
House
Book Club

Because
Stories Are
Better Shared

A BOOK CLUB GUIDE

Dear Reader,

I started this story in an airport, with a woman anxious about getting on a plane. That's relatable, right? Anyone can be a little anxious about flying. But there's a little more to it with Isadora.

The environment we grow up in determines our normal meter. It teaches us what to expect from close relationships and how to navigate the outside world. Isadora's anxiety—about a situation where she has to relinquish control—and perfectionism developed in response to a childhood with a parent with an undiagnosed mental illness. In the story, Karim supposes that it might be borderline personality disorder based on similarities with his diagnosed ex-wife's behaviors. I do not advocate self-diagnosis, or diagnosing others, particularly for Cluster B disorders. I'm not a mental health professional and the experiences in this book are only one reflection of how a Cluster B disorder might look. Disorders have an enormous impact on the lives of the people who suffer from them, and on their friends and loved ones. Borderline personality disorder is particularly insidious as it causes an intense fear of abandonment while simultaneously provoking behaviors that push loved ones away.

Having grown up practically one-on-one with her mother, Isadora needed to learn what the rules of the game were in order to get parental care and affection. There wasn't another parent to counterbalance. As an adult, Isadora had to continue following the rules. Here are some from the story:

Isadora had to place her mother's grief at the loss of her father above her own.

Isadora had to give her mother attention whenever it was demanded, even if she was asleep.

Isadora was told what her likes were, even when she was allergic to them (magnolias).

Isadora was only viewed as a child, not an adult.

Isadora was not allowed to put up boundaries.

When Isadora was in pain, no comfort was offered, only criticism.

Some may say that Isadora's mother was simply *difficult*. But it went beyond that. RJ mentions that he found some of Isadora's childhood stories nearly abusive, but more important, Isadora talks about the fact that people outside of the family who knew her mother spoke highly of her. A common feature in relationships with a personality disordered person is outsiders have a completely different view of the ill person, to the point that the (adult) child is not believed or is even shamed if they speak out about their experiences.

If Isadora's experience resonates with you, please know that you're far from alone. I cannot recommend the following enough:

https://outofthefog.website/ : in particular the forums

Stop Walking on Eggshells by Paul T. Mason and Randi Kreger

Adult Children of Emotionally Immature Parents by Lindsay C. Gibson

I wish you all the best,
GdC

QUESTIONS AND TOPICS
FOR DISCUSSION

1. Karim is still reeling from his marriage to Laila. Do you think he's truly moved on at the start of the novel? Why or why not?

2. How does Isadora's relationship with her mother affect her decisions?

3. Karim and Isadora both feel that there are risks to expressing their love for each other. Is it always a risk to admit to romantic feelings? Is the risk worth it?

4. Isadora and Karim have very different approaches to their careers. How do their career goals and ambitions differ and impact their romance?

5. Is Isadora's reaction to thinking Karim betrayed her justified? Why or why not?

6. How do Karim's anxieties and insecurities from his previous relationship manifest in his relationship with Isadora and in his career?

7. What are the support systems that Karim and Isadora have in place? How are they similar or different?

8. To what extent do gender roles play a factor in the ways Isadora and Karim view their careers and priorities?

9. Have you ever been in a situation where you felt like you had to make your emotions small for someone else, as Isadora does with her mother? How was your response similar to or different from hers?

10. Do you think Karim was overstepping a boundary when he stood up to Isadora's mother?

11. How does the drive for perfection manifest in Isadora and Karim? How are they able to escape this need to be perfect?

12. Discuss the Romeo and Juliet trope in the novel. Are there other ways it can apply besides the warring factions of the Senate?

PHOTO: © CÉCILE HUMENNY

GIA DE CADENET is the author of *Getting His Game Back* and *Not the Plan*. A Maggie Award finalist and lifelong romance reader, she is also a business school professor and a former translator and editor for UNESCO. A native Floridian, she currently lives in France with her husband and children.

giadecadenet.com
Twitter: @Gia_deCadenet
Instagram: @gia_decad
TikTok: @giadecadenet

RANDOM HOUSE BOOK CLUB

Because Stories Are Better Shared

Discover
Exciting new books that spark conversation every week.

Connect
With authors on tour—or in your living room. (Request an Author Chat for your book club!)

Discuss
Stories that move you with fellow book lovers on Facebook, on Goodreads, or at in-person meet-ups.

Enhance
Your reading experience with discussion prompts, digital book club kits, and more, available on our website.

Join our online book club community!
🅕 🅖 randomhousebookclub.com

RANDOM HOUSE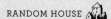